MEGAN HART

HOLD ME CLOSE

MIRA®

Recycling programs
for this product may
not exist in your area.

ISBN-13: 978-0-7783-1762-3

Hold Me Close

For questions and comments about the quality of this book, please contact us at
CustomerService@Harlequin.com.

www.MIRABooks.com

Printed in U.S.A.

First printing: December 2015
10 9 8 7 6 5 4 3 2 1

Praise for the novels of *New York Times* bestselling author Megan Hart

"Hart excels at creating female leads who know exactly what they want and don't make excuses for their lifestyle. Following this heroine's journey is exciting."

—*RT Book Reviews* on *Vanilla*

"Meticulously sensual details and steamy interludes make this an achingly erotic read."

—*RT Book Reviews* on *Flying*

"Hart's beautiful use of language and discerning eye toward human experience elevate the book to a poignant reflection on the deepest yearnings of the human heart and the seductive temptation of passion in its many forms."

—*Kirkus Book Reviews* on *Tear You Apart*

"[Hart] writes erotica for grown-ups...[*The Space Between Us*] is a quiet book, but it packed a major punch for me.... She's a stunning writer, and this is a stunning book."

—*Super Librarian*

"*Naked* is a great story, steeped in emotion. Hart has a wonderful way with her characters.... She conveys their thoughts and actions in a manner that brings them to life. And the erotic scenes provide a sizzling read."

—*RT Book Reviews*

"*Deeper* is absolutely, positively, the best book that I have read in ages...the writing is fabulous, the characters' chemistry is combustible, and the story line brought tears to my eyes more than once.... Beautiful, poignant and bittersweet...Megan Hart never disappoints."

—*Romance Reader at Heart*, Top Pick

"*Stranger*, like Megan Hart's previous novels, is an action-packed, sexy, emotional romance that tears up the pages with heat while also telling a touching love story.... *Stranger* has a unique, hot premise that Hart delivers on fully."

—Bestselling author Rachel Kramer Bussel

"[*Broken*] is not a traditional romance but the story of a real and complex woman caught in a difficult situation with no easy answers. Well-developed secondary characters and a compelling plot add depth to this absorbing and enticing novel."

—*Library Journal*

This book is for the wild ones who open their eyes wide into darkness, the ones who love when they should not; this is for the ones who count and take comfort in the stars.

This book is for those who would rather be haunted and driven mad than left behind.

HOLD
ME
CLOSE

People are complicated, and they hurt each other.

Effie Linton had known this for a long time, just as she knew that sometimes those wounds were inflicted deliberately, over and over, and not with fists or weapons.

Sometimes, they did it with love.

chapter one

Smooth, smooth skin, warm beneath her fingertips. The scent of him surrounded her—cigarettes, fabric softener, the faintest hint of cologne that smelled as though he'd splashed it on days ago. That familiar tang of sweat. He would taste of salt and liquor and something sweet and indescribable. She knew this man inside and out. There had been times over the years when she'd been certain she would never touch him again. She shouldn't touch him now, but she did it anyway, because not touching Heath would've been worse than turning away.

He shivered when she drew a fingertip up the hardness of his belly muscles to circle one dark brown nipple. He always shook when she touched him like this. Trembled and moaned, that mouth open just enough for her to catch a glimpse of his teeth and tongue before he pressed his lips closed. Embarrassed. He was always discomfited at his reactions, just as Effie was always aroused by them.

She murmured his name until he focused on her, his pupils so dilated that his pale green eyes had gone almost black. She pinched his nipple lightly, never looking away from his gaze. She pinched harder as his mouth opened on another moan. When she leaned to kiss him, Heath's hand went to the back of her neck so his fingers tangled and tugged in her hair. She sucked his tongue gently, then more fiercely until he opened for her. Then she broke the kiss but didn't withdraw. Their lips brushed as she whispered again, soft, low, filthy words of love.

She breathed his air. They didn't move, not for some long moments, while beneath her now-flattened palm, Heath's heart thudded faster and faster. His fingers snarled deeper into the length of her hair, pulling it from the loose bun so it fell over her shoulders and halfway down her back.

"Say it," Effie breathed.

Heath said nothing, but his grip tightened. It hurt. Effie couldn't hold back a tiny gasp when he tugged her head back, but that pain, oh, yes, she wanted more. Her fingers curled over his heart, digging into his skin. Harder. Deeper.

"Say it," Effie repeated. "Tell me you want to fuck my mouth, Heath. Tell me to get on my knees and take your cock down the back of my throat. I know you want it. Say it!"

His lips pressed closed, thinning. She pushed away from him, but he didn't let go of his fist in her hair, and she gasped again. Louder this time. Her nipples had gone tight and aching; her cunt clenched at the stinging throb in her scalp.

She slapped his face. Once, hard. When she tried again, Heath caught her wrist. His strong fingers ground her small bones against one another. With one hand on her wrist and the other still locked in her hair, Heath held her in place as she struggled.

Effie snapped her teeth at him. "Say. It."

"You want my cock." Heath submitted, finally, in that low and rasping voice that had more than once been enough to send her hurtling over the edge into orgasm. "You want to get on your fucking knees for me and suck me dry? Is that what you want?"

Now she wouldn't say it, would not give him the satisfaction of knowing that yes, yes, oh God yes, it was what she'd been thinking about all day. All this week and all the endless ones before it, too. Months. Every night and every morning without him, until she'd been unable to stop herself from calling him to come over.

He would have to take it from her, that admission. Slap it out of her. Fuck it out of her. That's how it was with them, and she loved that as much as she hated it. Probably *because* she hated it so much.

Effie fought him, but Heath held her so tight she couldn't even twist in his grip. Slowly, he drew her closer until his mouth grazed hers. She bit his lower lip, catching it between her teeth and pulling until he jerked her head back. She tasted blood, but she'd barely left a mark on him.

Breathing hard, Effie slowed her struggles at the sight of Heath's face. His tongue crept out to swipe along the wound she'd left—maybe she couldn't see the evidence of her teeth, but she was sure Heath could feel it. The thought that she'd hurt him sent a wave of gut-punching heat through her. Her hips rocked a little before she made herself go immobile again. Silent and challenging.

Without letting go of her wrist or her hair, Heath pushed her down, down, onto her knees, and Effie closed her eyes as she resisted. He was stronger than she was. Always had been. She went to her knees in front of him with her head tipped back and the pain arcing through her as hot and electric as pleasure, so little difference between the sensations that she could not have said which she was actually feeling. Everything was tangled up, knotted and twisted, one feeling useless without the other.

Heath kept his grip on her wrist but let go of her hair so he could tug open the button and zipper on his jeans. His fingers fumbled and faltered as he managed to get his cock out. Thick and long, glistening at the head with clear, sweet pre-come... Oh, God, how Effie loved his cock.

She closed her eyes and whispered the words once more. "Say it."

"I want to fuck your mouth, Effie."

She cried out, low and aching. Her head fell back again, and she opened her eyes to look up at him. Heath, her Heath. He stroked his length up and down, then held himself at the base and dragged his cock along her lips until she opened for him. She took him deep, all the way, letting her throat muscles go lax.

Nothing mattered but this. The taste of him. The feeling of his flesh against hers, her lips stretched wide to take him in, the clutch of both his hands on the sides of her head, forcing her to let him do exactly what she'd ordered him to say. To fuck her mouth, slow and deep, then faster until her teeth grazed him and he wrenched her head back again to stare down at her with that open mouth.

His open. Fucking. Mouth.

Heath's mouth made her crazy with longing. She wanted him to kiss her. To eat her alive and spit her out. To say her name the way he said it now, full of warning and that softness more dangerous than any threat. The sound of his love for her.

It hurt worse than anything ever could, that sound. It made it impossible for her to pretend he was just another man. It made it unimaginable for her to remember that there had ever been anyone for her but Heath.

Effie opened her mouth, unvoiced, offering herself to him. She'd begged him in the past, more than once. She might do it again now, if demanding didn't work.

Once more, Heath drew his cock along her mouth. Her lower lip. The upper. He eased the hot, thick flesh inside, then out before she could take more than the smallest taste, and at this denial, Effie moaned.

"You want it." His voice, deep. Hard. And somehow, always, always with the tiniest hint of wonder, as though he couldn't believe she was doing this.

That doubt made her hate him.

He must've seen it in her face, because his expression hardened. So did his grasp in her hair again. When she didn't wince or cry out, Heath pulled harder.

"You want it," he repeated.

"Yes. Fuck my mouth. Let me taste you. I want..." She lost her words. There was only that pleasure-pain. Only oblivion.

Heath pushed himself inside her mouth, then withdrew. He did it again. Effie lost herself in the leisurely rhythm of it. When he pulled her off his cock, she murmured a protest.

"I want you," Heath said.

You have me, Effie thought but didn't say aloud. *You will always have me.*

She got to her feet and turned as he pushed her dress up over her hips. Heath hooked her panties down over her ass and thighs, then off. He kicked her feet wide as he pushed her forward over the back of the couch, one strong hand at the nape of her neck. The other guided his cock inside her. She cried out again at the forbidden stroke of his bare heat inside her.

Heath was always risk and danger.

He was always her safe harbor.

"Tell me how much you love fucking me," he said.

Effie stretched out her arms and pressed her cheek to the backs of the cushions. She gripped the couch. She tilted her ass to urge him to fuck deeper inside her, deep enough to hurt.

"I love you fucking me."

Heath's fingers dug into the scant flesh above her hips. He would leave marks she'd have to explain away. Or maybe not. Maybe Effie wouldn't say a word; she'd simply let the bruises speak for themselves.

"Touch yourself." Heath spoke on a grunt.

Her hand slid between her legs, fingers finding her clit and rubbing, rubbing as he moved inside her. She would come from this, or from his thrusts, or from nothing but the *thought* of fucking him. That had happened, too. The pressure and slickness of her fingertips pushed her closer to orgasm. Faster, too, matching Heath's pace. The sound of his breathing and the quickness of his pace told her he was close. Effie stopped her circling touch.

Heath wasn't having any of that. He slapped her ass, a sharp, stinging crack. "You're going to come for me, Effie."

She wanted to come. She might not, in fact, be able to stop herself from it. They both knew it, though she sometimes wondered if Heath doubted the inevitability of her orgasms the way he doubted her love. She kind of hated him for that, too, for being unsure that he was getting her off even as he got closer and closer to coming himself.

He slapped her ass again, harder this time. More bruises. The thought of dark purple and blue fading to green and yellow on her pale skin, that was what bucked her hips forward. Pushed her clit into her touch. That's what, in the end, made her come with a harsh and rasping cry. She shook with the ecstasy, was made blind with it.

Heath pulled out. Wet heat slapped her buttocks and lower back. It would stain her dress. She didn't care.

"Effie, Effie, Effie," Heath cried. "I love you."

That was the thing about love, though, wasn't it? When you loved somebody, you wanted to give them everything you could. You wanted what was best for them, no matter what. You wanted them to move beyond what was awful and terrible, beyond anything that had ever hurt them. She would never be able to do that for him, nor he for her. They would forever and always be a reminder to each other of all the things Effie wanted them both to be able to forget.

So, although she knew he was waiting for her to say it back to him, Effie only listened.

chapter two

"Where's Polly?" Heath, hair wet from the shower, tucked the towel tighter around his lean hips and slid onto the stool at Effie's breakfast bar.

"School, hello." She glanced at the clock as she flipped the grilled cheese she was making. Just past noon. She had work to do, several paintings to finish and some paperwork to deal with. Updating her Craftsy store with photos of her new pieces was going to take some time, too.

"What've you been working on?"

He always asked her that. Effie shrugged. "Same old. I got a few new orders for some licensed products from a new company. They do mugs and mouse pads and stuff, not just T-shirts. And you know Naveen?"

"He has those two galleries, right?"

Effie nodded. "Yes. He hangs my pieces there in between regular shows, the stuff I feature online, and ships it for me when I make a sale. Well, I have a few things I need to get sent off to him, and I got some custom orders recently, too."

"Sounds like you're busy," Heath said.

"It's work," Effie said. "Keeps the lights on. Pays the bills. Lets me afford grilled cheeses."

The first painting Effie had ever sold went for just over ten thousand dollars. Now her pieces went for under a grand. She priced them that way on purpose. More work, more sales, a steadier income. She was too aware of the precariousness of her popularity—people who collected bones from sideshow freaks and signed poems from incarcerated serial killers could be fickle, and she'd done her level best to stay as far out of the victim spotlight as she could. She could've sold more, earned more, if she'd been willing to keep talking about her ordeal. There were websites and forums devoted to that sort of masturbatory, voyeuristic exploitation. She settled for living within her means and being grateful she could make a living at all with her art.

That first painting had gone for so much because she'd actually painted it in Stan Andrews's basement. She heard it was hanging in a billionaire's entertainment room, which made her think she ought to have held out for more money, but at the time ten grand had seemed like a fortune.

Effie made a career out of skewed landscapes and still lifes, of things seen from the corner of the eye. Her paintings looked normal until you slightly turned your head. Then you saw the maniacal dancing figures, the squirming maggots. The destruction. And if you looked very, very closely, you could always find a clock woven into the design. Those details were what made the collectors go crazy. They were her bread and butter. But to Effie, they were not what made her paintings art. They had kept her from losing her mind, and that, she'd always thought, was the difference between a paint-by-numbers kit of an Elvis on velvet and a piece that someone paid thousands of dollars to hang in their entertainment room.

She hadn't been genuinely inspired to paint anything in a long time. At least a year, maybe longer. It hadn't bothered her, losing her muse. Painting on commission or regurgitating old

themes for a few hundred bucks had kept her busy. Licensing
her images for postcards and T-shirts had paid her bills. She
and Polly didn't need much, and so long as Effie was careful
about putting money away for college, she didn't feel bad about
not taking her kid on expensive vacations or buying her all the
latest trendy fashions.

"You can afford better than grilled cheese, Effie."

She laughed and pushed a plate with a sandwich and some
potato chips in front of him. His clothes were still in the
washer. She'd told him to put on something from her dresser.
God knew there was more than one of his shirts and probably
a pair of boxers in there somewhere. He'd chosen the towel
on purpose to get under her skin.

"Maybe I can," she said, "but grilled cheese is what you
get."

He studied the sandwich, then smiled as if he had a secret.
"You put pickles on it."

"Of course I did." Effie crossed her arm over her stomach
and put her first two fingers of her other hand to her lips. She'd
given up smoking when she was pregnant with Polly and had
never taken it back up, but that posture had never gone away.

After the sex they'd just had, she wanted a cigarette. Badly.
He would give her one if she asked, but of course like cookies or orgasms, one was never enough.

"You're not eating?" Heath hadn't taken a bite. He watched
her, heavy dark brows furrowed. That mouth, his fucking
mouth, pursed in concern.

She had to look away or else she'd kiss him, and where
would they end up after that? His kisses were worse than
cigarettes. "I have to get to work. Anyway, I'm not hungry."

"You should eat," Heath said flatly.

She looked at him then. Silent. He was one to talk. His
hip bones were jutting. Every rib clearly defined. Heath was

fit and strong, but she'd known him to be heavier than this. She, on the other hand, had been noticing softness and curves where she'd once been sharply angled.

He broke the sandwich in half and held up one piece to her. She frowned and shook her head. He set it back on the plate and sat up straighter on the bar stool.

"I can swear to you, there's no ground glass in it. No hairs. No floor sweepings. No pills." Effie's throat worked at the thought of it, but she forced herself not to gag. She hadn't been hungry before, and now she was a little nauseous.

"I know that." Heath turned the plate around and around, then lifted a chip. Keeping his gaze on hers, he put it in his mouth and crunched loudly.

"You can open up the sandwich and look inside," Effie said, too loud. Too harsh. Her voice cracked and broke. "Go ahead! Make sure!"

Heath was off the stool and had her in his arms in seconds. She fought him for a second, but it was a useless protest. When he pulled her against him, she relented. Her cheek pressed his chest. She'd left marks of her own there, half-moon slices that would scab before they healed.

At least those wounds would heal, she thought. Some never did.

"I thought you'd be hungry," she whispered. "That's all. And it's from me, Heath. You should know that something from me would never... I would never..."

"I know. Shh." His hand stroked over her hair. "I was just being an asshole, Effie. I'm sorry."

Countless times Heath had said those words to her, but Effie couldn't remember if she'd ever apologized to him even once in all the time they'd known each other. She clung to him, though, for a few seconds longer before she forced herself to let go. She pushed away from him as the towel loosened and fell.

"You need to put some clothes on," she told him.

Heath grinned. "You sure?"

"Your stuff will be done in an hour or so. Aren't you cold?" Effie went to the fridge to pull out two cans of clear cola that she poured into glasses and held both up to the light without a second thought. She turned to hand him one but paused at Heath's chagrined head shake. "What?"

"You do it, too," he told her.

She frowned and set the glass on the counter with a thump hard enough to splash the contents out. "Yes. Well. Not from something you made for me."

Heath wrapped the towel around his waist again and took up the sandwich to bite into it, chewing slowly. It eased her a little to watch him do it. They weren't going to keep fighting, then. At least not about that.

He ate slowly, deliberately, pulling the bread and cheese apart into bite-size pieces, but she didn't call him on it. There were some things that would never go away, no matter how long ago they'd become a habit or how you tried to get rid of them. Like the way she stood even though she had no cigarette.

"I have some cookies if you're still hungry," she told him, but Heath rubbed his belly and shook his head.

When he held out his hand to her, she took it and let him pull her closer. Even sitting on the bar stool he was a little too tall to rest his head on her chest, but he managed anyway. He nestled against her, his hands on her butt and the heat of his breath seeping through the thin material of her T-shirt. Her dress had gone into the washer with his clothes.

They stayed that way for a minute or so before she tried to retreat, but Heath held her close. She sighed and shut her eyes, stroking the silky thickness of his dark hair. It had been too long since they'd been alone together like this.

And why? Stupid reasons. A disagreement that had turned

into an argument, and both of them too stubborn to give in until enough time had passed that they could pretend it hadn't happened.

Heath nuzzled against her. "Can I stay until Polly gets home from school?"

"I'm taking her to my mother's."

He looked up at her face, his expression so deliberately blank she knew he suspected something was coming that he didn't want to hear. She didn't have to say it, Effie thought suddenly. She didn't even have to *do* it. She could stop herself. If she wanted to.

She traced his eyebrows with her fingertips, then cupped his face. "I'm going out later. Polly's going to stay overnight with my mom."

Heath didn't flinch. He turned his face to press his mouth into her palm but didn't kiss her. Not quite.

"Okay," he said.

"Heath." Effie tried to let go of him, but his hands came up, quick as spit, to grab her wrists and hold her in place. He didn't open his eyes or turn his head. His breath was hot and wet on her skin. "Stop it."

"With who?" he asked.

"You don't know him."

"Oh, I know him. He wears polo shirts and khaki pants," Heath said with a sneer. "He works in an office and drives a sedan."

Effie twisted in his grip, but Heath held her tight.

"It's none of your business."

"Has he met Polly?"

She'd met her date on LuvFinder. He'd messaged her first. They always did. Since signing up about six months ago, Effie had gone on a bunch of first dates, and this one would make it a baker's dozen. "Of course he hasn't."

Heath released her. "Are you going to fuck him? Oh, wait. That's why you invited me over. So you wouldn't have to."

She slapped his cheek. Lightly, not enough to turn his head. He didn't flinch. She cupped his face in her hands and stared into his eyes.

"Fucking you now won't make any difference in what I do tonight."

Heath put his hands up to circle her wrists without pulling her hands from his face. "You'll do what you want to do, Effie. You always have. All I can do is wait for you. Right?"

"I wish you wouldn't!" Effie cried and pulled herself free of him. When he grabbed for her again, she was ready for him and danced out of his grasp. Backing up, she hit another of the bar stools with her foot and stumbled.

Heath caught her by the upper arms, holding her tight until she stopped trying to get away. "But I do. You know I do, Effie. I always do and always will. I love you. I love you. I love you."

"You have to stop," Effie said.

This time he was the one who went to his knees. He yanked down her cotton pajama bottoms and her panties, and when she tried to slap him again, to shove him away, Heath held her wrists at her sides. He pushed himself between her legs. The swipe of his tongue opened her to him.

She struggled for a moment, her wrists aching in the cuffs of his fingers. The right had been broken and left too long without proper setting. It hurt more than the other one, and his grip was looser. Because he knew. Heath knew everything about her. But he didn't let her go, even when she pulled. He pressed his mouth against her, his tongue finding her clit without hesitation.

She didn't climax so much as she unravelled. Sharp and fierce, the pleasure overtook her until she gasped and sagged, her knees weak. Heath let go of her wrists to support her as he looked up at her. He licked his lips.

"I will never stop loving you," he told her. "If we live a thousand lifetimes, I will never stop."

Effie disengaged herself from him, pulling up her panties and pj bottoms and stepping back. She wanted him to get off his knees, but he stayed there. She turned away so she didn't have to look at him.

"We don't have a thousand lifetimes. We only have one, Heath. Only this one."

He stood then. She continued refusing to look at him. She thought he might touch her, and she braced for it, but he didn't.

"Then this one has to be enough, doesn't it?"

She'd told him to leave a dozen times or more in the past. She'd screamed it at him. Begged him. She'd been polite and cold. None of it worked, not in the long-term. He came back to her, or she came back to him, one the waves and one the shore. So this time she said nothing, letting the silence grow between them until he had no choice but to sigh.

"Tell Polly I love her. I'll call her later. Maybe take her to the movies. If that's okay with you," Heath said finally from the doorway, and when she wouldn't answer him, "Effie."

Still she said nothing, not trusting herself to find a voice that didn't shake and break under the weight of her emotions. She waited until he left, not slamming the door behind him but letting it shut with a slow, solid and undeniable click.

Heath's love for her had been as solid and undeniable as the closing of that front door for almost twenty years. The problem was not that Effie didn't believe him when he told her that he would never stop. The problem was that she did.

chapter three

"Don't eat that." The boy standing in the doorway is too thin for his height. Shaggy dark hair falls over his eyes and almost to his shoulders. He wears a pair of raggedy jeans, holes in the knees, and a dirty flannel shirt rolled up to the elbows to expose bony wrists. A black T-shirt beneath. "He puts stuff in it."

"Like what? Spit?"

"Sometimes. Or worse."

Effie can't imagine something worse than spit in the small bowl of thin, cold oatmeal she'd found on the wobble-legged table next to the bed. The oatmeal had been waiting for her when she woke up, a scribbled note next to it saying *EAT*. No spoon. Later, she will understand just how awful the man can be, but for now, the idea of spit is enough for her to set the bowl aside. After all, she's not starving.

Yet.

She should've been startled when the boy spoke, but everything right now still feels hazy, as if even if she blinks hard over and over, she is unable to entirely clear her vision. It's the weird orange light from the wall sconces, but also the lingering pain in her head. She stares at the bowl in her hands. Then at him.

"Where am I?"

"You're in a basement."

She looks around, then sets the bowl back on the table and rubs at her eyes. The hazy feeling is fading. On her right thigh is a bruise that hurts when she presses it. Vaguely, she remembers a needle, and she closes her eyes for a moment. "He gave me a shot."

"Yeah. He likes those. Sometimes it's pills, ground up. But he likes the shots, too. They last longer."

The boy comes through the doorway. The ceiling in this room is so low he has to hunch to stand, but although there's a chair in front of her, he doesn't sit in it. He looks around the tiny, dank space, then crosses his arms. When he looks at her, his face is a puppet's. Blank, yet somehow menacing.

"How'd he get you?" the boy asks.

Effie doesn't want to say. She feels so stupid now. She knew better than to believe the man when he asked if she wanted to see the cute puppy in his van. She knew never to trust a stranger. It hadn't mattered, though, when she tried to run, because he'd caught her within half a minute. Her stupid shoes, the new ones her mom had insisted she wear, had given her blisters. She'd been limping. She could've run fast and gotten away, except for those stupid shoes.

"He told me my mom was in an accident," the boy says. Too casual. As if he's setting Effie up for a joke, but there doesn't seem to be a punch line. "He said she'd been taken to the hospital and my dad sent him to get me."

"That was stupid of you to believe him."

The boy looks at her with bright green eyes through the fringe of shaggy dark hair, and incredibly, he laughs. Really laughs, as if she said the funniest thing he's ever heard. As if Effie is the one telling jokes.

"No shit, right? I mean, my dad wouldn't give a flying fuck

if my mom was chopped into little pieces, and she sure as shit wouldn't bother to tell him if she was in an accident. Even if he found out, he wouldn't have sent someone to get me. I haven't seen my dad in eight years. He wouldn't even know what I look like now."

Effie blinks. She has a few friends whose parents are divorced, but most are amicable with each other, at least enough. She doesn't hang around with the sorts of kids whose parents don't see them.

Her own parents must be frantic by now. She's not sure exactly how long it's been since the guy with the van grabbed her and put her in this room, but her mom goes into panic mode if Effie is even fifteen minutes late from art lessons. It has to be so much longer than that by now.

She rubs her hands on her pleated skirt, but they're still sticky and gross. "So…why'd you go with him, then?"

"Because you always hope, don't you? That it's true?"

"That your dad sent someone for you?" Effie is confused.

"No," the boy says. "That your mom's been in an accident."

Is he joking? Effie doesn't know what to say to this. Somehow, being grabbed and shoved into a van and waking up in a smelly basement is not quite as creepy as the idea that she could ever be happy her mom was hurt.

"That's pretty messed up," she says.

The boy nods, one side of his mouth twisting. "Yeah. I'm kind of a mess."

"He grabbed me," she says suddenly. "He told me he had a cute puppy in his van, and when I tried to run, he…he was just so fast. He grabbed my backpack and yanked me back and I lost my balance, and then he hit me on the head. He pulled me into the van, and he stabbed me in the leg with a needle. Then I woke up here."

"Shit, he hit you on the head? You feel sick or anything? You're not supposed to sleep if you have a concussion."

Effie frowns sourly. "Well, it's too late now if I do, because I've already slept. My stomach hurts, but it's because I'm hungry."

"Don't eat that," the boy warns again. He sits at last. His legs are so long that his knees seem to reach his chin. His hands are really big, too, when he rests them on the worn denim. His fingers play with the torn threads around the holes where his knees poke through.

"I heard you the first time." Effie eyes the bowl again. "Everything? He does something to everything he feeds you?"

"Sometimes it's just too much salt or pepper or hot sauce, stuff like that. But sometimes it's pills or...other stuff. So you never really know. You just get so hungry you'll eat anything, eventually," the boy says. "But I try to at least pick through it, make sure there's nothing really bad in it."

"Worse than spit?" She can hardly imagine it.

The boy gives her a solemn look. "Oh. Yeah. Way worse than spit."

And then, just then, Effie knows there's no getting out of this. The man took her and he's going to keep her and probably he's going to do awful things to her that are worse than spitting in her oatmeal. Her stomach clenches and twists, but she forces herself not to choke or gag. She has to keep her head on straight. That's what her dad would say. If she's going to get away from here, she has to keep her head on straight.

"How long have you been here?" Effie asks.

The boy shrugs and looks away, again as if he's telling her a lie but not with words; this time it's with the things he doesn't say. "I don't know. A while."

Effie pushes herself up off the bed with a wince at the pain in the back of her head. A tentative exploration reveals a few tender spots but no blood that she can feel. Her blistered feet hurt at the scratch of the rough concrete. Her shoes were missing when she woke up. The man must've taken them off her along with her white cotton socks. She shudders at the thought of him touching her anywhere while she was unconscious. If he took away her shoes and socks, did he also touch her in other places?

Repulsed, she wants to run her hands over her body to check for any signs of being violated. She settles for forcing herself to stand up straight. Unlike the boy in front of her, she's not even close to touching the ceiling.

"I'm Effie."

"That's a weird name."

She shrugs. "It's really Felicity, but I hate it. I shortened it to F when I was ten. Now I'm Effie."

"I'm Heath."

"You're named after a candy bar," she says, "and you think my name is weird?"

Heath makes a small noise, not quite a laugh, and looks up at her again from under his bangs. He's older than she is, by at least a few years. Probably old enough to have his driver's license. If they'd met at the swimming pool or in school, she still wouldn't think he was cute. Effie likes soccer players. This guy looks like a stoner, the kind who'd hang around the metal shop making raunchy comments as the girls walk past. Effie knows how to deal with boys like that. You ignore them even when they say nasty things.

"Haven't you ever tried to get away?" she asks.

The boy shrugs again. His voice dips low. It's really deep, his voice. And rough. It's almost a man's voice, but not quite. Not yet, but it's easy to imagine how it will sound in a few years when he is a man. "Yeah. I've tried."

Obviously he didn't make it, but she asks anyway. "What happened?"

When he looks at her this time, it's not the cold room that sends a shiver all through her. "He caught me."

Effie is silent at this. She looks around the room, which is set up like a bedroom, though it's nowhere near as big as hers at home. One wall sconce casts that horrible, dull orangey light, and the one on the opposite wall isn't any brighter. The double bed she's sitting on sags, a stained patchwork quilt covering the otherwise bare mattress. Flat pillows in decorative shams rather than regular pillowcases. A battered white laminate dresser that doesn't match the rest of the furniture is in one corner. The chair in front of her. The table. Yellow wallpaper patterned with old-fashioned clocks peels off the walls, exposing dirty plaster. The doorway has no door, and she tries to see beyond but can't. Too dark.

"What's out there?" She points. "A bathroom? I really have to pee."

The boy looks startled and then embarrassed. "Yeah, but he has the water turned off. So you can't flush, really."

Effie's not sure if she ought to be afraid to push past him, but her bladder isn't going to let her wait much longer. The room outside this one, though, is dark, and she looks at the boy. "Is there a light out there?"

"Umm…" He shakes his head. "The bulb broke."

"Can you show me, then?" Effie only learned over the summer about the power of a smile when it comes to boys. It's not easy to find one, but she forces it.

It must work, because the boy stands up so suddenly he cracks his head on the ceiling and lets out a low, muttered curse. It shouldn't be funny. None of this is. But she laughs anyway before clapping a hand over her mouth to stifle the giggles that are going to become sobs if she's not careful. And she can't do that. Has to keep her head on straight.

"Please," Effie says. "I really have to go."

The boy nods and leads the way into a space not much bigger than the bedroom. She can make out the outline of a couch and what looks like an armchair along one wall. A small glint of metal that might be a doorknob. Same concrete floor, and Effie hesitates in the small square of dirty light spilling from the doorway.

"Be careful. There's stuff set into the concrete."

Her blistered feet already hurt. She doesn't want to cut them any more. "What kind of stuff?"

"Broken pottery and some glass. He put it there on purpose, I think. To make it hard to walk around out there, so you can't rush him when he comes in. I'll take you to the bathroom. You'll be okay."

"Thanks." After a hesitation, he moves and she follows. Three steps, then four, beyond the light as he guides her carefully, telling her where to avoid the sharp places in the floor. It's not pitch-black, but even so, the shadows here are thick and deep. When he stops, Effie bumps into his back. "Sorry."

"It's through here." He takes her hand, startling her, and puts it out in front of them.

She feels a wooden door frame, also without a door, and empty space behind it. There's no light at all in there. By now she has to pee so bad she's afraid she won't make it, but how can she go into that room without seeing what's there? What if it's all a trick? What if he's working with the guy and has been all along?

"Feel along the wall to the right," the boy tells her. "The toilet's there. There's no seat, and you can't flush unless we fill the tank with water. I usually, um…well, I try to only do it when it's full."

Effie cringes. "Oh. Gross."

"Sorry." He sounds truly apologetic.

She can't wait any longer, or she'll wet her pants. With mincing, timid steps, she feels her way in the dark along the wall until she bangs her knee against the porcelain. She bites her tongue to keep from crying out, but it hurts bad. She fumbles with her skirt, then her panties, and manages to get them down while crouching over what she hopes is the toilet. Her mom taught her to hover-squat over public toilets, but in the dark Effie's not sure she won't pee all over herself.

She risks it, letting go. Her bladder empties, urine spanging loudly against the porcelain. She lets out a long, low sigh of relief. Her thighs are almost cramping by the time she's done, and she did splash herself a little, but it's not as bad as she'd feared.

"Hey! Is there any paper?" She looks toward the sound of shuffling and sees a shadow moving.

"No."

"A paper towel? Scrap paper? A washcloth, anything?" She wriggles, trying to drip dry and balance while keeping her skirt up and out of the way.

From the open doorway, a shadow shifts. "Nothing. I used the last of it yesterday. Sorry."

"Stop saying that," Effie snaps as she pulls up her panties and stands to let her skirt fall around her thighs. "I guess you can't really help it, can you?"

He doesn't answer her. Effie holds out her hand, waving into the darkness to find him. She's afraid to move without him guiding her, although her eyes have started to adjust to the dark.

"Where are you?" she says.

"I'm right here."

Effie gives her hand another slow wave. "Help me?"

In a second, she feels the heat of his fingers curling in hers. Heath's hand is big and rough. He doesn't squeeze too tightly. Just enough to give her the confidence to take a step toward him. Then another.

As he guides her through the doorway into the other room, she can see the square of light from the bedroom. She lets out a small noise. She hadn't realized how much she'd been yearning to see it.

From above them comes the creaking of footsteps. Then... music? Effie stops short and loses Heath's grip.

She knows this song. Something about sailing away. Her mom sometimes listens to the soft rock station in the car, and this song is always on. Effie makes fun of her mom for singing along to the high-pitched lyrics, yet right now she thinks she'd give anything to be in the front seat of her mom's Volvo rolling her eyes and trying to convince her to change the station. Bright lights from above blaze so fiercely Effie has to cover her eyes, wincing at the pain.

"Hurry," Heath says in an urgent yet somehow flatly blank voice. "That means he's coming."

chapter four

Polly was settled at the breakfast bar working on her homework while Effie's mom pulled a pan of cookies from the oven. Oatmeal raisin, Polly's favorite. Effie hated raisins in anything, especially cooked. Their soft and gooey texture made her gag. But then, she wouldn't eat chocolate chips, either, even though she liked the taste. She simply couldn't bring herself to trust them, because they looked too much like rat turds or broken bits of cockroaches.

"Nana, I'm going to be in the school play." Polly's blond ponytail swung as she rocked a little on the stool.

"Polly," Effie warned. "Sit still, or you're going to tip the chair."

In perfect tween style, Polly sighed and rolled her eyes, so much Effie's mini-me that she couldn't even be annoyed. God help her when Polly hit teenagerhood in a few years. Her mother's wish that Effie would be blessed with a child just like her had never been meant as a compliment.

Effie wanted to squeeze and kiss her daughter but held herself back. Polly would suffer the embrace, of course, but Effie had decided when she was pregnant that she wouldn't be that smothering kind of mother. The kind who licked her thumb to clean a smudge off her kid's soft, fat cheeks, or who hovered. Anxious. The kind who baked cookies, she thought as Mom slid the edge of a metal spatula beneath each perfectly shaped cookie to lift them onto the cooling rack.

"What part are you going to play?" Mom turned with a smile.

Polly shrugged. "I'm in the chorus. I get to be in all the scenes where they need people in the background."

"That sounds like fun." Mom tugged open the fridge to pull out the jug of milk. She poured a glass and set it in front of Polly.

"It's not a *real* part," Polly said.

"It will still be fun." Effie went around her mother to open the fridge herself. She pulled out a can of cola and popped the top, then grabbed a glass from the cupboard. She poured the clear fizzy liquid into it and held it up to the light before turning.

Mom had been staring with that look on her face. The one that meant she was trying hard not to comment. Effie sipped slowly without looking away, daring her mother to confront her about the habit and knowing she wouldn't. Not in front of Polly, anyway.

"I'll wash the glass, Mom, don't worry," Effie said.

It wasn't that, of course. Mom was in her element when she was scrubbing and sewing and baking and cleaning. A single dirty glass was nothing to her. It was Effie's reason for using the glass instead of drinking straight from the can that bothered her, but what was Effie supposed to do about it? Some things never left you, no matter how much you wanted them to.

Polly closed her math book. "I have to be an office worker and a hot dog seller, with a cart. Meredith Ross gets to be the ice cream seller, which I think is better, but they wouldn't let us trade parts. Meredith thinks she's so great, though. Can I have a cookie?"

Mom nodded. "Sure. But only one. You don't want to spoil your dinner."

"Sure she does," Effie said. "Who wouldn't want cookies instead of meat loaf?"

"*You* used to love meat loaf." Mom's voice was sharper than usual.

Effie looked up. "I used to love cookies more."

"I like your meat loaf, Nana. And scalloped potatoes. And red beets," Polly said. "But no green beans!"

"No green beans," Mom said with another long look at Effie. She took a cookie from the cooling rack and gave it to Polly. "If you're finished with your homework, why don't you take Jakie out into the backyard and play for a bit until it's time for dinner?"

"Mama, when are you leaving?"

"Soon." Effie watched as Polly hopped off the stool. "Jacket."

When the girl had gone out the back door with Mom's aging Jack Russell terrier at her heels, Effie braced herself for the lecture. It was better to take it than avoid it. Otherwise, it would be twice as bad the next time. Kind of like letting a teakettle heat without the lid down on the spout—you could avoid the screaming, but you could also forget it was on the stove until it caught the burner on fire when the water all boiled away.

"You're too thin," Mom said flatly. "You have to eat, Effie. You're going to get sick, and then what will happen to Polly? You don't have health insurance!"

Effie had not actually been sick in years, not longer than a day or so anyway, and nothing more serious than a few sniffles or a cough. "I do, actually, Mom. There's a little thing called Obamacare, remember?"

"And if you get sick and can't work, how will you pay for it?"

"I just got a very nice royalty check from SweetTees, and one should be coming in from The Poster Place." The two biggest companies to which Effie licensed her images. "That's the great thing about doing what I do. The money comes in so long as stuff is selling, even if I'm not making something new. I have my Craftsy shop for new commissions that come in regularly, too. And I don't live above my means."

"A regular job with benefits, steady hours..."

Effie shuddered at the thought of going back to corporate work. "I spent the first few years of Polly's life working to afford day care for her, Mother. It's not like I don't know what it's like to work in a cubicle. This is so much better. I'm home to get her off to school. I'm there when she gets home. If I want to work until two in the morning and nap from ten to noon, I can do that."

"It's just...your work...it's so unstable," her mother said. "That's all. I worry."

"I'll eat an apple a day and keep the doctor away. Okay?"

"You need more than an apple. Look at you." Mom plucked at Effie's sleeve. "Skin and bones."

"Men like skinny women."

It was a mistake, Effie knew that at once, but the words had hurtled out of her before she could stop them. Mom frowned and backed up, then turned, shoulders hunching. She went to the rack of cookies and began putting them into a plastic container. They couldn't have been cool enough yet. They were going to mush and stick together.

"Well," Mom said. "I guess you'd know all about what men like. Wouldn't you?"

It made it hard to feel bad for her mother when she came back with a crack like that, even if Effie deserved it. Which she didn't. Not really. At least, not anymore.

"There's nothing wrong with knowing what men like, Mom. You could try it yourself, you know. Then you wouldn't have to sit around here alone all the time."

Mom didn't turn. "Maybe I like being alone."

"Nobody really wants to be alone, Mom. C'mon. Dad's been gone a long time…" Effie stopped. Her father had died of a heart attack, too young. She still missed him, and no doubt her mother did, too. "I'm just saying, there's nothing wrong if you wanted to go out sometimes."

"I have plenty to keep me busy. I have no need to paint myself up and whore myself around, Felicity. I don't believe my value as a person is reflected in whether or not a man wants to put his penis inside me."

"Liking sex doesn't make me a whore," Effie said.

"No," her mother said. "Letting them treat you like one does."

Effie's fingers curled into fists that she forced herself to open. "It's not the fifties, okay? If a woman wants to date a lot of different men, that's her…that's my choice."

Mom turned as she pressed the lid onto the plastic container. It shook a little as she gripped it in both hands. So did her voice. "What kind of example are you setting for Polly?"

"That's a shitty thing to say." Even during the height of what Effie thought of as her "experimenting" phase, she'd never brought any of the men home. Nor had she brought around any of her thus-far lackluster LuvFinder dates. "You know I don't expose her to strangers. What I do with my business as an adult person is just that. My business. Don't you dare give me grief about Polly."

"No, no, you don't expose her to strangers." Her mother's

voice dripped with derision. "Just that *one* man. Probably the worst of them all. Him, you let slink around all the time, don't you?"

It was an old and tired argument. "Heath loves Polly like she's his own. And she loves him. He's good to her."

"He's no good for you," Mom snapped. "He's the opposite of good, Effie. He's horrible for you, and that means he's no good for your daughter!"

"I know you hate him," Effie began and thought of more words but stopped herself before she could say them. They wouldn't matter. All these years later, all the same words. Nothing she said would make a difference.

"Of course I hate him," Mom answered. "What I don't understand is how you don't."

For a moment, Effie sagged. It was too fucking hard to deal with her mother sometimes, even on the best days. With this old argument rearing its head, all she could do was hold up her hands like a surrender. She shook her head, silent.

Her mother slapped the plastic container down on the counter. "You're better than he is."

"Why? Because his parents split up when he was a kid or his mother wears her skirts too short and his dad works in a convenience store, or because he never went to college?"

Those were all part of the reason, though she doubted her mother would ever admit to such snobbery. Effie ran a hand across her mouth, smearing her lipstick onto her palm. Now, shit, she would have to redo it. She rubbed the pink streaks into her skin.

"I'm going to be late," Effie said. "I'm just going to freshen up in the bathroom and then get going. I'll pick Polly up tomorrow after school, if that's still okay."

"And if I say no, I want you home tonight at a reasonable hour so you can pick up your own daughter and take her home so she can sleep in her own bed, where she belongs? If I tell you that, what would you say?"

Effie gave her mom a steady, unflinching look. "I would say that your granddaughter loves spending time with you and sleeping over here is a treat for her, and you know it, and you taking her to school in the morning is an even bigger treat, because we both know you always take her to the doughnut shop on the way. She loves that. She loves being here. She loves you. And so do I, Mom."

Her mother picked up and put down the container of cookies on the counter hard enough to rattle them inside. "Who is he tonight?"

"Someone I met online. Dating service. It's just a date, okay?"

"Have you seen him before?"

"No." Effie shook her head. "This is the first date. We're going to dinner and possibly a movie. Totally bland and lame. He works with computers, wears glasses and doesn't have any pets."

Mom sighed and rubbed at the spot between her eyes with her middle and third fingers, a habit she'd had for as long as Effie could recall. "What else do you know about him? Have you left his name and information somewhere, in case something…happens?"

Mitchell's dating profile had been witty, charming, detailed. He was seven years older than Effie. Divorced with no children, though he spoke warmly of nieces and nephews. He didn't smoke or do drugs or even drink to excess, or if he did, he was both lying about it and very good at hiding any evidence of it.

"He's probably not a serial killer," Effie said. Her mother didn't laugh. "I get it, Mom. Okay? I get it. You worry."

When her mother didn't reply, Effie took a step forward to

hug her. Her mom didn't yield at first but softened after a few seconds and rubbed Effie's back. Her mother sighed.

"I worry about you, Effie. I'm your mother. It's what I do."

And had always done. Effie understood it, perhaps more so now that she had a daughter of her own. She squeezed harder, breathing in the familiar scent of laundry detergent and, fainter beneath, a hint of Wind Song. Her mom had grown thin herself, the ridges of her shoulder blades hard under Effie's palms.

For a moment, Effie thought about canceling her date with Mitchell. She could stay here, hang out with Mom and Polly. They could watch a movie together, something funny. Her mother had kept Effie's old room pristine, exactly as it had been the day Effie left this house for good. A shrine to her mother's inability to let things go.

Effie could let go, though, and she did, putting some distance between them. "I'll pick her up after school tomorrow. I already sent a note to the school that she'll take the bus here."

Mom nodded stiffly. "Fine."

There was more to be said, but Effie didn't say it. It wouldn't change anything that had happened, and it wouldn't make a difference in anything going forward. Nothing would.

"I'll see you tomorrow," she said and left her mom behind.

chapter five

"When do you think she'll get up?" Heath paces beside Effie's bed.

With a sigh, she tosses back the covers so he can get in beside her. It's cold in their apartment and too early to turn up the heat. "She's three. She'll be up when it's light out, and then it'll be nonstop for the rest of the day, so I'd get another hour of sleep, if I were you."

Christmas. As a kid, Effie had woken before dawn to creep downstairs and peek at what Santa had left beneath the tree, but although Polly's excited about presents, she hasn't quite grasped the concept of getting up before the sun rises to open them. There isn't much under the tree for her anyway—going to school means only part-time work for Effie, and there are a lot of bills to pay before she can afford to spend too much on junky toys that will be broken within a day or two. There will be more gifts at Effie's mother's house later in the day, probably too many, and Polly will be overwhelmed with it all, but there's no telling Mom not to spoil her only grandchild.

"I can't sleep." Heath sighs and flops onto his back, taking up too much room in Effie's double bed.

She shoves him onto his side with another sigh and curls

against his back to make it easier for them to share the space. It's warmer, too. Her feet are icy, so she tucks them between his calves. His yelp of protest makes her giggle. In seconds, he's turning to face her, tickling until they're both breathing too hard.

That isn't all that's too hard. The press of his erection on her thigh is too familiar to deny. And it's Christmas, Effie thinks when they move together, when he kisses her, when he slides inside her. How could she say no to him at Christmas?

Because the "no" is on its way, and she feels it every time he tries to hold her hand. A few days ago, Effie got some mail addressed to "Mrs. Heath Shaw" despite never having signed up for anything, ever, using anything close to his last name. They've been living together in this apartment for nearly four years, and what had been meant as a temporary solution has started to feel far too permanent. Still, it's Christmas Day, and she lets the pleasure overtake her because it's too hard to resist him even without the shiny lights and promise of something special under the tree.

Heath slides a hand between them to stroke her in time to his thrusts. He's close, she can tell, but he's holding back to make sure she gets off first. It's perfect. She can't stop it. Heath's touch is magic, it's fire, it's fireworks and jingle bells. She comes with a low cry into his kiss, and Heath laughs, so pleased to have done that for her that he joins her in the moment after.

They sprawl in silence for a few minutes. She times the spacing of her breathing to his. Their hands are linked. He's falling asleep, but Effie is wide-awake.

It would be so easy to stay here with him and Polly in this tiny, bordering-on-decrepit apartment. Easy to keep struggling through school and work and raise this child with him. But what would not be easy is this, the linking of their fingers and the sound of his breathing next to her in bed. Love is not easy, Effie thinks as she pushes up on her elbow to look at Heath's face in the faintly brightening light coming in through the window. She keeps herself from tracing the lines of his face with her fingertip, because she doesn't want him to wake.

She loves him. She will probably never love anyone else, not like this. But how would she ever know if she could, if she doesn't try? If this is all they have because it's all they believe they *can* ever have, how is that good for either one of them? To never have even the illusion of a choice?

Down the hall comes the pitter-patter of little feet. Polly is awake. Effie shakes Heath and slips out of bed to pull on her robe as the faint squeals of joy come from the living room. Together, Effie and Heath follow the delighted laughter. Polly dances in the multicolored glow from the tree they left lit all night for just this reason.

"Santa!" Polly cries, clapping tiny hands. "Santa was here!"

"I'll make coffee." Heath kisses Effie on the cheek and squeezes her for a second.

"Wait. Hold me close," she murmurs when he moves away. She pulls him back for a longer embrace as they watch Polly shaking each package. She hasn't yet figured out she's allowed to tear into them. Effie squeezes Heath, her cheek pressed to his chest.

This could all be so easy, if only it weren't always so hard.

The phone rings. Her mother, frantic and desperate, incoherent. Heath holds out the phone and Effie takes it, alarmed, until she can get her mother to slow down long enough to speak.

"Your father is dead," her mother says. "I need you to come to the hospital."

Dead? That cannot be. Her father is always there, has always been. Her father can't be gone. What will Effie do, if this is true?

What she does is go to the hospital, leaving Heath to stay with Polly so Effie can help her mother take care of everything that needs to be taken care of. Phone calls. Arrangements. She stays for two days at her mother's house in the bed that had been hers for as long as she can remember, listening to the low, keening sounds of grief filtering to her from down the hall and finding herself incapable of going into her mother's room to offer her any comfort.

On the third day, Effie finds her mother sitting at the kitchen table with a cup of cold coffee in front of her and a grim look. She has a sheaf of papers. She pushes them toward Effie.

"There's money. Your dad's insurance policy. There's enough here for you to move out of that apartment. Get yourself a place. Unless you want to move back with me..." At the look on Effie's face, her mother laughs harshly. "Of course not. Of course you don't."

Effie looks at the numbers on the papers. It's like swallowing an icicle, this sudden realization that she does have a choice. With this amount of money, she'll be able to buy a house. Support herself and Polly while she tries to make a go of her artwork. This money is freedom, and Effie knows she's going to take it. She has to.

"I won't beg you to stay," Heath tells her. "I won't fucking do it, Effie."

"I don't want you to beg me. I want you to be happy for me."

He won't look at her. She can't blame him. Effie is upsetting this easy familiarity they've built together. She is breaking them apart. She can't explain to him why it has to happen, for both of them. She's not quite sure of it herself, except that before now she felt she didn't have a choice, and the money has made it possible for her to make one. Before, Effie thought

Heath was the only man she would ever be able to love, but she's never tried to find out otherwise, never fallen in love with someone new.

All they've ever known, really, is each other, but that was not a choice either of them made. It was forced upon them. How can either of them know if there isn't something better, if she doesn't do this now? If she doesn't try, for both their sakes?

She lets him believe she's selfish. She takes his anger. Then she steps back to let him go.

She is going to have to let him go.

chapter six

Effie loved the curve of a man's thighs. Muscles, crisp and curling hair. She let her mouth follow the bulge to Bill's knee, which she nipped lightly before letting her tongue trail slowly over his calf to the blunt knob of his ankle. This time when she pressed her teeth to his skin, he groaned.

Effie looked up at him for a second before moving up his body to straddle him. She let her fingers dig into his chest, not hard enough to break the skin. He wouldn't like that. When Bill grabbed her hips, she let her head fall back. The brush of her hair along her shoulders, almost to her waist, sent shivers all through her. Her nipples tightened, craving his mouth.

"Touch me," she said.

Obediently, Bill's hand slid between them until his knuckles pressed her clit. He rocked his hand against her. The pressure was good—not enough to get her off, but still nice. Bill had big, strong hands. He could circle both her wrists with one of them, though he never had and Effie doubted he ever would. He was too afraid of hurting her.

"Do you want to taste me?" she asked.

Bill groaned again. "You know I do."

She wanted that, too. Mitchell's dating profile had been witty and charming, but their date had been bland and unremarkable. He'd been nice enough. Polite. He'd insisted on holding the door open for her and pulling out her chair, which was a pleasant surprise.

He hadn't kissed her good-night.

It might be that he was too much of a gentleman or maybe he didn't like her enough. Effie didn't really care. He'd asked her if she might consider going out with him again, and she'd said sure, but she wasn't convinced he'd actually call her. She didn't really care about that, either.

Right now, Effie only cared about Bill's hot, wet tongue on her cunt. Making her come. All she wanted or needed was a thick, hard cock inside her.

"Eat my pussy," she breathed and moved up over Bill's face, her knees on either side of his head. She let her body hover over his lips, not close enough for him to touch her unless he made the effort. When he did, laughing, she pulled away, just out of reach.

With a small growl, Bill grabbed her hips again, his fingers digging in. He pulled her close. Got his mouth on her. His tongue swiped her expertly, delving into her folds and probing her entrance before moving up to start a steady pace against her clit.

"Fffffucccck," Effie breathed. She gripped the headboard, already rocking against him. No more teasing. No games. Pure pleasure.

Bill slid a finger, then another, inside her, fucking as he licked. The dual sensations sent her tumbling closer and closer, but her orgasm danced just out of reach. She needed something…more.

"Harder." She twisted to look at his cock. He had a hand on it, stroking. The man was nothing if not coordinated. He was going to come before she would; this had become a race. She didn't want to lose.

Gripping Bill's headboard until it creaked, Effie fucked herself against his mouth and fingers. He stretched her, too much. It hurt and not in the good way. It was a distraction that was keeping her from going over. She would be sore for days.

So close, so close and yet not close enough. Bill stepped up the pace, one hand jerking his cock while the other slipped away to grab her thigh. His tongue worked, swiping less steadily, the pace switching up at random.

She was going to lose it. Effie cupped her breasts, thumbing her nipples and then pinching them. Hard. The pain sparked a small surge of pleasure, but not enough.

Bill let out a low groan and rolled them both so he was on top. He fumbled in the nightstand for a condom and put it on before sliding inside her. He pumped a few times, then shuddered.

That was it for her. All done. Her cunt ached from the pounding of his fingers, but everything else felt swollen, throbbing, dissatisfied. Like menstrual cramps but worse. Women could get blue balls, too, she thought and shoved him until he rolled off her. Effie moved onto her back, head on the pillow beside his. They lay shoulder to shoulder until the slickness of his sweat repulsed her, and she shifted half an inch. He noticed, though. Bill always did.

"Don't let the door hit you in the ass on the way out," he said as he sat up to dispose of the condom in the trash pail by the bed.

Effie twisted to look at him. "Don't be like that. Jesus, Bill. Have a little more class."

"That's a good one." He snorted softly and lay back with an arm beneath his head. Somewhere in his house a clock chimed, though she knew him well enough not to believe the hour it was crying. He'd have forgotten to set it back for the time change, let the batteries run down, something. "You come over here after being out with some other guy, half-drunk, and all you want to do is fuck."

She hadn't been half-drunk or even drunk at all. She'd sipped from a glass of wine, just enough to let it linger on her breath. She just let Bill think that because it gave him an excuse to demand she stay until she'd sobered up. He was a cop. He didn't condone drunk driving, though he didn't seem to have a problem fucking her and letting her leave without so much as a cuddle after. Of course, that was why she came to Bill's apartment late at night after bland and dissatisfying dates in the first place.

Effie sat up, cross-legged, and poked him in the side. "Oh, don't act like it's your dream to have me here in the morning, making me eggs."

"You could make *me* eggs," Bill pointed out.

"I can't cook," she lied with a hint of a grin and poked him again. This time, he snagged her hand and held it for a moment as they looked into each other's eyes.

He settled her hand on his hip. She gave him a second or so before withdrawing it. He noticed that, too.

"You could stay," Bill said in a low voice. "The bed's big enough. You could have all your own space."

"I have to get home to my kid."

Bill frowned and pushed up on his elbow. "Bullshit. Your kid's with your mother tonight."

"How would you—" Effie scooted backward and swung her legs over the edge of the bed, then said over her shoulder, "What did you do, drive past her house? Check it out? Creeper."

"If you're with me, your kid's with your mom. Or with

someone. You wouldn't leave her by herself. I know you better than that."

She did not like that, not one bit, this idea that he believed he could ever know her. That he was right only soured her further. Effie stood, searching for her panties and settling for her dress. That, at least, she'd hung neatly over the back of a chair. The underwear had come off at a rather more heated pace. She'd probably kicked her panties under the bed or something, but she'd be damned if she was going to get on her hands and knees to look for them.

"Ah, shit, Effie. Don't be like that." Bill got up, too, and came around the bed to grip her by the upper arms, though loosely enough she'd have no trouble getting free if she wanted to.

"It's late," she said. "I'm sure you have to work in the morning. And I have things I need to do, too."

She had a commission to work on. Laundry. Her tires needed to be rotated, she'd almost forgotten about that appointment, and then she had to get over to her mom's house to pick up Polly.

"Sure. Fine." Bill let her go. Stepped back. Naked, his belly and chest still glistening with sweat, he bent to grab his T-shirt and cleaned himself off before tossing the shirt in the direction of a pile of laundry on the floor.

"God forbid you should put it in a basket," she murmured.

Bill snorted soft laughter. "The hell do you care? I don't see you offering to do my wash for me."

"Does that mean you have to live like a pig?" Effie buttoned the shirtdress to her throat and smoothed the skirt over her bare ass. It was going to be cold outside without her nylons, but they'd been shredded within a few minutes of her arrival here.

Bill frowned again, harder this time. "You have a mouth on you. You know that?"

"So I've been told." Effie shrugged and turned away. Bill caught her arm again, a little harder this time. Surprised, she faced him. "Hey."

His grip loosened, but he didn't let her go. He pulled her closer. Shit. Was he going to kiss her?

"No?" he said when she turned her face at the last second so that his lips brushed her cheek.

Effie said nothing. It was such a fucking cliché. She usually didn't even care about kissing in that way, except right now when he wanted it from her, and she didn't want to give it.

"You come over here and fuck around with me," Bill said into her ear. "You won't sleep over. You won't let me kiss you. You don't let me get anywhere fucking close to you, do you?"

Effie shrugged out of his grasp. "Don't."

Bill sighed and scrubbed at his short, pale hair. "Go, then. I guess I'll see you the next time you have an itch that needs to be scratched."

He slammed the door to his apartment behind her, which made her want to thump her fist on it until he opened it again. He wasn't being fair. This was the way it worked with them. He should've been used to it by now. She'd needed and wanted him to get her off, but he hadn't. She'd wasted her time and his. She'd hurt his feelings and hadn't meant to.

Shit. Effie sighed and didn't knock on the door. In her car, she watched Bill's silhouette in the window. He would stand there until she drove away, so he could be sure she left instead of, what, being murdered in her car in the parking lot? Effie laughed without humor, hating the bitter taste.

Backing up, she pulled out into the street. In her rearview mirror, she watched the golden square of light from his window turn into darkness. Then she drove home.

chapter seven

"How was he?"

She wasn't startled. Didn't scream. She'd known Heath was waiting for her the second she came into the kitchen and saw the back door was slightly open. You'd think she'd be smarter about it, take a baseball bat or something to protect herself in case it was a serial killer who'd happened to pick her house out of all the ones lined up along this suburban street. You'd think she'd have been more careful about locking her doors, the way her mother had urged her over and over again to be.

When the worst had already happened to you, everything else seemed a lot less dangerous.

"None of your business." Effie went to the fridge and pulled out a bottle of water, listening for the sound of the crack as she broke the sealed lid before she drank greedily.

Her stomach rumbled. Mitchell had taken her to a Chinese place for dinner, and there'd been no way for her to eat any of that jumbled-together sort of food. Nor any good way to explain to him why she couldn't have anything touching each other on the plate. Not without sounding like a lunatic. She'd gone to Bill with a different sort of appetite and he'd left her hungry, too. She pulled out a block of sliced cheese and took a piece. She offered one to Heath. He refused.

"Dammit, Effie."

She turned and leaned against the counter. Heath wore all black. Ancient jeans, ragged at the hems. A black hoodie over a black T-shirt. He'd left his shoes by the door, and he wore no socks. She had to look away from his bare, long toes—his feet killed her with their perfection. His arms stuck out a few inches below the sleeves. Heath had a hard time finding clothes that fit him. Legs and arms and torso too long. At six-five he was gangly, even now as a man when he'd filled out with muscle.

Thinking of his body, Effie swallowed hard and drank more water. Her thighs rubbed together, slick from her earlier, unsated arousal. Her lower abdomen still felt crampy.

"Where did he take you?"

"Jade Garden." She chewed slowly. Swallowed. Washed down the rest of the cheese with a swig of water, then another.

Heath let out a short, sharp bark of mocking laughter. "No wonder you're hungry now."

"He was a nice guy," Effie said mildly. "He's a software engineer. He makes good money. He smelled nice. He wears glasses."

Heath moved closer. He'd been working in the cafeteria at a local private college for the past couple years. He did most of their catered events. He stank of grease and fried foods with an undertone of grass and smoke. He would taste like honey. Effie didn't move away, but she didn't lean into him, either. Didn't soften or bend, didn't open her mouth for him to kiss her.

Heath leaned in to sniff her neck. His lips moved against her skin. "You fucked him."

"No."

"You fucked someone," he said and slid a hand under her dress and between her legs. His fingers cupped her hard enough to force a gasp out of her. In the next second he'd pushed his fingers inside her. "He's still dripping out of you."

In, out, his fingers slid against her slick heat, but he was wrong. She wasn't wet inside from Bill, but from this. Oh, fuck yes, for Heath, always for him. He could look at her from across the room, no words. None needed. A glance, and she was weak-kneed and trembling at the thought of his touch. Of his mouth, that tongue. His teeth.

The water bottle fell to the floor, splashing her legs with chilly liquid. She put both her hands up flat on his chest. His T-shirt bunched under her fingers. She pushed at him, but Heath had put his other hand at the small of her back, holding her still.

He slid his fingers deeper until his thumb pressed her clit. His teeth took the place of his whisper, fierce on the tender skin of her throat. Effie's head tipped back; now her fingers clutched at his T-shirt not to push him away but to keep herself from falling. Not that Heath ever would have let her.

He would never let her fall.

"So fucking wet," Heath breathed into her ear. His hand moved faster. He added another finger, stretching her. His thumb stroked. Had it only been this morning that they'd been doing this?

He backed away from her so suddenly that Effie took a couple stumbling steps forward in order to keep her balance. She cried out, low, as she lost her grip on his shirt. Her head spun.

"I waited for you," he said. "I was worried."

What else could she do then, but draw him close to her and hold him? What else but to kiss him, first gently and then as though they each were the only meal the other would ever need? Here in the dark and in the morning's ugliest hour, it was surely all right to take him by the hand and lead him into her bedroom, where he stood in front of her as she undressed slowly, piece by piece until she was naked in front of him.

Heath hesitated before stripping out of his hoodie, then pulled his T-shirt over his head with one hand over his shoulder in that purely male way. He tugged the button on his jeans and then slid the zipper down notch by notch without ever looking away from her. He wore no briefs beneath, and at the first sight of the dark bush of hair, Effie let a low groan slip out of her. Heath pushed his jeans down and kicked them off.

Effie backed up slowly until she reached the bed, then scooted back on it. She opened her thighs to show him her treasure and reveled in the way his gaze flashed in the light coming from the window. Propped on her elbow, she let the fingers of her other hand toy with her cunt, easing inside and then up to circle her clit. Slow, slow, until her head fell back and her back arched at how good it felt to have him watching her.

"Did he eat that pussy?"

"Yes."

"But he didn't make you come."

A stuttering, sighing moan ground from her throat. "No."

"Look at me, Effie."

She managed to lift her head. Heath's cock was in his fist. He got harder as she watched. Long and thick, his cock was slightly curved upward. Effie had been with dozens of men. She'd seen a lot of erections. Long, short, thick, thin, bent, uncut. Low-hanging balls or tight and high. Some men trimmed or shaved their pubic hair and some let it grow dense and wild. Yet of them all, Heath's was the only one she could have picked out of the crowd. She knew his body as well as she knew her own.

And he knew hers. Moving closer, he knelt between her legs to rub his prick along the seam of her cunt, up and over her clit again and again until she fell back onto the bed, legs splayed wide to urge him inside her. He teased her with the tip of his cock, his hands planted beside her head, his hips barely thrusting. Slick, flesh on flesh. She wanted him to fill her.

When at last he began to move, her hands went above her head, palm to palm, fingers linked. She gave herself up to the pleasure of him rocking his cock against her. She lost herself in it. She came in slow, rolling waves, aware she was crying out but not caring. So many times they'd had to fuck in silence, careful not to let anyone overhear them, but now in this empty house she let herself give voice to the passion only Heath had ever been able to give her.

Over and over, she rose and crested and dipped; over and over, he took her body higher until she thought she might pass out. Or die. Yes, she could die right now with him making her come. Or maybe she'd already died and this was both heaven and hell, this never-ending climax.

When the shaking of her body eased and she was able to breathe again, Effie opened her eyes. Heath still held himself above her. The cords on his arms stood out. His mouth had parted, slack, but his gaze was sharp and focused on her face. It stabbed her, that look. Penetrating and intense.

Without putting a hand on his cock, he nevertheless managed to find her opening and push inside. She groaned at the way he filled her. She moved to touch him, but he muttered a command for her to stay still. He didn't move. He stared into her eyes and pressed his lips together.

"Please," Effie said again. "Heath."

A low noise like a growl rumbled out of him. He slid out of her almost entirely, then back in. So slow, but not gentle.

Sweat dripped from his face onto hers and she licked it away, drowning in the taste of him.

He fucked her that way forever. Each thrust began to sting. She couldn't come again, it was impossible, but the pain was a pleasure of its own and she rode it the way she'd done the string of earlier climaxes.

Heath drew a series of ragged breaths. His hair fell in front of his eyes as he ducked his head. His arms had begun to shake, but he didn't lower himself onto her. He fucked harder, desperately. Frustration twisted his expression. Finally, he stopped, pushing upward again on his hands. He shook his head, but when he tried to pull out of her, Effie hooked her heels behind his calves and kept him close.

When she slapped him lightly across the face, Heath shuddered. The next time, she did it harder. His gaze flashed. Angry, but also that other thing, that dark thing that never went away between them. So she did it again, and this time he let out a low shout that got lost inside her mouth as he dived to kiss her. It was brutal, a clash of teeth and slash of tongue. She raked his chest with her nails, and he took her lower lip between his teeth. Then her tongue, biting.

They moved together, rolling, until she was on top. His hands gripped her hips. He thrust upward hard enough to knock her forward, her hands flat on his chest. She kissed him, not kind or sweet or loving. They made war and love at the same time until at last he pounded his cock deep inside her again, crying out. Then he went still.

Breathing hard, Effie uncurled her fingers. She smoothed the crescents her nails had left in his skin and bent to kiss the marks. A few of them overlaid the faint bruises from the last time they'd been together. One or two of them had bled and she took some extra time to soothe them. Then she rolled off him and onto her back beside him.

Heath was silent for a while before he turned onto his side, away from her. Effie had been staring up at the ceiling, cataloging the aches and pains of the aftermath. She waited a second or so before turning to spoon him from behind. Her face pressed the warmth between his shoulder blades.

"You stink," she told him. "You need a shower."

Heath didn't move. He found her hand and tucked it against his chest. Effie nestled her crotch to his ass and breathed him in. She licked his skin. Tangy. She closed her eyes. They would sleep this way, if she wasn't careful. Tonight she wasn't sure if she cared.

"Are you going to see him again?"

He meant Mitchell, but he could've meant Bill. It didn't matter. She didn't need to think before she answered. "Yes. If he asks."

"Will you tell him about me?"

There was so much about Heath to tell, how could she begin to answer that? Effie nipped his shoulder blade instead of a reply. Heath rolled to face her.

"Will you?"

"No."

"Nothing? Not a word?"

She smiled. "It's not any of his business, is it?"

"Is he one of your *fans*?"

At that, she frowned and sat up. "That's not fair, Heath. You know I don't fuck around with them."

"So, how did you meet him, then?"

"LuvFinder." Effie laughed, embarrassed suddenly in a way she hadn't been before. "I thought I'd try it."

Heath snorted. "Better than trolling for dates at bars and insurance conventions, I guess."

She pinched his nipple hard, until he swatted her hand away. "Shut up."

"So," Heath said quietly, "you're looking for love this time?"

"Isn't everyone?" She said it nonchalantly, but she knew this admission changed everything. Until recently, she'd only been exploring. Considering her options. Having fun. But lately she had to admit that she was searching for something more—something real. She wasn't sure she could find it with anyone but Heath, but she'd be damned if it wasn't worth trying.

"Not everyone," Heath said. "Some of us have already found all we ever want."

He ran a fingertip over her cheek then, and along her jaw. He finished by tracing her lips. When she opened them as though to bite him, he didn't pull away, so she kissed it instead. Then she took his hand and turned it over so she could press a kiss to the inside of his wrist and the scars there.

"I just want something normal," Effie whispered. A confession. It felt good to say it loud, like prying the last tiny piece of a splinter that had been festering beneath her flesh. "Is that so much to ask for? To be the same as everyone else?"

At that, Heath sat up and got out of bed. With his back to her, he said, "Effie, don't you know that in a million years you could never be the same as anyone else?"

She watched him gather his clothes and leave her room. She waited until she heard the back door close. Then she went, naked, into the kitchen to lock it.

chapter eight

"My mother says I'm not allowed to see you anymore." The words come easier than Effie had thought they would. She'd practiced them in front of the mirror at home for an hour, every time stuttering, but now they sound as casual as if she were asking Heath about the weather. "She says it's not healthy for us."

Heath stares at her with large, hollowed eyes. He's been smoking. He stinks of booze. There's a blossoming bruise on one cheekbone that Effie didn't put there. She's sure it came from his father or another kind of fight, not from another girl, but that doesn't matter. It makes her want to kiss him and also to slap him harder on the other side to make one to match it. It makes her want to hold him close.

Still without a word, Heath pulls a joint from the pocket of his denim jacket. He licks the end and tucks it into the corner of his mouth. The Zippo lighter comes from his jeans pocket, and the sight of it makes her mouth dry. That lighter had been Daddy's. She hadn't realized Heath had kept it. All these years later, and seeing it is still…it's hard.

"Say something," Effie demands.

Heath shrugs and lights the joint. He offers it to her. She

should refuse. She doesn't even like weed. It makes her sleepy and sometimes anxious. It reminds her of those hazy, blurry basement days when neither of them had the strength to get off the bed because Daddy had dosed them up with something to keep them from trying to get away. Yet the joint had been in Heath's mouth, it will taste of him even if only the barest amount, and this could be the last she'll ever have of him.

"She's not wrong," Effie says a minute or so later when they've passed the joint back and forth a couple times. They're alone here in the picnic pavilion, but the park is officially closed. This is a risk, but then so is being here with him at all, even without the weed. "You know she isn't, Heath."

"She hates me."

Effie shakes her head, already swimming from the pot. "She doesn't… She's only trying to protect me."

At that, Heath pinches off the joint and tucks it away. "From me."

"From everything," Effie says.

"Where was she when you were getting pulled into the back of a van?" Heath's voice is low, hard, sharp. Knife-edged. "Or when you were kept like a dog in the dark for days on end, or when you almost died? Who protected you then?"

He is angry. She can't blame him. She understands why, but she understands why her parents worry, too.

"What does your dad say? Oh, right. He goes along with whatever your mother says." Heath sneers.

Effie frowns. "Look, your parents might not give a damn about you, but mine do."

He doesn't flinch, but she knows she's poked him someplace tender. It should make her behave more sweetly toward him, knowing she's being hurtful, but there's something dark with the two of them that makes her only want to hurt him more.

It's that dark thing her mother worries about. To be honest, it's scares Effie, too.

"I'm only seventeen, Heath. What do you want me to do? Run away from home? Live on the streets? I'm going to college next year. I'm going to make something of myself. Not like you." Her voice rises. Her fists clench.

"You think I'm nothing."

She doesn't. Effie thinks, in fact, that Heath is everything. He is too much to her and she to him. Even at seventeen she knows it. The girls in her class, her "friends," are worrying about who will ask them to the prom, and none of them have any idea what it's like to love someone so much you'd die for them. Literally die.

Heath rakes a hand through his dark hair, which has been cut shorter than she's ever seen it. He told her he was going on job interviews again. Without a high school degree, without the hope of getting a further education, there isn't much out there for him. Gas station attendant. Stock clerk. It's been a year since they got out of the basement, and Heath's quit or been fired from a dozen jobs. He can't make anything stick. Nothing but Effie, anyway.

"I have to go," Effie says. "I told my mom I was going to the library. She thinks I was going to write you a letter instead of telling you in person."

"Why didn't you?" He paces a little, hands shoved in his jacket pockets. His boots are scuffed, and the way he kicks at the gravel shows how they got that way. He won't look away from her.

"I wanted to see you."

Something small and hopeful glimmers for a second in his gaze before vanishing. "You should've written a letter. It would've been easier."

"I don't care about it being easy," Effie says.

Then he is kissing her. Hard and hot and leaving her breathless. His hands on her. Over her clothes, cupping her breasts, then under her shirt to touch her bare skin.

Last weekend Effie went to a slumber party with some girls from school. She'd been best friends with a couple of them in middle school, but they're not close anymore. She pretends they are, hoping maybe it will become the truth. They all played Truth or Dare and the biggest question was about who'd "done it" and who had not. None of them had.

Effie had lied and said she hadn't, either.

"But I thought—" Wendy Manning had started to say before Rebecca Meyers shushed her.

Effie knew what all those girls thought. In the year since she's been home, the rumors have flown fast and thick. But Daddy had never touched her. Not like that. He'd done a lot of things, but he'd never done that. It was a lie to say Effie was a virgin, but faced with that solemn-faced group of girls, Effie was not about to say anything else. They still giggled about touching "it" or French kissing. None of them understood sex at all.

When Heath pushes a hand between her legs now, Effie pulls away. "No."

She hasn't slapped his face, but she might as well have. Heath frowns. He reaches for her, but she dances out of his grip again.

"I said no!"

"You don't have to worry. I brought something," Heath says. "We'll be careful this time."

Effie's lip curls. "You want me to fuck you right here on the picnic table? Classy."

"I want to be with you, and I want you to feel safe, not worried about anything happening again. But you know if it did, I'd take care of you."

Effie hops off the picnic table. She doesn't want to talk about what happened. She doesn't want to think about it. "No."

"You don't love me," Heath says.

This is too much. All this time and all that happened with them, and now he wants to tell her that he *loves* her? What is it supposed to mean, what is she supposed to do about it now, when everything has changed?

"I already told you how I feel about that," she snaps. "It's easy to love someone when they're all you know."

"Effie, please..."

"No." She holds up a hand, backing away from him. "We can't go back to where we were, Heath. Don't you get it? What happened to us, it was totally fucked up. Okay? We had a super shitty thing happen to us, but we got out of it, we made it through, and now...it's over. You can't hold on to it. It's not normal. It's crazy. It's wrong between us. You have to let it go. You have to let *me* go."

"I don't think I can."

"Not wanting to and not being able to are not the same things!" Effie wants to punch him with her fists but settles for hitting him with her words, forcing him back a few steps.

Heath holds up his hands. Turns his face. He stops moving so that if she keeps advancing she will be pressed against him, and she stops herself from doing that. They stand less than an arm's length apart. Close enough she can see the throb of his pulse in his throat.

"Loving you has nothing to do with choice," he says.

"Because we never had one!"

Heath is silent.

Effie lifts her chin. "You'll find someone else to love. We're still kids. You never find the one you're supposed to be with forever when you're a kid."

"There is no forever for me without you," Heath says, and Effie knows he means it. "If I never see you again, Effie, there will still never be anyone else but you."

She'd learned about sex, but whatever she'd believed she knew about love shatters in that moment, leaving her broken in its wake. Shaking her head, Effie says nothing as she backs away. Three, four steps take her to the driver's side of her father's car. She's behind the wheel a moment after that. Staring straight ahead at the road, wondering what would happen if she drives herself straight into a tree.

She unbuckles her seat belt.

She puts her foot on the gas.

But in the end, Effie is not about to die for love. Not again. Not ever.

When she walks in the front door, her parents are waiting for her. So are two uniformed policemen who exchange looks when her mother flies up off the couch to grab her. Effie recognizes one of them. He was the one who found them in the basement. Effie remembers that he held her hand while they waited for the ambulance.

"What's going on?" She tries to slip out of her mother's clinging, desperate grasp.

"You're all right," Mom says.

Her father swipes a hand over his face. "Thank God."

Effie, staring over her shoulder at the cop, turns her attention to her mother. "Yes, I'm fine. I told you I was going to the library."

"Effie, we know you weren't at the library," Officer Schmidt, that's his name, says. "You were with Heath Shaw in Long's Park."

Effie fights off her mother's grip. Panic rises. "Where is he? What's wrong? What happened to him?"

"You don't need to worry about him anymore," Mom says, but Effie won't even look at her.

Her father takes a step forward but stops when Effie shakes her head. She glares at the cop. He should understand, more than any of them.

"Where is he?"

"Heath attempted to take his own life shortly after you left him. He was discovered by a jogger and taken to Lancaster General Hospital. He's in stable condition, but he'll be remanded to a psychiatric care facility for the next few days while he's monitored."

"He tried to kill himself?" Effie sags, vaguely aware her mother is tugging her arm to get her to sit on the couch. She allows herself to be pushed. She shakes her head. "What did he do?"

"He cut himself." Officer Schmidt's voice is gentle, and he doesn't look away from Effie's eyes, not even for a second. "It was unclear whether or not he'd harmed you, however. He told us you'd been together, but not if you'd left safely."

"Of course I did. Heath would never hurt me. Not ever." She shakes off her mother's attempt at a hug and buries her face in her hands. The world spins. She thinks she might vomit right there on the rug, and won't her mom be upset then, when Effie makes a mess?

"Now that you're home safe, that's all we need to know." Officer Schmidt comes closer to squeeze Effie's shoulder. He looks again deep into her eyes, then takes a business card from his pocket and presses it into her hand. His fingers are strong and warm. "If you ever need anything, Effie, anything at all, I'm here for you."

Lots of people will tell her that in her life, but only a few of them ever are.

chapter nine

Polly had brought home a thick folder stuffed with information about the science fair. It was not optional. It was going to be a nightmare.

Effie, paint smeared all over her hands from the projects she'd been working on all day, gestured. "Okay, so what are some of the choices?"

"Testing the amount of sugar in sodas. Raising baby chicks. Ooh—"

"No," Effie said. "No way."

Polly rolled her eyes but ran her finger down the rest of the list. Her small mouth pursed, her brow furrowed. She looked a lot like Effie's mom when she did that, and a wave of love for her daughter forced Effie to the sink so she wasn't caught being all mushy. Sometimes Effie wondered if in her pursuit of not being too attentive, too hovering, she'd somehow ruined Polly. The girl was blessedly and casually independent, not at all clingy or a hugger. Still, not needing someone and not believing they would be there to help you when you needed it were two very different things, and although it never seemed as if Polly didn't trust Effie to take care of her, there were plenty of times Effie felt as though she'd come up short in the parenting department.

Polly paused with her finger on the paper. "I could grow plants in different soils with different kinds of water. Like, with acid and stuff."

"Acid, that sounds pretty dangerous." Effie scrubbed at the paint under her fingernails. She'd been working on a commissioned piece and was hating it, which was why she'd still been painting when Polly got home. Usually she tried to be finished by the time school ended so she could spend time with her kid. Procrastination, thy name was "Chuck Norris Riding a Unicorn."

"Not, like, superbad acid, Mom. Like, I dunno. Baking soda or whatever."

"Baking soda is acid? Since when?"

Polly shrugged. "How about I could try to design a thing for an egg that protects it from breaking when you drop it off a roof?"

"Does that involve you going up onto a roof to drop things off it?" Effie scrubbed a little harder, looking over her shoulder.

Polly grinned. "Maybe."

"Also no way. You're the kid who broke her leg tripping over a shadow on the sidewalk. I'm not letting you up on the roof." Drying her hands, Effie turned to lean against the counter. "Can't you pick something easy and delicious, like testing different types of chocolate chip recipes to see how they change when you add or subtract vital ingredients?"

"Is that on the list?" Polly shook the papers.

"I have no idea, but if it's not, it should be." Effie came closer to look over Polly's shoulder. "It would be fun. And I could be your taste tester."

"You don't eat cookies with chocolate chips in them," Polly said matter-of-factly, then paused. The girl had always worn her emotions all over her face. She looked scared now, and sad, and Effie's heart sank.

"What is it, Pollywog?"

"Meredith Ross said… She said…" Polly caught her breath and bit her upper lip with sharp white teeth.

Meredith Ross was a shitty little princess diva whose mother had gone to school with Effie. Delores Gonzalez had been a few years older than Effie, but she'd lived two houses down from Effie's parents, so the walk back and forth to school had often been made only a few steps behind her. Effie had very vivid memories of the back of Dee's head. They'd never been friends. Dee had been there the day Effie came home. The entire neighborhood had turned out to welcome Effie with a party like something out of a nightmare. It had been her father's idea, God bless him. He'd meant well. He'd had no idea how hard it would be for Effie to come back home and face all those people.

This wasn't the first time Polly had complained about Meredith. Once, when Effie was eight and Dee ten, the older girl had made fun of Effie's favorite dress. It sounded as if Dee's daughter was following in her mother's footsteps. Effie kept her expression neutral, though. Polly already looked on the verge of tears.

"What did she say?"

Polly ducked her head. Her shoulders heaved on a sigh. She shook her head, not speaking.

It wasn't like her to be so reticent. Effie pulled up the chair next to Polly's. Their knees touched. She took both of Polly's hands.

"Hey. Tell me what's going on."

Polly shook again, this time with silent, wrenching sobs. When she looked at Effie, blue eyes wide and confused, Effie's heart broke. She pulled Polly close, stroking the girl's blond hair over and over.

"Mama, is Heath my dad?"

Effie paused as her fingers snagged in Polly's hair. She untangled them gently and squeezed her daughter harder. "No, honey. No."

"Meredith said Heath is your brother, *and* that he's my *dad*! Both!" Polly's voice broke, agonized. She pushed away to stare at Effie. Her mouth worked. Her cheeks had flushed crimson.

"Oh, Polly. Honey…no. Heath isn't your dad. He loves you very much, but he's not your dad. And he's not my brother." Her voice hitched on that word. *Brother. Sister. Daddy.* She tried so hard never to think about Heath in that way, no matter how many times she'd been forced to call him that. Effie grabbed a couple of paper napkins to wipe Polly's face. "Why did Meredith even say such a thing?"

"Because she's a bitch!"

Effie choked back laughter and made her voice stern. "Polly."

"She's jealous because I got invited to Sam Walsh's party, and she didn't. Because she's mean, that's all. And Sam's mom said she could only have four friends over, and I was one of them. But Meredith got mad." Polly sniffled. "So she told everyone that Heath is your brother and I'm his kid. She said it was illegal and gross, and that I was probably deformed, because that's what happens when brothers and sisters have kids together."

Effie's stomach turned over. "Polly. No. I promise you, Heath is not my brother. If he was, then Nana would be his mom, right?"

Polly sniffled again but looked relieved. "Yeah. And Nana doesn't like him."

"No, she doesn't." There was no point in lying about it.

"Because something happened when you were younger," Polly said with some more confidence.

Effie hesitated. She'd never discussed with Polly what had happened to her from the ages of thirteen to sixteen. She'd meant to when Polly got older, probably when she was closer to thirteen herself, but she was only eleven now. There hadn't seemed a need to get into the details. It was actually something of a surprise that nobody had ever told her anything about it before now.

"Yes. That's why Nana doesn't like him," Effie said.

"It happened to you and Heath together?"

Effie nodded. "Yes."

Polly frowned and plucked at the hem of her shirt before looking at her mother. "Meredith said the only reason you ever sell any paintings is because people on the internet are perverts."

"Meredith Ross needs to keep her mouth shut, and so does her mother." Effie's voice rose, and she forced herself to calm. "Don't listen to her, honey, okay? She's a jealous little brat. You don't need to worry about my paintings or anything else. It's none of her business. You just concentrate on being the best Polly you can be, and ignore her."

Polly didn't look entirely mollified, but she nodded. Effie hugged her again, squeezing tight before letting her go. She held the girl's shoulders gently for a moment, though, looking closely at her daughter's face.

"If she gives you any trouble, Polly, you tell me. I'll talk to the teacher."

"No!" Polly looked alarmed. "Mom, no. Don't do that, I'll get called a tattletale."

"Is she telling everyone this stuff?"

Polly shook her head. "I don't think so. And if she did, I'd just tell them it's not true. Because it isn't. Right?"

"Right." Still angry but not showing it, Effie looked over Polly's list with her as they tried to settle on a project. Leaving it to be decided another time, she shooed her kid off to watch an hour of television before dinner.

Her phone buzzed with a call she picked up without looking to see who it was. Expecting her mother or Heath, Effie was ready to launch into a bitter tirade against tween girl bullies but stopped short at the sound of a male voice. "Oh. Mitchell. Hey."

"Hi, Effie. Is this a bad time?"

She looked at the pot of water she was boiling to make boxed macaroni and cheese. "I'm just putting together a gourmet feast for me and my kid. How are you?"

"Good, good. I thought I'd give you a call. See if you wanted to chat."

Effie hesitated. "I'm kind of in the middle of some things. Maybe later tonight?"

"Oh, sure. Dinner and stuff. Right. I should've thought." Mitchell laughed softly. "Bachelorhood tends to make you forget about things like regular mealtimes."

Somehow, she doubted that. Mitchell had not impressed her as the sort of guy who survived on day-old pizza. Was he angling for a dinner invitation? That was the problem with this dating stuff, Effie thought. It was so much more complicated than bringing home a guy from a bar and sending him home in the morning with a phone number one digit off so he wouldn't be able to call her again.

"I had a great time with you. I wanted to let you know," Mitchell said when Effie didn't speak.

"Me, too." She cradled the phone against her shoulder to pour the pasta into the water.

"So…we'll talk later. Okay? Looking forward to it."

"Me, too," Effie repeated and let him disconnect the phone call first. She stared at the phone for a second or so. She hadn't assigned him a special ringtone or added a picture to his contact information, so for the moment, Mitchell remained nothing but a string of numbers.

"Give him a chance," she murmured to herself. "This is what you want."

Something nice, something tame. Something normal. That was what she was looking for.

Wasn't it?

Polly was so quiet at dinner that nothing Effie said got a smile out of her. Clearly, she was still bothered by what had happened with Meredith. So, after they'd polished off the mac-n-cheese and Polly had cleared the table, Effie sent her off to her room to do homework.

Then she picked up the phone.

"Hi, Dee?" Effie fell into the old nickname before thinking it was possible Delores didn't go by it any longer. Then she decided she didn't give a rat's ass what the other woman preferred to be called. "This is Effie. Polly's mother. Your daughter's in Polly's class."

"I know who you are, Effie, of course." Delores sounded bubbly, as if maybe she'd already started on the early evening cocktails. No wonder, since her husband had left her several years ago for not a younger woman, but an older one.

Maybe that was unkind.

"So listen, Dee, I'm going to cut straight to it. Keep your mouth shut about my daughter, your speculation about her father, and about Heath." Effie drew in a breath as if she was dragging on a cigarette. "You know damn well he's not my brother. And not that it's any of your business, but he's not Polly's father. Get your own house in order before you start talking shit about mine."

Dee sputtered. "What... I... Wait a minute. What?"

"My kid's eleven years old. She should be worried about her science fair project and growing out of her favorite jeans

too fast. Not any other bullshit you want to spread around."
Effie paused long enough to hear a snuffle from Dee through
the phone. She smiled to be sure the other woman heard it
in her voice. "She has a lot of people in her life who love her.
She hasn't suffered for the lack of knowing who donated the
sperm that made her."

"Oh." Dee sounded confused. She'd never been the bright-
est shade of pink in the palette. "Oh, I didn't know you had
a sperm donor."

Effie had in fact been knocked up the old-fashioned way
and had been making a sarcastic comment, so now she sighed.
"Dee, Jesus. It's none of your business. Okay? Why would you
tell your kid anything like that anyway? And as for my paintings, also none of your business. What difference does it make
to you who buys them or supports them?"

Silence. Effie waited. Through the phone line she heard
another snuffle.

"I'm sorry," Dee said finally. "I didn't tell Meredith any of
those things. She must've overheard us talking."

"Who was talking?"

"Friends, I guess." Dee made a small, apologetic noise.
"The subject came up at the last mommy meeting I had here.
I guess she overheard us..."

It was far from the first time Effie had known herself to be
the topic of conversation. For years after coming home she'd
been approached by reporters and curiosity seekers wanting a
piece of her story. After the debacle with the coming-home
party, her dad had forbidden any of them from contacting her,
but after he died, there'd been a few who managed to find
her contact information. Some had been ballsy enough to ap-
proach her instead of just posting voyeuristic bullshit about her
on that stupid fucking forum for sickos who liked to collect
memorabilia from crime victims. Someone had even made a

documentary. Effie had been offered money to participate, but she had refused.

To hear it now, though...her stomach twisted again. She wanted a drink, something strong. Instead, she forced herself to breathe.

"Why the hell are you gossiping about me anyway?"

Dee made another of those noises. "They asked me. Some moms from school, I guess they found out we went to school together, and when they heard about Andrews being up for parole..."

"Wait a minute. What? What the fuck?" Effie froze, her fingers cramping and curling around her phone.

"An alert came up, I guess, about how a convicted sex offender was possibly going to be living close by. I guess you know where the house is."

Effie swallowed bitterness. "Yes."

The same house. It had passed to Andrews's children when he went to prison, and as far as she knew, they'd never sold it. Nobody had ever seemed to be living in it anyway, whenever she drove past, which was only on the rarest of secretive occasions. It had always been empty, the grass a little too long, merchandisers littering the driveway. At Halloween, no local kids egged it or strung toilet paper in the trees. The house had gained its own reputation.

Dee coughed. "Well. It's only a couple blocks away from where I live now. If he gets out on parole, he'll be living there. So, you know, they put out this petition to sign so that there wouldn't be a pedophile living there."

"I don't think you can keep him from moving back into a house that he owns," Effie whispered through her clenched jaw. "No matter what he did."

Dee was very quiet then, only the sound of her breathing coming through the phone. "I didn't tell anyone Heath was your brother, Effie. I told them that Andrews made you and Heath call him Daddy, that's all. And that's the truth, right? I didn't make it up. I wasn't lying! They asked me, and it's not like any of them lived around here when it happened. They don't remember the stories."

"Oh, God. Well, aren't they lucky they have you to catch them up." Effie swallowed again, her throat closing. All those women in their yoga pants and matching hairstyles, matching smiles. She'd never quite fit in with them, and now they all knew about her…this, the worst thing. But that wasn't what upset her the most. "Look, when it affects my kid, Dee, I get really pissed."

"I'm sorry," Dee said after a minute. "They're really worried about him getting out and living so close. That's all."

"He's not going to get out of prison." Bill had told her so, enough times, and all she could do was believe it or live every moment of her life waiting in dread for it to happen.

"Well, there was something on the internet…"

"Rumors about it go around every few years when he's up for parole, but he won't get out. He was served with two consecutive life terms for kidnapping, indecency, cruelty to children and a bunch of other stuff. He's not getting out, not ever." Effie laughed, harsh and sour. "Tell all your biddy friends not to worry so fucking much. And tell your kid to back off my kid."

"I'll talk to her," Dee said.

Effie took a slow breath. "Thanks. I'd appreciate it."

"Effie, if you want to come to our moms' group…" The other woman trailed off.

Effie didn't answer. The idea alarmed her. When Polly was younger and Effie had been struggling to get through school and working two jobs to make ends meet, she'd often eyed those put-together matchy-matchy moms in their playgroups with envy. Their fancy strollers and designer coffees. The way they all seemed to know how to keep their kids clean and dressed with what seemed like very little effort. There'd been days she swore finding two matching socks was a feat akin to Frodo's journey to throw the ring into the volcano.

"So you can all talk shit about me to my face instead of behind my back? No, thanks."

Dee sighed loudly. "I said I was sorry. They started to ask me questions. It's not like any of this stuff can't be found out on the internet. I mean, Effie, you make your living off it. Do you really think people don't talk about it?"

Effie knew her work's value lay in her past. She knew her story was public knowledge. She rubbed at the spot between her eyes. "Look, just…be more careful, okay? And tell your kid to back off."

"She's upset because her dad left," Dee said after a second. "I know she's been a pain to some of the other kids lately. She feels left out. Maybe if you could ask Polly to be a little nicer to her, you know, include her in some things…"

"You want me to have my kid befriend yours?" Effie frowned, thinking of all the little stories Polly had told her about Meredith's bullying tactics.

"She used to have a lot of friends, and now she's the outcast. She thinks they're making fun of her because of her dad leaving."

"It's because she spreads rumors and makes fun of other kids."

Dee coughed. "Girls like Polly… If she was nice to Meredith, the other kids would like her, too."

Effie rolled her eyes. "I'm not sure that's how it works, to be honest. Polly's not the one being nasty, you know."

"I know."

This conversation had not gone at all the way Effie had

imagined it would. Consequently, her righteous outrage was fading in the face of Dee's apologies and pleas on behalf of her lonely, socially alienated daughter. "I'll talk to Polly."

"I'll talk to Meredith. And, Effie...if you don't want to join the moms' group, maybe you'd like to grab coffee one day? Catch up? I'm really sorry, I never meant for anything to be hurtful. It got blown out of context. It's easy to forget there's a real person on the other side of the gossip. Let me make it up to you."

"Sure," Effie said, to her own surprise. "That sounds great."

Dee sounded pleased. "Great. I'll call you next week."

They disconnected and Effie tucked her phone into her pocket. She went into Polly's room to wish her good-night, only to find her daughter already asleep. Another rush of love washed over Effie, so strong it made her want to cry.

It was only later as she was falling into sleep that Effie jerked awake with that feeling of falling. She'd forgotten to call Mitchell. She twisted in her sheets to look at the clock. Too late now. He really wasn't the one she wanted to talk to anyway, but although she tapped in Heath's number, she deleted it before the call could connect.

chapter ten

Serving her father coffee, Effie feels incredibly grown-up but far from mature. Not even with the small bump of her belly sticking out from the front of her maternity dress. It's a horrendously ugly outfit and does nothing to hide the pregnancy she and her father have not yet discussed.

He takes the coffee and sets it on the table to look at her. "You don't have to stay here, you know that? Your mother…"

"She made herself very clear." Effie sips from a glass of ice water, the only thing she can stomach right now.

Her father sighs. "She's sorry about that."

"I'm sure she is." Effie shakes her head. "But I'm fine here. Really."

"If that boy wants to step up and take responsibility," her father begins but stops when Effie holds up a hand.

"This isn't Heath's baby. I told Mom that. But Heath is willing to let me live here. It's my best option. And it will be fine. Good. It's going to be great." As always since she came home, there's an awkward silence in the space where once she'd have called him Dad. She can't bring herself to do it anymore. It's not Daddy, but even so, the name is soured for her. It's not as if she can suddenly start calling him Pop or something like that. So Effie doesn't call her father anything, and it's obvious and uncomfortable, but neither of them ever mention it.

"I know you think so." Her father frowns. "I understand."

Effie sighs, sounding very much as he had only moments before. "You don't."

"I'd like to," her father says.

This is never the sort of conversation a girl should ever have with her father. It involves trauma and awful things. Also sex, which wasn't awful nor a trauma, despite the fact she ended up in this delicate condition when she ought to have known better.

Her father sighs again, looking so much older than he had even when Effie came back home, and she'd been shocked then at how much he'd aged in the three years she'd been gone. His smile reminds her of when she was younger and he'd take her on a Saturday to the hardware store to look at the tools. He's the sort of father any girl would dream of, the kind who will get choked up when he dances with her at her wedding. Not that she's planning a wedding anytime soon.

"The father. He's not in the picture?"

Effie has not told the baby's father that he's the one who knocked her up. She hasn't seen him since she found out. If he has by some reason heard about it, and he might've, because it's a small town, he probably assumes, as her mother had, that the baby is Heath's. And it should be, she thinks with a sudden, fierce twist of her mouth. This baby, the one she's going to get to keep and not the one she lost, *should* be his.

She shakes her head. "No. He doesn't know."

"You could come home, Effie. We'll take care of you." Her father sounds sincere.

Effie believes him. But... "I'm almost nineteen. I'm in school, I'm working, and I'm having a baby. Living with Heath is helping me. We're going to be all right. I don't have to come home. I can't."

"Why not? Because of your mother? She's just having a hard time with all of this. Honey, I know your mom likes to talk. But that's all it is. She'll come around. You know she will."

"No, not because of her. Because I'm not a kid anymore."

"You're still our daughter. You'll always be our little girl. Effie, your mom and I want to help you. That's all." Her father lifts the coffee mug as though he means to drink from it but puts it down without so much as a sip. He shakes his head. Sighs again.

Effie wants to make this easier for him, but she doesn't know how. "This is the best thing for me."

"To live in a crap-hole apartment, working and going to school, with a baby on the way? Living with a guy who can barely hold down a job of his own? I give him credit, don't get me wrong, if the baby really isn't his—"

"It's not," she says sharply. "And he knows that. So he *does* deserve the credit, and for more than just that. Heath works hard."

"He's been in and out of mental hospitals, Effie."

"Once. That's it."

"Once is one too many."

"Better than just going in and never coming out," she snaps, not caring if she hurts her father's feelings now. "Has he fucked up? Yes. We both have."

"I understand. You went through something terrible together."

"Yes," Effie says quietly. "Together. And we're going through this together, too."

"Is he good to you?"

It's not the question she expected, and she's taken enough by surprise to nod. "Yes."

Her father stands. "Well. I can't promise you anything about your mother, but…I'll try to give him a chance. I just want you to know you have choices. But if you need something, anything, you come to me, okay? I'm still your father, Effie, and I love you."

"Love you, too, D-dad." She stumbles on the word but gives her father a huge, long hug.

When he finally lets go to hold her at arm's length, he looks her up and down. Her mother would have lectured, but her father smiles. He puts a hand on her belly.

"I bet it's a girl," he says. "And she'll be beautiful, just like you."

chapter eleven

Effie missed her father every day, but there were some times when the ache was worse. Tonight, crammed into the middle school auditorium with her mom on one side and Heath on the other, she missed her father very much. He'd have been there with flowers for Polly, even though she only had a part in the chorus. Front row. Clapping until his hands fell off. Effie wisely did not mention this thought to her mother, who was already supremely uncomfortable with the fact Heath had shown up late and, to her, unexpectedly.

"Stacey," Heath said with a nod and a smile so genuine even Effie believed he wasn't being sarcastic. In Effie's ear, he said, "Parking was shit. Sorry."

"It's okay. You got here before they started, that's what counts." Catching sight of her mother's dour expression, Effie settled herself more firmly between them.

When he took her hand a few minutes into the show, she let him hold it for at least a minute before gently disentangling their fingers. She pretended it was so she could dig in her purse for a tissue, but she knew Heath wasn't fooled. Dammit, though, he didn't have to insist on trying to make them into a couple when they weren't. It put Effie in a bad place, made her the bad guy, and he knew it.

Heath gave her a glance and a smile that Effie didn't return. He rolled his eyes a little and turned his attention back to the stage. Three hours and one fifteen-minute intermission later, the show had ended and a bright-eyed Polly rushed to greet them in the school lobby.

"Everyone's going to Buster's for ice cream, Mom. Can I go?" Polly still wore the heavy eyeliner and blush from the play, and the sight of how she was going to look in a few years as a teenager sent a pang through Effie's heart.

"I can take her," Effie's mother said. "I have some errands to run in the mall. I can shop while she eats with her friends, then pick her up and bring her home."

Effie hesitated. "Are you sure?"

"Positive." Her mother smiled and put an arm around Polly's shoulders. "It's no trouble at all."

It was also a way to one-up Heath, something that only Polly didn't guess. Heath knew it but visibly shrugged it off. Effie gave her mother a lifted eyebrow that she pretended not to see, but refusing would punish Polly, not Effie's mom.

"Give me your things and I'll take them home so you don't have to worry about them," Effie said, then to Heath, "Are you going to hang around a few minutes, or…?"

"I'll wait until you get back. I want to tell my girl how great she was." Heath hugged Polly, then ruffled her hair. From his inside jacket pocket, he pulled out a single, somewhat crushed, carnation. "Here, Wog. You should always get flowers after a performance."

Oh. Flowers. Effie blinked at the sting of emotion and shot her mother a look that was far too triumphant to be appropriate. Polly was already heading down the narrow hallway to the band room, and Effie followed her through the throng of overexcited tweens. The noise level was insane. She waited while Polly gathered her stuff and piled it into her mother's arms.

"Polly," Effie said before her daughter could head back into the lobby. "I just wanted to tell you...you were amazing."

"It was just a part in the chorus," Polly said. "I messed up the one dance, too."

"You were amazing," Effie repeated.

Polly grinned and hugged her, squeezing too hard and crushing the book bag between them. Effie laughed. "Go on, so you're not too late."

A dark-haired girl wearing too much eye makeup even for the school musical paused as she passed them. "Are you going to Buster's?"

"Yeah." Polly paused. "You wanna come?"

The other girl smiled and nodded. "Yeah, sure, my mom said I could. I wasn't going to, but..."

"Nah, you should come. Everyone's going." Polly waited until the girl had moved out of earshot, then gave Effie a long-suffering look. "Meredith."

"Wow. I didn't recognize her."

"She stuffed her bra," Polly said with an arch sniff that said exactly what she thought about that little trick.

Effie stopped herself from laughing, but only barely. Back in the lobby, she hugged her daughter goodbye, gave her mother some money to pay for the ice cream, despite Mom's protests that she could cover it, and when they'd gone through the front doors toward the parking lot, Effie looked for Heath. The crowd had thinned drastically, and at six-five he usually stood head and shoulders over everyone else. He shouldn't have been difficult to see. Maybe he'd left despite telling her he would wait.

Effie shrugged Polly's book bag over her shoulder and patted her pockets to be sure she had her keys before heading out into the cold. She spotted Heath as soon as she came out the front doors. She should've known to look for him in the smoking area. "Oh, hey."

He wasn't alone. The blonde with him wore stiletto ankle boots with skinny jeans and an impossibly tight leather jacket that did not look very warm. It couldn't have been, not by the way she shivered and shifted from foot to foot as she smoked. She tossed her hair when she saw Effie, but it took Heath a few seconds longer than that to turn.

"Hey," Effie said again. "I'm heading out."

"Hi, Effie. I'm Lisa. Collins? My son Kevin's in Polly's grade. He was the zookeeper." The blonde stubbed out her cigarette and offered a hand that Effie took only because it would've seemed really antisocial to refuse.

"Oh. Right. Kevin. He was in Polly's class last year. Mr. Binderman." Effie had no recollection of ever meeting Lisa Collins before, but that didn't mean anything. She gave Heath a curious look.

Heath shoved his hands into his back pockets and rocked a little on his heels, looking from Effie to Lisa and back again. *Oh,* Effie thought. *Oh, shit.*

"Hey, well, I'm going to get out of here. Thanks for coming to the show, I know Polly appreciated it." Effie gave Lisa a nod and Heath a neutral look, then went to her car.

It took her a minute or so after putting the key in the ignition before she could force herself to pull out of the parking spot. She wasn't trying to watch and see if Heath and Lisa left together. Definitely not. But if she drove slowly enough, she might be able to catch a...

No, Effie thought. *Hell, no. You're not going to be that kind of jealous bitch.*

Heath had every right to flirt or date or fuck whomever he wanted. Effie had made that abundantly clear. It was not the first time he'd done it. There'd even been a girl named Theresa who, for a while, had been officially his girlfriend. She'd been decent to Polly and respectful without being obsequious or a bitch to Effie. She hadn't lasted long, not even a year, and Effie had never asked what broke them up, but she hadn't been sad to see her go.

Anyway, a pot could call a kettle any color it wanted to, but it would still be black. Effie and Heath were not together. She did not want them to be together, not like that. So good luck to Lisa, Effie thought and pulled into the line of cars leaving the parking lot. She made it all the way home without so much as a shaky tear or stifled sob. She even made it into the house.

There she poured herself a glass of white wine and leaned against the counter, waiting for the jealousy to hit her. It was going to. She deserved it to.

The back door opened before she had time to do more than take a few sips. Startled, Effie spilled the wine down the front of her shirt. "What the hell!"

"Sorry. I texted you. You didn't answer." Heath took the glass from her hand and drained it, then pinned her against the counter. "How long until your mom gets back with Polly?"

Effie put her hands flat on his chest to hold him off her. "Hey. You. No. This… No."

He tried to kiss her, but she turned her face. He didn't let that stop him. He licked her neck, then nibbled in the best way to get her shivering for him.

"Dammit, Heath," Effie said. "What the hell…"

He laughed into her ear and moved away from her. "Your face. When you saw her. Your fucking face, Effie."

At that, she was no longer jealous. Vindicated, though she'd never admit it. Also pissed, which she would.

"You're an asshole," she told him.

Heath frowned. "C'mon."

In response, Effie went to the fridge to pour another glass of wine. She didn't offer him one. With her back to him, she said, "Trying to make me jealous is an asshole thing to do."

"You do it to me all the time."

"No," she said, spinning. "I don't. I don't *try* to make you jealous. I try to move on and live my fucking life, Heath, and be honest about it. There's a goddamned difference."

"I went out to smoke. She was there. She started flirting with me. She's cute. I didn't start it up to make you jealous. But did it?" He looked angry but also hopeful.

Effie sipped wine without an answer. She pushed past him and went down the hall into her bedroom, where she shut the door firmly behind her. Her hands were shaking, but she didn't want him to see it. She put the glass on the dresser and unbuttoned her blouse, turning quickly when the bedroom door opened.

"I'm changing. Get out."

"It's not like I've never seen you naked," Heath said in a low voice, still trying for humor, although he wasn't laughing.

Effie paused, lifting her chin, her fingers no longer working the buttons. "I said get out."

"If you want me to leave, I'll go." Heath's gaze fell to the open V of her shirt, then moved to her eyes.

Effie scowled. Unbuttoning. One at a time, slowly, so slowly. "I said I wanted you to, didn't I?"

She let the fabric fall off her shoulders, leaving her in the pretty A-line skirt with the vintage styling and her lacy push-up bra that was definitely of a more modern fashion. Without ever looking away from him, Effie tossed her shirt onto the chair in the corner and put her hands on her hips. She drew in a breath, pushing out her tits and sucking in her gut. Cocked a hip.

"Get out," she said. "I'm trying to take a shower."

Heath didn't move. She hadn't really thought he would.

Effie reached behind her to undo the zipper on her skirt. That joined the blouse so she stood in front of him in only her underwear.

"Get out," she repeated one last time. "Or get on your knees."

She knew which Heath would choose, yet still she held her breath until he dropped to his knees and slid across the hardwood floor to get himself in front of her. He could say no, one day. It could happen, but it had not happened now, and when he ran his fingertips up the backs of her calves and thighs, Effie shifted her stance to give him ample access to the heat between her legs.

The sound of voices stopped him. He looked up at her. Effie put her hand on his head, running her fingers through his hair, but then she stepped back.

"They're home," she whispered. "I'm going to take a shower."

Under the water, she closed her eyes and let herself shake a little, thinking of his touch. Then she turned the water to cold and forced herself to endure the frigid sting long enough to numb herself to even a thought. Teeth chattering, Effie dried herself and put on a pair of comfy pj's and her fluffy robe.

Heath, to her surprise, had not left. Her mother had, but he and Polly were at the kitchen island with huge bowls of ice cream topped with candy and chocolate syrup. Effie paused in the doorway.

"What happened to Buster's?"

Polly waved her spoon. "It was too crowded and they didn't have enough tables, and some of the kids were being jerks about sharing, so I told Nana to bring me home. She didn't want to stay. She said she had to get back to let Jakie out."

"And I made Polly a better sundae here, anyway," Heath said. "Want one?"

Effie put a hand on her belly. "Whoa. No. I'm going to have some hot tea, though. Do you... Would you like some?"

She and Heath shared a look. She could've asked him to leave, but that would've raised a question and probably a protest from Polly. Besides, there was the promise of finishing what they'd started, later, when Polly had been safely put to bed and was asleep.

She and Heath drank tea. They played a few hands of Uno with Polly, who unashamedly wheedled them into letting her stay up late because it was a Friday night. When Heath slapped a card on top of Effie's and pulled them both out of the pile with a cry of triumph, Polly shook her head.

"That's not in the rules. I played this with Sam at her house, and she says that's not how you play it."

Heath shrugged and gave Effie a look. "It's how we play it."

They'd played Uno for hours, in the basement. They'd made up their own rules for the tournaments. Now Effie looked carefully at her own selection of cards.

"Lots of people make up their own rules, Polly. It's late now. Bedtime."

"C'mon," Heath said, "I'll tuck you in."

Polly rolled her eyes. "I don't need to be tucked in. Sheesh."

She hopped off her chair and went around the table to hug him, though, tight around the neck. Effie watched the two of them quietly before she got up to put the dishes in the sink.

"Brush your teeth" was all she said to her daughter. "And lights out, no playing around on your phone."

Polly sighed with another roll of her eyes but left after kissing Heath on the cheek. "Night."

Effie watched her go, then turned to him. "Remember run around the table?"

"Yeah. If you put down three of the same in a row." He leaned back in his chair with a laugh and a shake of his head.

"And if you used a Reverse card, you had to sit backward until the next one was played."

It was a surprisingly good memory. Effie smiled. When he came to the sink, she thought he'd kiss her, but Heath only pushed her gently to the side to take over the rinsing of the bowls before she could put them in the dishwasher. Effie was of the opinion that if you had to wash the dishes before washing them, you were making too much of an effort. She leaned against the counter to watch him, though.

"I have a floor that needs a good mopping, too," she said mildly.

Heath laughed and closed the dishwasher, then rinsed his hands under the tap. He dried them on the seat of his jeans and reached for her. Effie let him pull her closer.

"It wasn't bad every second," she said. "Sometimes we made it almost okay."

"Yes."

"Someone told me they heard something. About him. Getting out," she added quietly.

"He won't."

She nodded against his chest, her eyes closed.

"And even if he did…"

She looked up at him. "What?"

"He won't. That's all. He's in for the rest of his hopefully short life." Heath passed a hand over her hair and let his fingers tangle in the length for a second. "I should go."

Frowning, Effie stepped back. "So go, then."

"Kiss me first."

She did, a quick peck that made him laugh and pull her closer. She put her hands flat on his chest to hold him off and shook her head when he tried for another. "Lisa will get jealous."

It was a shitty thing to say, and she regretted it at once,

because Heath did not take it as the joke she'd meant it to be. With a scowl, he backed up a step. Effie reached for him, but he danced out of her reach.

"If you think I want her instead of you, you're insane," he said. "But you know what really sucks, Effie, is I think you want me to want her instead of you."

It was the last thing in the world she really wanted, but it *was* what she thought they both needed. She shook her head. Heath scowled.

"I'm not you," he said.

Effie put her hands on her hips. "Clearly."

Heath shook his head but said nothing. He grabbed his coat and paused to look at her over his shoulder as he stood in the doorway. "I love you, Effie, but sometimes…"

"Sometimes, what?" she demanded.

"Sometimes, you make it really fucking hard."

chapter twelve

Effie was looking forward to this date with Mitchell the way she anticipated a flu shot. It was going to be slightly unpleasant, but in the long run it would be good for her. Still, she'd been procrastinating about getting ready for it all day, using her work as an excuse. At least it had made her productive. She'd finished up three different pieces for her Craftsy store as well as one larger piece someone had commissioned.

Now she was going to be late. Not by a few minutes, either, but probably by almost an hour, since she hadn't yet showered and was covered in paint. Effie prided herself on being a woman who didn't need a lot of time to make herself date ready, but even she needed more than fifteen minutes.

Shit.

I'm running really late, she texted Mitchell. Sorry. Will that mess up dinner?

I'll change the reservation. What time?

Effie typed a reply while stripping out of her paint-spattered work clothes, asking for an hour and a half, just to be safe. Then she called down the hall to Polly. "Hey, is Nana here yet?"

"No." Polly appeared in the doorway. "I thought you were leaving at five."

Effie glanced at Mitchell's text long enough to see he'd said the timing was okay, then tossed the phone onto the dresser. "I was. Got caught up. What have you been doing all day? You've been very quiet."

Polly looked caught, which made Effie pause before stripping out of her underwear to head for the shower. "Nothing."

"You must've done a lot of nothing." Effie put her hands on her hips.

Polly shrugged and gave Effie a look of bland innocence she'd learned directly from her mother. Effie sighed and looked at the clock. If she showered quickly, she'd have time to shave all her important bits and blow-dry her hair, and still make it to the restaurant within the time frame she'd asked for. If she had a heart-to-heart motherly chat with her child, it was very likely she wasn't going to end up going on this date at all.

Choices, choices, choices.

"Text Nana for me, would you? I need to get in the shower," Effie said over her shoulder as she went into her bathroom and turned on the shower. She quickly tweezed her eyebrows while she waited for the water to heat, then called to Polly, still in the bedroom, "Did she answer you?"

"She says she's sick!"

Effie stuck her head around the bathroom door. "What?"

"She says she texted you and called you an hour ago." Polly held up her phone. "She said she's sick and she can't come."

"Shit." Effie's phone had been off while she worked and her mother wouldn't have canceled if she weren't truly sick. It was her own fault for not checking the text or voice mail she had seen but assumed was her mother asking her a question she could answer when she got there.

"I could stay home alone," Polly offered hopefully.

Effie snort-laughed at that one and hopped into the shower. Too hot. She hissed and turned the faucet handle while she grabbed her razor. "Um, no."

"Why not? I'm almost twelve. Meredith stays home alone all the time."

Effie started shaving, wishing she'd bothered to manage at least some of this upkeep a little better over the past week, because damn, she'd turned into a Sasquatch. Not that she intended to be in any sort of position with Mitchell that would give him even a glimpse of the parts she was grooming. "Since when are you and Meredith such bosom buddies?"

"You're the one who told me to give her a chance," Polly said.

Effie peeked around the shower door. "That means I was hoping she'd pick up your good habits, not that she'd teach you bad ones."

"Staying home alone isn't a bad habit!"

Effie ducked back beneath the water to rinse off the shaving cream and start on her hair. "No, but arguing with your mother is."

"Ugh!" Polly said, disgruntled. "If you're not going to let me stay home alone, then why are you still bothering to shower?"

Good point. Effie scrubbed shampoo through her hair, making sure to strip out the blobs of paint. "I'm going to call Betty Grover."

"No! No, Mom!"

Effie laughed again but held it back so Polly wouldn't hear. "She's not that bad, Wog."

"She smells like pee, and she makes me watch stupid TV. She treats me like a baby."

Effie bit back another chuckle. Betty had lived in the house next door for fifty years and had been very kind to them when they moved in, but she did, in fact, smell faintly of urine and was prone to babying both Polly and Effie. Still, she was almost always available to come and sit with Polly for a few hours and refused to take money, and with Betty here instead of Effie's mother, Effie would have a real excuse to get home early if she needed one.

"Can't I see if Heath will come over?"

Effie muttered a curse at the sudden sting of shampoo in her eyes. Polly had no idea, really, what a shitty thing it would be to ask Heath to babysit so Effie could go on a date, but there was no way to explain it to her. "No, Pollywog, if Betty can't do it, I'll stay home."

"He already said he would," Polly said.

Effie pulled open the shower door again to glare. "What? You already asked him?"

"Yeah, he said he would." Polly held up her phone without even a glimmer of remorse.

"That's not... Shit, Polly. Shit." Effie tipped her face under the water to rinse away the last of the shampoo. If she couldn't explain why it was a problem, how could she also explain why she was angry? Heath had taken Polly hundreds of other times when Effie needed someone.

"He'll be here in about ten minutes," Polly said. "You'd better hurry up and finish getting ready."

It took her about twenty to finish with everything else, and admittedly, Effie did not put as much effort into getting her glamour on as she should have for a date, even a second one. The look on Heath's face, though, as she came into the kitchen, was proof that even the underwhelming effort she'd made had been impressive. The gleam of admiration in his eyes actually made Effie blush.

"Hey," she said. "Thanks for this."

"No problem. You know I'm always here for you when you need me."

Effie pressed her lips together but met his gaze steadily.

Heath gave her a bland grin. He knew exactly what he was saying.

"I won't be out late," Effie said.

Heath shrugged. "Take your time. Have fun."

"I won't be out late," she repeated, then kissed the top of Polly's head. "Be good."

"So, tell me about what you do." Mitchell waited for the waiter to finish pouring the coffee before he leaned forward a little to look across the dessert plates at her.

It was an inevitable question for a second date, and one for which Effie had a standard answer. "I work from home, handling the details of an online retail store specializing in handcrafted items."

"Cool." Mitchell pulled the sugar packets toward him and added a few, then cream. "Do you like it?"

She laughed. "Sure. Do you like what you do? Tell me what you do, exactly. Software engineering. What does that mean, exactly? Programming? Writing code?"

It was almost always a cinch to get men talking about themselves so she could avoid talking about herself. Mitchell laughed and sat back in his chair. He shrugged.

"I put out fires," he said.

Effie sipped coffee. "Huh?"

"People bring me problems, and I fix them. Writing code, yes. Mostly for websites, but sometimes for internal company functions like, for example, if a company needs an internal instant message system, I might work on that."

"Sounds exciting," Effie said.

Mitchell laughed again, ruefully, and tilted his head. It was charming, the way he did that. Something about the slant of his smile.

"Oh, it doesn't. And it mostly isn't. Do I like what I do? Not really. I mean, it's a good job, I guess. But mostly at this point I'm just lazy about it. I do what I have to, and that's about it."

It was not a confession she'd expected from him, yet it made her like him better. No false modesty. "So why keep doing it?"

"Money. And lazy," he repeated. "I don't feel like trying to find a new job or do something else. I envy people who follow their dreams, I guess, but I'm too practical."

For a second, Effie considered telling him the truth about what she really did, but it would have only been to brag and would've opened doors she wasn't ready to unlock. "There's a lot to be said for being practical. What would you do, if you could do anything in the world?"

"I'd knit sweaters for ducks."

He said it so deadpan, so serious, that Effie didn't know what to say. When he laughed, though, she joined him. Mitchell shook his head.

"Sorry. It's something my dad always said when someone asked him what he was doing. He'd say, *knitting sweaters for ducks*. I have no idea why. But, really, if I could do anything? I'd be a ski instructor in the winter. In the summers, be a rafting guide."

Effie sat back in her seat. "Really?"

"Really." Mitchell shrugged and gave her that head tilt, that tilted smile. He had no idea how cute it was, that was evident, which meant that no woman had ever told him so. Maybe no woman had ever thought so.

Watching him gave Effie a warmish feeling all over, thinking that perhaps there was something about him that would be fresh and new with her. That she might be the first, in some way. Which was vanity and arrogance, she reminded herself.

"I've never gone skiing. Or rafting."

Mitchell shifted in his seat and leaned a bit closer, his gaze on hers. "I'll have to take you, then. Next summer."

Next summer was a long damned time away, but his words sent another round of tingling heat through her. They were only words, she knew that, but even so, it gave her something to think about. Something beyond a third date, anyway.

The conversation drifted after that, interrupted by a buzz from Effie's phone. She excused herself to check it. "My kid."

It was a photo of Polly and Heath at the bowling alley, both with wide grins and thumbs up. Another came in a moment later of Heath doing what looked like a victory dance after a strike. This one had the corner of Polly's eye and someone else in the background. A blonde someone. Effie frowned and didn't reply. She looked up to see Mitchell's curious look.

"She's out with her…my…friend. They're bowling," she explained.

"Everything okay?"

No, because apparently Heath had taken Polly on his date with Lisa Collins. Effie didn't say that aloud. "Yep. I should be getting home soon, though. He's doing me a huge favor taking the kid. My mom was supposed to, but she was sick. I promised I wouldn't be out late."

"Seems like they're having fun, though. Are you sure you have to rush home? I thought we could check out this local jazz band at Mooney's. A friend of mine's the bass player."

Effie hesitated. Jazz made her ears bleed. She must've done a poor job of hiding her distaste, because Mitchell frowned.

"No?" he asked.

"I just… I really… I hate jazz." She gave an apologetic smile.

"You know what?" Mitchell said. "Me, too."

She laughed and shook her head. "So…why?"

"My friend really is the bass player. He's been asking me to come out for months. I figured if I had to suffer through it, at least the company would make it all worthwhile." Mitchell, Effie discovered, had a really great, genuine smile.

They sat in smiling silence for a moment or so. She liked him, Effie realized. Really liked him and his great smile and his sense of humor and the fact he was up front about being lazy with his job. She liked that he knew without a doubt what it was he'd like to do, if he threw away the restrictions of practicality. She liked that he hated jazz but would listen to it so he could make a friend happy.

"We could wear earplugs," she suggested.

Mitchell waved for the check without ever taking his gaze from hers. "You're on. Let's go."

It was not even close to what Effie would've considered early when she got home just before midnight, though she was ready to argue that it also wasn't late. She didn't have to defend herself, though. The house was dark and empty when she went inside.

Polly hadn't texted her since sending the pictures. Heath had sent no updates. Effie turned on the lights in the kitchen and poured herself a glass of water as she considered whether she ought to start worrying. As it turned out, she didn't have to, because ten minutes after she got home, Heath and Polly came through the back door.

"Mom! Guess what, I bowled a one-eighty and I beat Heath and his friend twice. We bowled five games." Polly sounded giddy the way she always did just before she crashed from exhaustion, but her eyes were bright and her cheeks pink with excitement. "It was awesome! Heath said there's a kids' bowling league on Saturday mornings, and I should join! He said he could take me."

"We'll see." Effie met Heath's gaze over the top of Polly's head. "You should get to bed. It's late. Make sure you thank Heath."

"My pleasure." Heath squeezed Polly and kissed her cheek with a loud smack. "Do what your mom says."

"Love you," Polly told him, then gave her mother a hug and a kiss, too. "Mom, next time you need to come."

"We'll see." Effie waited until Polly had disappeared down the hall and her bedroom door closed before turning to Heath. "You should've told me you were taking along a friend."

"Hey, I had made those plans beforehand, and what was I supposed to do?" He helped himself to a can of cola from the fridge and leaned on the counter.

Smug. *Jerk.* Effie poured the rest of her water down the drain so she didn't throw it at him.

"I don't think it's appropriate to be taking my daughter on your dates. That's all. I don't take her on mine," Effie said quietly, refusing to let even the tiniest hint of anger drift into her tone.

Heath drained the can and wiped his mouth with the back of his hand. He put the empty can in the sink and moved toward her. She let him pull her closer, but she did not kiss him.

"Jealous?" Heath whispered into her ear.

Effie closed her eyes. All she had to do was turn her face the tiniest bit and she could kiss him. She wanted to. It would be so easy for them to slip back into what they'd been doing with each other, on and off, for so many years.

"No." She let her lips brush his cheek before she pulled away, turning so it wouldn't be so easy for him to embrace her again.

Heath took the hint and stepped back. "Effie…"

"It's fine." She looked at him sideways with a small smile. "Thanks for taking Polly. I appreciate it."

"Anytime. You know that."

She nodded. "Yeah. I do."

For a moment, Heath looked as though he meant to say something more but thought better of it. "I'll call you."

"Sure," Effie said. "Talk to you later. Thanks again."

When he'd gone, Effie went to Polly's room. She was sure the girl would be asleep, but the light was still on. Polly lay wide-eyed, staring at the ceiling.

"Hey, Wog. What's wrong?"

"Can't sleep." Polly turned onto her side, tucking a hand beneath her chin. The earlier giddiness had faded. Now she looked sad.

Effie sat on the edge of the bed. "What's wrong?"

"Mom, how come you and Heath aren't boyfriend and girlfriend?"

"We're better as friends, that's all." Effie rubbed Polly's leg under the blankets. "It's late. Go to sleep."

"You used to be. When we all lived together, weren't you?"

Effie hesitated. "Heath and I have always had a really special friendship. And we always will."

"I didn't like Lisa," Polly said.

Effie held back a smile. "Nobody says you have to. But you could give her a chance. Don't automatically not like her, Pollywog, just because you think I won't."

Polly was quiet for a moment or so, her eyes drifting closed. She wasn't quite asleep, though. Effie could tell by the breathing. Effie waited.

Polly spoke. "I love you, Mom."

"Love you, too, Pollywog." Effie waited another minute or so, letting the sound of her daughter's breathing soothe her. When she was sure Polly had at last fallen asleep, she turned off the light but left the door cracked so the night-light in the hall could shine in. Polly hadn't asked for that in years, but tonight it seemed like the right thing to do. To leave some light on in the darkness.

Effie left her own door cracked open, too.

chapter thirteen

"Effie! Hey!" Dee waved furiously from the table in the corner. "Over here!"

Effie waved and pointed toward the counter to show that she was going to grab a coffee first. She got a latte and a muffin and headed for Dee's table. "Hey."

"Have you tried the cranberry walnut? Super yummy." Dee grinned.

Effie had ordered a plain corn muffin. "I don't eat here very often."

"No? It's my favorite place. I come in, check out the cute guys, drink a latte. Catch up with my reading." For a moment, Dee looked sad. "Since Brad left, I haven't been reading as much."

"But maybe you've been checking out the cute boys more often, huh?" Effie glanced around to see if she could find any, but the coffee shop was mostly empty.

Dee still looked sad when Effie turned back to her. "Yeah. It's hard, though. You know? Finding someone nice."

"Yeah…yeah, I bet." It seemed like the right thing to say, until it came out. Then it sounded sort of condescending, which wasn't how she'd meant it, at all. To make up for the fact that she'd sounded like a straight-up bitch, Effie admitted, "I've been on a dating site for about six months. God, no. Longer than that now."

"Any luck?" Dee waggled her eyebrows.

"Not much. Well. There's one guy. He's all right."

"Yeah?" Dee looked thoughtful. "I thought you and…"

"No," Effie said when Dee didn't finish. "Not for a long time. We're friends, that's all."

Dee looked embarrassed. "Hey, do you remember Mrs. Kettle?"

The twelfth-grade English teacher. She'd almost failed Effie, keeping her from graduating with her class. "She made me do a bunch of extra credit work in order to get a freaking D."

Dee nodded. "She was a tough one. Well, she published a book!"

"Really?" Effie laughed at the thought of it. "What kind?"

"A romance," Dee said. "A really smutty one, apparently. We're going to read it for our book club. You want to join?"

Effie hadn't read a book for pleasure in years. "Umm… how smutty is it?"

"I don't know, but I think it's got…you know, spanking and stuff in it." Dee looked so gleeful that Effie had to laugh again. "What? It's kinky, right?"

Spanking. The thought of it twisted Effie's smile a little. She'd done so many things more fucked up than that, though she doubted they'd count as BDSM. "Yeah. Totally."

Dee lifted her coffee cup. "I'm in!"

Effie shook her head. "Okay. Sure. I'll read it."

"Good. The meeting's at Nancy Gordan's house at the end of the month. Peter's mom? I'll email you the information." Dee beamed. "You know, Effie…I know we weren't really friends in school. But I hope we can try to be friends now."

"High school was a long time ago," Effie admitted slowly.

"I always admired you," Dee blurted.

Effie's eyebrows went up. "You did?"

"Yeah. Even...before. When we were younger. You were always so good in art class and stuff. I'm not surprised you sell your paintings." Dee nodded.

"Well. Thanks." Heat crept up Effie's cheeks and throat, but the compliment pleased her.

"And I'm really sorry, again, about the stuff with Meredith and Polly. I talked with her about gossip." Dee looked rueful. "It's a lesson I should've learned myself a long time ago. I guess it made me feel important or something, because I remembered when it happened and none of the other women in the group did. I mean, most of them had no idea."

Effie frowned. "And now they do. Thanks."

"I don't blame you for being mad," Dee said hastily. "I just hope you can forgive me."

"Holding a grudge doesn't really do anyone any good." Effie shrugged. "What happened to me and Heath was a long time ago. I try to forget about it as much as I can. Move on."

Dee was quiet for a second before she said in a low voice. "But you don't, do you? I mean, the artwork. It's all related to the...what happened. You paint it, right? I've seen your stuff. It's good. But a little scary."

Good, but a little scary. It wasn't the first time someone had called Effie's paintings that. It was better than hearing that her work was boring as shit, pretentious and tried too hard to capitalize on her notoriety, which she'd also heard more than once.

"Yes. Sometimes. The art helps. Like cutting out an infection," Effie told her.

"Yeah. I can see that." Dee nodded and sipped her coffee.

She didn't mean to ask, but the words came out anyway. "Dee…when you told me about him getting out of prison…"

Dee looked embarrassed. "Yeah, that was crappy. I'm sorry."

"No. It wasn't. It's not true, I don't think," Effie said. "But if you could tell me where you heard it, so I could look it up?"

"Oh. Shoot. Well, I heard it from one of the moms. I'm trying to remember who." Dee bit her lower lip, frowning. "I can't think of it, or where she heard it. But I'll ask around, okay? If you really—"

"No, that's okay," Effie cut in quickly with a small laugh and a wave of her hand. "I've heard for years, off and on, that he's getting out. It's never true. I'm sure it's not this time, either."

Awkward silence. Dee still looked embarrassed. Effie didn't quite know how to fix it. At last, Dee shrugged and smiled.

"So, tell me about this dating site. Think I should join up?"

chapter fourteen

Effie is down to her last piece of paper in her drawing pad. She's worn her colored pencils to nubs and the charcoal pencils that were in her backpack are entirely used up. She tries to shade a line with her fingertips the way Madame Clay taught her, but the paper tears, and with a sigh, she crumples it into a ball and starts to toss it into the trash can before thinking again and smoothing it instead. She adds it to the small and precious pile of paper they hoard for the bathroom. They hide the spare paper under the mattress, behind the dresser drawers, under the couch cushions. Somehow the indignity of having to use scraps of paper for the bathroom is worse than the awful food or the bad lighting or the relentless monotony. It makes them into animals.

Heath looks at the picture, then at her. "You drew me?"

"Yeah. The nose is all wrong, though." Effie gestures at him. "I couldn't get it right."

She studies him. Locked in these three small, dank and often dark rooms, at the mercy of a crazy, moody man, Effie would never have thought she could be bored, yet she is. The days have blended into one another, which is why she started keeping track with the hash marks on the wall beside the bed.

She thinks she's been here about two weeks so far, but it could be longer. The only way to really tell for sure is that every morning the orange lights come on and every night they go off, except sometimes it feels as if the day lasts forever and other times it's definitely much shorter.

Twice since she woke up here the blazing white overhead lights have come on, and the man who insists on being called Daddy brought them food. A half a jug of water. The first time, he also brought two glasses of chocolate milk he forced them to drink. It made them both fall asleep. The second time, he gave them each a shot of "vitamins." Effie knows it was a sedative. Maybe she'd rather be unconscious than awake. It passes the time.

Effie has asked Heath a few times about escape, but he won't give her the details about what happened when he tried it before. There has to be a way out of the basement, but though she cuts her feet by navigating the other room, there are no windows that she can find. The door, of course, is locked. There's always a warning before Daddy comes into the basement, the music and the bright lights coming on overhead. They could jump him, couldn't they? Force him to let them out. Next time, Effie thinks and stifles a yawn. She'll do it the next time.

"Try again," Heath says.

"I can't. I'm out of paper. And pencils." She holds up the drawing pad, flipping through the pages to show him.

Heath snags the book from her and sits on the rickety chair to slowly page through it. Every so often he pauses to look at one page longer than the others, and Effie tries to figure out why but can't. She doesn't see anything special in the pictures Heath seems to like best—a rose with a bee circling it, a bowl of fruit, a stop sign. The ones Effie is most proud of, the castle and the koi pond, he barely glances at. Finally, he looks at her.

"You're good."

"Thanks." She shrugs and scoots back on the bed to rest against the wall with her knees drawn to her chest.

They have spent most of their time in the bedroom because the small living area is so dark and the couch out there has springs poking through the cushions. In here, at least, the orangey light from the wall sconce is better and the bed provides a softer place to sit. Effie could tell you the exact dimensions of this room. Ten short paces in one direction, ten slightly longer paces in the other. None of the walls seem to align. Everything's skewed. If she looks too long at the corners, she'll get a headache. Everything is an effort.

Heath reaches the end of the sketchbook, closes it and hands it back to her. Effie clutches it to her chest for a moment, remembering when all the pages had been fresh and clean. She'd wasted so many of them, but how was she supposed to know she'd end up here?

"We should hit him with something," Effie says.

Heath looks around the room, then at her. "There's nothing to hit him with."

"I could stab him with a pencil," Effie says. "If I hadn't already used them all up. I was so stupid!"

"He doesn't look strong, but he is." Heath frowns. "You'd have to do it in the eye or something. How good is your aim?"

Effie closes one eye to keep his face from blurring. Both eyes are gritty. Sore from rubbing them. "I don't know. Why aren't you trying harder to think of a way?"

"He said he'd kill…"

The searing bright lights come on overhead. The music starts, but it's not the same song. This one's not that soft-voiced, high-pitched one about sailing; it's harder edged. She knows it after a minute, though. "Maxwell's Silver Hammer" by the Beatles. Effie laughs, confused, but the sight of Heath's face stops her.

"What?" She was hot a moment ago, the basement is almost always too hot or too cold, but her skin crawls and bumps into gooseflesh now. "What's wrong?"

"Go get under the covers. Pretend you're asleep."

"But what..."

"Go," Heath says as he backs up into the living area, already turning away from her. "Please, Effie, just do it."

The rasp in his voice convinces her. Effie hops into the bed and pulls the blankets up over her ears. Beyond the doorway, she hears Daddy saying something, but it's not in that too-bright and jovial voice he's used every time before. He sounds worse than angry. He sounds as if he's gone...dark.

"Sister, Sister, Sister. You stay in here," Daddy says from the doorway. "You be a good girl now and stay where you are. You won't like what happens, if you don't."

Nearby, there is a woman's voice. She sounds drunk. Laughing, but slurred. Effie sits up, meaning to get out of bed and run, run to this new person, because surely whoever it is will save them. Before she can, though, there's a crack of flesh on flesh and a low, soft cry. Daddy's voice, louder.

"Don't just look at it, boy. Put your face in that goddamned mess and eat it."

Another rise of drunken laughter. Another sound of slapping. A moan, it sounds like pain but could be something else.

Effie pulls the covers over her head and turns herself to the wall. Her parents weren't much into going to church, and Effie's not even sure she believes in God, but she prays now.

Whatever he's doing, please, oh please, don't let it happen to her.

Please, oh please, don't let it happen to her.

When the sounds get louder, she plugs her ears with her

fingers. It lasts forever, whatever it is, until her stomach is sick with anticipation and she has to press a hand over her mouth to keep herself from gagging. Her eyes are closed, but she can tell when the bright lights go out, leaving her in the pitch-dark again.

She waits and waits, but Heath doesn't come into the room. Effie does not want to get out of bed, but she makes herself. Bare feet on the cold floor. She takes each step, sliding and shuffling so she doesn't accidentally step on something that could hurt her, reaching with tentative hands into the blackness until she finds the door frame. She stops.

"Heath?"

At first, no answer. She's sure he's gone or, worse, dead out there on the floor in the dark and if she stumbles forward she will land on his cooling body. Effie shakes. Her fingers grip harder into the wood. She calls his name again, voice catching, and this time, he answers.

"I'm here."

"Are you okay? Did he hurt you?"

"I'm okay." There's a scratching on the concrete. "Go back to sleep."

Heath has always let Effie sleep in the bed while he takes the lumpy, stinking couch. She should go back and dive beneath the blankets again, but she can hear him crying. Low, strangled sobs.

Effie has found her way to the bathroom and back in utter darkness enough times by now to know where to walk to avoid the sharp things set into the concrete, but this time she eases her way to the couch. She can't see more than shapes and shadows, but she can hear Heath breathing. She can smell him, too. Both of them stink. You'd think they'd get used to it, but so far she hasn't.

"It's cold out here. Come to the bed."

"No," he says immediately. "You take it. I'm..."

"Heath. Come to the bed." Effie finds him with her hands. He's shivering. He's naked. She pulls away, startled. Embarrassed. Then, with more determination, she puts out her hands again and finds his shoulder, his arm. Finally, his hand. She links her fingers in his. "Where are your clothes?"

"I don't know."

She thinks about this. They could stumble around in the dark, trying to find them, or they can wait until the morning lights turn on and find his clothes then. For now, he's cold and shaking and something bad has happened to him.

Effie tugs Heath's hand. "Come on."

Together, they make their way into the bedroom. She urges him into the bed and makes him get in first, facing the wall. She lets him be the little spoon and curls herself around him. She's never been in bed with a boy before. She's never seen a naked boy, never even kissed a clothed one, but when she presses her face to Heath's bare back, all Effie can think is that he needs this, and needs her.

Heath is crying again. Effie is quiet at first, but she has to know. "I heard a woman. Won't she help...?"

"Her name is Sheila. He gives her drugs so she'll do... things. He likes to watch."

She wants to ask what sorts of things but is too afraid. "Won't she help us, Heath?"

"He said if I ever tried to escape again, he would kill her." Heath's voice is flat and darker than the basement could ever be. "Not me. Her."

"He wouldn't! And if we got out, he wouldn't have the chance to."

Heath shifts a little. "I think he would. And I'd have to live with that for the rest of my life, that she died because I tried to get out."

"We *have* to get out, Heath," Effie says.

"Someone will come looking for you, Effie. Nobody gave a damn about me, but you… Your parents are looking for you. They're going to find us."

Effie isn't so sure. "Will she… Would she tell anyone about us?"

"I don't think so. He tells her I'm his son," Heath says. "And she's so out of it, she believes him. And she doesn't know about you."

"Next time, I'll come out there. I'll tell her who I am. She'll have to help us—"

"No!" Then softer, "No, Effie, you can't. He will kill her. I know he will."

Heath doesn't say anything more. So she holds him, quietly, until they both sleep. She wakes when the bright lights come on. The sailing song filters through the speakers, and disoriented, she struggles out of bed to find herself alone. Heath is in the living room, fully dressed.

Daddy comes with food. He is wild-eyed and frantic with hilarity, telling joke after joke. He praises Effie. What a good girl she is. What a good, good girl.

He's brought soap. He's turned on the water in the bathroom so they can shower. He's brought books, magazines. Chocolate candy. It's like Christmas morning, and he's some kind of demented Santa. He focuses on Effie, ignoring Heath, and by now she knows it's better to laugh when Daddy tells a joke, so she does, even though it feels like glass grating in her throat.

Daddy has brought her a dress, pink with ribbons and bows, appropriate for a much, much younger girl. White stockings. The outfit would be complete with black patent leather shoes, she thinks, but of course there are no shoes down here.

"Go take a shower, Sister. Be Daddy's pretty girl," he tells her with that wide, horrible grin that wrinkles his face and makes him a troll.

The hot water feels so good she stays in the shower longer than she should, taking more of her turn than is fair, but it feels so freaking good to be clean, really clean, that she can't help herself. When Effie comes out of the bathroom, Daddy is gone. Heath stays in the bathroom even longer than she did. When he comes out, his eyes are red-rimmed.

They don't talk about what happened. Together, without a word, they sort the goodies Daddy left, hoarding the things they know they'll need later. At the creak of the floorboards overhead, they both look up. Heath shakes his head.

"He won't be back down for a while." From next to the bed, he pulls a box Effie hadn't noticed before. "Here."

"What is it?"

Heath shakes his head. "Just open it."

It's an art kit. Paper, brushes and a watercolor palette. Stunned, Effie stares at him. "What is this?"

"I told him to bring it for you."

"When?" Effie asks.

"Last night."

She doesn't understand. "Why would he...?"

"Because," Heath says in a dull, expressionless voice, "he always brings me what I want. After."

"And you asked him for this, for me?" Effie, an only child, is used to getting almost everything she's ever wanted from her parents. Christmas and birthdays were sometimes embarrassing, she got so much loot. She's never had anyone do something like this for her, though. Never.

Effie closes the kit's lid. She thinks about the wealth Daddy had brought them this time. "Heath...what did you have to do?"

In reply, he turns away, and Effie doesn't ask again.

chapter fifteen

Effie hadn't been active on LuvFinder in months, though she hadn't hidden or deleted her profile. She simply didn't answer the messages that pinged her inbox three and five at a time from men who obviously liked what they saw. She took a good selfie, that was all she could think when she scrolled through the "Hey" and "Hello, there" and paused occasionally to read a "Hi, Gorgeous." She *had* made herself invisible for the chat function, though, so nobody would bother her in the few minutes every couple of weeks that she bothered to check in.

She'd logged in now to show Dee how easy it was to use the site. "You can chat, like instant message, right here on the site. You can set yourself to invisible. That's what I did. Otherwise, you're getting pinged nonstop while you're trying to do other stuff."

"Or you're not," Dee said ominously.

"You're a female. You'll get pinged." Effie laughed. "If there's a green dot next to the username, that person is online. Pretty standard. And here's where you see who they match you with, but you can also do custom searches. And here's where you see who you've been chatting with, and you can keep track of your dates and rate them. Privately. They can't see your rating and you can't see theirs. Thank God."

"Ugh, can you imagine?" Dee said. "I wouldn't want to see my rating."

Effie shook her head, scrolling through her own ratings. "No, me neither... Oh."

Mitchell was online. Two nights ago, he'd kept her up until just after one in the morning, making her laugh. They'd planned to go out again soon, and he texted her at least every other day, though he hadn't yet today. It hadn't occurred to her to wonder if maybe he was still dating a lot of other women. Effie tried to think if it bothered her, the idea that she wasn't the only woman he was pursuing. It wasn't as if she had the right to be upset. She was glad now, though, that she'd set herself to invisible, so he couldn't see that she was online.

Quickly, before she could dwell, Effie logged out and pulled up a new page so Dee could start filling out her own profile. The other woman had about ten different selfies to choose from for her LuvFinder profile picture, but none of them were quite right. Effie took up her phone and started snapping, asking Dee questions to get her reactions. Snap, snap, snap.

"There," she said. "There's the one."

She turned the phone to show Dee the shot that was going to work. Dee's head, thrown back in laughter, her dark hair tumbling over her shoulders. It was an incredibly sexy and fun picture. With a few edits using a photo app, Effie played with the colors and smoothed some rough edges.

"It's not cheating. It's enhancing," she explained and emailed the photo from her phone so Dee could upload it to her profile.

Dee was still hesitating before hitting the submit button that would take her profile live. "I don't know, Effie. I've heard some nightmare stories."

"Just keep this in mind. You don't have to go out with

anyone. You're not obligated to be nice. And if someone doesn't return your messages, you've just saved yourself a whole lot of wasted time." Effie leaned over Dee's shoulder to study the screen. "C'mon. Do it."

With a sigh, Dee clicked her mouse, and within seconds, the LuvFinder site populated her "matches" section with suggestions. Giggling in much the way their daughters were doing from the other room, Effie and Dee scrolled through the possibilities. Effie saw a few names she recognized from her own suggestions list. She steered Dee away from one or two of them but recommended a few others.

"You wouldn't think it was weird if I went out with one of them after you did?" Dee asked.

Effie shrugged. "Would you?"

"Yeah. Maybe. What if I meet someone amazing and we fall in love and get married and then you're my maid of honor and you'd already slept with my future husband?"

For a second, Effie started to protest that she hadn't slept with any of the guys from the site, before she saw Dee's grin. "You'd never make me your maid of honor."

"You never know." Dee waggled her eyebrows and turned back to the computer. "So, should I send a message to any of them, or should I wait for them to… Holy shit. I just got… one, two…four messages in my inbox?"

Dee looked stunned. Effie laughed. "Yeah, get ready. It is a little bit like tossing chum in the water. The sharks come out right away. Remember what I said. You don't have to answer everyone."

Dee scrolled through her inbox and clicked on a profile picture. "What about this guy? He sent me a nudge."

"That means he's interested, and if you are, you nudge back, and then eventually one of you gets the balls to send an actual email." Effie laughed and took a seat on the lumpy futon in Dee's office.

Dee moved her mouse over the list of suggestions, pausing at one. "Oh, my God. Jon Pinciotti."

Effie remembered him. She'd had a crush on him in the seventh grade. He was a soccer player.

"He was my first kiss. My first everything, really," Dee said and spun in her computer chair to look at her. "Holy shit, he's on LuvFinder."

"Send him a message!"

"No. No way." Dee shook her head. "I couldn't."

"Why not? You could just say hello." Effie leaned forward to try to get a glimpse of Jon's profile.

"Sure. To my high school boyfriend. My first love. Right. That's going to work out so great."

"You never know until you try," Effie said.

Dee took a deep breath and put her hands on the keyboard. "Okay. Fine. I'm going to do it."

A half minute later, she let out a low hoot of triumph and spun her chair entirely around a few times before stopping herself abruptly to give Effie a scandalized look. "I can't believe I did that. What if he doesn't answer me? Oh, shit. What if he does?"

"One step at a time," Effie said with a laugh.

Dee groaned, then giggled, her cheeks flushed. "Thanks, Effie. None of my other friends have done this."

"No? That's crazy. It's the age of internet dating."

"I should know," Dee said, the gleam of giddiness in her eyes fading. "It's where my ex met his new wife."

Effie frowned. "Sorry."

"Nah. It's fine. He's better with her than he ever was with me, and she can deal with all his shit now. I don't have to. I just wish that Meredith had handled it better. He swore he wasn't going to let his new family interfere with his relationship with her, but I guess his stepkids that actually live with him take up a lot of his time." Dee's voice rasped.

"Sorry," Effie said again, softer this time. "That sucks."

Dee wiped away the brightness in her eyes and gave Effie a sad smile. "How did you help Polly deal with it? Not having a dad, I mean."

"I guess I never had to, really. She's always had Heath. We've been up front that he's not her father, but...yeah. He's always been there." Effie's smile felt sad, too.

Dee spun her chair in a circle with her head back. "He's very good-looking."

"Yeah." Effie laughed lightly. "He is."

"You've been with him a long time," Dee said.

Effie nodded. "I've known him since I was thirteen."

"He was *your* high school boyfriend, then," Dee said and looked stricken. "Shit, Effie, I'm sorry, that was a really stupid thing to say."

"No. It's okay. It actually means you forgot about...it. The thing." Effie made air quotes around the last word. "And you're right. He *was* my high school boyfriend, if anyone was. He was my first kiss, and my first everything, too."

Dee looked solemn. "Kind of hard to get over it, huh?"

"Not really," Effie said lightly, the lie coating her tongue with the taste of copper and smoke. "Nothing's that hard to get over, if you try hard enough."

chapter sixteen

Effie had mapped Bill's body over and over again. She knew every scar, and he had quite a few. There was the one running up the back of his calf from when he'd burned himself on a motorcycle pipe. There was a dimpled button in his lower right side from a stab wound. Not a knife, a fountain pen. Bill liked to joke he'd bled ink for weeks. He was always making jokes about the scars, as though they made him feel self-conscious but proud at the same time.

This wound on his arm was new. She stroked her fingers along it gently, barely touching the angry black stitches around the red, sliced flesh. Dog bite, he'd told her. He had to take antibiotics and get a rabies treatment.

"Seven shots in the belly," he told her with barely a wince. "Fucking people who shouldn't fucking own fucking dogs. I had to put it down. Right in front of..."

Bill's voice broke. He covered his eyes with one big hand. His shoulders shook.

Effie pressed her mouth to his bare shoulder. She took his other hand. When he curved his fingers into hers, she lifted his hand to her mouth and kissed the back.

There were few times when she'd ever been the one to

offer him this kind of comfort. She felt ill-suited to it. For anyone, really, other than her kid. Effie had not often sought the solace of an embrace. A hard cock inside her? Oh, sure. But this softness, this consideration, was not as natural.

"Right in front of the kid." Bill swiped at his eyes and gave her an angry stare. He shrugged out of her grip and went to the small sideboard he used as a liquor cabinet. He poured himself a healthy slug of whiskey and tossed it back. Then poured another. He wiped his mouth with the back of his hand and contemplated the amber liquid in the glass. He shook his head. "Four, maybe five years old. The dog came after me. Bit the fuck out of my arm. I kicked it, and it went for the kid. I had to shoot it, Effie. It was going to maul that baby."

She got up and took the shot glass from his hand to drink it herself. She set down the empty glass and put her hand over it when he lifted the bottle. The last thing Bill needed right now was to get hammered. He was already taking painkillers, which, more than anything else, told her how bad he hurt. Bill had broken his ankle once and walked on it for two days before seeking treatment.

"You did what you had to do," she told him.

After dropping off Polly with her mother, Effie had planned to spend the night working—she had to finish up one commission and had a new project that had been circling her mind, gnawing at it, for a week now. Ever since she'd had coffee with Dee. The idea had come to her as they usually did, in the faint light of morning when she'd woken but wished she were still unconscious. Instead of dancing sugarplums, Effie dreamed of a dark room lit by faint orange light and the lengths of shadows. In the light of day, the normal light of day instead of eye-searing brightness used to diminish and control them, Effie was almost always able to put aside the dreams, but sometimes they lingered long enough to become inspiration.

It wouldn't sell, of course. What she thought of as her "real" art never did. But she would paint it anyway, because if she couldn't do something for herself once in a while, she'd lose her fucking mind.

Bill's text had come in when she was at the art supply store buying some new brushes and paints. The message had surprised her. She hadn't heard from him in weeks. Like the painkillers, his text meant he was really hurting.

Since seeing Mitchell online at LuvFinder, she hadn't heard from him, not even once. She hadn't texted him, either. The thought that he might not answer her because his interest had been taken up by someone else…it didn't hurt, exactly, but it sure as hell smarted.

Effie held out her hand. "Come to bed."

"I didn't ask you to come over here to fuck me."

Effie laughed. "Yes, you did. And that's why I came over. So come on. Unless you want to do it right here."

She hadn't exactly dressed for seduction, but that had never much mattered to Bill. The first time they'd ever fucked, she'd been wearing a pair of ratty sweatpants and a stained T-shirt. She'd been soaking wet from running in the rain. He'd pulled up beside her in his car and offered to take her home. Instead, he'd taken her to his place.

Bill nudged her hand aside and poured himself another shot. Then one for her, and what the hell. She wasn't leaving anytime soon. The painting could wait a few hours. Who knows, maybe it would be better if she was a little toasted when she did it, anyway. Maybe she'd be able to let herself go without that inner critic warning her she was fucking it all up.

Bill licked his lips. Without a word he pushed past her and went down the hall and into the bedroom. After a few seconds, Effie followed. She found him in bed, already naked, but not hard.

She eyed him. "Hey."

"Come suck my cock," Bill said as if he was offering her a gift.

Effie tilted her head and crossed her arms. "Oh, that's how it's going to be?"

"Like you don't like it that way?" Bill didn't even crack a smile.

She did like it that way, of course. A lot, as a matter of fact. It wasn't as if she could be offended. With a shrug, she tugged her shirt and sweater off over her head and folded them neatly to put on the chair, then unbuttoned her jeans and did the same. In her bra, panties and a pair of knee socks, she cocked a hip and watched his crotch for any signs of life.

Bill crossed his arms behind his head, watching her. Slowly, Effie went to the bed and knelt on it next to him. She ran a hand up his thigh, scratching lightly with her fingernails. She dipped her head to stroke her tongue along the path of her fingers. At the sound of Bill's soft sigh, she smiled.

She took him in her mouth, his cock still mostly soft, but not for long. All the way in, until her lips brushed his belly. Then out. By the time she'd done that a couple times, he was thick and pulsing on her tongue. She cupped his balls, stroking downward with her thumb along the seam between sac and ass.

After that, she lost herself in the delight of sucking his cock. There was no complication in it. He didn't need any special tricks to get him off. She sucked. Bill came. He flooded her mouth with salty heat and she swallowed, then sat back to wipe the corners of her mouth.

Bill had closed his eyes. His chest rose and fell in the aftermath of the pleasure. He hadn't touched her at all.

"Everything's going to be okay," Effie said quietly when he didn't move. "You're good at your job, Bill. You did what you had to do."

He put a hand over his eyes and swiped over his face, then looked at her. "Thanks."

"Welcome." Effie shrugged.

"Come here. Let me do you."

She glanced at the clock. The whiskey had warmed her but was now wearing off. She wasn't usually one to turn down a ride on Bill's tongue, but the painting picked and poked at her brain, more intriguing than an orgasm. "I have to get home. I have work to do."

Bill sat up. "Right, I forgot. You only stop by for this."

"Don't start," Effie warned. "Next time, I won't come at all."

"You didn't come this time," Bill pointed out. "I'm trying to be a gentleman."

Effie didn't roll her eyes, but she didn't move to kiss him or anything, either. They stared at each other until Bill sighed. He gestured toward the door.

"Go on, then. If you want to. Or you could stay and eat with me. I'm starving."

Wrapped up in her latest project that she'd promised to ship off a week ago, Effie had skipped lunch. She put a hand on her stomach, empty and complaining. Polly wasn't home, so there'd be no reason for her to cook a dinner only she would eat. And, while she could take or leave the orgasm, food wasn't quite as negotiable.

"Sure," she said. "I can stay for a bit."

Bill gave her a slow, grudging smile. "Wow. Should I be honored?"

"Always," she told him with a grin and got off the bed to put her clothes back on.

In his kitchen, she watched him putter with pasta and olive oil. He put together a simple salad. Toasted some bread. It was totally a bachelor's meal, but it smelled delicious. Tasted good, too, she discovered when she took a tentative bite.

She'd watched him slice the garlic cloves in front of her, seen him choose the spices from his cupboard. She had no reason to believe Bill was trying to poison her or make her sick, especially since he was eating out of the same pot from which he'd served her. Still, she couldn't stop herself from using her fork to separate the strands of pasta and poke away some stray bits of oregano.

"What?" she said when she looked up to see him staring at her.

Bill gave her a neutral look. "Is it okay? Everything good?"

"Yeah. Great. Delish." She forked a bite of pasta and tucked it into her mouth to chew elaborately. Making a show.

Bill shook his head. "Maybe I should get you one of those plates with the dividers, so you can make sure nothing touches anything else."

"Huh?" Effie paused at this, fork halfway to her mouth. Once she'd started eating, it was hard to keep herself from gobbling.

Bill gestured at her plate. "Like a kid's plate. My sister's kid, he screams if anything touches the other things. So she got him these plates with dividers so he can have his meat loaf not touching the peas and not touching the mashed potatoes. I think it's stupid to cater to a kid like that, but what do I know. I don't have any kids."

"Yeah," Effie said after a second in which she forced herself to swallow the pasta suddenly threatening to stick in her throat. "What do you know about it?"

Her eating habits were fuckery. Pathological. She knew it. The annoying thing was, Bill should've known she couldn't help it. Now instead of hungry, she felt self-conscious. Embarrassed.

"Hey," he said when she put her fork down and wiped

her mouth with the napkin. "Eat up. I was just yanking your chain."

"I'm full."

"Bullshit. You ate, like, two bites." Bill leaned to pick up the fork and hand it to her. "C'mon. You have to eat."

"Now you sound like my mother." Effie rolled her eyes but took another bite.

Bill grinned. "Ah. Good old Stacey. How is she, anyway?"

"Fine." Effie pointed her fork at him. "And you don't get to call her that. To you, she's Mrs. Linton."

"Right," Bill said. "Because she has no idea I've been fucking her daughter."

Effie frowned. "You're not my boyfriend, Bill. We've been over this. What, you want me to take you home, show you around? Introduce you to my family as my, what, boyfriend?"

"Would that be such a terrible thing?"

"I think we both know why it wouldn't go over that well," Effie said.

Bill dragged a piece of bread through the garlicky olive oil and took a huge bite. Oil dripped down his chin, glistening in the cleft. He chewed loudly.

"It shouldn't matter anymore," he said when it was clear Effie had finished speaking.

"It still would to my mother, and you know it, Officer Schmidt. Anyway, you told me yourself, you don't want to get tied down. You like the bachelor life. Go where you want, when you want. Fuck who you want," Effie said flatly, her expression matching her tone. "You don't have a nine-to-five life, that's what you've always said. Maybe I'm just trying to respect that."

Bill snorted laughter. "Nah. You're trying to convince yourself of that, maybe, but we both know the truth. You don't want a boyfriend or a husband any more than I want to be one."

"You have no idea what I want." Annoyed, Effie took her plate to the garbage pail and scraped it empty before putting it in the dishwasher. She turned to look at him staring at her. "But even if that were true, why is it that when a guy wants that, he's a player, but when a woman wants it, she's a whore?"

"I didn't say that. Jesus, Effie, you put words in my mouth." Bill got up and advanced on her fast enough to keep her from being able to get away. His hands anchored on her hips. She turned her head when he tried to kiss her with that garlic-tasting mouth. Thwarted, he pressed his lips to her ear. "But you like it when I call you a whore, sometimes. Don't you?"

It was as true as when he'd told her she liked blowing him. Still, annoying. Effie pushed him so she could get past him.

"Not if you mean it," she said.

Bill looked surprised. "I would never mean it."

"No?" Effie paused to look him over. "You see a girl on the street in a short dress, you call her a slut. You head over to a domestic violence call, you say later that if any woman talked to you the way that one did to her husband, you'd probably want to slap her around, too."

"Shit. I said that one time." Bill's jaw dropped.

"But you said it."

He shook his head. "I would never hit a woman without provocation, Effie, and you fucking know that. But I don't think a set of tits and a vagina get you off the hook for bad behavior. If you want to dish it out, you should be ready to take it back. That call you're talking about? The woman had been needling that guy for days, and when he wouldn't rise to her taunts, she slapped him in the face. Four times before he finally hauled off and punched her, and she called us."

Effie pressed her lips together. "How do you know?"

"Because they made a report," Bill said as if she was stupid. "She admitted to it. She signed her fucking name to the report, and the two of them went off together making fucking goo-goo eyes all over the place, I almost had to arrest them both for public indecency."

"Oh."

Bill put his hands on his hips. "Yeah."

"Well," she said after a moment. "You still think it's okay to judge a woman based on what she's wearing."

"Everyone does that!"

"Does that make it okay?" she shot back. "You think it's all right to catcall a girl as she walks down the street because she decided to put on a pretty dress today that had nothing to do with you? And if she answers you, she's a slut, and she's a whore bitch if she doesn't."

Bill looked utterly stunned. His mouth opened, then shut. Opened again.

"The fuck is wrong with you tonight? I was talking about how you like it sometimes when I talk dirty to you, Effie. You asked me to! And it's hot, sometimes, sure, but I didn't really mean… Dammit. A guy can't get a break. You want us to notice you when you look good, and if we don't, you get all bent out of shape."

"I'm just saying, what if that was your daughter walking down the street?" she said abruptly and clamped her mouth shut before she could totally lose her shit all over him.

"But I don't have a daughter," Bill said as though that made it all okay.

Effie let out a long, slow breath. "Right."

Bill took a step closer to her but stopped and put his hands up when she bristled. "Right, okay. So what the hell is all this about?"

"If you ask me if I'm on my period, I swear to God I will punch you in the junk."

Bill laughed. "Uh-huh. See? Totally okay for a chick to threaten violence, but not a dude. Yep. That's equality, all right."

"Thanks for letting me suck your dick. And for dinner." She lifted her chin and crossed her arms over her chest. "I'll get out of here."

"Fine. Whatever. You'll do what you want to do. You always do."

Effie frowned. "So do you. Don't act like you don't."

"Look, let's not fight. Okay? I feel like shit enough as it is. I wanted you to come over because I…wanted to see you," Bill said with a brief hesitation. "Not so we could circle each other like fucking feral cats. I wanted to see you."

"I'm here," Effie said.

After a second, Bill reached for her. This time, she let him pull her closer. Her head fit neatly under his chin. Against his broad chest, she could rest her cheek and feel the thumping of his heart. She could put her arms around him and let him hold her. She could, if she wanted to, pretend she loved him.

But she didn't.

She let him hold her anyway. Bill had been there when she needed him more than once. She could be there for him now.

With her face still pressed to his bare skin, she finally asked him the question that had been burning in her mind since she'd first heard it was possible, no matter how many times she'd tried to rationalize it away. "Is it true?"

"Is what true?" Bill asked and pushed her away to look into her face. Then he looked guilty. "It's really unlikely he'll get out, Effie. You know that."

"You did hear! And you didn't tell me?" Effie backed up and cupped her elbows, forcing herself not to make fists or to pace. "Dammit, Bill. You told me you'd always tell me if you heard anything about him."

"It's one of those things. He's up for parole, he's ancient, he has people making appeals for him." Bill took his plate to the sink.

Effie frowned. "But...he won't get out."

"I don't think so, no." Bill looked over his shoulder at her. "It's just something that comes up every so often. It has before, and it's been okay. It will be all right this time, too."

When she didn't say anything, he wiped his hands on the dish towel and came over to her. His big hands took her gently by the shoulders. He looked into her eyes.

"If I hear anything otherwise, I'll let you know. Otherwise, it's all just rumors. Soccer moms getting bent out of shape so they have something to gossip about."

"You're not responsible for protecting me, you know," she told him.

Bill shrugged. "I'm responsible for protecting everyone. It's my job."

He was good at it. Being a cop. Neanderthal attitude aside, Bill cared very much about keeping the world safe.

"You don't have to worry about him. I promise," Bill said.

How could she explain that she wasn't worried? Not in the way anyone would expect. She wasn't thirteen anymore, and Stan Andrews was an old man. Even if Daddy got out of prison, he wouldn't come for her. She was too old now, to be his little girl.

"He deserves to rot and die in there, that's all," she said. "For what he did to us."

"Right. The two of you. You know your boyfriend got picked up for drunk and disorderly, right? He got in a fight over at the Shamrock. Punched a wall, and also Dickie Alonzo. He was with Sheila Monroe. Apparently, he punched Dickie for impugning Sheila's honor." Bill paused as though to gauge Effie's reaction to that, but she had none.

Sheila Monroe was both the town drunk and the town pump and had been forever. She had no honor. But Heath did. What Heath did with her was complicated and none of Effie's business. Also, she'd long ago stopped correcting Bill when he referred to Heath as her boyfriend. She was never sure if Bill knew she and Heath still fucked on occasion. She'd never actually admitted to Bill that she'd ever fucked Heath at all.

"I didn't. But you just couldn't wait to tell me. Could you?"

"I thought you'd like to know, that's all. If he's not careful," Bill said, "he's going to end up in prison right alongside his Daddy."

For a moment, all she could see or hear was the blank, wretched noise of her own beating heart. She was aware of the chair clattering to the floor behind her as she whirled. Of the rattle of plates and silverware on the table. Then Bill had her in his arms, gripping her tight with his good arm while she struggled.

"Don't touch me," Effie said.

Bill let her go. "I'm sorry. It's the pain meds. They make me say dumb shit."

"You *are* a dumb shit," Effie said. "Jesus, Bill."

Bill didn't look sorry. He looked as if he scored a point off her in some game only he'd known he was playing. Effie headed for the front door.

"You don't have to worry about that guy, Effie, I told you that!" Bill called after her.

Effie flipped him the finger and slammed the door behind her.

chapter seventeen

Mitchell had lost his phone, and it had taken him a while to get a new one set up. Warily, Effie had accepted this excuse because, besides seeing a small green circle next to his name on a dating site when they'd never even skated close to talking about exclusivity, she had no reason to think he was jerking her around. Because if she wasn't going to take a chance and trust someone, why the hell should she bother trying at all?

He really was a nice guy. Normal. He did wear khaki pants and a polo shirt and his hair was rumpled, but adorably so. He had rimless glasses that somehow made him cuter than he ought to be. A nice, normal man without a dark past who wrote computer programs for a living and didn't seem bothered that she listened more than she spoke.

She was going to try this, Effie thought firmly as she and Mitchell exited the movie theater. She was going to figure out this dating thing, once and for all, and she was going to do what she'd told Heath she was doing. Moving forward with her life.

"I thought the movie was pretty good," Mitchell said.

Effie eyed the smokers gathered around the ashtray to the side of the theater doors and craved a cigarette fiercely.

Wouldn't she always? It was one of those habits you could quit but never really leave behind. "It was violent."

"Oh." Mitchell paused to give her a sideways glance. "I'm sorry?"

She laughed and, on impulse, linked her arm through his. "No, it's fine. I like that sort of thing. Guns and fast cars, hot women. It was a perfect date movie."

"I thought for sure you'd pick that other one." Mitchell looked pleased at the contact of her hand on him, his step falling in time with hers. "I'd have gone with that one, if you wanted."

"Of course you would. You're a gentleman." Effie spoke sincerely but lightly, testing him.

Mitchell smiled. "I'm glad you think so."

He eased them around a puddle on the sidewalk in front of them. She noticed that. Also how he switched sides to be between her and the street. He relinked their arms, keeping her close. She liked that, too, though while other women might've giggled, flirting, she kept her gaze on the path in front of them.

"It's been three dates and you haven't even tried to kiss me," she continued as though it didn't matter.

At that, Mitchell stopped, but slowly. He turned her to face him. There on the sidewalk in front of the empty storefront that had once been the local hardware store, he pulled Effie close and kissed her lightly on the mouth.

"Better?" he asked.

She hadn't even had time to close her eyes. It wasn't terribly romantic, but it was horrifyingly sweet. It made her want to kiss him back, to force his mouth open with hers and push inside it with her tongue. She didn't. She smiled, though, ducking her head in what appeared to be coyness but was really a way to keep from laughing in his face. There were lots of ways to hurt someone, and that wasn't the way she wanted to do it.

"Effie, I really like you."

Of course he did. He had no idea who she really was. If he did, wouldn't he run screaming down the street?

"I like you, too, Mitchell."

"Can I take you for coffee, maybe some dessert? Do you have to get back to your daughter?"

"She's with my mother. Coffee sounds amazing." Shivering, Effie looked up at the sky. No stars. It smelled like snow. To kiss him again, she pushed up on her toes, but only a little, because Mitchell was only an inch or so taller than she was.

This time, the kiss lingered. Open mouths. Tongue. It was better than the first time. When she pulled away, he looked a little dazed. His mouth wet and slightly open. She didn't kiss him again but waited to see if he'd go for it.

He did and, gentleman or not, his hands wandered to her hips, pulling her closer. She closed her eyes and let herself sink into the taste of him. Her breath caught. It was easier than she'd thought it would be, she thought before it ended and she had to open her eyes to look up at him. Mitchell looked up to the sky, then glanced back to her with a grin.

"It's starting to snow." He held out his arm to show her the small flakes on his dark coat sleeve.

"Oh," Effie said. "Pretty."

"Not as pretty as you," Mitchell said, and she wanted to laugh at that, too, because he had no idea, did he? All he saw was her face and her body, and yes, Effie knew that she was pretty. The problem was not those outside bits but what was inside her, and so far, Mitchell saw only the outside.

For the first time in forever, Effie was glad of that, of still being a stranger to someone who thought she was nice and pretty and normal, too.

"There's a great place a block over. They have amazing chocolate cake. How about you take me there?" she said.

And he did.

chapter eighteen

Heath had shown up with a casserole in a thermal bag and a fancy salad in a bowl. He also brought a bottle of white wine and a two-liter bottle of Coke. Why? Because he somehow knew, as he always did, when Effie was up to her ears in work and hadn't had time to cook a full meal in days. Okay, for about a week. She and Polly had been eating leftover pizza and frozen french fries. Effie, as she always did while caught up in a project, had demolished a case of ramen noodles and a dozen mini cans of Pringles chips. She liked them because you could tip out the entire sleeve of chips onto a plate and see every single one before you ate them.

Breathing in the scent of chicken, garlic, broccoli and butter, Effie grinned. "Ohmigod, fresh vegetables. Did you make this at work?"

"Yeah." He pulled out the casserole and set it on the stovetop, then found a serving spoon and dug it into the steaming contents. He gave her a look. "It's not rice. It's couscous."

Effie paused for a second before saying, "I've been eating rice."

"No shit. Since when?" Heath turned with a goggle-eyed look.

"I don't know. A few weeks." Effie shrugged and tried to

blow off the conversation, but Heath snagged her elbow until she looked at him. She wasn't going to tell him that she'd been seeing Mitchell, that Mitchell liked rice and that she'd finally done with the food what she'd done with the dates. Given it a chance.

"I made this myself and watched everything that went into it," he told her.

Effie nodded and pushed onto her tiptoes to give him a hug that didn't linger. Her fingers stroked down his back once, twice, before she pulled away. "I trust you."

For a moment, all he did was stare. Then a small smile twisted his mouth. She thought he might kiss her, but Heath only went back to setting out the food he'd brought while Effie watched.

"You need a haircut," she told him.

He looked at her over his shoulder. "After dinner? Will you?"

"If you want to look like a shorn sheep." She laughed and shook her head, but Heath was serious. Effie sighed, pretending to be annoyed, though secretly she was pleased he came to her for things like that.

Polly, without being asked, had set the table. She was being too quiet, something Effie noticed but hadn't yet approached her about. She suspected it had something to do with the sleepover party Polly had been at last night. So far, Polly hadn't talked about the party, but she'd been sleeping all day since Dee had dropped her off at ten this morning.

"Pollywog, get me a beer, would you?" Heath shrugged out of his battered canvas jacket and hung it on the hook next to the kitchen door. *His* hook. Nobody else ever used it.

Why Effie should think of this now, she couldn't say, except that she hadn't noticed how empty the rack looked without his coat on it. She shoved that thought aside and focused on getting out the plastic containers of chopped fruit and veggies with ranch dressing from Heath's bag.

"I got lemon bars for dessert." Heath's gaze swept her up and down. He put out one long arm to turn her slightly, side to side, then nodded.

Effie put her hands on her hips. "What?"

"You're looking good."

"Chubby, you mean."

"Too many dates," Heath said. "All those fried appetizers."

Effie knuckled his upper arm. Heath grabbed her to hold her off, then tickled her ribs until, squealing and breathless, Effie tossed up her hands. She looked to see Polly watching them with a small yet somehow humorless smile. Carefully, Effie extracted herself from Heath's grip.

"It looks good on you," Heath said. If he noticed anything off about Polly, he wasn't showing it. He took the beer the girl handed him and cracked off the top to take a long swig. When he let out a low, rumbling belch, Effie and Polly both gave disgusted cries. Heath patted his belly and gave Polly a wink. "Better out the attic than the basement."

Usually Polly would've giggled at that, but today she gave him only a faint smile and took her place at the table. Effie hadn't raised Polly with any kind of religion beyond secular observances, but a few years ago she'd decided to pray before meals. What Polly said or whom she said it to, Effie didn't know, because Polly always did it in silence. Today, though, she held out her hands. One to Heath, who took it at once. One to her mother, who hesitated.

"It won't kill you," Heath said.

Polly looked expectant. Effie frowned but linked her fingers with her daughter's. Polly bent her head. Effie waited for her to speak, but she prayed as she always did, without words. A few seconds passed, and in the quiet, Effie looked across the table at Heath. Their eyes met.

He smiled at her.

In that moment, there was nothing else in the world for her. This, the two people Effie loved most in the world, at her table. They were a family. In that moment, she couldn't imagine anything other than this.

Sister, Brother, Daddy. Here we are. Isn't this nice? All of us together, a family.

The memory reared up, twisted and ugly, and Effie jerked away from it physically, knocking over her wineglass. Liquid spread across the table and she jumped up to grab a towel, grateful for the chance to hide her face from Heath, who would've looked at her and known something was wrong. He did give her a curious glance as she blotted the spill with an airy, forced laugh at her clumsiness, but he didn't say anything, and when he tried to help her, she shooed him away.

"I got it." When he tried again, she snapped at him. "I said I got it."

He backed off.

"My friend says she's going to grow beans," Polly said when the conversation turned to her science project.

"Can you do something that doesn't involve taking care of any living thing?" Effie got up to pour herself a new glass of wine and brought another beer for Heath. "No peeps, no beans. How about that diet cola and mints experiment? That looks like fun."

"Someone else is doing that one." Polly dragged her fork through the casserole, separating the chicken from the rest of it and pushing it to the side.

Heath tipped the beer bottle against his lips, then swallowed. "You're not going to eat that?"

"I think I might become vegan." Polly shrugged.

That was news to Effie. "You realize that means no cheeseburgers, right?"

Polly laughed. "Duh!"

"And you'll have to actually eat vegetables," Effie added as Polly pushed the broccoli to the side, as well.

"Yes, Mother," Polly said with a sigh. "I know."

Heath poked his fork into a piece of chicken on Polly's plate. "More for me."

Polly eyed them both. "So, you're okay with it? If I become vegan?"

"If that's what you want," Effie said. "I think it's going to be harder than you think it will be, but okay."

Polly looked faintly surprised, then frowned. "Sam's mom told her she wasn't allowed. She said that Sam could do whatever she wanted when she grew up, but while she still lived at home she had to eat what her mom made for dinner."

Effie had never forced Polly to eat anything she didn't want to, never made her clean her plate. Eating and food were complicated issues for Effie, and she wasn't about to make them so for her daughter. She gave Heath a look.

"Well, Polly, I can't promise you I'll make all kinds of elaborate meals for you—"

"You don't anyway," Polly pointed out.

Effie made a face. "Thanks, kid."

Polly laughed again, and this time it sounded more natural. "I can find recipes on the internet."

"I can help you cook some vegan meals." Heath stabbed another bite of Polly's discarded chicken and chewed slowly, and that was that.

"Where do you think that's coming from?" Heath asked when they'd finished eating and Polly had gone to her room to do her homework.

Effie looked at him from the sink, where she was washing the casserole pan. "Wanting to be vegan? Who knows. It's trendy?"

"She's growing up." Heath leaned against the counter next

to her, close enough that she'd knock him with her elbow if she wasn't careful.

Effie blew a palm of soap suds at him, keeping things light. "That's what they do."

"Yeah. I guess so."

She faced him. "What's up with you?"

"Nothing." Heath shrugged and ran a hand through his hair to get it off his eyes. His phone rang from his pocket, but instead of answering it, he pressed the button to send it right to voice mail.

Effie kept her voice casual. "Your girlfriend won't be happy if you don't answer her calls."

"She's not my girlfriend."

"Of course not." Effie rinsed the pan and set it on the dish rack, then washed her hands and dried them before looking at him again. She touched the fading bruise on his cheek.

Heath closed his eyes at the touch, which was not quite a caress. He turned his face to let his lips press her palm in not quite a kiss. Effie took her hand away.

"Let's cut your hair," she said.

Seated in front of her in a kitchen chair, a towel clipped around his neck, Heath shook his head until his hair fell over his eyes. Effie dragged her fingers through the thick, silky darkness. She scratched his scalp lightly, and he let out a sigh. She finger-combed it, letting the length tickle her fingers. Heath had gorgeous hair, and it seemed a shame to cut it, but he also couldn't go around looking like a sheepdog.

She took her time, trimming a bit here and there. Humming under her breath, she drew the hair to the tips of her fingers and let it fall over his face to judge the length. Trimmed some more. Caught up in what she was doing, she didn't notice him staring at her at first, but when her gaze snagged on his, she paused.

"Kiss me," he mouthed.

Heat flooded her, but with a small smile, Effie shook her head. Heath's eyes glittered. She was standing between his spread knees, the scissors in one hand and his hair in the other. He let his hands run up the backs of her denim-clad thighs to anchor her hips and inch her a step closer.

"Kiss me," he said in a low voice.

"No. Sit still."

Heath closed his eyes and gave Effie a sleepyish smile. She put her knuckles beneath his chin to tip his head back, then stroked her fingers through his hair, once, twice, again. She watched his smile thin, but he didn't open his eyes.

She wanted to kiss him, of course. Wanted to do more than that. Simply touching him this way, when he was acquiescent under her caress yet on the constant edge of a plea, made Effie feel as though she were slowly treading water but waiting for the inevitable moment when she knew she was going to drown.

Instead, she focused on finishing the haircut. Brushing the hair from his shoulders and catching as much of it as she could in the towel, Effie stepped back. "All done."

Heath opened his eyes and scrubbed both hands along his scalp. "Thanks."

"You don't want to look at it?"

"I'm sure you did a great job." He stood, looming over her. Stray hairs clung to his face here and there, and he held out the collar of his shirt to shake it. "Itches. I need a shower. Then dessert? You want to watch a couple episodes of *Runner* with me?"

Over time, they'd slowly been working their way through the entire ten seasons of the show, although they'd seen them all already. Effie shook the towel over the garbage can. "I have a project to finish. But I bet Polly will watch with you. Make sure she's finished with her homework first."

"Of course." Heath snagged her by the belt loop to pull her a few steps closer. He would kiss her now, she thought, but he only passed his thumb over her lower lip for a second before letting her go.

Twenty minutes later, the familiar sounds of *Runner*'s opening theme song hummed through the wall as Effie stood in front of her easel. She'd bought this house because of the glassed-in back porch, which was too hot in the summer and too cold in the winter, but had amazing light all day long. It didn't matter much now, since the sun had set, but she'd rigged up a pair of strong work lights.

This piece would probably be better painted in the dark.

She stood in front of a canvas still mostly blank. She'd stroked a few tentative lines over the surface. Letting her fingers get a feel for the image. At this point, the picture was still all in her head. It had taken her a few weeks to get started, for the idea to move from concept to actual planning. This piece would be different from the ones she put up for sale at her Craftsy store or the ones people paid her to create based on their own specifications. This one was going to be all Effie.

She'd thought she would sketch an outline first, but now she picked up several tubes of paint instead. Black, crimson, shades of blue. The faintest, palest pink. She squeezed out liberal amounts onto her wooden palette and took up a brush. She began to paint.

Happy little trees.

People could make fun of Bob Ross all they wanted, but Effie has spent hours with his soft drone and those landscapes. The TV in the basement gets only one station, PBS. It's almost worse than having no television at all, but Daddy gave it to them as a "reward" for good behavior, and Effie wouldn't complain about it, not even to Heath. Especially not to him, when he's been the one to suffer for the reward.

She's always loved drawing and painting and art, but she's learned more about technique in the past few months of *The Joy of Painting* than she had in the years of taking classes with Madame Clay. Yesterday, Effie painted a pretty landscape with trees and mountains and a lake. Then she painted crossbars, like a window, so they could hang it on the wall and pretend they had a view. Her perspective is all off. If her painting was truly what they could see from their window, the water of the lake would be lapping at their toes. She doesn't care. She'd give anything to stand on a sandy shore with warm water teasing her to dive into it.

Today, Effie wants to finish the landscape she started last week, but she woke up feeling sick to her stomach. It's the drugs. Sometimes there are too many. Daddy's going to kill them one day. Maybe that's what he's going for.

Effie wants to be still and quiet in the dark and sleep until all of this goes away. She could sleep through the music, that same song over and over, the one about sailing. She can't sleep through the bright lights, though, and he always turns those on just before he visits.

Daddy. That's what he insists they call him. He calls them Brother and Sister. He's a small man with round glasses and a balding head, a belly a little too big for his pants that hangs out under his too-tight belt. But he's stronger than he looks, Effie knows, because the time she did try to jump past him and head for the door, he was on her before she could get more than a few feet. He'd backhanded her, sending her reeling. Worse, he'd punched Heath in the face over and over until Effie begged him to stop, and then Daddy promised her that if she tried another stunt like that, he would make sure Heath gets worse than a knuckle sandwich.

Effie believes him. It helped her understand why Heath is so reluctant to try to escape, too. The burden of knowing that your actions will hurt someone else. He's still convinced someone will find them. Effie is losing hope.

"Good morning, children," Daddy always greets them. "Wakey wakey, eggs and bakey!"

Sometimes there *are* plates of eggs and bacon, the smell so good it makes her mouth squirt saliva. Sometimes there is fresh fruit cut into artful shapes like flowers or panda bears. When he's angry, there's plain, cold oatmeal or undercooked noodles made bitter with the dust of pills and other things. Sometimes for days and days there's nothing at all, and that's all right, because it's easier to deal with hunger when there isn't a plate of steaming, fluffy scrambled eggs sprinkled with cheese in front of her.

Still, there's only so long either of them can go without eating something, and last night Effie had broken down and gobbled the entire plate of pasta with butter. Heath only picked at it, watching her with a concerned expression. There'd also been garlic bread, and he'd passed on that entirely, but Effie had been ravenous, incapable of resisting once she'd taken a few bites.

Effie has learned the hard way to believe Heath when he told her not to eat what Daddy brings them.

She regrets it now. Her stomach aches, her guts cramp. She's been up half the night with the shit-shivers and had almost thrown up several times. She managed to keep herself from it only because the thought of the stink it would leave for days or weeks in the basement was too much to handle.

Today when the song starts and the lights come on, Effie pulls the shabby, stinking blankets up over her head and rolls onto her side with a groan. There's no way she's getting up, no way to put a smile on her face the way Daddy demands. Not even for the promise of being allowed to go upstairs, an event Daddy assures them both over and over will happen "one day." When they've both been good enough. When he knows he can trust them. Effie knows better than to believe him. The only way either she or Heath is going to go upstairs, she thinks, is if one of them is dead.

"Effie," Heath says now. "Get up. He's coming. C'mon."

"I'm sick."

"You shouldn't have eaten the garlic bread," Heath says.

Effie whips the blankets off her face and scowls. "Gee, thanks, Captain Obvious."

Overhead, the creaking floors tell them Daddy's heading for the basement door. Then the wooden steps and the door at the bottom that leads into their living space. The rooms she and Heath share have been soundproofed so thoroughly they can't hear anything else outside it, but sure enough, in a few minutes, the door opens. Heath shakes his head and moves away from her to stand. Effie curls into a ball.

"Wakey wakey…" Daddy begins. "Well, now, Sister. What's going on? Why aren't you up and at 'em, Adam Ant?"

"She's sick," Heath offers.

Daddy moves closer to the bed. "Is that so? What's wrong?"

"My stomach hurts." Effie presses her hands to her belly.

Daddy looks as if he's pleased but trying to hide it. "Ah. Well. You'd better let me take a look."

Effie does not want this man to touch her, and she tenses when he sits on the edge of the bed. She's ready for him to get freaky. That's what perverts do, right? Touch young girls inappropriately? But Daddy simply probes her belly with soft fingers and then puts the back of his hand to her forehead.

"Chicken soup," he declares and slaps both his knees at the same time. "That's the ticket."

"I'm not hungry."

"It will make you feel better." Daddy stands and turns to look at Heath. "And you. How are you feeling?"

Heath shrugs. "Fine."

"Fine, what?"

"Fine, Daddy." The word grinds out of Heath's mouth as if the taste of it is making him sicker than the garlic bread made Effie.

Daddy frowns, as though maybe he was hoping for a different answer. "I'll be back."

When he's gone and locked the door behind him, Effie sits. Everything hurts, aching, throbbing. Her head pounds. She makes fists and rams them into the sagging mattress over and over.

"What does he want?" she cries. "What is the matter with him? Why does he keep us down here? Why does he feed us things to make us sick, Heath, why?"

Everything spins. She's going to throw up, she knows it, but she can't force herself to walk, much less run, to the toilet. Gagging, Effie spits into an empty bowl, but nothing comes up. She swipes at the snot dripping from her nose, not caring how gross that is. She stands and tries to overturn the table. She wants to break things, but the cramping in her guts doubles her over.

Heath takes her by the arm, and he's too strong for her to shake off. He holds her still until she stops struggling. For a second, Effie thinks he's going to hug her, but then he lets her go.

"He makes us sick so he can take care of us. Make us better. So we're grateful to him," Heath says in a low voice.

Effie sits on the edge of the bed. Her eyes feel wide and

wild. Her throat feels tight, as if she can't breathe. She's frantic and desperate and yet overcome with a lethargy so strong it's all she can do not to fall back onto the bed.

"Why?" she says again, softly this time.

"Because he's crazy."

Before she can ask Heath more questions, her stomach cramps again. This time she does get up to rush to the toilet. Heath must've filled the tank with water to flush sometime during the night; she'd be more embarrassed about the mess and stink if she didn't feel as if she was going to die.

Daddy has left the bright overhead lights on, something he usually turns off when he leaves. Effie's grateful for them now, though, because they shine into the bathroom enough that she can see what she's doing. Though her belly is cramping as if she has diarrhea, nothing comes out. When she wipes, though, the paper comes away covered in dark red fluid. Effie stares at it, uncertain at first. Then she starts to cry.

All of her friends have been getting periods for over a year. Mom told her it would happen any day and had taken her to the store to pick up pads and tampons that Effie has dutifully carried in her purse, waiting for this moment. Now here she is on a broken toilet in a crazy stranger's basement, getting her period for the first time, and all she can do is weep.

"Effie?"

"Go away!" Embarrassed, cringing, Effie tries to clean herself up, but there's too much blood and not enough toilet paper.

Heath peeks around the door frame. "Are you okay?"

"No." With a shaky breath, Effie pushes her knees together. "I need help."

"With what?"

She doesn't want to say it. Not to *this* or any other boy, but what choice does she have? "I got my period."

"Oh." Heath doesn't sound embarrassed or even curious. He sounds sympathetic. "Shit."

Effie cries again, though she hates the tears. "I don't have anything!"

"I'll ask Daddy for something when he comes back."

"He won't have anything," Effie says. "Will he?"

Heath moves a little closer. "He'll have to, won't he? He can't expect you to just...not have something. I mean, girls need stuff. He should know that."

"He's crazy, though." Effie sniffles. A slow, rolling cramp ripples through her.

"He likes to take care of us so we're grateful," Heath reminded her.

The floor creaked above them. That freaking song was still playing. Effie wants to cover her ears, but she doesn't. It wouldn't block out the song, anyway.

Outside in the other room, the door opens. "Sister, I brought your soup... What's going on in there?"

Heath straightens. "She needs some, um...girl supplies."

Effie can't see much over Heath's shoulder, just the top of Daddy's balding head. He sounds surprised, though. "What?"

"Tampons!" Effie screams suddenly. "I'm on the rag, it's the curse, I'm on my dot. Aunt Flo came to town!"

"Oh, my goodness," Daddy says.

"She needs things," Heath tells him.

There's silence. Effie hears the door close. She gives in to tears again, her face in her hands. This is awful, all of it, but particularly this. It's worse than when Robin Sanders got her period for the first time when she was wearing white pants and had to tie a sweatshirt around her waist for the rest of the day. Worse than any story about getting your first period that Effie's ever heard, and girls in school passed around those horror tales like trading cards.

After a minute or so, Heath leaves the bathroom and returns to press something soft into Effie's hand. It's a dish towel, folded into a rectangle. She looks at him.

"I can't."

"It'll be okay," Heath tells her.

"Go out of here." Effie waits until he leaves, then stands to tuck the towel between her legs. She pulls her panties up to hold the towel in place, and another sob leaks out of her. It's worse than a diaper.

She tips the last few drops of water from the gallon jug into her palms to wash her hands and hopes that Daddy will bring them more water when he comes back. In the other room, Heath looks up expectantly when she comes out of the bathroom. He looks at her face, not between her legs. Effie notices that, and if there's a moment when she starts to think of Heath as something other than a stranger she's been forced to live with, it's right then. When he is more than kind to her. When he helps her not be ashamed of something she can't help.

"Effie. Hey. Effie." Heath's voice drew her back to this room, this reality, and out of that basement.

Blinking, Effie let him turn her. He gently took the brush from her cramping fingers and set it down. Effie looked at her hands, encrusted with paint. The colors had blended and blurred, but there were hints here and there of individual shades. She rubbed her fingers together, feeling the rubbery dried texture in some places, still-slick in others.

"Hi," she said.

"It's late. I made sure Polly got a shower and brushed her teeth before she went to bed." Heath let his hands run down Effie's arms until he could lightly circle her wrists before letting her go. "Is it finished?"

Effie turned to look at the painting. It was bigger than most of her other work. It would be a bitch to ship, if she could find someone to buy it. Naveen was going to go ape-shit, she thought and smiled with a sudden, fierce brightness that nevertheless felt as if it twisted her mouth into a grimace. She hadn't sent him anything this good in a long time.

"It's probably the best thing I've ever done," she said. "But I'm not sure that it's finished."

"You want something to eat? You were at it for hours." Heath tapped her shoulder to turn her attention back to him, and like a woman waking from a dream, Effie turned.

She blinked, really seeing him. With a faint shake of her head, she sighed. "No, I'm not hungry."

"Tired? Let's get you to bed."

"I'm covered in paint." Effie looked down at herself. She wore yoga pants and a white wifebeater tank top that stuck to her bare skin with paint and emphasized the fact she'd taken off her bra hours ago, when she'd been painting hard. "I need a shower first."

As always in the aftermath of painting something that had truly inspired her, she felt fragile, delicate, the Little Mermaid walking with her steps like knives. She wasn't hungry, but she should at least drink something. Her mouth was parched, lips dry, tongue like sand. Yet she couldn't make herself move, not yet, still caught up in the power of creating something she knew, she fucking knew to the core of her soul, was really art.

Heath brushed the hair out of her eyes and rested his hands on her shoulders. His thumbs stroked briefly along the sides of her neck. "So, let's get you a shower."

She stumbled on the step from the porch into the den, her legs aching from standing in essentially one position for so long, but Heath was there to hold her up. One hand snaked around her waist, guiding her. Through the kitchen, down the hall, past Polly's half-closed door, where they both paused to peek inside.

"I love her so much," Effie whispered.

Heath's fingers tightened on her hip. "I know you do."

In her bathroom, he pulled her tank top over her head, and though he gave a soft intake of breath at her bare breasts and hardening nipples, he didn't touch them. He helped her step out of her yoga pants, at first bending, then going to his knees to push the material over her ankles and off her feet. Head bent, he let himself lean forward a little to press his face to her thigh. Effie's fingers trailed over his hair, her body already reacting to the idea of him kissing her there, but Heath let only his fingertips skate up the backs of her thighs for a second or so before getting to his feet. He didn't look her in the eyes as he turned on the shower and tested the water before stepping aside so she could get into the shower.

"You don't have to stay," Effie said as she got into the water a minute too early. She shivered at the lukewarm spray, rapidly warming. In another minute it would be too hot, scalding her. She tipped her face into the spray, already knowing his answer.

"I want to make sure you get to bed all right."

"I'm not an invalid," Effie told him. She took a mouthful of water and spit it out, eyes closed, hands flat on the shower's tile wall. She didn't need to see him to know he'd stayed within arm's reach. She could feel him with every part of her. "Just tired."

He left her alone. She'd have stayed under that hot water forever, if she could. Somehow there could never be enough of it for her. Too many years fighting to bathe in cold water from a jug, running water a luxury, hot running water a reward for unspeakable acts she'd never had to perform. There were days she showered three or four times, simply because she could. Tonight, though, knowing the clock was ticking toward morning and she would have to be up and awake to get Polly off to school, Effie couldn't allow herself to indulge in anything longer than the time it took to scrub herself clean of the paint.

The bedroom was dark, but she didn't need light to navigate. She'd towel dried her hair but left it hanging over her shoulders and down her back, and the tickle of it between her shoulder blades became an itch that spread throughout her entire body. Naked, Effie took several careful steps, sliding her feet as had become her habit so long ago so she didn't step on something sharp. Heath was a shadow, but just as she had in the shower, she didn't need to see him to know where he stood.

She kissed him.

She ran her hands up the front of his shirt to link her fingers behind his neck, not caring if she stained his shirt or his skin with the leftover paint. His mouth opened, as she'd expected, but his hands went to her hips and pushed her gently back, which she did not. Frowning, Effie moved to kiss him again.

Heath turned his face just enough that her kiss skidded past his lips. They stayed that way for a moment or so, until Effie reached between them to cup his crotch. He was already hard, his cock hot and pressing the denim. He sighed when she did that. He shivered. But he didn't kiss her.

"No?" Effie whispered, moving closer to say it directly into his ear. She let her tongue drift out to flick at his sensitive earlobe. Then the flesh of his neck. She nipped, then bit, as her hand between his legs squeezed gently. Then a little harder. At his noise of protest, she eased off but kept her mouth close to his ear. "Kiss me. I want you."

With that, Heath groaned and pulled her close. His lips found hers. Then his tongue. His hands slid from her hips to cup her ass and grind her against him.

Oh, it was always a mistake to think she was in control

when she was with him. He pushed her back toward the bed, and they fell onto it together in a protest of creaking headboard and mattress springs. They rolled until Effie was on top, her knees pressing his sides in the sweet, hot places where his shirt had ridden up, and she loved that, fucking loved it, skin on skin. She needed more. Her hands slid up his arms to pin his wrists at the sides of his head, and she bent to let her breasts tease his mouth. At the touch of his lips on her nipple, she ground against him harder, harder, not caring if she hurt him. Trying, in fact, to make it hurt.

Heath groaned and muttered her name.

"Yes," Effie said. "It's me. It's always me, always, always and forever."

She wanted to move up and over his face, to press her cunt over his mouth and nose until he couldn't breathe. She wanted him to drown in her. She took his mouth again instead, kissing cruelly until he growled and rolled them both again so she was beneath him and her wrists were pinned as his had been.

She could've gone soft, compliant, submissive, but that wasn't what Heath wanted from her. She fought him, bucking her hips. Her naked flesh scraped against denim. She snapped her teeth at him, scant inches from his skin, and he pulled away only far enough to keep her from biting him. His fingers bit into her wrists harder, harder until she cried out.

Then he let go of one of her hands to cover her mouth with the other.

Ah, fuck, yes, it was wrong to love this, but she did, she did, she could not stop herself from loving it. Or him. Effie bit at Heath's palm but couldn't get more than a taste of him. Her bite became a kiss, helpless and longing, and he pressed his fingers tight into her cheek as he let go of her other hand so he could unzip and unbutton.

With her hands free, she could fight him, and she did, but

he was bigger and stronger, and did she really want to get away from him? Of course not. When she slapped at his chest and dug into him with her nails, it only urged him on. Later, she could feel guilty for this love that was nothing like the books and movies told her how it should be, but not now. Never in the moment, when his body on hers became her everything.

Effie cried out against his hand when Heath fucked into her—she was turned on but still a little dry, and he scraped. As he pulled out, Heath nudged her knees apart, sliding a hand beneath one to lift her hips. Opening her. His mouth crushed onto hers, taking the place of his hand. His next thrust took him even deeper, and it was easier this time because now she was getting slick, wet and hot and slippery for him. This time when she made a noise, he sank his fingers into the hair at the base of her skull and yanked her head back.

Fuck, that hurt. Pulling her hair, the awkward arch of her back, the way his cock rubbed her inside. It hurt and made her crazy at the same time. When Heath pressed his face to the side of hers and took her earlobe in his teeth, Effie shuddered.

"Quiet," Heath said in a low rasp. "You don't want anyone to hear."

Oh, quiet, oh yes, there it was, they had to be quiet and not let anyone know. This had to be done in secret, in the dark, in furtive, guilty moments they were supposed to regret but never, ever did.

She *never* did.

He fucked her steadily. He knew her rhythm. How to press his pelvis to her clit the right way, over and over, until her hips lifted and she arched, raking his back with her nails and hooking her heels over his ass to shove him deeper. Harder. That's when he eased, slowing, teasing, pulling almost all the way out and using the tip of his cock to barely dip inside her while he put a hand between them to tweak her clit.

With other men Effie could control herself, but not with Heath. Never with him. She did not give up to her orgasm so much as she was swept away by it. Rushing waves of pleasure shook her, and she cried out into his mouth over and over as his thrusts got deeper again.

When he bit down on the curve of her shoulder, another wave of ecstasy ripped through her. Heath caught her flesh in his teeth, sucking hard. He would leave a mark, oh, fuck yes, she thought, she would see it in the morning, that bruise, that place where he had left the proof of this.

Effie came again.

Heath soothed the pain in her neck with his tongue and captured her mouth once more, this time teasing her with his lips the way he'd been doing with his cock. She couldn't manage another orgasm. She was broken from the pleasure, wrung out, but when he rolled his hips and groaned into her mouth, Effie put her fingers in his hair and pulled him tight against her.

Heath finished with a low, soft cry against her. He buried his face against the side of her neck, lips pressed to the spot he'd bitten. He pressed deep and went still. It took him a few minutes to soften inside her, but then he pulled out and moved to lie on his side, turning her to spoon against her ass. It was wet. Effie thought distractedly of her clean sheets, of at least pulling up a blanket to cover them, but in the end all she did was wake to the morning light streaming through her windows and a dozen aching sorenesses all over her and an empty bed beside her.

chapter nineteen

Shit. It was late. Effie had stretched, cataloging the places she ached, but now shot up and tossed off the covers. Polly would miss the bus and be late for school, Effie would have to drive her, she stank of sex and needed a shower, there was no time. With a frustrated groan, Effie slung on her robe and went out into the hallway.

Heath was in the kitchen. "Hey."

"Hey, I need to get…" Effie paused. "What time is it?"

"Almost nine. I got Polly up and on the bus, don't worry." Heath held up two mugs of steaming coffee. "Thought you might need this."

Effie clutched the robe tighter around her throat. "Shit. I'm sorry."

"I always wake up early. It's okay. And I like getting my girl off to school." Heath shrugged. "I miss her, Effie."

Effie took the mug of coffee and sipped carefully. He'd put too much sweetener in, forgetting or maybe not knowing that she'd gone off it several months ago when she'd read on the internet that artificial sweeteners could cause skin irritations and she'd been plagued by a round of distracting itches. Still, the coffee was hot and welcome.

She sighed, though. "It's confusing to her, that's all."

"You both lived with me for the first four years of her life," Heath said flatly. "The only person who's confused about that is you."

"I'm not going to fight with you about this." Her stomach rumbled.

Heath put his mug on the table, plucked a couple pieces of toast from the toaster and set them on the table, along with the butter and jelly and a knife. Then he crossed his arms over his chest and stared at her while she made herself a fresh mug of coffee.

"The sweetener," Effie said without looking at him. "I take it with real sugar now, or black."

"I let her think I slept in the guest room, you know," Heath said. "I'm not a total fucking moron. I do get it, Effie. But I love Polly, and you can't tell me that it wouldn't be helpful to have someone here with you to help out."

Effie, mug cradled in her hands, turned. "Are you behind on your rent again?"

"No, and fuck you," Heath said evenly. "Don't be a bitch. You know I've been working. I have a decent job. They like me there. I don't need your fucking charity. I'm probably doing better than you are."

Effie sipped carefully to keep the hot coffee from burning her tongue. "There are other reasons why living together does not work out for us, Heath."

"Right. Because your mother hates me. Because you want to be free to fuck other men."

"Because we don't work as a couple," Effie reminded him without letting him push her into anger. They would fight. Then they'd fuck. In the light of day she had no more regrets than she had in the dark, but she did have some small measure of sense.

Heath took a seat and started spreading butter on the toast. Then jelly, strawberry, always jelly and never jam because jam had chunks in it. Watching him, Effie failed to push away the immeasurable sadness that crept inside of her. She sipped her coffee and looked out the kitchen window, giving him her back. She was hungry but now couldn't eat.

"Why won't you just let me help you?" Heath asked. "When you know it would make me happy?"

Effie put her cup on the counter and faced him. "Because it comes with a price, doesn't it? Making you happy."

"Everything comes with a price, Effie." Heath pushed the plate away and stood. He gave her an open, yearning look that she could not bear to see. When he came up behind her, she closed her eyes and let him pull her back against him. "Don't you get tired doing it all yourself?"

"Yes. That's why I'm using a dating service," she said.

Heath breathed against the side of her face. "How's that working out for you?"

"Good," she said without missing a beat. "I've met someone nice. We've gone out a few times."

"Same guy more than once?" Heath pulled away to look at her face.

Effie nodded. "Yes. Same guy. More than once."

"But you never—" he began and stopped himself. "You're not going to find what you're looking for. You know that, don't you?"

She didn't want that to be true. Effie put her hands on the counter, bending away from him but unable to move because of the cabinets in front of her. She closed her eyes. She breathed in, then let out a hiss of air.

"Do you think anyone else will make you happy, Effie? Really?"

She shook her head. "If you rely on another person to make you happy, you're always going to be disappointed."

"When you love someone," Heath said, "you want them to be happy more than you want it for yourself. You don't care about the price."

Effie breathed.

Heath backed up a few steps. "Fine. You want me out of your life?"

"I didn't say that."

"Being with you only halfway, it kills me," Heath muttered. "You know that."

She did, but she said nothing. Did not turn. Effie kept her eyes closed. Her fingers curled on the countertop, finding no purchase. A fingernail bent, bringing pain that she refused to acknowledge with so much as a sigh.

"And every time we're together, I tell myself not to hope that this time you'll just fucking see that there is nobody else for you. That you'll give me a chance to prove we're good together, really good, no matter what your mother says. Or anyone else. And every time that hope, it fucking slaughters me, Effie, because in the end it's so obvious that you could not possibly love me," Heath said. "If you did, you wouldn't keep pushing me away."

"Can't you just be happy with what I can give you?" she cried, still not turning. "Does it have to be everything or nothing with you?"

Heath didn't answer her. She heard the rustle of fabric and clink of metal—he was getting his coat from the hook that was his and only his, and would always be his. She turned, finally, unwilling to let him leave her this way one more time, with harsh words between them. She wanted to tell him she loved him and always would, but the look on his face stopped her.

"The problem is, Effie, that you don't give me anything. Not really." Heath shrugged and opened the back door.

"That's not true."

Heath paused. "You don't give me anything you don't give a dozen other guys. Or maybe now, I guess, just that one."

That stung, and it wasn't true. It had been true in the past, when she'd gone through men like wind through reeds, but was not now and hadn't been for a long time. Effie's chin went up, though. She wasn't going to defend herself against him. Not about that.

Heath didn't smile. He looked at her with those green, green eyes and ran a hand over his too-short hair. "Thanks for the cut," he said, and she didn't know if he meant his hair or something else. Something deeper.

In the end it didn't matter, because he walked out the door, and she let him go without calling him back.

chapter twenty

Effie wakes with a pain down low in her guts. She's grown used to pains like that. Sudden sicknesses. This is different, though. This is a deep and grinding pain deep inside, and though she feels as though she could possibly puke, this doesn't feel like illness. It feels as if something's wrong, though. With her hands on her belly, she sits up.

Disoriented. Blinking at the faint light from the hallway through the door her mother insists on keeping cracked open, Effie swings her legs over the edge of the bed. Soft, clean linens, pillows, an unstained mattress. Her feet touch fluffy carpeting.

She's home, oh, God, she's home, she's home.

It's not a dream, this is real life, and she'd cry with the relief of it except that Effie is trying hard to unlearn how to weep. She listens for the sound of her mother hovering outside her door, but all she can hear is the faint noise of her father snoring. That noise is the background of her childhood and should soothe her, but something's wrong now. Maybe nothing will ever be right again.

Standing, Effie grunts at the force of a cramp. She needs the toilet, and fast. Halfway there, something tugs itself free from inside her, soaking her cotton panties, and begins an inexorable slide down her thighs. She knows it's blood before she even gets to the bathroom. She doesn't turn on the light. She fumbles with the toilet seat lid with its fuzzy yarn cover, something she also remembers from her childhood but that brings no comfort now. All she can think about it is how dirty that cover must be, how impossible to clean and how her hands have probably stained it.

If she doesn't turn on the light, she doesn't have to know. She doesn't have to see it. If she sits here in the dark with her sopping panties around her ankles, she can pretend she's had an accident. Embarrassing, but nothing she's never dealt with before. She will sit here until the cramping fades, and she'll take a long hot shower and clean off. She'll put her soiled clothes in the laundry and hope her mother doesn't notice.

But Mom notices everything.

It's been six weeks since Effie came home, and in that time, there hasn't been a single thing Effie's done that Mom hasn't seen. Effie ought to be glad she's home in her soft, warm bed, a fridge full of food she can't quite bring herself to eat, loving and caring parents. Yet this constant scrutiny, the lack of privacy, the way everyone stares at her no matter where she goes, all have left Effie sometimes dreaming of the basement's darkness. She misses Heath's warmth in bed beside her. A legion of stuffed toys could never take his place. Her mother won't allow Effie to see him alone. She sits with them at the kitchen table while they drink hot cocoa and play cards, or in the living room when they try to watch a movie. Heath is not Effie's boyfriend. He's more to her than that, so much more. Her father seems to understand at least a part of that, but her mother never, ever will.

Except now Mom will know everything that went on. She won't be able to pretend she doesn't. No more denying. The truth of what happened in that basement won't be hidden anymore, unless Effie can figure out a way to get herself up and off this toilet, clean herself up. She needs to take care of this. But even as she tries, her hands pressing to her cramping, aching belly, she wants to weep at the loss.

She didn't want to be pregnant at seventeen, but she hadn't wanted to be abducted by a crazy guy and kept in his basement for three years, either. The baby is not a surprise. Effie's long known about how babies are made. You couldn't fool around without risking pregnancy, and she and Heath had been anything but careful.

"Effie? What's going on in there? Are you sick?"

"I'm okay," Effie manages to say. "Just ate something that disagreed with me."

Mom raps lightly. "Let me in."

"No, I'm fine. I'll be…" Effie rasps a groan.

"Let me in, Felicity!" Mom knocks harder. "Phil! Something's wrong with her!"

"No, no, no," Effie says under her breath, but it's too late. The knob rattles. She locked the door, but it doesn't matter; her father has one of those little metal tools that pops the lock. The door opens. The light comes on, too bright, and Effie puts up a hand to cover her eyes.

Mom screams. Effie wants to get up and tell her to stop, it's all right, there's nothing she can't take care of, but in the light there is blood. So much blood. It's splashed all over her legs, the floor, the toilet seat. Her hands. Effie clenches her fists, feeling the stickiness there. That small life, lost now.

"Oh, my God," Mom cries. "Phil, get out of the way. She needs to get to a hospital."

"No ambulance," her father says at once, and Effie wants to hug him, but she can't. "We don't want everyone in the world finding out."

Effie says, "I'm sorry. I'm so sorry."

"Shh, kiddo. It's all going to be okay." Her father grabs a couple towels from the shelf and wraps them around her waist.

Together, they get into his car, Effie in the front seat and Mom muttering over and over from the back while her father drives. By the time they get to the emergency room, Effie expects the entire car to be overflowing with what's coming out of her, but it seems to have slowed. Her father has given her his trench coat to cover her so that nobody in the waiting room even really knows what's going on.

She's taken to a room at once. Settled onto a gurney. Feet in stirrups, her body opened and probed and examined while her father holds her hand tight on one side and Mom on the other dabs at Effie's forehead with a damp cloth until Effie asks her to stop. Then Mom mutters something that makes the nurse standing between Effie's legs frown and ask her to leave the room.

"I'm very sorry," the nurse says when her mother has left in a huff. "You've lost the baby. I... Did you know that you were pregnant?"

"Yes," Effie says.

Her father makes a small, sad noise, but his fingers grip Effie's tighter. A doctor comes in. He does some things that hurt, but they've given Effie some pain medication in an IV drip, and she doesn't care what's going on anymore. The nurse cleans her up. They give her a gown to wear. They take away her stained nightgown and the towels.

"Mom's gonna be mad," Effie slurs. "About the towels."

Then there's a far-off humming and she sleeps for a bit until someone shakes her awake. She's in a hospital bed and she sits up, terrified, not sure what's going on, because the last time she was in the hospital, it was after the basement, and yes, there's Officer Schmidt again.

"What's he doing here?" Effie remembers now why she's there.

"I called him," Mom says. "He's going to need to take your statement. About what happened. It's for the case, Effie. So we can make sure that man never hurts anyone ever again."

Officer Schmidt has nice blue eyes and blond hair carefully combed back from his forehead. He has a nice smile. "Hey, Effie. I just need to get some information from you, okay? Do you feel up to it?"

When the questions begin about Daddy, and how often he touched her, Effie looks for her father, but he's gone. Sent for coffee, Mom says. Effie shakes her head, still woozy with the drugs. Now there's pain again, dull and aching deep inside her, but she's not sure if it's from what they did to her or if her body is somehow simply mourning. All she knows is that they want her to say that Daddy did this to her, and that's not true.

"No. It wasn't. He didn't." The words are thick in her mouth. Her tongue clumsy. Lips dry. She looks for water, which Mom gives her in a cup with a straw, and she gulps it too fast and then feels sick.

"Effie," Mom says quietly, without even a glance at Officer Schmidt. "If it wasn't that man who did this to you, if you're going to tell me it was that boy, well… You're underage. He's an adult. There will still be charges made."

Against Heath. Who is nineteen but not an adult; he's still a kid, like her, only neither of them are kids anymore. Not really. Effie feels about her childhood the way she feels about movies she saw or dreams she had. It existed, somewhere, but not for her.

She looks at her mother. At her father, standing in the doorway with two paper cups of coffee in his hands and a look of such strained grief that Effie can't stand it. She looks then at Officer Schmidt with the nice blue eyes and the big strong hands and the uniform, and Effie speaks.

"Yes," she says. "It was Daddy."

chapter twenty-one

The plan had been to go to the movies, but after looking at all the choices on the marquee, both Effie and Mitchell had agreed that nothing was tempting enough to waste their time on. That's how they'd ended up back at his place with a pizza and some wine and a movie streaming on Interflix. She could've blamed the movie, which had sounded great in the description but had been a total snooze fest. She could've blamed the wine. But in the end, she had to admit that it was her own curiosity that had shifted her closer to Mitchell on the couch so that he could put his arm around her.

She'd gone to bed with men on the first date, or without a date at all, and she and Mitchell had surpassed that a few weeks back. Yet something made her shy when he turned to look at her with the shadows of black and white from the TV screen flashing over his face. When he leaned to kiss her, she turned her face, just enough.

"No?"

Effie laughed. "Not no. Just…slow."

Mitchell tugged a strand of her hair that had escaped the low bun at the base of her neck. He moved closer, a hand on her thigh, but not pressing upward. He nuzzled at her cheek, then lower to her neck, and there, yes, okay, that was good. Like that. The soft brush of his lips on her skin, the heat of his breath. Now if only he would use his teeth...

Mitchell pulled away. She thought he would speak, but he only smiled. It was the right choice. Words would've meant she had to answer him with some of her own, and it was always so much easier to talk with her body than her voice.

She kissed him, harder than he had her. His mouth opened under the pressure of her lips, and when her tongue slid along his, Mitchell let out a low, very gratifying moan. Effie moved onto his lap, straddling him, her hands cupping his face. His went at once to her ass, gripping hard through the denim.

"So much for slow," he murmured into her mouth, which gave her pause.

"I..."

"Shh," Mitchell said. "It's fine. It's great."

They kissed for a long time. Slow, fast, hard, soft. She learned that he liked it when she sucked his tongue, but that it seemed to surprise him how much. She did not like the way he didn't move his hands around her body and kept them firmly planted on her ass—but she chalked it up to that politeness he'd shown her from the start. Maybe he was waiting for her to give him the go-ahead.

"Touch me," Effie breathed against Mitchell's throat as she rocked against him. He was hard, that wasn't an issue, for sure. Yet something in the hesitant, embarrassed way he laughed a little at her request made her sit back. Again pausing, trying to figure him out.

Mitchell leaned back against the couch. His eyes looked a little glazed. His mouth wet. He licked his lower lip, and she watched him, wondering what he would do if she leaned forward to take that soft flesh between her teeth. He wouldn't like it, Effie thought. He would not like that at all.

"Maybe we should go upstairs?" Mitchell offered.

"To your bedroom?"

He laughed. "Yes. To my, um, my bedroom."

She got off his lap and held out her hand. "Yes. Let's go."

Before he took her hand and stood, several seconds passed. Was he going to turn her down? Just before she withdrew her hand, Mitchell grabbed it. He pulled her into his arms for another kiss.

"C'mon," Mitchell said.

Upstairs, his bedroom was no shock. White walls, linens, decorative pillows on the king-size sleigh bed. Spare and sterile artwork in perfect frames on the walls. He had a fireplace, the mantel bare but for two matching vases on each end. Through a door she caught sight of a bathroom as blandly neutral as the bedroom.

"So clean," Effie murmured and looked over her shoulder at him as she went to the bed to sit on the edge.

Mitchell looked at her. "Umm...yeah, well... So, maybe we should... Do you want to pull the blankets back?"

"Oh. Yes. Of course." She stood to allow him to take off the pillows and watched him pile them neatly on the bench at the foot of the bed, where clearly they were meant to be piled instead of tossed haphazardly on the floor.

"Would you like to shower or anything?"

Shit. Was he being polite or was he asking her to shower first because he expected her to? Effie glanced toward the bathroom, uncertain. This wasn't going the way she'd imagined, but to be honest she hadn't spent a lot of time fantasizing about fucking Mitchell. At this point, it was beginning to seem as if one thing had led to another, going faster than it should have.

"I could...or...are you going to?" Effie asked.

"I could if you want to, or..."

She laughed, not because any of this was funny, but because none of it was. Mitchell joined her after a second. He shook his head and stripped back the covers and stepped back from the bed.

"I'll turn out the lights," he said.

She was glad for the darkness. It made it easier for her to strip out of her clothes, folding them neatly and putting them on the chair because she felt too self-conscious to do anything else. It made it easier, too, to slip into the clean sheets smelling faintly of lavender. She heard the click of Mitchell putting his glasses on the nightstand. She waited for him to touch her.

She waited.

The first touch came, finally, on her hip. His hand moved to her belly. He rolled to face her and kissed her mouth; there was a tangle of arms and legs and the brush of his cock, thank God it was still hard, against her side, and she reached to touch him, but he twitched when she did, so she let her hand rest on his leg instead.

She waited for him to kiss her.

He did, at last, and it was better than it had been on the couch. He touched her, his hands finally roaming. Exploring. Mitchell's touch was not tentative, but still softer than she liked or needed. When she moved beneath him, he went slower, not harder. Not faster.

She had told him to go slow, after all. Concentrating, Effie willed her body to respond. She wasn't used to passivity during sex and yet found herself unable to do much more than allow Mitchell to make all the moves.

He was patient, she gave him that. And had stamina. Inside her, appropriately sheathed, of course, he moved in a steady rhythm and stayed with it, until yes, yes, yes…

"There," she said. "Oh. Fuck. Yes, right…there…"

Orgasm. Small but genuine. He followed her into it with a

low grunt and some faster pacing, some harder fucking, and that would've sent her over the edge again if he'd kept it up, but it lasted only a few seconds more before he shuddered and buried his face against her neck. Moments after that he withdrew before he was even soft. He took care of the condom in silence and slid back beneath the covers next to her.

"That was…unexpected," Mitchell said after some more silence had passed.

Effie had been dozing, but now her eyes opened wide. She rolled to face him, a hand beneath her cheek on the pillow. She thought about snuggling close to him, but she didn't.

"Was it?"

He turned his head. In the dim glow from the night-light in the bathroom, she could still see the gleam of his eyes and teeth when he smiled. "It was great. I mean it was just a surprise."

She was afraid to ask why, not sure if he meant that he hadn't expected them to do it at all, or that he'd thought it would be better than it had been. Or that it had been better than he'd imagined. It was not the worst sex Effie had ever had, by far, but it was far, far from the best. She wasn't going to share that opinion, though.

"Surprises can be good," she said instead. "Can't they?"

"Yes. Absolutely."

They both slept after that, but Effie woke with a start and a gasp that fortunately didn't wake Mitchell. She crept from the bed and used his bathroom. She was gathering her clothes when his voice curled toward her out of the dark.

"You don't have to go."

"I…should get home. My kid…" She didn't have to pick Polly up from her mom's until the afternoon, but Mitchell didn't need to know.

"Right. Of course." He sat, a lumpy shadow among all the others. "Let me walk you to the door—"

"No," she said quickly. "It's fine. I didn't mean to wake you."

Mitchell made a soft noise. "I know you didn't."

She wasn't sure what to say to that. So she simply put her clothes on, feeling him watching her even though she knew he could make out only the shape of her and no details. She went to the side of the bed to kiss him before she left. She did that much, at least.

"I'll call you," Mitchell said.

She let another kiss drift along his mouth. "Okay."

Then she let herself out.

chapter twenty-two

Naveen's gallery wasn't the biggest around, but he did have two locations, one in New York City and one in Philadelphia, which was as far as Effie ever wanted to travel. He was also fair with his commission, and he put her work in front of the bigger buyers, at least when she had something they'd like. When the phone rang in her pocket with his distinctive ringtone, Effie pulled it out even though it was almost her turn at the cashier and she hated it when people took calls in the grocery store line and held everyone else up.

"Hello, lovely," Naveen said without preamble. "Is this a bad time?"

"For you? Never." Effie gestured to Polly to inch the cart forward so they could start putting the items onto the conveyor belt.

"Are you sitting down?"

She paused, bending to keep the phone pressed to her ear while she rummaged in her purse for her store loyalty card. She handed it to Polly to give to the cashier. "No, I'm in line at the grocery store. Why?"

"I sold your painting," Naveen said. "I think you're going to be very, very happy."

Effie laughed. "I'm sure I am. Are you going to tell me for how much, or do I have to get Elisabeth on your case?"

"She's not here. You have to settle for me." Naveen sounded as if he was grinning from ear to ear, a Cheshire cat. "Sure you don't want to sit down?"

The woman ahead of her had paid her bill, and it was Effie's turn. She shook her head to the question of if she had any coupons and gave the guy behind her an apologetic glance even though she hadn't done anything so far to hold up the line. "Polly, keep unloading the cart, please. Naveen, just tell me."

"Twenty."

"Twenty…dollars?" Effie paused, confused.

"Twenty thousand dollars. Twenty. Thousand. Bucks." Naveen sounded giddy with glee, and could she blame him, hell no, twenty grand?

"Twenty grand," Effie breathed and for a second or so wished she could sit down right there on the cool tile floor. Thinking she might have no choice but to at least bend and put her head between her knees, since everything had sort of tipped. "Are you f… Are you kidding me?"

Mindful that she had an audience, she lowered her voice. Polly gave her a curious look. Effie gave her a thumbs-up. Polly went back to loading eggs and yogurt and crackers onto the belt. Effie wished now she'd sprung for the pricey cereal the kid had wanted. Well, next time.

"I'm not kidding you. It's one of my best buyers. Her clients are all richer than Midas and trust her implicitly. Your piece, Effie, I have to tell you…I knew it was going to sell the second I saw it. It's the best thing you've ever done. And I mean that," Naveen said sincerely. "It was brilliant."

"And to think, if I could do a couple of those a year I'd be all set." Already the buzz was fading. By the time Naveen took his cut and she covered her expenses, there'd still be a respectable amount left over, but it would be whittled quickly into zeros by groceries and new tires and sneakers for Polly.

Still, it was worth a celebration, and when she disconnected with Naveen, Effie squeezed Polly's shoulder. "Let's get out of here, kiddo. We're going out for dinner to celebrate. I just sold a painting."

"Oh, Mom, great!" Polly grinned. "Can we go to the Melting Pot? Can Heath come?"

Effie, pulling out her credit card to slide it through the machine so they didn't take up any more time, gave Polly a glance. "Yes, we can go to the Melting Pot. Yes, you can call Heath."

She hadn't spoken to Heath in three weeks, though she knew he texted with Polly regularly and had picked her up from school a couple times to take her for hot chocolate or bowling or some other "Disneyland Dad" activities while Effie worked. She'd been swimming in an influx of orders from her store, last-minute rush orders she assumed were for holiday gift-giving. It was good for her own holiday budget, but it meant long hours of what could only occasionally be considered fulfilling work. She'd been grateful for the extra projects that kept her busy. Less so for the way Heath waited in the driveway for Polly to come out, and the way he wasn't answering Effie's calls.

With a quick stop at home to drop off the groceries, Effie and Polly were at the Melting Pot in less than an hour. Polly had texted Heath, who didn't answer at once. He called as they pulled into the parking lot.

"Let me talk to him." Effie held out her hand for Polly's phone. "Hey."

"Hey." He sounded taken aback. "I thought I called Polly."

"You did. I sold that piece. Naveen called me today. We're

at the Melting Pot to celebrate." Effie kept her voice light, casual. Not trying too hard.

"Congratulations, that's great. I knew you would sell it. It's an amazing piece."

Heath's voice shifted, getting fainter. She could picture him holding the phone to his ear while he slid behind the wheel of his beat-up Camaro. Effie hadn't realized how long three weeks was until they'd been without him. She closed her eyes against a sudden burning, twisting in her seat to keep Polly from seeing.

"So, dinner. My treat? I'll spring for the four-course meal."

"Nah, sorry. I can't make it. Another time, maybe." Heath's voice was as light and casual as Effie's had been, but his words struck her hard.

Not in the chest, not in her heart, but in that gag-inducing spot at the base of her throat. Swift and fierce like the stab of two fingers. It hurt to swallow. Effie drew in a breath to keep her voice calm.

"Polly was looking forward to it."

"I'll see Polly another time."

"Heath," Effie said sharply but with a quick glance at her daughter, who was pretending to be busy with something in her purse, but who gave her mother a sideways look that said she was listening to every word. Effie took another breath and let it out, forcing herself to smile. "Fine, then. Another time."

She disconnected without waiting for him to say anything and handed the phone back. Polly slipped it into her purse and gave her mother an expectant look. Effie took her keys from the ignition.

"C'mon," she said. "Let's call Nana instead. I bet she'll be excited."

chapter twenty-three

Effie wants out of the hospital. There's nothing wrong with her. Nothing physical, anyway. Nothing they can fix with bandages or stitches or a cast. She's sure there are pills she could take that would make a lot of the memories go away, but she's done with drugs. The doctors are concerned about withdrawal. They told her that, without knowing what exactly Daddy had been giving them, they can't predict how she'll react to not taking anything. They want to monitor her.

Heath, they sent home.

He's not a minor, and she still is. He doesn't have insurance, and Effie, through her parents, still does. It's not fair, she knows that, but she's not sure if it's because it feels as if Heath has been set free or shunted aside.

"I want to go home," she tells her mother, who is fussing and cooing over her until Effie wants to scream. "I just want to go home."

"Tomorrow." That's the promise Effie's heard for the past three days, but her mother seems to believe it. She pats and smooths the blankets over Effie's feet and offers her a drink from the plastic cup and straw and some pudding, and Effie chokes down everything because all she wants is to be out of here.

She wants Heath, too. They would not let him in to see her after that first day when the two of them, filthy and aching and sick and starving, had been brought in the ambulance with Officer Schmidt there to make sure everything was all right. Her father had told her Heath had been released. Her mother refused to talk about Heath at all.

Another day passes with tests and probing and being woken in the night to have her blood pressure checked. Effie is exhausted. She's gained a pound, which seems to make the doctors happy enough to send her home. She has to sit in a wheelchair, although there's nothing wrong with her legs. Hospital policy. When her father pushes her through the doors and out into the unexpectedly bright sunshine, Effie looks up at the sky and sneezes, hard, four or five times.

Her father laughs. "There's my girl."

All Effie wants to do is to stand under the shower in her own bathroom until the hot water runs out. Then she wants to put on clean pajamas and crawl into bed and sleep until she can't sleep anymore. Yet not even that simple desire is meant to be fulfilled, because as they pull up to the house, she sees too many cars. And there are people outside in the front yard. Balloons. A sign.

Welcome Home!

Oh, no, Effie thinks as she looks out the car window. *Oh, no.* There's nothing she can do about it, though. Her father has invited the neighbors. Family. And, once she gets inside, there are a few strangers who've made their way into the kitchen to stand with plastic cups of punch beneath the balloons. Strangers who want to ask her questions that Effie refuses to answer.

Her father throws them out, but it's too late by that point. Effie has broken into tears and screams, retreating to her room to slam the door in the faces of everyone who wants to point and stare. The only person she really wants to see, needs to see, was not invited.

All she really wants is Heath, but though he promised he would never, ever leave her, he is gone. Her father sits on the edge of Effie's bed and pats her shoulder awkwardly. In the past, he would have hugged her tight, but there's a distance now between them, and Effie knows why. She's not his little girl anymore. He thinks things happened to her in the basement, and he's right, of course. Things did. But it shouldn't matter to him, and it does. Maybe he thinks Effie would push him away, or that she doesn't want his comfort, but she does, desperately.

When she tries to lean against him, her father's stiff posture and the hesitant cough pushes her back an inch or so. She draws her knees to her chest and rests her chin on them. Her hair, wet and clinging to her face, annoys her, so she leans to reach in her nightstand for a hair tie. There were a whole bunch of them in the drawer before she was taken, and they're still in there.

That starts her crying again. Everything in her room is the same. The house, mostly the same. Her parents look older, and they, too, are mostly the same.

Only Effie seems to have changed.

"He's my friend," she says. "You don't understand."

"I understand that the two of you formed a special relationship. But your mother and I think that it's better for now if you have some time here, with us. To readjust. If he's truly your...friend...he'll understand."

"You filled the house with people I don't want to see. And strangers," Effie said. "Journalists."

Her father looks so sad that Effie wishes she hadn't said anything. "I'm so sorry, Effie. They must've found out about the party somehow and showed up. Believe me, I would never have allowed them in. I thought family and friends would make you feel more at home. I thought it would help."

"Heath would help me."

His shoulders sag. He sighs. Her father knuckles his eyes, pressing so hard for a moment that Effie's sure he must be seeing stars. Then he takes the phone from its cradle on her nightstand and punches in a number he must've memorized. At her look, her father gives Effie a sad, broken smile.

"He called every day while you were still in the hospital and left this number for you to call him back. So call him. If that's what you need. Call."

Effie would hug him, but something in the way her father stands keeps her from it. "Thanks."

Effie talks with Heath on the phone for three hours. Much of the time, they say nothing, but the soft sound of his breathing is enough to calm her. When at last they disconnect the call, Effie feels as though she can bear to venture from the safety of her bedroom and go to the kitchen for something to eat.

Does she imagine the warmth on the carpet outside her door, as though one or both of her parents had stood there, listening? Their bedroom door is cracked open, the soft murmur of a late-night talk show familiar as a lullaby. She considers knocking softly on their door, but in the end does not. Her mother will want more than a simple good-night, and the day has been too long already.

In the kitchen, she's startled to find her father sitting with a glass of amber liquid in front of him. She's not sure how much he's already had to drink, but since she can't recall ever seeing him drink alcohol, even beer, the very fact he has a bottle of Scotch in the house is enough to set her back a step. He smiles when he sees her.

"Hey," her father says. "Effie."

"I came to get something to eat."

"Good. Good." Her father gestures at the fridge but doesn't get up. "We have a lot of food left. From the party. It was a stupid idea. I'm sorry."

Effie can't tell him she forgives him—she's not sure it would matter, and she's not positive she does. She pulls a platter of lunch meat and cheese from the fridge and goes to the drawer where her mother always kept the bread. It's full of club rolls and sliced bakery loaves, the fancy stuff.

Faced with this reminder of once again how everything is very much the same while she is vastly different, Effie puts her hands on the countertop to keep herself from shaking. She breathes in. Out. Her fingers curl on the slick Formica. When she looks at her father over her shoulder, thinking she will need to make some excuse for her behavior, she finds him staring instead at the glass he is turning around and around in his hands.

Effie makes a sandwich, inspecting each slice of meat, cheese and bread before layering it. No mayo or mustard. Of course she doesn't expect that the condiments in her mother's kitchen would be spoiled, but the thought of it, the slippery slimy taste of mayonnaise that seems fine but which has gone horribly bad...she can't do it. The sandwich is dry and yet is also the best thing she has ever eaten in her life.

"That boy," her father says quietly, then stops.

"Heath."

"Yes. He's not going to have it easy."

Effie's not sure what to say to that. She takes another bite. Chews. Savors the food. Swallows.

"If you want to talk about what happened..." Her father pauses. The amber liquid spins slowly when he stops turning the glass, then settles. He doesn't drink. He looks at her.

It's an offer to listen, yet he can't quite force himself to make it. Effie thinks she understands. Her parents don't really want to know about what happened to her.

"Even the bad things make you into the person you are," her father says. "Never be ashamed of who you are, Effie. That's all I really want to say."

Then they are quiet together until Effie finishes her sandwich and her father gets up to pour the booze down the sink. He pauses to squeeze her shoulder as he passes. Effie waits until he's gone upstairs before she puts her plate in the dishwasher. She drinks a glass of cold, sweet water, then another because she can. She goes upstairs. The noise of the television is still coming from her parents' bedroom. Effie pauses with one hand on the wall just outside her bedroom door, her eyes closed, breathing in the quiet of the house. The smells. The soft carpet beneath her toes. The safety.

She's home.

chapter twenty-four

"Hey," Effie said into her phone from the comfort of her blankets and pillows. She'd already turned out the lights. "How are you?"

Mitchell sounded pleased. "Effie. Hi. I'm good, good. I was just thinking about you."

"Oh. Good. Is that good?" She laughed, stretching a little in the cocoon of warmth.

"Very good," he assured her. "What's up? How've you been? Haven't heard from you in a while."

It had been less than a week since the night she'd fucked him, and he hadn't called or texted her, either. It was not the first time he'd let a week pass without getting in touch with her, and she'd remembered that, just as she remembered that small green circle next to his name.

"I've been busy. Work. Kid. That sort of thing. I'm…sorry I didn't call you before now?"

Her voice tilted up at the end, a question, not a true apology. The sound of it curled her lip. Jesus, she sounded like every wishy-washy girl she'd ever disdained.

"Ah. Busy. Yeah." He paused. "About what happened…"

Oh, shit. He wanted to dissect the sex. Effie braced herself.

"Just wanted to make sure you were okay with it," Mitchell said.

"Oh. Yes. I mean, sure, it was fun. It was great," she added, thinking of his terminology.

He chuckled softly. "It was great. But then I didn't hear from you…"

"Maybe we were both busy," Effie said more gently than she thought she'd be able to manage. "It happens."

"Yeah. It happens. Work. Kid. They take up a lot of time."

"My kid's amazing," Effie said. "It's not like I mind."

"I didn't mean… Yeah, of course. I just meant… Hmm. Sorry?"

Effie relaxed a little at the same sound of uncertain apology in his voice she'd just had in hers. God. Relationships. Even when they weren't complicated, they were a pain in the ass to navigate.

The conversation continued. They talked about television—he'd never seen *Runner*. Effie had never heard of his favorite show. They talked about books. Mitchell devoured at least one or two a week. Effie barely one a year. They didn't have much in common, but it didn't seem to matter very much, because Mitchell made her laugh.

"It's been two hours," Effie said finally with a yawn and a glance at the clock. "I have to get up early to get Polly ready for school."

"Do you ever think about having any more?"

This surprised her. "Sure. I mean, in a vague sort of way, in that I'd want her to have a sibling. I never had a sister. I sort of want Polly to have one."

"Do you have a brother?"

Brother.

"No," Effie said with a small shudder. "How about you? Kids. Want them?"

"I've thought about it. They're a lot of work. I see my sister with hers and wonder how anyone survives the toddler years. But...yeah. I think I'd like to have some of my own. Five, maybe." Mitchell laughed.

"Umm..."

"Joking," he put in. "I'm joking. One or two would be fine."

Another baby. Effie put a hand on her belly. Polly's birth had been difficult and complicated. The doctors had told her there was little chance she'd conceive again. Not impossible, but not likely. At what point, exactly, was it appropriate to tell a potential long-term mate who was asking about having children that she might not be able to give him any?

Not at this point, she decided. Too soon. Too intimate.

"Well, good night," Mitchell said when the silence had stretched on. "Did you fall asleep on me?"

"No. Sorry. But, yes, it's late. Good night," Effie said.

"When will I see you again?" He snuck in the question before she disconnected.

"When do you want to see me again?"

"Right now," Mitchell said.

Oh.

"How about tomorrow? Lunch?"

"Lunch it is. Meet at the Blue Moon Café? Noon?"

They agreed. He disconnected. There it was. Dating, she *could* do this. Effie put her phone on the charger and tucked herself tight into her blankets, but she couldn't fall asleep.

Sex would help, and not the sort she'd had with Mitchell, but Polly was home and that meant Effie couldn't sneak out to knock on Bill's door. And Heath...she couldn't call him. He might refuse to show up, even if she did. That left her bedside drawer and her small collection of sex toys.

She got up to make sure her door was locked, then slipped

off her clothes and stretched out, naked, in the cold air. Her nipples peaked. She pinched them. Hard. It wasn't the same as someone else's touch.

She slid a hand between her legs, stroking the soft hair. Then her clit. Lower, she dipped two fingers inside herself, but she wasn't wet. Well, she had lube for that.

Rolling onto her side, Effie pulled out the smooth metal dildo she'd bought online. One end was bluntly curved. The other had nodules. Coating it in lube made it slippery and she had to be careful—once, she'd dropped it on her foot and nearly broken a toe. It was cold when she pushed it inside her, but the sting was good and she bit her lip to hold back a moan. Slowly, slowly, she fucked it in and out, deeper each time until the blunt end nudged her cervix.

It wasn't going to be enough.

One of the reasons why masturbation was never as satisfying for her was because...well, she could slap her own face, pull her own hair, but like pinching her nipples, it was never the same. Effie knew about pain play, BDSM, all that sort of thing. She didn't get off on being handcuffed or anything like that.

She liked to feel dirty when she fucked.

She didn't need a shrink to tell her why. She knew it was because of what had happened to them in that basement, of how they'd turned to each other without anyone else to turn to. She knew it was because pain and struggle were the first things that had ever accompanied sex for her, and she'd imprinted on them like a baby duck.

Effie knew everything about herself she wished she did not.

For a moment, she almost gave up and put away the toy. This was going to take more of an effort than she wanted to make. Again, she thought of calling Heath. He was angry at her. If she could convince him to come over, he would still be angry. He would bruise her. He'd fuck her. He would grab her tight and oh…oh, yes. There it was.

Effie arched, fucking the toy deeper inside her as she imagined Heath fisting his fingers into her hair and pulling tight. She thought of how it felt to hit him, the sound of his groans. She rolled her hips. The cold metal had warmed. The blunt end rubbed her G-spot with every thrust.

More lube. Slick fingers. She needed more. Rolling again, Effie pulled out the small glass plug and eased it into her ass. It stretched, hurting, but oh, fuck, yes, like that, so full, it felt good. She clenched on it, rocking as she fucked herself faster. Harder. Pinching her clit between her thumb and forefinger, she jerked it like a tiny cock.

Heath was the only man who'd ever fucked her in the ass. She thought of that now, being stretched and filled, his cock moving inside her while he fucked her cunt with his fingers. She thought of how once he'd spanked her clit at the moment of climax, how it had hurt but made her come so hard she saw stars.

She thought of biting him.

More than once, how she'd drawn blood.

How he begged her to hurt him, and she did, and he hurt her. Over and over. Desire and suffering, all wrapped up together in a way only the two of them could understand.

Carried by these memories, her ecstasy overtook her and left her shaking. Effie sobbed out a low cry, limp in the aftermath of her orgasm. Her body felt pounded, sore, aching.

So did her heart.

chapter twenty-five

"Mom…" Polly tapped her pencil on the table, then put it down. Her brow furrowed. "I have to talk to you."

Effie looked up from the sketch pad she'd been balancing on her knees. She'd been drawing Polly, smooth lines for her blond hair, rounded curves for the slope of her shoulders. Black and white, smudgy lines. She was no portraitist, but it was turning out better than she expected.

"Sure." Effie let her pencil shade another line and gave Polly a sideways glance. "What's up?"

"I did something bad."

At this, Effie set the sketch pad aside. "Uh-oh."

Polly's lower lip quivered. "I went on the internet."

Oh, shit. What had she seen? Effie flashed to some of the worst stuff she'd had the misfortune to stumble across, and she was an adult who could presumably filter out that kind of horror.

"What was it, Pollywog?" Effie leaned forward, bracing herself.

"It was about you."

That was shit of a different color. Effie sat back. "Ah."

Polly frowned and picked up her pencil again to tap it

rapidly on her math homework, a habit that usually drove Effie nuts but which she ignored at the moment. Polly looked at her mother, mouth working. Finally, she put the pencil down again and shook her head.

"I found this website that talks about you."

"Oh. That." Effie bit the inside of her cheek for a second. She should've known this discussion wasn't over with gossip from bitchy tween girls and their mothers. "Honey, those people..."

"There was a lot of stuff on it. They talked all about you and Heath and how that guy kept you in the basement and stuff."

The conversation between them was still fresh in Effie's brain, the details she'd given and the ones she'd kept still secret. Polly had listened and taken the story well, better than Effie had expected. Clearly, Effie had been wrong.

"Yes," Effie said. "I've seen that website."

Polly let one small fist pound the table. "They talk about you like they know you. But they don't!"

"No. They don't. They like to think they do."

"But...why?" Polly gave Effie a confused, agonized look.

Effie went around the table to sit next to her kid, putting an arm around Polly's shoulders and squeezing her. "Because people like to think they know stuff. I don't know why, honey."

"They're stupid."

"Yeah." Effie laughed. "But, Polly, sometimes stupid pays the bills."

Polly looked confused again. Effie chucked her under the chin and got up to get some milk from the fridge. From the cupboard she took the cocoa powder and sugar. A saucepan. Polly loved hot cocoa, and if there was ever a time to drink some, it was now.

"A lot of those people buy my paintings." Effie looked over her shoulder for a second before pouring the milk. "They like thinking that they know me somehow, which makes them like the art better. I don't know, kid, it's messed up. But you have to realize, they *don't* know me. They don't know you. Or Heath."

"Isn't some of what they say true?"

With the milk heating on low, Effie turned. "Some of it is. Yes. But there's a lot of what they call speculation. Which means they don't know, so they make it up based on what they do know. It's stupid."

"Yeah." Polly frowned. "Mom…"

Effie smiled. "Yeah?"

"It was bad. Wasn't it?"

"Yeah, honey. It was bad. But it happened." Effie paused. "And my father told me that even the bad things make you into the person you are. So I try really hard not to let that bad thing that happened keep hurting me."

Polly got up from the table to tackle hug her mother. Effie hugged back, hard. She stroked Polly's corn-silk hair. Love washed over her, fierce as fire.

"How do you stop it from hurting, Mom?" Polly's voice was muffled against Effie's stomach. Her arms tightened.

Effie had only one honest answer for that. "I don't know, Polly. I just try hard, every day."

"I love you." Polly tipped her face up, her eyes bright with tears.

Effie kissed her on the forehead. "I love you, too, Polly-wog. Don't go on the internet again without my permission, okay? Or I'll have to take away privileges."

Polly sighed and moved away. "I know. I'm sorry."

"If you have questions, you ask me." Effie stirred the steaming milk and added some cocoa powder and sugar.

"Are you and Heath fighting?"

Effie looked over her shoulder again. "Yes."

"Why?" Polly went back to the table to push her homework aside so she had room for the mug of cocoa Effie poured.

"It's really not your business." Effie put the mug in front of Polly and leaned against the counter to drink her own.

Polly looked chastened. "I don't like it when you guys fight."

"I don't like it, either, kid, believe me."

"Is Heath your best friend?" Polly blew on the cocoa to cool it while casting a side eye at her mother.

"Yes," Effie said. "He is."

"Can't you make up?" Polly frowned. "You tell me when I fight with my friends that we should make up."

Effie laughed ruefully. It was good advice, and she ought to take it. "I'm sure we will soon."

"Mom," Polly said again and, typically, stopped.

"Yeah?"

"Remember when I was a baby and we all lived together?"

"Yeah, of course I do," Effie said. "But I don't think you do. Do you?"

Polly looked serious. "Yes. I had flowers painted on the bedroom wall. And the same rocker I still have."

Effie was the artist, yet Heath had been the one to paint the flowers. Heath had bought the rocking chair from a used furniture store, cleaned it, refinished it. He'd put together the crib and, later, the toddler bed Effie had taken with her when she and Polly moved into their own place.

"It would be okay with me, you know. If you wanted to live together again." Polly shrugged.

Effie wasn't fooled by Polly's too-casual tone. "That's not going to happen, Wog."

Polly sighed. "But..."

"Did Heath tell you to ask me that?" Effie dumped her

cocoa into the sink and put the mug in the dishwasher. When Polly didn't answer, she turned. "Did he?"

"No." Polly shook her head. "I asked him. He said to talk to you about it."

That wasn't much better than if he'd actively put the idea in Polly's head. Effie felt the beginnings of a headache coming on. She dumped the dregs of the cocoa and began to scrub the saucepan, her back to Polly.

"Finish your homework," she said.

A text came through from Mitchell, but she chose not to answer it. Instead, Effie went to the porch to contemplate her half-finished canvas. Mitchell had seen her naked, but he still didn't know the most important parts of her. The longer it took her to tell him the truth about her work, her past, the harder it would get. The stupider she would look for keeping it a secret.

Heath knew everything about her, and always would. Together or apart, he was inside her. She could hate it, but it was the truth.

chapter twenty-six

Effie had sent Polly to her mother's house. Armed with a box of powdered doughnuts and a bag of Heath's favorite gourmet coffee beans, she drove to his apartment. She hadn't called first. She wasn't going to give him the chance to tell her not to come over.

She could've walked in without knocking, as she'd done so often in the past. She had lived in this same apartment for four years, after all. Still, she knocked and waited like a stranger on the doorstep, because that's how it felt to be there after all this time.

"Hey." Heath looked surprised and, before he could stop himself, so happy to see her that Effie's heart hurt when he quickly shuttered his expression. He didn't step aside to let her in. "What's up? Is Polly okay?"

"She's fine." Effie held up the paper grocery bag. "Are you going to let me in?"

Heath looked past her, into the dirty hallway. "What do you want?"

"To see you. Isn't that all right?"

He shrugged and opened the door. He followed her into the small galley kitchen and watched her set the doughnuts on the table. Effie put the bag of beans on the counter.

"Let's grind." Her joke fell flat. He didn't even crack a smile. With a sigh, she stepped away with a flourish, leaving him to make the coffee.

While it brewed, she opened the box of doughnuts and ate one. Heath put two mugs on the table, along with sugar and cream. He took the seat across from her but left the doughnuts alone.

"They're your favorite," Effie said quietly.

"I'm not hungry."

Effie licked sugar from her thumb. "Heath…"

He sat back, arms crossed over his chest. He had that stubborn look on his face, the one any smart woman would've taken as a warning. Effie had always prided herself on being smart. Mostly.

"I'm sorry," she said.

He looked away from her, his jaw set. A muscle ticked in his temple. For the first time, Effie noticed a glint of silver in the dark hair there. It made her feel suddenly small. All this time had passed, so much between them, and here they sat at his kitchen table and he wouldn't even look at her.

"I'm sorry," she said again and got up from her chair to go around the table so she could slide onto his lap. Straddling him, Effie cupped Heath's face and turned him toward her. "I'm sorry, I'm sorry, I'm sorry."

He allowed her to tip his face to hers, and his hands went to her hips to steady them both, but his expression remained shuttered and tight. He'd closed himself away from her, and she couldn't blame him, could she? Even if it broke her to see it.

She kissed him. He did not kiss her in return. Effie pressed her forehead to his, then her cheek.

"I'm sorry," she repeated.

"You don't even know what you're apologizing for," Heath said.

They sat in silence for a moment or so before she nuzzled

his neck. When he didn't resist, she pressed her teeth there and then, helpless against the taste of him, her tongue. She sucked his flesh into her mouth. He tasted better than sugar to her. Better than anything.

When he groaned, Effie grinned. Triumphant. She rocked against his crotch, feeling his cock harden between them. She cupped his face again. Brought his mouth to hers. The long, slow slip of her tongue between his lips. The soft intake of his breath, stealing hers.

"I miss you, Heath."

He'd closed his eyes to her kiss but opened them at her words. "Good. I hope it fucking kills you. Every day."

"Hush." Effie sat up, her hands on his shoulders so her thumbs could toy with the sides of his neck. "Don't be a dick about it."

"You make me so goddamned crazy. You know that?" His hands moved above the waistband of her skirt, fingertips questing beneath the hem of her shirt. "You make me hate you."

Effie shivered. Her nipples tightened. She ran her thumb over his bottom lip, opening his mouth at first gently and then hooking her finger inside to tug harder. Her breath caught when he moaned.

"I love it when you hate me," Effie said into his ear before she took the soft lobe between her teeth and bit.

With a low, muttered cry, Heath stood, lifting her with one arm around her waist to hold her. The other hand swept the table clean, sending the cardboard bakery box thumping to the floor. The mugs clattered, shattering. She was on her back seconds after that. Heath yanked her hips to bring her to the edge of the table. He tore her panties halfway down her thighs, then with another hard tug, all the way off.

Effie lifted her hips, offering herself to him. Heath opened his belt and undid the zipper of his jeans with the same swift desperation. Gripping his cock, he pushed inside her but did not thrust. Instead, he took her clit between his thumb and forefinger. Locking his gaze with hers, he pinched her sensitive flesh. Released. Again. Over and over until she was losing her mind.

"Fuck me," she breathed.

"No." His cock deep inside her, Heath refused to move anything but his fingers in the steady, inexorable squeezing of her clit.

Effie arched her back. Her shoulders pressed the table's hard wood. She would ache later, but oh, fuck, it was so good right now that anything that came after would be worth it. She gripped the table's edge, then her knees as Heath pushed them upward. The new position opened her deeper to him, but no matter how she begged, he still would not move.

"Shut up," he muttered. "Just shut up, Effie."

"Tell me how you hate me." She focused on his face, watching for the flare in his eyes. She gave a sobbing, breathless laugh. At the next slow tweak of her clit, she writhed, made helpless in her pleasure.

"Shut up!"

"Fuck me like you hate me," Effie said.

With a groan, Heath withdrew. He took his cock in his hand and rubbed the head of it over her slick, engorged clit. "No."

The torturous squeezing had been bad enough, but now this steady, rhythmic stroking of his cock head against her, sliding through her folds and up over her clit but never, never inside… He was going to kill her with this, and she would willingly die.

She came, then again, hard on the still-rippling edges of the first. Floating, distant, Effie was aware of her low, endless cries but could do nothing to hold them back. Nor the helpless, frantic shaking of her entire body. She looked between them to watch as Heath came all over her belly, and one final shudder of pleasure racked her. Heath, however, came in silence, not so much as a gasp or a whisper or a single syllable of her name.

When it was over, he moved away from her and went to the sink to dampen a clean cloth and wipe himself off before pulling up his jeans. Effie watched him, her elbows hurting from pressing the wood. So did the edge of her ass. She didn't want to pull her blouse down over the mess he'd left, but she did cover her bareness with the hem of her skirt. When he came to hand her the cloth, Effie reached to pull him down by his shirtfront for a kiss. She held him there longer than she needed to, and when he made to pull away, she kept holding him until he acquiesced and stayed still. Then she let him go, took the cloth and wiped him off her.

She had told him she was sorry, but that wasn't quite the same as asking him to forgive her. Effie rinsed and wrung out the cloth, formulating the words. So many hours, so many times they'd never needed to speak at all, and now she found herself unable to think of the right things to say. Heath knew her inside and out, upside down, frontward, backward, side to side. There wasn't a thought in her head he wouldn't have been able to determine without so much as a single uttered vowel.

So why, then, did she find it so hard to simply tell him how much she loved and wanted him?

"It does kill me," she told him, finally.

He turned. "So what, then? You're a ghost? Because that's how it feels to me sometimes, Effie. You're a fucking ghost, and all you do is haunt me."

"I don't want to!" she cried, then lowered her voice. "Don't you understand? That's why it's no good for us to be together. All we do is remind each other of the past. It will keep us both…crazy."

"I would rather have you haunt me, driving me mad, than have you leave me."

From his front door came a brief, timid rapping. Effie looked at Heath, who shrugged, unsmiling but also unapologetic. She had herself put back together by the time he opened the door, and Effie had put a blank smile on her face, expecting a neighbor, a delivery person, a stranger.

"Hi," Sheila Monroe said in her breathy, low voice. She pushed past Heath and was already in the kitchen before she looked up to see Effie, which stopped her short. Sheila gave Heath a startled look.

"Hi, Sheila," Effie said.

Heath went to the fridge and pulled out several plastic containers of food that he put into a cooler bag with an ice pack. He added some bottled water and a loaf of sliced bread. Sheila shifted from foot to foot as she watched him, every so often flicking a glance toward Effie. She also took in the doughnuts and dishes on the floor. When Heath finally handed the bag to her, Sheila's scrawny arm shook with the weight of it.

"Let me take that out for you." Heath looked her over. "Did you drive?"

"Reggie gave me a ride. I don't got my license back yet. He's waiting for me in the parking lot." Sheila gave Effie another uncertain, wavering smile that was more like a grimace. "How are you, Effie?"

"I'm great, thanks."

Sheila nodded as though she'd expected nothing less. "How's your little girl?"

"She's fine."

"She's, what, ten now? Eleven?"

"Almost twelve," Effie said. "If you can believe it."

"I can't." Sheila's laugh was bolder than her smile had been. She was missing a tooth toward the back. She hefted the bag of food over her shoulder and hesitated before opening her other arm to Heath for a swift hug. "Thanks, Heath."

"I'll talk to you next week, okay?" Heath walked her to the front door and followed her out, closing it behind him enough to keep Effie from seeing or hearing what they were doing or saying.

Not that it was any of Effie's business. She gathered her own belongings. Coat, purse. Slipped into her shoes. She brushed her hair off her face, wondering if Sheila had seen the evidence of their fucking on her face and not only on the floor. She decided she didn't care.

When Heath came back inside, Effie was ready to go. Heath watched her button her coat without saying anything. She waited for him to ask her to stay. He didn't.

"Well," Effie said stiffly. "I guess I'll get going."

Heath cleared his throat. "She needs help. She has nobody else. She doesn't take care of herself right. She lost her license for a DUI and is having a hard time getting hours at her job. You know it's not... I'm not..."

Effie held up a hand to stop him. "You don't owe me any explanations."

"You don't want one, that doesn't mean I don't want to tell you."

She shook her head, not meeting his eyes, not wanting to fight with him again, not about this or anything else. Moments ago she'd been ready to ask him to...what? Move in with her and Polly? Make a life, a family, try to see if they could make things work? Right there, knocking on his door, was the reason why that could never happen. Why they could never forget their past. Not in any way that could ever be good for either of them.

"Polly asked me if I could live with you guys," Heath said.

Effie looked at him. "Yes. I know."

"Effie." He sighed, and his bland expression twisted into sadness.

"Hold me close," she whispered.

He had her in his arms then, and she didn't want to leave him. She clung to him, cheek to cheek. They held each other in silence for a long time, until at last she stepped back and out of Heath's embrace. She kissed him gently on the corner of his mouth.

"Haunt me," he whispered. "Make me crazy for the rest of my life. But please, Effie. Don't leave me. Just let me love you."

"I don't think I can..." Baby. Honey. My love. *Brother.* At the last, Effie turned from him, steeling herself against the voracious crescendo of sorrow threatening to send her to her knees.

"But, Effie," Heath said, cold as ice, cold as a void, so cold it burned her worse than any fire. "Don't you know? Not wanting to and not being able to are not the same things."

She made it to her car before the sobs came. Wretched, wrenching, they shook her even though she clasped both hands over her mouth to keep even a single sound from leaking out. The spatter of icy rain on the roof covered the noises of her grief, but nothing could stop her from feeling it.

Effie can hear them in the next room, even with her hands over her ears. Low, rhythmic slapping. Daddy mutters commands.

"Harder. More. Slap her up a little. Good. Yeah. That's good."

Effie knows what's going on, but she has never been made a part of it. Nothing stops her from leaving the bedroom and going out there. Well, nothing except fear. She doesn't want to see what Daddy makes Heath do.

"I'll kill her," Daddy has told them, over and over. "Don't think I won't. If you come out? If you make a noise, Sister, if you let her know you're in there? I will kill her. If you pull another stunt like you tried before? I will kill her. Not you, Sister. Not Brother. I'll kill that woman. Do you want that on your conscience?"

Daddy knows how to keep them in line, and not only with the drugs. He knows what to say. How to threaten. Later, Effie will be unable to explain why she and Heath didn't overpower him, why they didn't try harder to escape. It's too difficult to understand, even for herself, when she looks back and tries to think what kept them there.

Tonight it goes on longer than it has before. There is more talking. Daddy sounds angry. The soft, surprised murmur of a woman's voice, protesting, is quickly silenced by the crack of flesh on flesh. A muffled sob.

"I don't care," Daddy says. "I don't care what you want. I told you to get over there and make her cry!"

Effie does not cry. She plugs her ears with her fingers and rolls to face the wall, hoping it will be over soon. Because after, Daddy gives them whatever Heath asks for, and the food will be safe to eat for at least a day or two, and after this it will be some long weeks before they have to go through this again.

She doesn't think she could sleep, but she must have, because the next thing she knows is the bed is dipping beneath a familiar weight and the lights have gone out. Heath moves against her back, carefully, cautiously, as if she's ever turned him away. As if she ever could, after everything he's done for her.

His breath hitches. She feels it against the skin of her neck. He's respectful and hesitant, but Effie wriggles back against him so he can be the big spoon. She takes Heath's arm and pulls it across her to tuck his hand beneath her chin. She is aware he's touching her breasts, but it's not until she wriggles again and feels something against her butt that her eyes open wide and she goes very, very still.

Effie's a virgin, but she's not stupid. At summer camp when she was twelve, there had been a silent sort of competition among the girls to see if they could catch sight of "boners." They'd been easy to spot in the pool, where the boys made a game of trying to catch and dunk girls as an excuse to get closer.

She'd never been one of the girls who got caught. She'd seen the tented swim trunks and embarrassed expressions, but until this moment, Effie had never actually felt a boner. She wriggles again, experimentally. When Heath's breath hitches again, she turns in his embrace to face him. She slides a knee between his thighs to press herself against him, harder.

She says his name.

Heath shakes; has she hurt him somehow? Effie seeks his face in the darkness, finds it with her fingertips. Tracing the arch of his brows, the line of his jaw, she tries to tell if he'd been injured, but bruises are impossible to feel.

"Are you okay?" Effie asks.

"No."

"What happened?"

He kisses her, their lips mashing against their teeth. It takes her by surprise. It's nothing like Effie had ever imagined her first kiss would be. It's rough and fierce and takes her breath away. It hurts. She tastes copper, blood, her mouth opened in protest and Heath's tongue stabbing inside and filling her up until she isn't sure she can breathe.

She pushes at his chest, but he grabs her wrists and holds them so tight she gasps into his kiss. Between them, that hardness presses her belly. Heat. His fingers grind her wrists until pain flares, and she brings her knee up on instinct. She hits him in the upper thigh, but it must be close enough because Heath flinches and lets her go.

Effie slaps at him. Her hand connects somewhere on his face, a solid thud of skin on skin. Her other hand clutches at the front of his shirt. The fabric tears as he yanks himself away from her. The bed creaks, headboard scraping the wall and springs squealing.

He rolls until she's pinned beneath him, her wrists trapped above her head. She can see nothing, only feel him, but his weight presses her into the lumpy mattress hard enough to send the springs beating into her. His breath gusts over her face until his mouth finds hers again. Heath shoves her knees apart with one of his. That hardness presses her belly.

"You want to know what he makes me do?" Heath says this low into her ear. "You really want to know?"

No, no, no, Effie doesn't want to know, but something in the way Heath rubs himself against her, lower now, makes her incapable of answering. Her back arches as he finds the softness of her throat with his teeth. She cries out when he bites her.

No, no, this isn't what it's supposed to be like, she thinks, tossing her head from side to side as Heath's mouth moves across her skin. He's supposed to be gently insistent; she's supposed to push him away and make him wait. It's supposed to be on prom night, maybe, or the backseat of his car. She should be older than sixteen. It strikes her, suddenly, just how long she's been kept here. It's been *years*.

Heath's mouth moves lower, over her collarbones. Lower still, his mouth hot and wet through the thin fabric of her T-shirt, and then he's let go of her wrists to run his hands up, cupping her breasts. Her nipples are hard. When he pinches them both at the same time, Effie writhes and cries out a plea, but not for him to stop.

"Yes." Her voice harsh and guttural. She sounds like a

stranger. "Oh, please, Heath. Yes. I want to know what he makes you do."

Heath shakes when she says it. He moves down her body so quickly Effie doesn't have time to react. No time for protest. Heath pushes his way between her legs, her skirt shoved up to her thighs. He's going to put his mouth on her down *there*. Oh, no, that's not... She's not ready for that...

Too late, he's hooked a finger in the leg band of her cotton panties and pulled them to the side. His lips and tongue are hot and wet. She cannot stand how good it feels when he licks her.

Effie had thought she understood sex. Why people do it for reasons other than making babies. She understands it feels good, but this, oh, this is like nothing she thought she could imagine. This is the electric pain of being tickled until you think you're going to faint from it, but you don't.

There are words. She hears them. She can taste them. What they are, though, Effie doesn't know. All she can think about is what's happening to her, and how much she wants it to keep going on and on, maybe until...oh...yes, there, that...until she can't breathe or see or hear.

All she can do is feel.

When it's over, all she can do is lie there, limp and spent. When the bed shifts, she feels him drawing away from her, and Effie reaches into the darkness to snag Heath's shirt. The dark makes it easier for her to pull him back to her.

His kiss tastes like the sea, somehow, tangy and slick, and he shakes at the stroke of her tongue. Between their bodies, he is still hard. She finds his length with her fingers, exploring, at first uncertain, then bolder at the way he mutters her name.

Effie wants to make Heath feel the way she did. If she can. She's aware that something in the way boys and girls are built means it's going to be different, but she has no idea how. Still, she tries. With featherlight touches, she strokes that hardness.

At the first slippery wetness, she pauses, uncertain again. Is he...done?

When his hand closes over hers and keeps up the motion she began, Effie realizes he's not. There is more. The sound of his breathing. The way he thrusts into her grip. The moan of her name.

Then, finally, there it is. Heat and wetness. Not only the taste of the sea but something like the smell of it, too. Briny. It sends a rolling wave of electric tingles all through her again.

She finds his mouth with hers. He pulls her close. They stay that way until her hand is cramped and they both begin to shiver from the cold this time.

"I love you," Heath says into her mouth.

Effie thought she knew about sex; now she understands she thought she knew about love and had been wrong about both. She wants to tell him she loves him. It's what you do, isn't it, when you've both done what they just did? She wants to tell him because it's the truth, but what stops her is something that is also the truth.

"It's easy to love someone when you don't have a choice," Effie says. "When you're all they have."

chapter twenty-seven

Mitchell was a door-holding-open sort of guy. Effie had dated a few of them. It was something in the law of averages or something, wasn't it? That even in a sea of assholes, douchebags and egotistical thunder twats, there had to be a good guy or two among them.

It made her feel funny, though, having to wait for him to get out and walk around the car to open the door for her. She could handle him picking up the check. She could even handle him pausing to always let her go first through any door, and pulling out her chair, but this car door thing...

"It's very old-fashioned," she explained to him over a plate of decent pasta with garlic and olive oil. "That's all."

Mitchell grinned. "What can I say? My mama raised me right."

"She did." Effie returned his grin, which was surprisingly naughty, considering what a gentleman he was claiming to be. "It's nice. Just..."

"Makes you uncomfortable?"

She nodded after a second, her grin twisting slightly to become a grimace. "I'm sorry..."

"It's okay. But I like to," Mitchell said. "In case you think it was a pain in the butt or something. It's not. I like to do it."

"It makes me feel helpless," Effie blurted and immediately wished she hadn't.

Mitchell looked surprised, then concerned. "I didn't know that."

"Forget it." Effie twirled the pasta on her fork, pressing it into her spoon's deep bowl. It was an old trick, to make an elaborate show of eating to hide the fact she'd taken no more than a couple bites.

"No. I don't want to forget it. I don't want you to feel uncomfortable with me, Effie. I'm really sorry if anything I did made you feel that way."

Shit. Now she'd gone and done it. Brought out the white knight in him.

"It's just a thing I have. It's...really... I don't want to talk about it. I shouldn't have brought it up."

Mitchell sat back in his chair with a frown. "Okay."

She changed the subject, effortlessly, she thought. They ordered dessert. She wanted coffee but sipped a mug of hot tea. She'd demurred about cake, saying she was stuffed.

He hit her with it in the car, the ignition running but still in Park. "You didn't eat. You said you were full, but you didn't eat anything."

"I ate." She heard the defensiveness in her voice and softened it. "I wasn't that hungry."

The loud growl of her stomach at that inopportune moment proved she was a liar. Effie pressed a hand to her belly and looked Mitchell straight in the eyes. Daring him to comment.

Most men would've let it pass, but she supposed most men wouldn't have noticed. Mitchell tapped the wheel, looking away from her. He sighed.

"My sister's anorexic. She's been hospitalized for it a couple times. I know the tricks." He looked at her. "I noticed it the first few times we went out, but I didn't say anything because I didn't want to make you feel weird about it, and you don't look… Shit. I know that you don't have to look any certain way, but…"

"I don't have anorexia. Or bulimia." The words came out with the sharp edge of an addict swearing she didn't need the high. Effie pressed her lips together for a second before adding, "I have a thing about food. Yeah. But it's not an eating disorder, at least not the kind you'd think."

"I see."

He could not see, of course. Not without a long and detailed explanation that Effie was in no way ready to provide. She put her hands in her lap, fingers linked, and stared straight ahead. It had begun to rain again.

"We might never get any more snow this winter," she said. "Maybe it will all be rain from now on."

They didn't say much of anything on the way to her house. Mitchell turned on the radio, which should've been a relief but made the silence only all the more obvious and awkward. When he pulled into her driveway, the house was blazing with light. Her mother threw a fit if you left a light on in any room you weren't using, but only in her own house. Apparently, Effie's electric bill wasn't of her concern.

Mitchell put the car in Park but left it running. He did not, as he'd done every other time, get out to go around and open her door for her. Of course she missed it as soon as he didn't do it. Of course she couldn't say so, not without sounding stupid.

"Well. Good night. Thanks for dinner." Effie put her hand on the door.

"Effie…wait a minute."

She half turned. He'd apologize again now. Or try to get her to talk about "it," whatever the *it* was in his brain that he thought needed discussion. She should've just fucked him on the first date, Effie thought. Found out what was inside those khakis and been done with it. Moved on. What had ever made her think she could be anything like normal?

"I'm a good listener," Mitchell said.

Effie's eyebrows rose. "Okay?"

"Out of all the women I've met on LuvFinder, you're the only one who doesn't really seem to like to talk." Mitchell gave her another of those bad-boy grins that ought to have been at odds with the rest of his persona but somehow fit him just right. "It's kind of making me a little crazy, to be honest."

Effie laughed. "Oh, yeah? You like talkers?"

"It's not that I like them. I guess I just got used to it. We're all on that site to find someone, right? So you get paired up by whatever algorithms they use to show you profiles, or you hunt around, stalking, until you see something you like. And you can only hope that the other person likes you, too, at least enough based on whatever clever stuff you used to fill out your profile, and then, wow, if you do get someone to say yes to a date, well..." Mitchell pushed his glasses up on his nose and shrugged. "You can only pray that you like them enough to want to ask them out again. And that they like you, too."

"That's pretty much how it goes. Yeah." On Effie's front porch, her mother's silhouette appeared in the doorway. "She'll flash the light next."

"I guess I should kiss you quick, then," Mitchell said and leaned across the center console before Effie could stop him.

She let him kiss her, though, and it was as sweet and nice as it had been the other times. She wasn't expecting him to cup the back of her head, nor for his hand on her knee, high up and higher before she put a hand on his to stop him going any higher. The kiss got harder when she did that, only for a second or so before he broke it. He didn't move away from her.

"That night we spent together…" he said.

"Yes?"

"I think about it all the time."

Surprising heat washed over her, painting her cheeks and throat. "You do?"

"Yeah." His fingers inched upward, teasing. "All the time."

Effie kissed him again. She put her hand on his and moved it higher. His fingertips brushed between her legs, and she let out a sigh before pulling away.

"I want to see you again," Mitchell said.

"Even if I don't talk enough?"

Mitchell smiled. "Yeah. Maybe because you don't. It makes you mysterious. Like you're full of dark secrets that maybe I can get you to tell."

"If I told you my dark secrets," Effie said, "they wouldn't be secrets, would they?"

"I thought you were never going to come home," Mom complained when Effie at last came through the front door. "It's late, and the weather's getting worse. I was getting worried."

"I know you saw me sitting out there, Mom. You couldn't have worried too much. I was in the driveway."

Her mother huffed. "I know what you were doing out there."

"Kissing," Effie said to get a rise out of her. She shrugged out of her coat and hung it in the front closet. "Tongues and everything."

"Jesus, Mary and Joseph, Felicity. For the whole world to see!"

"They couldn't see anything. The windows were steamed up." Effie grinned and waggled her brows at her mother, then gave her an impromptu hug. "Thanks for watching Polly. If you don't want to drive home, you can stay over. We can make pancakes in the morning."

"I like to sleep in my own bed. And I need to let the dog out." Her mother shook her head, then gave Effie a sideways glance. "You like him?"

"He's very nice. By that I mean, like, nice, nice. I told you he was nice. You don't believe me?"

Her mother rolled her eyes. "A nice guy wouldn't sit in the driveway with his mouth and hands all over you."

"No," Effie said, "I guess he'd come inside and fuck me on the living room carpet in front of my mother."

Her mother scowled and shook her head. Then she laughed, at first softly and then a little as if it choked her. "Okay. Okay, I get it."

"I'm an adult, as crazy as that might sound and as insane as that makes you," Effie said. "And I know I've done my share of giving you trouble, Mom. But I'm trying to get at least some things in my life in order, okay? I really am. And if that means a guy like Mitchell…"

"What's wrong with a guy like Mitchell? You said he was nice." Her mom gathered her coat and slipped it on, then pulled a knit cap over her hair.

"He is. He's *too* nice." Effie rubbed her hands together, then found a hair elastic in her pocket and pulled her hair up on top of her head into a twisted, messy bun with a sigh of relief. Getting the weight of it off her neck was relief akin to taking off her bra, which was the next thing she intended to do. And after that, a bowl of soup from her freezer. She was starving.

"How can someone be too nice?"

"He's good. That's all. Too good." Effie caught sight of her mother's face. "What?"

Her mother shook her head again. "Oh. Effie. Never say that."

Effie swallowed against the sudden lump in her throat. "I'm hungry. Do you want something to eat, or are you really leaving?"

"I'm leaving. But, Effie…" Her mother paused, then came closer to take Effie by the shoulders. "You listen to me. No man is too good for you. It's the other way around. And I have other news for you, too. Your life *is* in order. I look at you, what a wonderful mother you are to Polly, and I could not be more proud of you. You're a talented, creative woman with a good heart and never, ever let anything ever make you feel any different."

They hugged, and Effie clung for a moment or two longer than she normally would have. "Thanks, Mom."

"Eat," her mother said. "You're getting too thin."

"You can never be too thin."

Her mother patted her rounded belly through the padding of her coat. "Don't argue with your mother."

Effie waited until her mother had pulled out of the driveway before she turned off all the lights. In the kitchen, she pulled a container of soup from the freezer and heated it in the microwave. Heath's soup, made in the university kitchen but brought home for her because he knew she would trust him enough to eat it.

She'd set her phone on the table while she went to the bathroom and had missed the message that came through. It was from Mitchell. No words, just a smiley face emoticon and one word: Goodnight

Alone at her kitchen table, Effie put her face in her hands and cried.

chapter twenty-eight

It's the first time Effie's ever taken a pregnancy test, though not the first time she's ever counted the days since her period was due, praying for a miracle. The instructions say she needs to wait three minutes, but she's hovering over it, watching for the plus sign she already knows will be there. She's felt this before, all the signs, and she knows she was stupidly not careful enough.

Sure enough, the clock ticks past and two pink lines, intersecting, appear in the small white window. There's no denying or ignoring it, no explaining it away. She is pregnant.

Again.

She's never been regular. All the doctors she's seen said women who don't eat right often skip periods. It has never been strange for her to go a month or two, or even three, without bleeding. So why has she taken the test this time, instead of assuming she was just skipping a few months the way she so often had? Simple. She remembers how it felt the first time.

In the mirror, Effie looks at her naked reflection. She turns from side to side, trying to see if there's any kind of bulge. Her hip bones jut. Her belly is slightly less concave than usual. Her mother has been nagging her about the weight loss. In these last few months before Effie starts classes at the local college, the tensions between them have been mounting, but they don't argue out loud. Her mother forces food on her, and Effie doesn't eat it.

Panic slaps her, and she drops to her knees in front of the toilet to dry heave. Nothing comes up but air and thin yellow bile. Effie presses her forehead to the cool tile floor and considers praying, but what god will listen to her now?

Outside the door, Mom knocks. She's never accused Effie of bulimia, but she has a way of lurking around the bathroom door when Effie's inside for any length of time. Effie pictures her now, ear pressed to the thin wood.

"I'm getting ready to go to the mall," Mom calls out, all casual, as though she hasn't been listening to the sound of Effie puking. "Why don't you come with me?"

"I have homework." She graduated on time, but barely, and has signed up for summer correspondence courses so she could forgo some of the lower level classes in college. Now, Effie thinks, she'll never bother to finish a math problem again. It's clear she already doesn't know how to fucking count.

"Effie."

Effie sighs and pushes herself up and off the floor to run some water in the sink. She wraps the pregnancy test in some toilet paper and shoves it to the bottom of the garbage can, hiding it beneath used cotton balls and tissues. She brushes her teeth to cover up the taste of bile.

With a bright, fake grin, she opens the door so fast her mom has to step back out of the way. Mom has the grace to look a little embarrassed. In that moment, all Effie wants to do is collapse into her mom's arms and be rocked like when she was young and had scraped her knee. She wants her mom to make her chicken soup and tuck her beneath a blanket and let her watch old episodes of *The Patty Duke Show* the way she had those first few weeks after Effie had come home.

Effie hadn't appreciated that then, but she would trade anything to have that time back now.

Instead, she makes sure to look her mom right in the eyes, because the easiest way to tell a lie is to make sure you keep the eye contact. Totally throws the other person off. "I told you, I have homework."

"I don't want to leave you here by yourself. I wish you'd come with me."

Effie keeps her expression neutral. All she can think about is those two pink lines making that plus sign. The rest of her life, summed up in the equation answered in that tiny little window.

"Mom. I really can't." Effie softens her tone. "But if I finish all my homework, maybe we can watch a movie when you get home? Make some popcorn? I'm craving some."

It's the promise of getting her to eat that persuades her mother to agree. Effie sees it on her face. A hint of relief, overlaid with a wariness Effie hates because it makes her feel so freaking guilty. Because she's caused her mom so much grief and worry, and she can never, ever make it up to her, and because she's about to cause her so much more.

Later, after a bowl of popcorn that Effie personally popped and inspected to make sure it didn't contain anything hidden, and a chick flick they got from the video store, her mother comes into Effie's room. She's carrying the pregnancy test, the handle wrapped in layers of toilet paper but nothing at all hiding that glaring pink plus sign.

"It's that boy. Isn't it? You've been sneaking around behind my back, seeing that boy!" Mom throws the pregnancy test at Effie.

It hits her in the face. Cringing, Effie knocks it off the bed, where it falls onto the floor, facedown. Her mother is panting, short sharp and hysterical breaths. Her eyes are wild. Her hair looks as though she's stood in front of a wind turbine.

Effie hasn't seen Heath in almost a month. Hasn't fucked him for much, much longer than that. He wanted more from her than she could give him. He always does, most people do, but Heath is the only person Effie can't bring herself to lie to. If anything, Heath is the only person to whom Effie can tell her every truth. He wants her to love him and only him, and she can't do it. Every time she looks at him, she's back in the basement. So they fight. They hurt each other over and over, and what Effie thinks is, she already knows that knife is sharp. Why does she have to keep slicing her fingers on it, just to be sure?

"Kill yourself for good this time if you have to," she'd snapped at his threats. "Maybe you'll be better off dead than always wanting what you can never have."

It's the cruelest thing she's ever said to anyone. She still runs hot and cold with shame at the memory of it. Yet sometimes the hardest thing and the right thing are the same. If you can't give someone you love what they want, sometimes you give them what you need.

"It's not Heath's."

Her mother's face drains of all color. Her fists clench. Her mother has never, that Effie can remember, hit her, but it sure looks as if she's about to now.

"Liar. I know you've been sneaking off to see him. I can smell it on you when you get home. You stink of it. You think I didn't know?"

Effie's lip curls. "I'm pregnant, Mother, but I'm not lying. It's not Heath's."

"Whose is it, then? Oh God, Felicity, oh my God, oh my God…" Mom's hands rake up her cheeks and anchor in her hair. Her mother stalks to the phone on Effie's desk. "I'm calling the police."

"For what?" Alarmed, Effie gets off the bed. Her toe nudges the pregnancy test. She scoops it up and tosses it into the garbage, and this time with no need to try to hide it, of course it sinks all on its own beneath the detritus of crumpled notebook paper and magazines.

"You were under eighteen! He's twenty. That's... It's rape. Or something. It's statutory rape, and I'm going to make sure he pays for it!"

"I've been over eighteen for months, Mom."

Her mother gives Effie a steady, solemn and completely venomous look. "You weren't that first time."

Effie knocks the phone from her mother's hand. It bounces onto the desk. The battery compartment pops open, the battery pack and a small tangle of wires comes out, and the phone itself lets out a loud, somehow startled buzz for a second before going silent.

"No. You can't! They'll arrest him!"

"He already has a record, Effie. That boy is nothing but trouble and always has been." Her mother's nostrils flare. If she knew how horrid she looks, she'd be embarrassed, she would hide her face.

"Heath..." But here Effie falters.

Her mother shakes her head. "He's a sad, sick boy. He will never amount to anything. He uses you. He's no good for you."

He isn't good for her, though not for the reasons her mother thinks. Heath is not good for Effie because he loves her too hard, wants to give her too much. He reminds her constantly of how empty she is inside.

"This baby isn't Heath's. You can't get him into trouble, Mom. Not for this."

"Then who did it to you?"

Effie turns. "Nobody did it to me! It happened. I wasn't careful enough. I thought I was, but I wasn't."

"Who?" her mother repeated.

Effie knows exactly who the father of this baby is, and she will never tell anyone. Not her mother, who would rage against him even more than she does against Heath, for whom she at least on occasion has felt a twisted, sanctimonious sort of pity. Her mother wouldn't feel that way about the baby's father. She would lose her shit completely. He'd lose his job, for sure. There would be a scandal. People would be looking at Effie again.

Effie won't tell *him*, either. He might be the sort of guy to step up to the plate when it comes to things like this. He's got a hero complex, Effie knows that for sure. He might do the right thing, but he would hate her for it forever. Besides, he lives in a one-bedroom apartment with battered furniture and no matching dishes, and he gets drunk too much and sometimes he asks her to do things to him Effie had never imagined a man liking. Or herself, for that matter.

He's not a man she wants to marry, that's for damn sure, and he's not one she wants to tie herself to forever, either. Not no way, not no how. Her hands go protectively over her belly. She will *never* tell him.

"I don't know," Effie says, then adds hastily, "only that it's not Heath."

"What do you mean you don't know? How can you not know? Effie, if someone hurt you…again…"

That old story. Effie's chin lifts. Daddy had never "hurt" her in that way, but there was no way for her to say it so that anyone would ever believe it.

"I mean there've been so many boys," Effie lies flatly. "It could be any of several dozen. It means I don't know, Mother.

It means I don't even know the names of some of them. Or where they live."

Mom takes a step back. She shakes her head. She looks broken, and why? Because her daughter admitted to having sex? To getting knocked up? Effie had spent three years as a captive of a sick man determined to steal someone else's children when he was denied access to his own, and this was what broke her mother?

Effie goes to the closet and pulls out a bag. Starts to fill it. She doesn't pay attention to what she's tossing in there. Shirts, pants, some underwear, socks, a sweater she hates but throws in anyway.

"What are you doing?"

Effie doesn't look at her mother. "I'm leaving."

"Effie. No. Wait. Please…we'll take care of this. We can have it dealt with. You don't have to ruin your life!"

Effie thinks of all the blood, of how it had slipped out of her so easily, before. In silence. All the worst things happen in the silence.

Effie pauses, again touching her belly. "Was your life ruined when you had me?"

"I was married and twenty-four years old," her mother says. "You can hardly compare. I want more for you than this."

"Maybe this is the best I can expect to have. I'm leaving. I'll call and tell you where I am."

When Effie shows up at Heath's door, he lets her in without needing to be asked. When Effie kisses him, he lets her. He takes her in his arms and together they fall down on the mattress with its rumpled sheets.

His hands roam over her body. Naked, she arches beneath his touch. Her nipples are more sensitive. When he slides one between his lips, she can't keep quiet. He puts a hand over her mouth to stifle her. They shouldn't have to be silent, not here in this shitty warehouse loft where the neighbors can't hear a thing through four-foot-thick brick. It's an old habit they might grow out of, someday, if they keep doing this. For now, his rough, warm hand tastes of salt, and he covers her mouth while she cries out.

His fingers move between her legs, finding her slick and secret places. He toys with her, teasing her to the edge without letting her go over. When she tries to fight him, to move so his fingers will press harder on her clit and make her come, Heath grips her wrists in his hand and forces her onto her stomach. For a moment, she fights harder, thinking of the child. Worried of hurting it…though she's lost a baby before. She knows what to expect. It wouldn't be the most awful thing in the world if it happened again, would it?

She fights anyway because it excites him. Because when he grabs the back of her hair to yank her head back and to push her again into the mattress, facedown and ass up, it excites her. He doesn't spank her. It's not about making this some kind of late-night Skinemax movie with handcuffs and feather masks.

Effie isn't sure what it is about.

Only that it…is. This. Heath behind her, ramming himself inside her so deep she's sure he will kill her with his cock. With the grip of his fingers so tight on her skin she will find the marks there for days.

There were times, long, long ago when she can remember exploring her body in the late-night darkness of her canopy bed. Tiny breasts, the surprising tingle of touching her nipples, the more exciting rush she felt when her hand slipped between her legs. The first few threads of curling hair. How her body opened the longer she touched and stroked. She hadn't known it was sex, but she had known it felt good.

Effie can hardly imagine doing that now. Making herself

come? She's not sure she could. The only pleasure she can really find is with him.

When her body clenches around him, he shudders and pulls out. Scalding lashes of ejaculate hit her back. Her arms. Her ass. She buries her face in the pillow, shaking with her climax. Then with tears.

Heath doesn't ask her who the baby belongs to. He simply nods when she tells him. He holds her close, curled in a ball, and he kisses her forehead. When she can't stand the closeness of the embrace any longer, he lets her go. It's what he does. Know when to let her go.

"I'm with Heath," Effie tells her mother over the phone. "But so help me, Mom, if you call the police or in any way get him into trouble, I will never come home. I will never let you see this baby. I will disappear, and this time, you will never get me back."

Effie's mother sounds as though she's been chain-smoking and sobbing. She probably has. "Don't you understand I only want the best for you? Maybe you'll get it now, when you become a mother. I want what's best. That's all. And Heath, Effie...he's ruined you."

"Don't you get it?" Effie says tiredly, wishing all of this would go away. "I was already ruined."

chapter twenty-nine

Naveen had called Effie early this morning about doing a gallery show, all on her own. Effie listened to the message as she sipped lukewarm coffee in her quiet house and thought about the work she'd have to do to paint enough pieces to have a real show. Her kitschy hidden clock paintings weren't going to cut it. They paid the bills, though, and she had orders to fill. She didn't have time to wait around for a creative muse to strike her, not to mention what paintings like the one he'd just sold took out of her.

"I don't know, Naveen," she said when she returned his call. "I won't be ready to do something like that for a while. You're talking about a lot of work."

"Think about it," he insisted. "Maybe you have some pieces you've finished that you haven't sold?"

Effie leaned against her kitchen counter and looked over at the empty glass ashtray she'd picked up years ago at a thrift store. Heavy, ornate, clearly made in a time when everyone smoked and drank and the world was lit in Technicolor. Now she kept loose change and buttons and paper clips in it.

She did have a number of pieces she'd done over the years. Work she'd painted in the dark, ones that left her sweating and sick and sometimes on her hands and knees with her face in her hands. Too big to ship, too dark and violent to appeal, even to the people who collected her other pieces. She painted them and put them away, hoping each time she'd exorcised some new demon. They did make a collection, though not one Effie was sure she'd ever expected or wanted anyone else to see. Those paintings were her lost hours.

She closed her eyes. "How many pieces would you need?"

Naveen made a soft, thoughtful sound. "Ten, minimum. I can fill in the rest with your current work, but I'd really like to have at least ten more like what you just gave me."

"Greedy." Effie laughed. She had at least twice that many hidden away under sheets.

"Hey, a lad's gotta eat. Don't tell me you don't love making money. And I can sell that stuff. You know I can. Your other work, too. But, Effie…"

"Believe me, I know. The hidden clocks aren't art."

"Not the same kind, anyway," Naveen said.

"I have commissions to finish first. Those clocks are my bread and butter. I also have to eat, you know. My kid needs new clothes. I can't promise you anything." Effie dumped her coffee in the sink, thinking about making a fresh pot and not sure she felt like bothering. She had to run out on a few errands anyway. She could pick up a cup of some fancy brew from the local coffee shop. Let someone else do the work for her.

"Think about it," Naveen repeated. "I can have Elisabeth put you on the books for the spring. That's five months away. I'm booked that far in advance, so it will be perfect. We can get you in there, have a big to-do, get you hobnobbing with collectors. It'll be great for your career, Effie. And I don't need to tell you that stuff like this isn't easy."

"What, making a living as an artist? No, you definitely don't need to tell me. My mother reminds me of it all the time. She thinks I should go back to school." Effie laughed, though a trifle bitterly. She had half a degree in business administration. The thought of sitting behind a desk all day made her want to stab something with a pencil, probably her own eyes.

"Most people can't, you know."

"No kidding. Naveen," Effie said after a pause. "Did the buyer...know? Who I am?"

Naveen huffed. "I don't know."

That meant yes. Effie frowned and rubbed the spot between her eyes. "Great."

"If it sells the work," Naveen said, "does it matter?"

It did to her, but she said, "No. I guess not. Like you said, gotta eat."

"I'll have Elisabeth call you about dates," Naveen said. "Ciao, bella. I'll talk to you soon. Send me some of your clocks. I can hang them in the gallery for you."

"Sure. I'll see what I have."

Disconnecting, Effie slipped her phone into her pocket and sighed. She was lucky, she knew that. Talent could take you only so far in the creative business. Luck was what pushed you into the right places, made you collectible or popular or whatever. And luck didn't last forever. She should take advantage of it while she could, or she really would find herself sitting behind a desk filing shit and answering phones.

When she stood in front of her easel, though, all she could think about was mimicking Thomas Kinkade except with a giant hamster sitting on top of one of his cutesy Christmas cabins. She could do a van Gogh with a Tardis swirling around in the stars—it wasn't original, though. She'd seen that on the internet, and she'd never watched *Doctor Who* anyway, so it felt disingenuous to cash in on the show's popularity. Mona Lisa with a mustache?

Fuck it all, this was shit. Worse than shit. At least her other stuff, the twisted clocks hidden in the landscapes, had been original. At least she'd felt something when she painted them, even if it was more of a secret, ha-ha, "see how clever I am" sort of feeling and not that all-encompassing frenzy, that draining almost-religious ecstasy that happened when she painted from her dreams of the basement.

She couldn't just command it to happen, though. No matter what Naveen wanted or how Effie herself wanted to make something real and meaningful that would also make her money. You can't command a muse, she thought and dunked her brushes into the vase of cleaning solution. Besides, she still hadn't had enough coffee.

"Dee," she said when the other woman had answered her phone. "Want to grab a coffee with me?"

"Oh. Hell, yes. I don't have to be in to work until later. Same place?"

Agreed on the location, Effie grabbed her coat, purse and keys and headed out. Fresh air, a fancy coffee, maybe even a decadent pastry. She could hang out with Dee for a bit and feel like a normal woman with a friend, then maybe sketch in the coffee shop and think about what might work for a gallery show. She could at least try.

The girl behind the counter wore a T-shirt sliced into fringes with a familiar design on the front of it. One of Effie's. As always when confronted with this real-life evidence that there were people out there who actually bought her shit because they wanted it and not because they knew her, she smiled.

"Nice shirt."

"I got it over at the Tin Angel." The girl grinned. "Johnny Dellasandro's place, he was having this big display. You been there?"

Effie shook her head. All of her licensed items were ordered and shipped from the company that made them, the T-shirts and posters and mugs. All she did was look at the royalties when they came in. "I should check it out."

"It's pretty cool, some really great stuff. What can I get you?"

"Large mocha latte, and a blueberry scone. No. Cinnamon bun." Effie studied the glass case, aware of someone next to her but not turning until she felt a tap on her shoulder. She turned, expecting to see Dee, but smiled in surprise. "Mitchell. Hey."

"Hey." He grinned and pushed his glasses up higher on his nose. "I thought that was you. Do you come in here a lot?"

"No, not really." Effie stepped to the side to pay for her order. "I thought you'd be at work."

"We have a SCRUM meeting in an hour. Everyone kind of rolls in just before it. I figured I'd grab something on the way." Mitchell pointed to a chocolate croissant and pulled out his wallet. "Coffee, too, please. Hey, I got this."

"No, you don't have to," Effie protested but stopped at his look. She laughed, ducking her head. "Okay. Sure. Fine. Thank you."

"That's better." Mitchell followed Effie to a table near the window and waited until she sat before taking the chair opposite her. "You look pretty today."

Effie's brows rose. She wore jeans, a concert T-shirt hidden beneath her winter coat, a pair of battered black Converse. Had she even put on makeup? She couldn't remember. "Umm. Thanks?"

"So, what are you up to today?" Mitchell stirred his coffee and sipped, then looked at her expectantly.

Effie settled her bag on the back of the chair but didn't take out her sketch pad. She still hadn't told Mitchell she was an artist. "Have some errands to run. Boring stuff."

Mitchell broke his chocolate croissant into pieces, setting them neatly on the plate and wiping his fingers carefully on a paper napkin. Effie watched him, amused. Attracted, too. Something in the way he made sure he'd cleaned his fingers of any scrap of chocolate reminded her that he could be very, very attentive to other kinds of details.

He'd caught her staring at his hands and gave her a bemused look. "I'm glad I ran into you. I was going to call you. Next week is First Friday here. All the stores and galleries on Front and Second are open late. There's music and food and stuff. Would you like to go with me?"

"I'll have to see if I can find someone to stay with my daughter, but yes. That sounds really nice." Effie smiled, tilting her head to study him. "I've never gone to First Friday."

"It's fun," Mitchell said. "It'll be more fun with you."

The bell over the door jingled, announcing a new arrival, but Effie didn't turn until a flash of navy blue caught her eye along with a glimpse of pale hair. Shit. She half turned in her chair toward the window, but of course it was useless. Bill's job was noticing things. She braced herself for him to stop by the table and make things awkward, but he ordered his coffee and bagel to go and headed back out without so much as a hello.

Mitchell had noticed her concern. "You okay?"

"Yeah. Just… It's nothing." Effie gave him a bright grin.

Mitchell leaned to the side to look out the window at Bill walking away, then back at her. "You in trouble with the law?"

He'd said it like a joke, but Effie didn't know him well enough to be sure of that. "No. God, no. Not at all. I know that guy, that's all."

"Ex-boyfriend?" Mitchell asked. "Or…current?"

"Neither," Effie said firmly. She put her mug on the table and reached to put a hand on Mitchell's wrist. "Just some guy

I've known for a while. Sort of a friend. Sort of. But definitely not a boyfriend."

Mitchell looked pleased. He pushed his glasses up again, then drummed the table edge in a little riff Effie almost recognized before he quit. "That's nice to know, I guess. Um, Effie, I have something I'd like to talk about."

That could never be good. It was the sex. It had changed things. Maybe she was overthinking it? But no…not from the way he was looking at her. Shit. "Okay."

"I haven't been seeing anyone else but you for the past month or so. I know we didn't talk about being exclusive, but I wanted to let you know. Would you… Would you like to just see me? I mean, it doesn't have to be anything super serious," he added hastily. "But I believe in being up front and honest. I hate all the game playing on that site, to be honest."

"Yeah, me, too," Effie said, though actually she'd never experienced any games because she usually didn't bother dating a guy more than once and had never had a problem using the block button.

"And I thought since we…already, well…"

She tried to answer but managed only to nod and smile. Mitchell frowned a little, as if she ought to have said something more, and dammit, she probably should have, but what was there to say? They'd fucked. It happened. People did it all the time and never spoke to one another again. Why did relationships have to be so much fucking work? Effie turned her mug in her hands. She had not, in fact, been dating anyone else from LuvFinder since she started seeing Mitchell, but that did not make them exclusive. Yet she'd told Heath and her mother and herself it was what she was looking for—and it was, wasn't it? So why, then, when faced with having to make it official, did everything inside her squeeze like a fist?

"So…?"

She bought herself some time by sipping some more coffee, then gave him a small smile she suspected wasn't going to make her answer any more palatable. She had to tell him the truth, though. She hadn't been entirely truthful about a lot of other things, so he at least deserved her honesty now.

"I'm not sure I'm ready to make that promise."

"Oh, sure, sure. Right." Mitchell nodded, his gaze going shuttered.

She'd hurt his feelings. "But I'll let you know about Friday as soon as I can figure out who can stay with my daughter, okay? I'd really like to go out with you."

"Great." Mitchell stood, his coffee only half-finished, his croissant barely touched. He wrapped it back in the paper and put the lid on his paper cup. "You have my number. Just give me a call. Or text. It was nice seeing you, Effie."

She stood and gave him a one-armed hug. Awkward, but not unpleasant. "You, too. I'll call you."

He gave her a little wave as he went out the front door. Effie watched until he disappeared from her sight, then sat back with a sigh to pull out her sketch pad. She'd made only a few strokes before her phone buzzed with a text. Mitchell, already? She grinned, then frowned when she saw who it was really from.

Nice looking guy.

Bill. With a sigh, Effie thumbed a reply. Don't you have some criminals to harass?

Would rather harass you.

She twisted to look out the window, expecting to see him watching from across the street, but all she saw were parked cars and a guy in a long dark coat and a striped scarf coming into the coffee shop. She didn't answer the text, but she couldn't manage to concentrate on any drawing ideas, either. *Fucking Bill,* she thought with the corners of her mouth turned down.

I'm getting off shift now. Come over.

NO, she typed and erased. Typed it again. But she didn't hit Send. Another text came through while she was debating.

I'll eat your pussy until you scream, Bill typed, and Effie had to stifle a groan.

She didn't answer this text, either, though she saw the three small dots that indicated Bill was still typing. Before he could finish, she got another message, this one from Dee, apologizing that she'd have to cancel because the school had called her to come get Meredith, who had a fever. By the time she finished typing her reply to Dee, Bill's next text had buzzed through.

I'll make you come so hard you forget your name.

Oh, universe, Effie thought. *What lesson are you trying to teach me?*

Promises, promises, Effie typed. I'll be over in half an hour.

On her knees, Effie took Bill's cock down her throat. Her hand at the base kept him from going too deep and gagging her, while her other hand cradled his balls. He thrust with a groan. He wasn't pulling her hair. She wanted him to, she'd asked him to, and he had for a minute or so, barely hard enough, and then let go.

Effie loosed his cock from her lips with an audible pop and looked up at him. "Fuck my mouth."

Bill looked down at her with narrowed eyes, hazy gaze. His mouth was wet. From his tongue or from her cunt, she wasn't sure, but she liked to think it was because a minute or so ago he'd been face-first in her pussy. Her clit throbbed, and she slid a hand between her legs to stroke herself as she went back to sucking him.

She was close, so very close, but she hadn't quite made it when he flooded her mouth. She'd barely swallowed when Bill pulled her to her feet and kissed her. Their teeth clashed. His hand went between her legs, found her slick and open. He fucked into her with his fingers, his thumb on her clit. Still, wasn't nearly enough. She wanted it to be. Effie wanted to come so much it was all she could think about. Too long without that pleasure, even from her own hand. She wanted to come the way normal people did, easily or with effort, but she hadn't had an orgasm since the last time with Heath.

She didn't want to think about him now, but it was the memory of his taste that washed away Bill's flavor. Heath's touch, his kiss, his face in front of hers. She might hate it, she might not want it, but there it was, and oh, fuck yes, then she was coming and coming and coming while Bill murmured words of encouragement to her.

They were on his bed before she quite knew how they got there. Not cuddling, though the way she was feeling, she might have let him. Bill snored lightly and Effie curled onto her side but facing him, so she could, if she wanted to, reach out and touch his face.

Quietly, she got out of bed and went into his bathroom to take a shower. She would be cutting it close, getting home in time for Polly to get off the bus, and she didn't want to greet her daughter stinking of sex. She didn't luxuriate but scrubbed herself quickly and got out without even wetting her hair. At his sink, she rinsed her mouth and spat, then again. She could still taste him.

He was still sleeping when she came back into the room, and she sat on the edge of the bed next to him. She put her hand on his bare hip, thinking he might wake up and hoping he wouldn't. Then they'd have to talk, and she didn't feel like talking to Bill right now. She let her fingers slide down his flank, feeling the crisp hairs curling against her knuckles.

She used him. He used her. They'd been doing this a long time, and there was no reason for her to think it had to change. But it would, if she gave Mitchell the answer he'd been hoping for. Everything would change then.

"Bill." He didn't answer, so she poked him a little harder. "Bill, wake up."

"Shhh… Wha…" Grumbling, he opened his eyes and frowned. "What?"

"I was on a date with that guy in the coffee shop. I've seen him a few times. He's asking me to make it exclusive."

Bill yawned. "Yeah. So?"

"So, doesn't that bother you?" She poked him again, taking a small pleasure in the way he winced and put a hand over hers to stop her from doing it again.

Bill let out a low, muttered string of curses. He sat up. "No. Should it?"

"Maybe. I don't know."

"Do you want it to bother me? Christ, Effie, I'm tired. I worked the night shift," Bill complained.

Effie got up. "You weren't too tired to have your dick in my mouth."

"And you put it there, so what's the fucking problem?" Bill yawned again. "You want to go on dates? So, what? Go. Hell, get married if you want to. Isn't that what all girls want, eventually?"

"What's so wrong with that?" Effie demanded, crossing her arms. "What's so wrong with wanting to find someone to be with who cares about you? It's what people do, Bill, unless they're too fucked up to ever even try."

"Well, that's you and me, isn't it? Too fucked up to even try?" Bill winked.

Effie sneered. "I hate you. You know that?"

"You wish you could hate me," Bill said and rolled back into the blankets, pulling them up over his shoulders. "Keep trying. Maybe you'll get there."

The whispers stop when Effie enters the locker room. It's been months since she came home. You'd think everyone would have something else to gossip about, but nope, it's still her. Her father says she could stay home, get private tutoring. Switch schools, even, but Effie said no. This story will follow her anyway, no matter where she goes. At least here she knows these kids. It's easier to brush off the rumors and looks when she knows that Rachel Franklin wet the bed up until the sixth grade and Courtney Spenser's dad went to jail for drunk driving.

Nobody takes a shower, even though the gym teacher said they have to. Effie does, though. She'll shower any freaking place with hot water. What does she care if it means being naked in front of other girls? None of them ever had to spend weeks feeling filthy. Effie will never pass up a chance to scrub herself, especially after sweating on the track the way they did today. And it's last period. She can take her time, no rush to get to her next class.

She closes her eyes to let the hot water stream over her face. Dreamily, she scrubs her hair, luxuriating in the way the shampoo leaves it squeaky clean. She lathers beneath her arms, over her belly, her thighs. She looks down to see the suds swirling down the drain around her toes. When she looks up, Cindy Jones is looking at her from the shower room doorway. Cindy wears too much black eyeliner and teases her hair high on one side, leaving the other side shaved. She's the antithesis of a teen drama cheerleader, but she's still a popular girl with a covey of followers who bill and coo around her. Now she's staring in at Effie.

"What?" Effie says, challenging.

Cindy's smirk says it all. When Effie comes out of the shower with her towel wrapped around her breasts and her wet hair still hanging in sopping strands over her back, Cindy is hovering around her locker in the next row over. Her voice rises enough to be sure Effie hears her.

"Yeah, she took a whole bunch of crazy pills with a bottle of Scotch. They had to send her to the hospital to get her stomach pumped." Cindy says this with such confidence there's no way anyone could dispute her.

Effie slips her panties over her still-damp skin. Then her bra. She wraps her hair in the towel, refusing to give them the satisfaction of knowing she heard them, but Cindy isn't satisfied. She *wants* Effie to know they're talking about her. She wants a reaction.

"It was a suicide pact," Cindy says, a little louder. "With her and that guy she was with. Her parents found her in the bathtub with a razor on her wrist."

Effie can't take it. She steps around the row of lockers. "Shut up."

Cindy turns with another of those smirks. Why she has such a fucking hard-on for Effie isn't clear, except that maybe compared to Effie's story, Cindy is not even close to being the kind of badass she makes herself out to be. What has Cindy ever survived but the wrong pair of jeans under the Christmas tree?

"Everyone knows you were in the hospital two weeks ago. And you didn't have the flu."

The bleeding and cramping had stopped only a few days ago. Effie missed only three days of school. Now her hands fist with rage she forces herself not to show.

"So you assume I tried to kill myself?"

Cindy's smirk falters for a second. She's not expecting Effie to stand up to her, because nobody ever does. Effie takes the towel from her hair with a quick, drying scrub, then tosses it to the bench. She puts her hands on her hips. Nobody can look directly at her, whether they're ashamed or because she's standing so boldly in only her underwear and that intimidates them, her easy nakedness.

"If I tried to kill myself, they wouldn't let me out of the hospital the same day. They'd send me someplace for longer than two days." It's Effie's turn to sneer. She holds out both wrists. "I don't even have a scratch there. So much for your razor blade theory."

Cindy's chin goes up. "Look, it's not like it's a big deal. Lots of people try to kill themselves. I mean, they're losers, but whatever."

Effie looks at each of the girls in the group, one at a time. None of them will meet her gaze. Her mouth tastes sour. She wants to spit.

She can't tell them the real reason she had to go to the ER and why she missed school. The truth is worse than Cindy's lie. Thinking of it all over again breaks her with the slow, spreading crackle of glass shattering. She thinks of her father saying, "Effie, you don't have to go back to school right away. Nobody would blame you if you wanted to stay home." Of her mother responding, "She needs to get back into normal life, Phil. Or she never will."

If Effie ever wants to get back into normal life, here it is.

The bullshit of high school, right in front of her. She's already older than all of these girls, even if they're still the same age. It's not enough that she struggles with the curriculum in classes that are technically two grades behind so that she can catch up in time for graduation. She also has to eat shit or be an outcast.

"I didn't try very hard." The words are ash on Effie's tongue. She sees the way their faces light up. The way Cindy looks around with smug satisfaction, even though she has to know her own story was a lie.

"My cousin tried to kill himself once," pipes up Rachel.

Courtney nods. "Yeah, I went to summer camp with a girl who tried."

One by one, the small group chimes in with their own stories. They all know someone who tried, but nobody seems to know anyone who succeeded. There's acceptance in their eyes and voices, in the way they reach out to her without actually reaching, and Effie lets them take her into their circle because she doesn't want to be outside it.

She can't stop thinking about it, though. Later, after dinner when she's supposed to be doing her homework, all she can do is stare at the pages of her history book and think about how she will never need to know who wrote the Magna Carta. Her stomach is empty, growling, because her mom made some kind of chili and there were simply too many...things...in it for Effie to eat.

She calls Heath, but his father answers, drunk. He doesn't know where his son is. Effie's sure he doesn't care.

She needs to get out of this house.

The only way to do it is by sneaking. Mom will flip her shit if she knows Effie wants to go running out in the night, along dark streets, alone. If nothing had ever happened to her, Effie knows her mother would still cling too hard, but now there is no way for her mom to let her go and do normal things, no matter how much she claims she wants Effie to be normal. Everything is fucked up. It will never get better.

So she sneaks out, careful on the creaking stairs, inching past the door to the family room, where her parents sit in silence on separate sides of the couch and stare at the television. Through the kitchen and out the garage door, then out into the cool and misty autumn air. She breathes it in, shivering, and runs.

It starts to rain. She keeps running. Feet slapping the pavement. Fists pumping. She will never be caught again, never.

She can run fast, or she can run far, but she can't do both. Not with a stomach that's been near to empty for days. She's weak, and Effie lets out a curse as she bends over, mouth open, waiting to see if she's going to heave. The rain is turning to speckles of ice. She's not wearing gloves.

The car that pulls up beside her does not have flashing red and blue lights, but it's still a cop car. Effie straightens. She's out past curfew. She has a story, or she'll think of one, but when the window rolls down and she sees that familiar face, she doesn't have to say a word.

"Get in," Officer Schmidt says.

"Did my mother call you?"

"No. Get in."

She gets in the front seat next to him, warming her hands on the air blowing from the vents. She's not soaked through, but she would've been in a few minutes. She should be grateful for him. For saving her again.

They drive, but he doesn't take her home. Officer Schmidt pulls into the hardware store parking lot, but around the back where the deliveries are made. He parks in a patch of darkness. He sits with his hands on the wheel, facing forward, not looking at her.

"You shouldn't be out past curfew," he says. "Running alone in the dark is a good way to get yourself in trouble."

"I had to get out of the house. I was going to go crazy." Effie's voice cracks. She leans into the warmth, bathing her face. Closing her eyes. When she opens them, he's looking at her.

Oh, there's a look she understands.

She is kissing him before she can think to stop herself. This, kissing him, is saving of a different sort. She thinks he will push her off him—he has to, doesn't he? He's an adult, she's only seventeen, he's a police officer, she's a fucked-up mess, but all she can think of right then is the sight of that blue uniform when he came through that doorway into the basement with his gun drawn. How he lowered the weapon at the sight of them, she and Heath, both of them still so stunned by Sheila's drunken intrusion and her screaming that neither of them had moved.

All she can hear is his voice, saying over and over, "It's going to be okay. It's all going to be okay."

So she kisses him, and he does not push her away. His mouth opens. Their tongues stroke. His hand goes up to the back of her neck, holding her off him but not pushing her away. She can feel the battle in him, and it's one Effie intends to win.

"Not here," he says. And later, when she's on top of him in his bed with the plain white sheets and lumpy pillows, "Call me Bill. My name's Bill."

chapter thirty

The trip to Philadelphia was, on a good day, a two-hour drive. That is if you could avoid traffic on the Schuylkill, and honestly, that was an impossible dream. Still, Effie had made it in just under three hours and didn't have to be home at any certain time because she'd made arrangements for Heath to be there when Polly got off the bus. It had been an olive branch from her to him, and he'd taken it, but she wasn't sure it had made much of a difference, overall.

She didn't want to think about that now.

"Effie! Hi." Elisabeth had worked with Naveen as long as Effie had been selling her art to him, though it had been only in the past few years that she'd taken over acquiring pieces on her own. "Can I get you something? Coffee, tea, soda? I have a bottle of wine somewhere around here, if you want a glass of that."

"It's a little early, even for an artist." Effie laughed and hung her coat on Elisabeth's rack, then took a seat on the plush red couch. "Your office looks amazing. Wow."

"I told Naveen that if we wanted to get to the next level with clients, we had to show ourselves off as being worth the time. He was happy with bare-bones spaces, but I had to convince him that, sure, they like to go look at the pieces hung in the gallery, where they look spectacular, but they're only going to buy what they can imagine will look fantastic hanging in their homes." Elisabeth poured herself a mug of coffee from the maker on the small stand next to her desk and held up the carafe with a raised brow.

"Yeah, thanks. Black is fine." Effie took the mug the other woman offered and sipped the strong, hot coffee hesitantly at first. It was fine, of course. She took another drink.

"So," Elisabeth continued, "I redid my office here to have this little area that's set up like a living room. Even if the clients don't have the same decor, at the very least, they can picture the piece in a living room or foyer, not simply hanging in perfect lighting with neutral backgrounds. It's been working out really well. I move so many more pieces since I did it. But, hey, tell me what's up with you. I saw the piece you sent to the New York gallery. My God, Effie, it was amazing."

Warmed by the praise, Effie sat back against the cushions. "Thanks. Sometimes it comes out right, you know?"

"I couldn't make art if you put a gun to my head." Elisabeth took a seat in the retro-styled chair across from Effie. "So I don't really know, but I understand. Does that make sense?"

Effie laughed. "I think so."

"Anyway, let's go over the ideas I had for the show. We can start by looking at the calendar and going from there."

Together, they worked up a date and time for the show, how long it would run, how many pieces Effie would need that were similar to the one she'd sent in. Elisabeth assured her they'd fill in with the other work. It was going to be great, she said. Effie wasn't so sure.

"I've never had my own show. I'm not sure I can carry it." The coffee gone, Effie had nothing to do with her hands but link her fingers in her lap.

Elisabeth shook her head. "You're going to be great. Really. And honestly, it's as much about marketing and publicity, these days, getting people into the gallery. And if we can get them in, I can guarantee you'll sell. You want to see the new gallery space? Check out what we have room for? I don't know if it will help you figure out what you want to paint or not. I work with some people who insist on being guided by the muse no matter what form it takes, and others who are really more interested in making a living."

"I'm totally interested in making a living," Effie said absently as she got up to check out the piece hanging on Elisabeth's wall, not in the client section but to the side of her desk next to the window. "I make art like it's my job so I don't have to get another one."

It was a photograph. An 11 x 20 print, scattered stones on a bed of velvet with one heart-shaped rock set off from the others. It was more than just a photo. Someone had added lines and color to it, little hints here and there, using ink and pen to transform an already-beautiful shot into something unique. Special.

"This is good," Effie said, turning to look at Elisabeth, who'd stopped, still and silent, to also stare at the photo.

"It was a gift," Elisabeth said.

Effie had bitten her own tongue for silence enough times to see the struggle in someone else. Wisely, she changed the subject as she followed Elisabeth out of the office and into the gallery space. It was bright, airy, welcoming. Various paintings, photographs and sculptures occupied well-designed spaces. Effie spotted a couple of her hidden clocks along a back wall but didn't go closer to see them. She knew what they looked like.

"Can you envision your work here? Oh, hold on. Excuse me." Elisabeth pulled her buzzing phone from her pocket to look at the screen. Her brow furrowed. She slipped the phone back in her pocket and gave Effie a pained smile.

"You need to take that?"

Elisabeth shook her head. "No. It's…"

The phone buzzed again. Elisabeth put her hand over her pocket. Effie gave her a sympathetic look, woman to woman. That had to be from a guy.

"Excuse me just a minute. Take a walk around, make yourself at home." Elisabeth walked away to look at her phone, shoulders hunched, furiously texting.

Effie watched her for a moment and took the chance to tug her own phone from her pocket. Messages from her mother, of course. One from Heath saying he'd be taking Polly bowling tonight if she got her homework finished in time, so if they weren't home when Effie got there, not to worry. One from Mitchell, a simple smiley emoticon and one word.

Hey.

Hey, Effie typed.

Immediately, the three small dots that indicated Mitchell was typing showed up on her screen. With an eye on Elisabeth, who was now pacing and typing, Effie waited for his reply. He typed. Then stopped. He typed, then stopped.

Finally, Hey.

She laughed, gave another look to Elisabeth, who was still occupied with her phone, and responded. That was a lot of typing for a single word.

I was going to try for clever, but I didn't know how the joke would go over, so I just went with the safe route. How r u?

Fine, Effie began, meaning to write more but at that moment Elisabeth returned.

"Sorry." The other woman looked as if she'd been trying not to cry.

"Everything okay?"

"No, not really," Elisabeth said with a tired smile that didn't reach her eyes. "But it's also nothing new. So, let's take a look at the spaces I was thinking of using for you, okay?"

This time, Effie's phone was the interrupting buzz. The first time it hummed from her pocket, she ignored it. The second time, she assumed it was because she hadn't checked the first message—her phone could be impatient with alerts. The third and fourth times it buzzed, she figured she'd better peek to be sure it wasn't Heath with an emergency with Polly. She caught Elisabeth's curious look.

"This is something kind of new," she explained, then after a second thought, she showed her phone to Elisabeth. "Boys being pouty? I don't know how to deal with it."

I wanted to follow up about next week, First Friday?

Hey, r u there?

Guess you're too busy to chat.

Give me a ping when you have some time for me.

"Ugh," Elisabeth said, but she laughed. "Maybe he didn't mean it to come off as pouty?"

"I don't know him well enough to say," Effie admitted. "I've only just started dating him. But if that's how he's going to be, I'll have to tell you, I'm not gonna have it."

Elisabeth gave her a commiserating look. "Let's go back to

my office for the final details. And yeah, I know what you mean. It's fine for them not to pay attention to your messages, to leave them unanswered for days at a time, but boy oh boy, you'd better be jumping to answer them the second they text you, huh?"

As if on cue, Elisabeth's phone jangled. A call this time. She slid her finger across the screen and gave Effie a twisted little grin.

"Nope," she said. "I'm not answering him this time. He can wait on me, for a change."

Effie had known Elisabeth through Naveen for years but hadn't spent much time with her. Effie thought the other woman was married, had some adult kids, but something in the way her phone was blowing up didn't sound like a husband. At least not the loving kind.

"Oh, hey, I wanted to ask you if you'd consider bringing a few special pieces, too. I saw them on your website store. I…" Elisabeth paused, looking almost embarrassed. "I really like them. They spoke to me. I know you prefer to sell those yourself, so I'd be willing to take them here without charging a commission, if you sell them. I want people to see them."

Surprised, Effie nodded. "Sure, I guess. What pieces?"

"Let me show you." Elisabeth pulled up Effie's Craftsy store on her desktop and spun the monitor to show her. "I've noticed these pieces have been for sale for a long time. Your stuff usually moves pretty quickly on there, so I thought…well, art is so subjective, you know? I know you have that collector audience who buy the clocks…"

A beat of silence fell between them, and Effie filled it by moving closer to look at the screen. "Oh. Those? You like those?"

Elisabeth had pulled up three oils Effie had painted, not a triptych on purpose, though they'd ended up being one.

Similar themes as the ones the collectors bought—straight lines, simple subjects, with hidden images you had to search hard to find. They had clocks, but they were barely hidden, no challenge to find. She'd always assumed that was why nobody had wanted them.

"They're a secret. Aren't they?" Elisabeth shifted in her chair to draw some lines in the air above the picture on the screen. She glanced at Effie, but her voice and her gaze were somehow...*reverent* didn't seem to be the right word, but *respectful*. Yeah, maybe that.

Effie tilted her head. "Why do you say that?"

"Well, the reason why people love your work is because it's a challenge. Finding the clock. Right? You make them not only appreciate the piece as something enjoyable to look at...not always pretty," Elisabeth amended. "Sometimes a little disturbing. But always enjoyable. Yet you also make them look behind what the picture is to what's hidden in it. I've been on the forums. They love it, like a grown-up version of *Where's Waldo?*"

"Yes, but for freaks," Effie murmured.

Elisabeth didn't laugh. "Yes. There's the voyeuristic aspect to it. Yet these three...well, you barely have to glance at them to see the clocks. It's not super obvious, but it's there and there and there." She pointed. "But that's not the real hidden picture. Is it?"

Effie sat back to study the other woman. "No. It's not. What do you see?"

Elisabeth used the mouse to click something, blowing up the picture on the screen. Her grin turned kind of secret, assessing. Something in her eyes glowed as she glanced at Effie.

"You have the clocks, of course. You always do. But here, here and here—" Elisabeth traced the lines "—you have this. It's the shape of a heart and two initials. *E*...and *H*."

It was true, and real, and nobody else had ever seemed to see it. Effie had shown the three pieces together and separately to several people and had featured them in her store. Elisabeth was right about that—they'd been in the inventory for a couple years, never selling. Nobody had ever inquired about them.

"I'd always thought they were some of my best work," Effie said quietly. "Not like the piece I sent to Naveen. But really good."

"They are more than really good. The piece you sent to Naveen is art. If you do more like that, they will also sell. They will make people talk, there's no question about that. But these, Effie…" Elisabeth sat back and pressed her fingertips to her eyelids. She drew a hitching breath. In a broken, rasping voice, she finished, "You made these for someone you love. Didn't you?"

Effie swallowed against the tightness in her throat. "Yes. Someone I love very much."

Elisabeth gave her a watery smile and grabbed a tissue from the box on her desk to wipe her eyes and then her nose. "I can tell."

"Maybe that's why they didn't sell." Effie reached for a tissue herself.

They stared at each other across the desk.

"Does he know?" Elisabeth asked after a moment.

"About the paintings?"

"No," Elisabeth said. "How much you love him?"

Effie shook her head. "No. He couldn't possibly. I've never told him."

Elisabeth spun in her chair to look at the photo on the wall. "You should tell him, Effie. Even if he doesn't love you back. Trust me on this, you'll regret it if you don't."

The problem had never been about Heath loving her back.

Effie pointed to the photograph on the wall. "Did you tell him? The guy who gave you that picture?"

Elisabeth looked at her. "Yes, I did. More than once."

"Do you still love him?"

"Yeah," Elisabeth said. "Still."

Effie frowned. "And what happened?"

"Nothing," Elisabeth said. "But at least I can take comfort in the fact he knows. No matter what else happens, he will always know it."

"Even if you can never be together?"

"Especially then," Elisabeth said, and after that the conversation moved to other things.

chapter thirty-one

"Fucking you is like fucking a skeleton," Bill says. "Jesus, Effie, what the hell's going on with you?"

"Thin is in."

She's drunk. She raided Bill's liquor cabinet the second she came through his door. He didn't try to stop her, even with her being underage. Some cop. She lifts the bottle of whiskey in offer to him, and Bill takes it from her.

"You've had enough. Let me make you a sandwich or something. Christ. Are you going to puke or anything? Go to the bathroom."

Effie's not going to puke. She feels good, glowing, happy, full of…something, she doesn't know what. It's summer. The sun takes forever to set. She doesn't have to be in the dark for hours.

"I graduated," she tells him.

Bill looks at her over his shoulder. He's still naked, and something about that makes Effie giggle. He frowns, brandishing the mustard-smeared butter knife.

"Why are you laughing?"

"Your butt has dimples." Effie giggles again. "Hey. Hey, Bill. Hey, Officer Schmidt. I graduated. I fucking made it."

"Don't curse, it's crude."

Effie rolls her eyes. She wears Bill's T-shirt and nothing else, and she pirouettes in place. Points her toes. She's a terrible dancer, but she's trying to make him laugh. She and Heath laugh together until they can't breathe, but she and Bill...they hardly ever laugh at all.

"I didn't know if I could, you know? Like, all that time I missed, right, but I worked hard and I managed to make it happen, and I did it. I graduated with my class. Aren't you proud of me, Bill?" She dances closer, letting the hem of that shirt ride up on her thighs.

His gaze drops there, and to the shadow between her legs, and his gaze also shadows. Effie lifts the hem higher. Higher. She wants him to look at her. She wants him to *see* her.

"So what's the plan now? Go off to college? Get married, get the white picket fence, have a couple of kids?"

Effie's buzz is wearing off. She'd applied to the local college on the advice of her guidance counselor, who said she could take two years of interim classes before she'd have to think about applying someplace else. Two years to Effie feels like a very long time. "I don't know. I'm just glad I did it. I guess I can think about what happens next later. Maybe after you fuck me again."

He tells her not to be crude, but it excites him. She sees it in the way he licks his lips, the way he shifts from foot to foot. Fucking Bill is everything anyone would ever say is wrong, but Effie can't manage to stop herself from doing it, because fucking Bill makes her feel as though possibly, maybe, there's a chance for her to do something with her life exactly like what he just described.

"And what's wrong with getting married or having kids anyway?" Effie spins again, slower this time. She pauses with her back to him so she can look over her shoulder through the filter of her hair. "Haven't you ever thought about it?"

"Yeah, sure. Doesn't mean I want to do it."

"No?" Effie grins. "I could be a nice little housewife. Cook and bake and fuck…"

Bill laughs, sharp and hard. "You? You're eighteen years old. You have a whole life ahead of you. The hell you want to think about getting married for?"

"It feels safe." Effie frowns. Her stomach has started hurting, and her head, and the soft warm glow she had earlier from the way Bill kissed and held her is almost gone.

"Well," Bill said. "There's nothing safe about it. Eat your sandwich, and I'll drive you home."

There's a bit more to it than the sandwich, several hours of it as a matter of fact, but when it's over Bill does drive her home. He drops her off a block from her house so she can walk to her front door without her parents seeing them together. She made it home just as night is falling, so there's no reason why they should be worried or waiting for her, but someone is there on the front porch. The sight of that long black trench coat, the dark and spiky hair, stops her heart from beating for a long second before her pulse thumps hard and fast in her throat and wrists.

Heath has taken to lining his green eyes with black. He runs with a bad crowd. Effie hasn't seen him in months, because the last time they were together, he'd been drunk and high and argumentative. They'd fought about something so stupid she can't even recall what had prompted it, just that in the end he'd spat out a bunch of insults that Effie had returned with an even fiercer venom.

They've started hating each other, sometimes, and she doesn't know what to do about it.

He stands when she comes up the walk. Metal glints on his

belt, rivets and buckles. And on his boots. He's so tall she has to crane her neck to look at him, and she knows him, this boy who's struggling so hard to become a man. She would know him in any guise. In any darkness.

"I graduated," Effie says. "I did it."

"Congratulations," Heath says.

Confused, her mouth dry and tongue thick, too much to drink, it's catching up to her, Effie frowns. "What are you doing here?"

"I came to see you."

She twirls, dancing. "Here I am."

Heath reaches for her hand to stop her from moving. "I see you. You've been with him again."

"I haven't been with anyone." She doesn't mean to lie, but there it is, words tumbling from her mouth like stones. "What happened to your face?"

Heath touches his cheek where a dark bruise blossoms. "My dad and I got into it. He kicked me out. For good this time."

"Oh. I'm sorry. You want to come inside?"

Heath glances over his shoulder at the house. "Your parents are home."

Her father has never seemed to hate Heath the way her mother does; still, he's married to her and supports her even when she's being kind of a crazy bitch. Effie pushes past him on the front step to get at the door, but her keys are slippery and she drops them. Laughing, she bends to pick them up but can't make her fingers find them.

"You're drunk," Heath says.

"Come inside." Effie lets him open the door for her and, putting a finger to her lips, shushes him. Her parents are home, though the house is dark and they're probably watching television in their bedroom. Her mother would be waiting up anyway, no matter how late it might've been. She claims she can't sleep until she knows Effie is home, safe and sound.

Effie supposes she can't really blame her, all things considered. At least her mother has stopped waiting for her in the living room. At least she makes a pretense of trusting Effie at becoming some semblance of an adult.

In the kitchen, Effie pours them both glasses of clear cola and sips at hers to settle her stomach. She loves the way being drunk makes her feel, but she's never happy about the aftermath. Heath gulps his soda and she refills his glass.

"Are you hungry?" she asks. His father never feeds him. Without waiting for him to answer, she pulls out the fixings for a sandwich and lays out the meat, cheese, bread on the counter. She makes two sandwiches and puts his on a plate.

Together, they sit at the kitchen table. Heath devours his food while Effie picks at hers. When he's not looking, she drinks in the sight of him.

"What are you going to do?" she asks after a while. "Where are you going to live?"

"I'll get an apartment."

Effie presses the soft white bread with her fingertip and watches it spring back. Spongy. The thought of eating it turns her stomach, and she pushes the plate away.

"How will you pay for it?"

Heath sits back in his chair and wipes his mouth. Effie watches the motion of his fingertips against his lips. She's kissing him before she can stop herself, straddling his lap. His arms go around her. His tongue in her mouth.

She presses her forehead to his and closes her eyes. Between them she can feel him, hard. They have to be quiet here in the kitchen, but she wants to make him scream.

"I have a job," Heath says against her throat.

She runs her hands through his hair, pushing it off his forehead, and cups his face. "You got a job? Where?"

"Line cook at the diner. Hey, at least you'll be able to eat there if you know I'm the one scrambling the eggs. Right?" He tips his face to look at her.

"Don't go away from me again," Effie says.

There it is between them, fierce and yearning, a darkness that won't ever go away. She touches the bruise on his face, imagining his father punching him. Her slap is sharp, on the other cheek, and won't leave a mark. It's not meant to hurt him. Not really. She does it because she knows what the crack of her flesh on his does to him.

They've never talked about it, why Heath craves that sort of treatment, why he likes her to be the opposite of soft to him. Effie has never tried to figure out why she likes the feeling of heat beneath her palm when she hits him; it's the same to her as the taste of his mouth when he kisses her. One with the other, always, tied up and tangled so tight they can't separate their desires.

From upstairs, the creak of the floor turns both their heads toward the kitchen doorway. Effie's mother is not even pretending to be quiet or subtle about the fact she's awake and waiting for Effie to come to bed. If Heath doesn't leave in the next few minutes, Effie's mother will come into the kitchen and make it so supremely uncomfortable for him to be there that he won't have a choice.

Effie kisses the corner of his mouth, then the bruise his father left. She traces the curve of his cheek and imagines she can still feel the heat her slap left. She doesn't want him to go, but he'd better, or there will be trouble and neither one of them want that.

"I didn't go away from you," Heath says as he stands and settles her on her own feet.

Effie is no longer drunk, but she wishes she were because it would make it easier to talk to him. "You did. I haven't heard from you in months…"

"I've been trying to get my shit together."

"Good luck with that." Effie laughs. It's cruel. She can't help it.

"Of all the people in the world, I thought you'd be the one to believe I could," Heath tells her.

She should cry out after him and tell him to wait, that she does believe in him. Of course she believes. Shouting will bring her mother downstairs, and Effie doesn't want to deal with that mess. She wants to call Heath back, but in the end, it's better if she doesn't. Those small hatreds they've started fostering between them…well, one of them just reared its nasty face.

If Heath gets his shit together, Effie will have no excuses for continuing to be a fuckup, herself. And what if, in the end, no matter what she tries, she can't get beyond what happened to them? College, a job, that white picket fence Bill mocked her for wanting? All of those things feel so far away and out of reach, as if she will never be able to touch them.

chapter thirty-two

Effie had never been inside the Tin Angel art gallery, a tiny studio tucked inside a lovely restored brownstone on Front Street in Harrisburg. She usually avoided art galleries, to be honest. It was too hard to judge the work on the walls against her own and find either it or hers lacking. She took a glass of white wine, though, to hold instead of Mitchell's hand as they made their way through the different small rooms in the building.

To her surprise, in the small back corner room, hung on a plain white wall and lit with several pinpoint spots, hung one of her pieces. Effie pulled up short, uncertain. It was one of the ones she sold on her site, she knew that much. And she'd been credited as the artist, according to the placard discreetly placed beside it.

"I don't… This is…" Effie gestured at the painting.

Mitchell looked closer at it. Then at her. "Felicity Linton? Do you know her?"

Of course he didn't know her real name was Felicity. Effie laughed and took a long gulp of wine to keep herself from sounding like a crazy person. She shook her head.

"I just… It's interesting, isn't it?" She turned to leave.

Mitchell didn't. "You like that?"

She paused. "Do you?"

"I don't know." Mitchell studied it, looking closer. "It doesn't look like much of anything to me, honestly. It looks like something anyone could do if they tried a little."

Effie frowned. "It always looks easier than it really is. I mean, I'm sure."

"Yeah, but this…" Mitchell looked again at the placard. He leaned close to the painting once more. "I don't know, it feels like there should be something more to it."

There *was* something more to it, Effie thought. It's what made people like it. She didn't point that out, though. She watched him look it over, then turn to her with a shrug.

"I don't get it," he said.

"That's the thing about art. It's different things to different people." Effie finished her wine and lifted her empty glass. "Another drink?"

"There are other places to see, if you want. There's a great little vintage shop a block over. We could check it out, then head to dinner?" Mitchell smiled, no clue how he'd insulted her.

"Sure," Effie said with a smile to match his. "Let's go."

It was better in the other shops, although Effie found herself unable to forget what Mitchell had said about her painting. It wasn't as if she'd never had criticism before, but fuck if hearing it face-to-face didn't suck extra hard. She couldn't even defend herself without outing that she was the artist.

"You're quiet," Mitchell said.

He'd taken her to the Capital City Diner instead of a fancy place, and Effie liked that. It meant she could order something safe and cheap and not feel bad if she didn't eat all of it. She was making sure to actually eat at least some of it, though. She didn't want another discussion about her weird habits.

"Kind of tired, I guess." Effie cut into her eggs over medium with her fork to let the yolk spread out over the plate so she could sop it up with the buttered toast. She caught him looking at her and gave him a smile. "But it was fun. Did you have fun?"

"Yeah, I like looking in all the shops. They have some cool stuff. I never end up buying anything." Mitchell looked contemplative. "I should. Maybe some decorative balls in, like, a bowl or something, for the coffee table. My house is pretty bland."

"I know. I've seen it." She said it, knee-jerk, knowing it would be slightly insulting and also knowing she was still stewing over the fact he'd basically shit on her artwork. It wasn't fair of her. She knew that, too.

Mitchell didn't look offended, though he did pause before answering. "I bet your house is decorated with lots of color and funky throw pillows and stuff."

"My house is mostly decorated with clutter. Nothing matches. I'd make a terrible housewife. I hate mopping." Effie laughed and shook her head.

"To be fair," Mitchell said mildly, "mopping sucks."

Mitchell had not picked her up tonight, so in the parking lot they prepared to part ways. It was too cold to stand outside talking for long. Effie pulled her scarf closer around her throat, wishing she'd worn jeans because her legs were freezing.

"Thanks for coming out with me tonight," Mitchell said.

"Thanks for asking me."

He pulled her a little closer but didn't kiss her. His cheeks and the tip of his nose had gone pink with cold. Effie had thought his eyes were blue, but now in the diner's bright parking lot lights, she could see they were more green.

"I'm not going to ask you again, about being exclusive. I get that maybe I jumped the gun on it." Mitchell tugged her one more step closer. "But I do like you, Effie. And after we…well, that night at my house…I kind of got the idea you thought we might've rushed into that. And we did, I guess. Not that I wouldn't like to do it again, of course."

"Of course," Effie said.

"I didn't want you to think I was the kind of guy to sleep with a woman just casually," Mitchell said. "Like it didn't mean anything. I tried that a few times, and it's never really what you think it will be."

Effie would not have said never. Sometimes it was terrible, true, but she'd had plenty of great sex with men whose names she barely knew. "No, Mitchell. I didn't think that."

"I figured I'd tell you, because…well, I'm looking for something long-term, and if that's not where you see us going, then I wanted to be up front about where I was."

"Are you saying you don't want to go out with me again unless I agree to be your girlfriend?" Effie frowned.

Mitchell nodded after a second, then shook his head. "I guess we don't have to put a label on it. I just think that if you're not interested in moving forward into something long-term…"

"You're not going to go out with me again." Effie pressed her lips together. "Well, Mitchell, I am looking for something long-term, eventually."

He grinned but didn't speak.

Effie's smile was a little more tentative. "But I don't like to make promises I'm not sure I can keep."

"I won't expect you to mop," Mitchell said.

She chuckled. "Okay, well, that does make a difference."

They looked at each other. She waited for him to kiss her, and when he did, it was really nice. That's all it was. Nice. But what was wrong with that?

"I'll call you later," Mitchell said. "Drive safe."

In her car, Effie checked her phone before pulling out of the lot. A message from Bill. She opened it.

Come over.

No, Effie typed. I told you. I'm dating someone.

Come over anyway. I'll fuck you. He'll never know.

She deleted it without answering.

chapter thirty-three

They've been talking about the plan for days. They've saved the bits of paper, the small bits of butter or salad oil, anything they think will light. Heath has Daddy's lighter, picked from his pocket while Effie distracted him. When Daddy comes downstairs, Heath will light the trash in the garbage pail on fire and use that to force Daddy to open the door. Effie will run, through the door, up the stairs. She'll call the police.

"Too tight?" Heath asks. He tears off the piece of duct tape from the roll and smooths it gently onto Effie's bare foot.

Without shoes, she'll need something to protect her feet. She looks down at the silver sole and flexes her toes. "It's kind of hard to move my toes."

"It'll have to do." Heath sits back. "Okay. So when he comes down, I'll set the fire. If I have to hit him, I'll do that, too. When he opens the door, you run as fast as you can. Don't look back, and don't worry about me."

She does worry about him. It's been weeks since either of them had more than a few nibbles of food that hadn't been contaminated in some way with something disgusting, but they've been holding off on the food because of the drugs. They have to be clearheaded, and the only way to make sure of that is to not eat more than the few bites it takes to keep them alive. When Effie stands too quickly, hazy lights flutter in the edges of her vision. Heath can't be feeling much better.

They could starve to death before they have the chance to get out of here, but she's willing to die if that's what it takes.

Still, they've decided they have to try. Time is passing, and the longer they wait, the harder it will be. Lying in bed next to each other, holding hands, Effie listens to the in-out of Heath's breathing. The orange lights have gone out, but the overhead brights could come on at any moment. Or in a couple days. They simply never know. So they have to be ready.

She sleeps and wakes to more dark. Sleeps again. Wakes to orange lights. They move throughout their day, playing cards. Sleeping. Portioning their small bits of food. Effie tests out her duct-tape shoes. The tape is starting to irritate her skin.

She's not sure how long it is before the overhead brights finally come on, but she is instantly awake. Eyes wide. Heart pounding. Heath gives her a solemn nod. He lights the lighter, then closes the lid to extinguish the flame. He stands over the pail they've prepared.

It's a good plan. It should work. When Daddy comes through the doorway with a tray of steaming scrambled eggs, toast slathered in butter, the smells turn her stomach inside out, her mouth is watering, she's starving, but when Heath lights the flame and drops it into the pail, it blazes up. Faster than either of them thought it would. A great gust of heat and smoke. With a shout, Daddy drops the tray.

Daddy is screaming and batting at the fire, but it scatters. Burning paper lands on one of her art pads, and it begins to burn, too. Daddy punches Heath in the face, knocking him to his knees. Effie, frozen, watches as the torn shreds of wallpaper begin to smoke.

"Open the door!" Heath shouts through bloody lips. He

spits a mouthful of red and tries to get to his feet, but Daddy punches him again, and he goes down.

Daddy rips the blanket off the bed and tries to smother the garbage pail, but all he manages to do is spread another dancing flutter of burning papers. They land on the shitty cabinet, the table, some cling to the walls and wink out, but others take hold and grow. A dozen mini flame flowers sprout.

"Open the fucking door!" Heath stands and kicks over the pail, scattering the fire across the concrete.

Flames begin to lick the bed's dangling sheet. Daddy laughs, his mouth twisted and gaping. He pulls something from his pocket—a syringe, a glinting needle. He gestures toward the door.

"Go ahead," he says. "It's not locked. That door is never locked when I'm down here with you."

Effie and Heath look at each other. Never locked? All this time, never locked? She runs through the living room, over the scattered bits of glass and broken pottery set into the concrete. One stabs through the tape, but she keeps going. She bends, using her hands to pull herself up the staircase faster than she could by standing. Up, up, and at the top, the door. She slams into it, already imagining the kitchen beyond it, the phone, how she will call the police or, better yet, run screaming out into the yard to beg the neighbors for help.

She hits the door at the top of the stairs with a thud and reels back. For an interminable moment, she hangs there, hands pinwheeling, her slippery, taped foot on the edge of the stair. At the last second, the very last, she grabs the railing to keep herself from plummeting all the way down. She hits the door again. It doesn't budge.

At the bottom of the stairs, Daddy appears. "That door, now, that one is always locked. Ten bolts, and you need a key for each of them."

Effie looks at the row of holes lined up along the door. She's never seen a door with so many keyholes but only one doorknob. She hits it again. Again. Her hands hurt. She's cut herself.

Daddy comes up the stairs and grabs her by the back of the neck. He yanks her to the bottom of the steps. She skins her knees on the concrete floor as he drags her back into the bedroom, where the fires are still burning. Heath is in a small pile on the ground, not moving.

"Put them out," Daddy says. "Unless you want to burn to death down here, or suffocate from the smoke. Put them out."

It's too late, Effie thinks. The fire's out of control. All she has are her bare hands and her duct-taped feet to stamp out the flames that moments before seemed so enormous but are now puttering into ash, but she does it while Daddy watches.

"I'm going to kill that woman the next time she comes over," he says quietly. Calmly. "I hope you know I'm going to kill her, and it will be all your fault."

"No. Please... We didn't mean... It was a joke..."

"I'm going to kill her right in front of you, and you'll understand then, the consequences of your actions." Daddy nudges Heath with his toe. "He'll be out for a while. Clean up this mess."

chapter thirty-four

Effie had offered Polly a birthday party at one of the local kids' hot spots, the one with the laser tag and trampolines and video games, but Polly had declined in favor of some friends sleeping over. And she'd requested her favorite dinner, cooked by Heath. Had it felt a little like manipulation on her dearest daughter's part? Of course, but knowing that didn't make it any easier for Effie to say no.

It had been over a month since she'd seen him last. He answered her texts now, at least there was that. They were being cautious with each other, stepping as carefully as winter-softened feet on summer's first rocky beach.

What had started as two friends had turned into six for dinner, though two of the girls weren't able to spend the night and would be leaving after the movie and popcorn. Effie didn't mind. Watching Polly with her friends reminded her of how it had felt to be turning twelve. Giggling with friends, pigging out on junk food, everything stretching out bright and shiny. Adulthood impossibly far away.

Twelve had been safe.

Effie had added the leaves to the dining room table and brought out the good china her mother had given her when she bought herself something new. She'd even set the table with a pair of fancy candlesticks and long tapered candles. There was sparkling grape juice in plastic champagne glasses and a vase of flowers that Heath had brought, and a white linen tablecloth with matching lacy napkins.

Watching the girls tip their glasses to each other to pretend they were at a fancy restaurant, Effie's chest grew tight. Behind her, Heath's warmth tempted her to press herself against him, but she didn't. She did look over her shoulder, though, to find him smiling.

"You did a great job," he said.

"So did you."

Then for a moment their fingers linked and squeezed. She could've kissed him then, if things were different, but they weren't, and so Effie let go of his hand so she could move into the kitchen to help serve the food. Her mother was there, dishing up pasta and vegetables.

"How's it going out there? Look at this. What a lovely presentation." Her mother gestured at the platters Heath had brought. She didn't look at Effie when she added, "He's very talented."

Effie paused, sure she hadn't heard that correctly. "Who? What?"

"Heath." Her mother straightened. "He's talented."

"Yes," Effie said. "He is."

"And Polly clearly adores him."

Effie eyed her mom. "Uh-huh."

"Well. I'm just saying."

Effie didn't reply. She helped her mother finish dishing up the portions and took them into the dining room to serve with a flourish and a fake French accent that had Polly rolling her eyes but all the other girls guffawing. Effie gave a grandiose bow.

"Would Madame require any-zing else? More cham-pan-yuh, perhaps?"

Polly gave in to laughter. "Mom!"

"Fine, fine. We'll get out of here and let you girls have your privacy. C'mon, you," she said to Heath. "Let's go have an adult beverage."

In the den, she poured them both glasses of gin and added sweet lime and club soda. Heath sipped his with a grimace and shook his head. Effie laughed.

"I'm trying to expand your palate," she said. "Man cannot live on beer and Mad Dog forever."

Heath took another slow sip but didn't laugh. "So, cake and ice cream after dinner? Then I'll head out."

"Oh." Effie looked toward the dining room to the rising sound of girlish hilarity. Then to the kitchen, where her mother was still presumably puttering. "I thought maybe you'd stay."

"Nah. I have some plans."

"Ah." Effie drank. If he was waiting for her to ask him what plans, he'd be waiting a long damned time.

Heath didn't offer any more information. He gave her a steady, solemn look, though. That was answer enough.

She didn't care, Effie told herself as she polished off the drink but did not make another. She couldn't get shit-hammered with a house full of other people's kids. She didn't care what Heath was doing when he wasn't with her.

When the doorbell rang, they both turned in the direction of the sound. Oh no, he did *not* invite *her* here. With a scowl, Effie set her glass on the end table and went through the living room to answer the front door.

"Mitchell!"

"Hi." He grinned, holding up a pizza box and a paper sack that clinked inside, like glass. "I brought… Oh. I didn't realize you had company."

From behind her, Heath said, "I guess I'll just get going now, then."

"No. Wait." Effie turned, her cheeks flaming. "Um, Mitchell, come in."

He stepped through the doorway. Rapidly melting snow coated the shoulders of his navy blue peacoat and clung to the dark strands of his hair, falling over the top rims of his glasses. He shook it, set down the bag on the stairs to hold out his hand.

"Hi. I'm Mitchell."

"Heath."

The men shook firmly, one-two pumps of their hands before Mitchell stepped back to look at Effie. "I should've called first. Sorry."

"It's okay. We're having a birthday party for my daughter. Heath made pasta. My mother's here. It's a family thing."

"Oh," Mitchell said and seemed relieved. He gave Heath a chin tip. "Nice to meet you."

Heath stepped backward, out of the foyer. "I'll say goodbye to the Pollywog and head out. Nice to meet you, too."

Shit.

Effie held out her hands for the pizza box. "Let's take this into the kitchen."

"You sure I shouldn't leave, too? I don't want to interrupt." Mitchell followed her into the kitchen, where her mother looked up, startled, from her place over the birthday cake she'd been decorating with candles.

"Mom. This is Mitchell." Effie put the pizza box on the counter.

There must've been more awkward silences in her life, but at the moment Effie couldn't remember any. Heath came through the dining room door and grabbed his coat from his hook. Her mother looked from one man to the other, frowning, before she caught herself and gave Mitchell a wide grin.

"Mitchell. So nice to finally meet you. Effie's said so many nice things about you." As she moved forward to shake his hand, Heath opened the back door and Effie moved toward him.

She followed him onto the back porch. "Hey. Listen…"

"It's fine. He seems like a nice dude. I have to get going anyway." Heath looked past her, into the house. "You should get back inside. You're going to catch a cold."

Effie shivered and looked up at the dark sky and the snow coming down like cotton balls. Heavy and wet, it was sticking to everything, and the bite in the air promised there'd be ice later. She sighed.

"I didn't know he was coming over."

"No. Of course you didn't." Heath shrugged and shoved his hands into his pockets. He scuffed a trench in the couple of inches of snow on the walk. "Have him shovel this for you before it gets too heavy."

"Heath."

He leaned suddenly to hug her, but not long enough and clearly as though it were a duty, not desire. "Later."

She watched him get into his car and drive away, and by the time his taillights had blinked red one last time, the snow had almost filled in the furrow he'd made. It also covered her hair and shoulders, and she brushed it off before she went inside. She stamped her feet on the mat. Mitchell and her mother turned.

"Hey," he said with a slowly widening grin that lit his hazel eyes. "I was just thinking I needed to send out a Saint Bernard with a barrel."

"You'd think she'd have more sense to come in out of the weather," her mother said.

Effie smiled at them both. "You'd think so, huh?"

"They're about ready for the cake," her mother said.

Effie nodded. "So, Mitchell. Do you want to help us sing 'Happy Birthday'?"

The snow hadn't stopped. Effie's mom had insisted on heading out to get home, but the two girls who were supposed to leave ended up staying so their parents didn't have to come out in it. Now they were all settled in the den in sleeping bags with bowls of chips and cans of cola, watching episodes of whatever the currently popular teen show was.

Effie and Mitchell were in the living room. He'd helped her clean up the kitchen after dinner, moving around her kitchen with an easy efficiency that had unsettled her. By the time they'd finished, his car had vanished beneath a blanket of snow.

She'd invited him to stay.

She regretted it now, with the rise and fall of voices from the other room reminding her they were anything but alone. He'd lit a fire in her cranky fireplace. He'd suggested they play cards and offered to teach her to play gin rummy. He hadn't tried to kiss her, but what would happen later, when even the girls in the next room started to fall asleep? Was he expecting to share her bed?

"They're being really quiet," Mitchell said as he dealt another hand. "My sister and her friends were always so loud my parents had to holler at them."

"They're a good bunch of girls. We can just hope there isn't going to be any drama. So far, so good."

"Uh-oh. Are you expecting some?" Mitchell looked at the cards in his hand, fanning them out.

Effie took her own cards, sorting them. "You never know. There's been a little bit already with one of the girls, but hopefully it's resolved. But they're preteen girls. Drama happens."

"My sister used to have frenemies. Hell," Mitchell said with a thoughtful pause, "I think she still does."

"How old is she?" Effie studied her cards, trying to strategize.

"Twenty-two."

She looked up, surprised. "Oh. So she's much younger than you."

"Yeah, about fifteen years. I had an older brother who died in a boating accident when I was pretty young." Mitchell said this easily, an old pain that had diminished enough to be made casual. "My parents never quite got over it. Then when I was fifteen, lo and behold, a baby sister."

"That must've been a surprise."

Mitchell smiled faintly and shrugged. "It was a surprise to my dad, for sure."

Ah. So there was a story. Effie put down a card, picked up another. Laid down a set. "Am I getting the hang of this?"

"Yep."

They played in silence for a minute or so, until Mitchell won. Effie tossed down her cards in mock disgust, though she didn't care about winning or losing. As she leaned to gather the cards to shuffle for her turn as dealer, Mitchell leaned, as well.

He kissed her. Effie didn't pull away. Mitchell was the one to withdraw first. When she opened her eyes, he'd gotten to his feet to go to her mantel to look at the framed pictures arrayed there. He ran his finger along the wood, pausing at the large collage frame Effie had put together years ago when she and Polly had moved into this house from Heath's apartment.

"Is he Polly's father?"

"No." Effie gathered the cards and tapped them into a tight deck, then slipped them into the box. She closed it and went to stand beside Mitchell.

There was a photo of her with baby Polly, wrapped in a pink blanket. Tiny face screwed up on the verge of tears.

Heath next to them, making a face. His hair had been long then, past his shoulders, and tied at the back with a shoelace. Effie had been fat in the face and soft in her belly, the remnants of pregnancy. There was a picture of Polly in a baby swing on the playground, Heath pushing her. A photo of the three of them she'd had taken at one of those mall stores, the background a covered bridge and trees with brightly fake fall leaves. She hadn't looked at any of these pictures in a long time, but she could remember when and where each of them had been taken.

Mitchell turned. "He might as well be, though. Huh?"

"Yes. I guess so. He's been in Polly's life since before she was born." Effie looked at the picture next to the collage. That one was Polly's school picture from last year. She'd changed so much in those few months.

"When I first got here, and you said it was a family party, I thought he was your brother. Like, he had to be. And then I thought, maybe a cousin. But he's not, is he?"

"No, Mitchell. Heath's not related to me." Effie looked at him. "But he *is* family."

"Ah." Mitchell took a step or two back. "I knew I should've called first."

Effie frowned. "Yes. You should have. But you didn't, and you're here now. He's not. So if you have something you need to say to me, or ask me…"

She waited, sort of breathless, for him to say something. To ask those questions she'd avoided until now but had known would eventually come up. She would tell him everything. She would do it, let him see her.

"Is he the reason why you're hesitant about committing?"

"Yes," Effie said.

"You were together?"

Effie turned to the mantel and the photographs. "We've known each other since I was thirteen."

"Oh. First love," Mitchell said as if he knew what that meant.

Effie looked at him. "Yes."

First. Last. Only.

"But it's over?"

"Yes. That part of it, anyway," Effie said and wanted to cry because of how much it felt like the truth.

Mitchell was quiet for a moment. He looked at all the pictures again. Without looking at her, he said, "It's admirable that you can be friends for Polly's sake."

"We'll always be friends."

"Got it," Mitchell said.

From the other room came a swell of giggling that broke the mood that had, for a moment, threatened to turn somber. Effie smiled at him. She went to the mantel and pointed at the collage.

"I got pregnant at eighteen with someone I was only casually seeing. Had Polly just after I turned nineteen. I knew better but hadn't been careful. My mom flipped out. Heath was there for me. He's always been there for me." She touched the frame briefly, then turned to Mitchell. "He's my best friend. Anyone who's with me should be his friend, too."

"Fair enough." Mitchell nodded. He hesitated, then said, "Effie, I feel like you have a lot going on that you don't share. And I'm not trying to push you or whatever. All in good time, I guess."

Only minutes ago she'd imagined herself telling Mitchell everything, answering any question. Faced with the reality of it now, though, Effie found herself unable to offer anything. She'd have stripped down bare in front of him and felt less naked than telling him why Heath meant so much to her.

"Another game?" Mitchell suggested, and she gladly agreed.

They played cards, then watched a movie until the girls in the den quieted down. Effie tiptoed in to check on them. All sleeping. She moved half-full soda cans and popcorn bowls to the side and turned off the lights, leaving on the one in the hall in case any of them needed to get up in the night to use the bathroom.

Back in the living room, she found Mitchell had straightened up the sofa pillows and was looking over the photographs on her walls, most of them Polly but a few of Heath there, too. He turned when she came in. He gestured toward the window.

"It looks like the snow's stopped. A plow went by, and a salt truck. I bet the roads are okay now. If you wanted me to leave."

Effie paused before answering while she thought about what she wanted. "Do you want to go?"

"If it's going to be weird in the morning," he said, "I probably should."

She thought about Polly having to face a stranger over the breakfast table while her overtired and possibly bitchy friends giggled and whispered. "Yeah. That's probably best. I don't want you to go if it's not going to be safe, though."

"I have four-wheel drive. I'll be okay."

They both stood without moving until Effie took the two steps toward him and Mitchell met her halfway. She kissed him. Slowly at first. Then harder when his mouth opened and his arms went around her.

"You really shouldn't go out in this weather," Effie said.

Mitchell studied her quietly for a moment. "I can take the couch."

"You don't have to…" Effie paused at the look on his face. "I mean, I have a guest room."

Mitchell kissed her again, then hugged her close. He said against her cheek, "It's not that I don't want you."

Effie laughed and nuzzled against his neck for a second, thinking of kissing him again. Or nudging her knee between his thighs and sliding her hands down his sides to cup his ass. She could seduce him. She'd already done it once, right? But Polly was here, along with a bunch of other people's kids, and Effie had long made a point about not fucking strangers with her child in the vicinity.

"God, I really do want you," Mitchell said before Effie could answer him. "But with the kids all here…"

"We don't have to have sex, Mitchell. You can sleep in the guest room or the couch, your choice. But the guest room is way more comfortable."

Down the hall, she showed him the spare room and gave him fresh towels. A toothbrush from her supply of extras. A pair of sweatpants that were too big for her.

He kissed her in the doorway when she turned to leave, and Effie let it linger until Mitchell had backed her up against the wall and her breath caught in her throat. She closed her eyes, feeling his hands. His mouth. His tongue. And yeah, there it was, the press of heat and hardness on her belly.

She opened her eyes. "Good night, Mitchell."

"Yeah," he said after a second, his voice raspy rough. "Good night."

He left a note on her pillow in the morning, saying he'd snuck out before any of the girls could wake. He would call her soon. He'd put the borrowed sweatpants and the used linens in the laundry room. Mitchell's handwriting was painfully neat and straight, nary a stray loop or slant. It was sweet, his intentions. His consideration.

How long, Effie thought with a shudder, had he stood over her, watching her sleep?

chapter thirty-five

The house is big and quiet and, damn, she'll admit it, lonely. Effie had insisted on having her own bedroom in the apartment, but it had been a pretense. She'd slept in Heath's double bed or he in hers every night, waking in a tangle of arms and legs, often with Polly tucked up somewhere between them. In this house that her father's death allowed her to buy, Effie has a king-size bed. She'd thought stretching out, waking up alone without an elbow in her side or stinking morning breath gusting over her face would be luxurious.

All she feels is alone. She didn't sleep well, either. Every small noise and creak had left her wide-eyed and straining in the darkness, trying to figure out the source of the sound.

The worst had been the dreams. Back in the basement, the overhead scratch of Daddy's footsteps, the orange light and then the glare. The sharp pieces of glass and ceramic stuck into the concrete floor. The stink. The fuzzy, blurry feeling in her head that had taken so long to get rid of.

Effie has never been so happy to see the sun rise. She's up and showered and making breakfast when Polly's tousled blond head peeks around the kitchen doorway. The little girl carefully navigates the four steps down into the kitchen from the hall, biting her lip as she rubs her eyes and looks around the kitchen.

"Where's Heath?"

Effie turns from the pan where she's making scrambled eggs. "Pollywog, Mommy and Heath talked to you about this. About how you and I were going to live in this house, and Heath was going to live in his house. But you'll still see him all the time."

Polly's lip quivers, but she nods and doesn't cry. She eats her breakfast more quietly than usual, though, and later in the afternoon she voluntarily takes a nap, something she hasn't done in about two years. Effie pauses outside the door to listen to the soft huffing of her daughter's breathing, and she gives in to tears she stifles with both hands clapped over her mouth.

She and Heath have no formal custody agreement. He's not Polly's father. He and Effie weren't married. Still, single parenthood has turned out to be harder than Effie ever imagined, and when Heath offers to take Polly for a weekend visit to give Effie time to work on her painting, she takes him up on it so she can have some time to herself. Polly looks so small next to Heath's lanky, towering six-foot-five frame that Effie has to turn so she doesn't watch them walk away.

She spends Friday night and Saturday painting, working on finishing enough stock so she can open her Craftsy store with enough inventory to keep her from feeling stressed out. Optimistically, Effie hopes to have a steady stream of orders, enough so she doesn't have to go back to working part-time jobs to support herself and Polly. It's not vanity. She knows there are collectors who'll be willing to buy her paintings. Maybe not for as much as that first one sold for, the one she actually drew in the basement, but these others will go. She feels it.

By Saturday night, Effie's hands are cramping and her head spins from the scent of the solution she uses to clean her brushes. She has paint grimed into every surface of her skin. She's tired and thirsty and hungry and the paintings have stirred up an array of emotions she knows are probably good for the art but are hell on her sanity. If she were with Heath, she would take him to bed and slap his face and make him pull her hair while he fucked her. He would mutter her name in that pleading tone and she would come and come and come, and forget everything but that pleasure. She'd be able to get lost, at least for a little while.

She can't call him. Not for sex. They've only barely begun talking again after the fight about her moving out.

Effie has slept with two men in her life. Heath, her first. Bill, her second. Tonight, she thinks, she would like to find a third.

It's both easier and more difficult than she expects. For one thing, she celebrated her twenty-first birthday nursing a toddler with an ear infection. Effie hasn't spent a lot of time hanging out in bars, especially not alone. For another, she's not very good at flirting. It's like a complicated dance with a lot of fancy steps, and she's stuck doing the back-and-forth shuffle.

The easy part is finding a guy who offers to buy her drinks. The hard part is getting him to offer to take her home. Effie took a cab to the bar, a local divey sort of place, for the sole purpose of not having to worry about her car. But after three gin-and-tonics and a round of darts, her "beau" is showing no signs of wanting to get frisky.

Finally, when the bartender is announcing last call, Effie decides to go for it. Jason, his name is, looks surprised when she asks him for a ride home, but then a sly sort of grin tips his mouth. In his car, when he asks her where to go, she gives him that same sort of grin.

The sex is fumbling but adequate. Her orgasm comes at her own hand while he fucks her from behind, but she does manage one. After, Jason is gracious and offers the use of his shower.

"You can't stay, though. I mean, I'll give you cab fare. It's pretty late." He runs a hand over his hair. His smile this time is guilty. "I...um... Look, I should've told you before. I have a girlfriend."

Effie doesn't need his cab fare and she doesn't want to sleep over, and she really doesn't want to see him again. She frowns at his admission, though. "Oh."

"She's out of town. We're kind of on a break."

"For the weekend?" Effie asks as she slips into her panties and jeans and finds her bra.

Jason coughs uncomfortably. Effie has no desire to make this easier for him. She's kind of pissed off, to be honest, if only because of all the men in the bar tonight, Jason had been the first to buy her a drink and she might've found someone else if she hadn't been so damned eager to just get this out of her system.

"Listen, don't worry about it. It's cool. Thanks for the ride," Effie says.

"You want to give me your number?"

She glances at him over her shoulder from the doorway. "No."

"Oh," Jason says. "Okay."

She thinks about him all the way home, and in the shower when she scrubs away the scent of sex, and later in bed when she stares up at the ceiling and tries to figure out how she feels about what she did. When the morning comes, though, Effie doesn't think much about Jason again. There will be many, many other men.

Sunday afternoon, she goes to the apartment that still feels like home no matter how much she tries not to let it. She knocks on the door like a salesman. At the sight of Heath, a dish towel slung over his shoulder and a smudge of flour on his cheek, a surge of love sweeps over her in a rush so strong she's sure, for a moment, that it's going to send her to her knees.

Together, they finish baking the sugar cookies Heath and Polly had been baking. He wraps a platter of them with plastic and Polly proudly carries it. Heath and Effie both watch her, waiting for her to stumble and drop them, but she makes it all the way through the front door without so much as a crumb being spilled.

"You know," he says to Effie as they very specifically don't hug in the doorway, "you and Polly can always come back."

For a moment, she almost says yes, but the truth is, if Effie wants all of them to keep moving forward, looking back is not the way to do it. She kisses him instead of speaking, a brief brush of her lips on his cheek. It's the last time she will kiss him for a very long time.

"I'm really doing it. A whole show. In the spring. So, yeah, I need to work on a lot of things. I'm going to pull out some older pieces," Effie told Heath. "See if anything's worth showing."

"I'm sure they're all worth showing." Heath had not taken off his coat. Effie noticed but pretended she didn't. "Wog! Let's go, we're going to be late for the movie!"

"Thanks for taking her," Effie said.

Heath shrugged. "You know I'm happy to, anytime. I've missed taking her on the weekends. It's been a long time. I'll have her back on Sunday before I have to head into work for an event."

"The show will be a lot of work." Effie paced, already thinking ahead to the hours she'd have to herself over the next couple of days. How much she might be able to get done. Heath was right, it had been a long time since he'd had Polly for the entire weekend. Years, probably. "I've been making sketches. I have some ideas. But I won't know until I start if I can really pull any of it off."

"Effie."

She stopped to face him. Heath's smile, so familiar, so beloved, urged her own in response. "Heath."

"You're amazing, and you're going to make this happen. Wog! C'mon! I told Lisa we'd pick her up on the way!"

Effie had been about to hug him for his support, but at his words, she kept herself still. Heath caught her look. They both stared.

"It's not serious," he said finally.

"Does she know that?"

He shrugged. "We haven't talked about it. She's fun. You'd like her, Effie."

"I'm sure I would." Effie's chin went up, but only a little. She forced a smile. "You should bring her around. Maybe we could all have dinner or something."

"Sure. Me, you, Lisa, Polly. Mitchell," Heath added lightly. "It would be awesome. Supercool. A big old family get-together. Invite your mom, too, she'll have a great time."

Effie laughed. "Your sarcasm is showing, love."

Heath flinched. She couldn't miss it, and it killed her. Again she thought of hugging him, and again she kept herself from it.

"We are a family," Effie said. "We'll always be."

Heath nodded and called again for Polly, who hollered back that she'd be there in a minute. He cut his gaze from Effie's. "You know what, Effie, I think I need to take a break from you for a while."

"Again?" was all she managed to say.

"Yeah. Only this time, I mean it. I'll still be here for Polly, of course. Always. But she's old enough now that she and I can make any arrangements we have to. I don't want you to call me anymore, or text me, unless it's about her." Heath's voice had gone low but smooth, as though he'd rehearsed what he was saying.

The thought of it, that he might've practiced this speech, slaughtered her into speechlessness. When Polly bounced into the kitchen with her backpack bulging and a wide grin, Effie managed to steer her toward the door with hugs and kisses and muttered words that sounded as if they made sense. At least enough that Polly didn't even give her a curious glance as Heath told her to wait in the car. When she'd gone, he turned to Effie.

"I want you to be happy, and if it's with that guy, then you should go for it. And you can't do that if I'm still hanging around, messing it up," Heath said.

Effie shook her head, still silent.

Heath coughed into his fist, then straightened and looked at her, dead on. No more flinching. No more evasion. "You were right. We can't move forward if we're both hanging on to the past. We both got out of a really bad situation, and all we do is remind each other of it. We're bad for each other. You're right about that, too."

No.

No.

We're not bad for each other.

She shook her head again and put a hand on the back of a kitchen chair. Locked her knees so she didn't stumble, though she wasn't even moving. Every word was a stab in her heart, a slice in her soul, but there was nothing she could say to stop him, because she'd been the one to put this in motion, and now she had to live with what she had begun.

"I want you to be happy, Effie. I do. But…I guess I'm a

shit-heel son of a bitch, because I just can't bear to watch it. It makes me want to fucking die. Do you understand?"

"Yes," she said through numbed lips. "Yes. I understand."

"I'll bring Polly home on Sunday."

Effie nodded, and they stared at each other in agonized silence until the sound of Heath's car horn bleating turned him toward the door. Surely he would say something else, or hug her, or kiss her, even on the cheek. He had to, she thought, even after the door closed behind him without another word or even one more look.

He had to, but he didn't.

chapter thirty-six

Mommies and Margaritas. That was Dee's clever name for the moms' group. She'd sent Effie one of those funny e-cards with a line drawing of a Victorian woman holding up a glass and some joke text about how the only way to get through the day was by being drunk. Effie didn't find jokes like that to be particularly funny. Yet here she was with a glass serving dish of chili cheese dip she'd made herself and a bag of tortilla chips, and why? Because it was that or sit alone in an empty house weeping into her glass of wine and making bad life choices, and she'd done too much of that lately.

"Effie! Great, you came." Dee looked surprised but pleased, holding the door open wide for Effie to enter. "Everyone's in the den. You can put the food in the kitchen. Yum, that looks delish."

Effie followed her into the spacious, immaculate kitchen and set the glass dish on the waiting hot pad. Dee gave her a bowl for the chips, and Effie took her time filling it. She could see the sunken den from where she was. Lots of ladies with plastic margarita glasses filled with frosty green liquid. Low music played and the propane fireplace crackled. This was it, time to make some friends.

It was easier than she expected to smile as she was introduced to Dee's friends. She knew a number of the mothers from the years of volunteering for Polly's classroom when she was younger. She'd done flash cards with a bunch of their kids. Chaperoned more than a few field trips. She'd held the hair of Amy Kendig's daughter once when the bus ride had made her sick.

"Hey," Effie said with a nod at Amy, who lifted her glass in reply.

Dee clapped her hands twice. "Everyone, this is Effie Linton. Polly's mom. I finally convinced her to join us."

The greetings were effusive and seemed sincere. Effie accepted a margarita. She'd walked over here, just two blocks, and she suspected that after a couple of drinks the walk home would be a lot warmer than the one over had been. She took a seat on the couch next to a woman she didn't recognize. Becky turned out to be Amy's sister-in-law. She sold makeup, and since Effie had an unapologetic fetish for liquid eyeliner, they spent twenty minutes talking about how to do the perfect cat's eye line.

"I'll drop off some samples," Becky offered and shook her head with a grin when Effie protested. "Hey, first taste is free. After that, I hope you'll buy more."

Amy brought over the pitcher of margaritas to refill their glasses. "I can't even show my husband how much I spend with Becky every month. He'd kill me!"

"But my husband loves you for it, especially when he's ordering new parts for his Jeep." Becky laughed.

"I don't have a husband," Effie said, not meaning to be a downer, but it was the truth. At the sight of the other ladies' faces, she realized, a little too late, that she was on her way to being drunk.

"I have an *ex*-husband," Dee piped up, and the moment passed.

Effie had a third margarita, because that was the problem

with margaritas. They went down so smooth that before you knew it you were dancing on a tabletop wearing a lamp shade… or worse, exchanging Crock-Pot recipes as if you knew what the fuck you were talking about with a woman wearing a sweatshirt with a pair of Christmas kittens on it. Effie didn't even own a Crock-Pot, though the way Cissy was evangelizing about it made her want to go out right now and buy three of them, just so she could make all the things. All of them.

"I fucking love tequila." Effie lifted her glass to tap it against Cissy's.

Cissy blinked. "Oh. Um…"

Shit. She shouldn't have let the f-bomb drop. This crowd probably said *goshdarnit* or *shucks*. This crowd, Effie thought with a look around the room, probably didn't like blow jobs. And that was just too fucking sad.

Effie drained her glass and wisely looked for a sink to put it in. She wanted another, of course. You always wanted another one. But she wasn't going to have one. Nope. She was going to restrain herself from making that mistake. At least that was the plan before Dee brought over the pitcher again, swirling the dregs of melted margarita in the bottom.

"Top you off?" she said to Effie. "I'm not sure I should make another pitcher. It might go to waste."

"No more for me," Cissy said.

Effie held out her glass. "Sure. I'll take the last bit."

Cissy eased away and Dee set the now-empty pitcher on the kitchen island. She pulled the decimated platter of veggies and dip toward her and plucked out a carrot stick. She dipped it directly into the bowl of dip, an action that made Effie shudder. She hadn't eaten anything here, not even the dip she'd made herself. The drinking had gotten in the way, and by the time she thought to put something other than booze in her stomach, the chili dip had already been besmirched by chip crumbs and double dippers. Sober Effie would have forced herself to eat some, but she'd passed sober two hours ago.

"I'm really glad you came." Dee scrunched another carrot and held out the platter to Effie.

"No, thanks." Effie sipped her drink. "Yeah, it's fun, thanks for inviting me."

Dee looked past Effie into the den. A lot of the women had left half an hour or so ago, and when Effie glanced back to see what Dee was looking at, she saw a couple more putting on their coats. She laughed.

"Shit, I'm going to close this party down." She drained the last of the drink, waiting for the brain freeze, but it had melted enough that she escaped that torture.

"Where's Polly?"

"She's with Heath." Effie paused, trying to gauge Dee's reaction. "Who is not my brother. Or her father."

Dee laughed, but uncomfortably, with another glance over Effie's shoulder. "I know that. I told them all that, too."

"It's okay." Effie shrugged. She'd been drunker than this, but not for a long time. She put a hand on the kitchen island to make sure she wasn't weaving. The floor beneath her felt a little tilted. Was she slurring?

From behind her, a waft of perfume announced Becky's presence. The other woman reached past Dee to also grab a couple carrot sticks, slathering them with dip. Effie kept her lip from curling, but barely.

"I feel like I can pretend I'm eating healthy," Becky explained with a longing look at the plate of cookies next to the vegetable tray. "But let's face it, I'm about to murder those cookies. Wish I had your willpower, Effie."

Effie laughed. "Trust me, there are plenty of things I can't manage to resist."

Several of the other women came through the kitchen,

saying their goodbyes, and Dee moved off with them to walk them to the front door. Becky took a piece of celery and crunched it with a sigh. Effie tried to think of something clever to say, but all she could manage was a smile.

Dee came back. "That's almost everyone. Beck, is Gene coming to get you?"

"Yeah. I called him. He's on the way."

That was Effie's cue to leave. "I'll get going, too."

"You didn't drive, did you?" Becky asked.

Effie laughed. "No, no. I walked. It's only a couple blocks."

"We can give you a ride home, if you want."

"No, that's okay. I like to walk." Effie looked around, trying to remember where she left her coat. Dee had taken it from her when she came in, she remembered that much.

Becky snagged another carrot stick but didn't eat it. "You're not...scared?"

The circle of Effie's vision narrowed, like the closing of a camera aperture. Becky's face swam for a second. "Why would I be scared?"

"After what happened," Becky said. "I think I'd be afraid to walk by myself anywhere."

Effie let go of the kitchen island, no longer afraid of weaving. Her back felt as stiff and straight as if someone had replaced her spine with an iron rod. "It was a long time ago. If I was still too afraid to go by myself anywhere, I'd have a helluva time, wouldn't I?"

"At night," Becky amended. "In the dark, I guess."

"He took me at three o'clock in the afternoon," Effie said.

Dee coughed uncomfortably. "Hey, Effie, let me get your coat."

"Sorry." Becky looked embarrassed. "Liquor loosens the tongue. I didn't mean to offend you."

"I'm not offended. Better to ask me to my face than whisper

behind my back." Effie ran her tongue along the inside of her teeth, hating that leftover booze flavor. "Can I get a drink of water before I go?"

"Sure, of course." Dee bustled to the cabinet to get her a glass, filling it from the fridge's filtered water spout. She handed it to Effie with a glance at Becky, who'd stopped pretending to be healthy and was now eating a cookie.

Effie drank the cool, sweet water, letting it fill in all the leftover space in her stomach. "If there's something you want to know, Becky, you should ask me now. I'm fucked up on tequila."

Becky gave a small, uncertain laugh. "No, I shouldn't have said anything. It's not any of my business."

"Here's the thing." Effie went to the fridge to help herself to another glass of water. "Nobody asks anymore. In the beginning, when I first came back, it was all anyone could seem to talk about. But it's been fifteen years, you know that? Most people don't even remember it happened."

"But you do," Dee said quietly.

"Me and a bunch of freaks who talk about me on some sicko forums," Effie said flatly. "And women who go to moms' groups."

The silence would've been way more awkward if she hadn't had so much to drink, but all it did now was make her laugh. Becky bit her lower lip, looking away. Dee frowned.

"I was thirteen. I was coming home from my art class. He grabbed me and took me into his van. He hit me on the head and jabbed me with a needle, and I woke up in a basement lit only by these weird fucking orange lights. I should've run away from him, you know? And I tried. But my mom had made me wear these new shoes—" Effie kicked out a foot to demonstrate "—and I had blisters. And he was fast. Nobody even saw him take me, at least that's what the story was. I mean, I was missing for three years. He kept me in a house not twenty minutes away from my own. If someone had seen him take me, don't you think they'd have said something?"

Becky winced. "That's horrible."

"Yeah." Effie nodded and drank half the glass of water, then added ice. She looked at both women. "They did a documentary on it. Part of one, anyway. They interviewed a whole bunch of people about him. They interviewed his ex-wife. His kids. The neighbors who called the police, finally."

"Oh, my God! Oh, my God, what the hell? Where's Stan? Who are you? What the hell?"

The woman's words echo in the basement, hurting Effie's ears. It's been days without food. A week since the last time Daddy came into the basement. They're down to the last scant cups of water in the jug. They've been huddling together for warmth. Heath hasn't spoken for hours, though the rasp of his breathing tells Effie that at least he's still alive. The woman's voice echoes around them again, and then there's some muffled shouting. The thud of feet on the stairs.

A cool breeze.

Then there's light, a faint square in the blackness. The door.

The door is…open.

"But I didn't talk to them about it," Effie continued. "They offered me money, but I didn't need money. I had my dad's life insurance. I always wondered if my dad knew he was going to die young. If that's why he paid for that policy for me. I never asked my mother how long he'd had it."

Becky stared, but Dee drew her own glass of water to gulp before saying, "They talked to my mom. She didn't make it into the final cut of the film, but I remember them interviewing her in the kitchen."

Effie searched for some affront, some offense, but couldn't find any. "Most of it they got wrong, anyway. The forums do, too, all the time, because of it. The guys who made the documentary thought they had all the facts, but they didn't. So those freaks who post online about it, about my art, about everything…they think they understand the significance of it all, but really they're going by that movie. My paintings," she added when Becky looked confused. "They have hidden designs. People collect them because they're part of this group that idealizes victims of crimes. Or I guess the criminals. I don't know. I stopped looking at that forum a long time ago. It's disgusting."

"I'm sorry," Dee said.

Becky coughed. "Yeah, shit, Effie. Me, too. I didn't know."

"It's like it's a big secret." Effie couldn't stand the thought of drinking any more water, so she dumped it in the sink and set the glass carefully, carefully, on the counter. It would've been easy to shatter the glass with her tequila-infused fingers. She looked at both of them. "Only it's not, really."

Becky opened her mouth as though to say more, and Effie waited for it. Fuck, she wanted it. She wanted to talk about this, finally, to get it all right out there so they could gossip about it if they wanted to, or maybe fucking forget it the way she wished she could. Because Mommies and Margaritas might be the lamest fucking name for a group of friends Effie had ever heard, but fuck all if she didn't want to be invited back. She wanted friends. She wanted to giggle over movie stars and eat tortilla chips and she wanted, goddammit, to bitch about a husband who didn't like it when she spent too much money on eyeliner.

So she waited for Becky to ask a question, something, anything, so that Effie could tell her whatever it was she wanted to know. Instead, Becky's phone buzzed from her pocket. With an apologetic look, she took it out.

"Gene's in the driveway," Becky said. "Are you sure we can't give you a ride? It's late. And it's cold."

Effie uncurled fingers she hadn't noticed she was clenching. She nodded. Took a deep breath. Gave both Dee and Becky a smile that made her face ache but that must've passed as genuine because neither of them seemed to mind.

"Thanks. I really don't mind walking. It's good for me. And it's only a couple blocks. Fully lighted streets," she added, then tacked on a small lie. "I have pepper spray."

Becky looked doubtful. "If you're sure…"

"I'm positive." Effie took another deep breath. "I'm good."

With Becky gone, Dee made a halfhearted effort at putting some food away while Effie got her coat from the dining room table, where she remembered Dee had put it. Dee stopped, though, after putting away the platter of veggies in the fridge. She gave Effie a look.

"I'm sorry about Becky."

"No. It's fine. I told you, I'd rather have you ask me than talk about it behind my back. It's not like I'm ashamed of anything," Effie said. "It's shit that happened to me, you know, when I couldn't help it. We all have shit, Dee. Mine just made me famous in the papers for half a second fifteen years ago."

Dee gave her a tentative smile. "If you ever want to talk about it, I'll listen. If you don't, that's fine, too. I'm really sorry about everything, that's all."

"I'm glad I came tonight." It would take hours for the drinks to fully wear off, and Effie was already regretting how she was going to feel in the morning, but she meant it.

"Text me when you get home, okay?" Dee looked worried. "Are you sure I can't have Jon give you a ride? He'll be here in about an hour from work. I don't mind hanging out with you until he gets here. I won't be able to sleep until he does."

"Jon," Effie said. "No way!"

Dee looked pleased. "Yeah. It's going really well. I kind of owe it to you, Effie. I sent him that message, and then the next thing you know, we were seeing each other every day. It's like no time at all passed, yet everything's different."

"You're not kids anymore," Effie said.

"But he makes me feel sixteen," Polly admitted in a whisper. "All lit up and tingly every time I see him."

"Happy for you." Was a hug appropriate? Damned if Effie knew, but fuck it. She embraced Dee and squeezed her until they both laughed and Effie stepped back.

"You sure he can't give you a ride home? It's really cold out."

"Nah. Really. I'm good." At the front door, she paused. "Dee, I'm sorry I was a bitch to you about Meredith. And everything."

"I deserved it." Dee smiled. "Anyway, that's over and done with. We'll get together again soon, okay?"

Effie nodded. "Sure. That sounds great."

On the sidewalk, she looked back to Dee's front door, but it was closed, and who could blame her? The night had turned frigid, so cold Effie's breath stung her nostrils and she dug in her pockets for her mittens. For a second, she regretted not taking a ride, but then she thought about having to sit in a moving vehicle and gulp-swallowed a slight burn rise of bile in her throat.

She should have turned right to head for home. Down two streets, then across one and over a block or so. She'd be home and in her bed in fifteen minutes, walking fast so she stayed warm.

Instead, she turned left.

Four blocks down. One block over. Another half a street because of the alley. And there it was. Daddy's house. Unkempt yard, too-long grass glistening with frost. The driveway, cracked and never patched. And in the front window, something she'd never seen in all the years she'd driven past.

A light.

chapter thirty-seven

"You lied." Effie had shouted this several times already until Bill had clamped his hand over her mouth. She could still taste his palm. She had not bitten him, although she wanted to. Now she lowered her voice because he would not hesitate to put her on the ground if he thought she would wake the neighbors.

"I didn't lie to you, Effie. Jesus." Bill wore only a pair of low-hanging pajama pants. His hair stuck up all over. He'd been asleep when she pounded on his door. Of course he had been, at eight in the morning when she'd sobered up enough to drive herself over there and wake him.

Effie had not slept. She'd spent a couple wretched hours wishing she could make herself sick to get rid of the roiling in her guts, then another few hours sipping hot tea and nibbling on saltines. By the time the sun rose, she'd managed to fend off the worst of the hangover, though her head still throbbed and her eyes felt as if she'd ground glass with them.

"You told me," she said, "you would let me know if he got out. Fuck, Bill. He's out. Someone's in that house. It's him. I know it is."

"I could make some calls." Bill yawned and scrubbed at

his face, then padded to the counter to pour a mug of coffee before the pot had fully filled. Spatters hissed and bubbled on the hot plate before he put the carafe back without asking her if she wanted some. He looked at her over his shoulder. "Find out for sure. But, shit, Effie. Does it matter now?"

"How can you ask me that?"

Bill looked chastened. "All I mean is, he's an old man now. He did his time…"

"He didn't. He didn't do his time," Effie said. "He wasn't supposed to get out, ever, and there he is, back in that fucking house."

"Anyone could be in that house, Effie." Bill reached for her, but she danced out of his grip. "C'mon. Don't be like that."

"Any time a man doesn't like the way a woman acts, that's what he says. 'Don't be like that.' Like I don't have a right to feel this way? I don't have the right to be upset? Fuck you, Bill."

"Effie," he said warningly.

But she knew him. Oh, how she did. Effie got right up in his face, pushing on her tiptoes to do it, their mouths bare inches apart when she spat the words.

"Fuck. You."

Then his hand was in her hair, yanking her head back, and she cried out but didn't struggle. She waited for him to kiss her, or maybe to turn her around and bend her over the table. Effie tensed, never looking away from him even as her eyes burned with tears of pain she refused to shed.

Abruptly, Bill let her go. She stumbled back. His mouth twisted and he turned from her, wiping it with his hand. His shoulders slouched.

"It's too fucking early for this, Effie. Go home."

She straightened. She smoothed her hair over her shoulders. "Fine."

"Don't be like… Shit. Effie." Bill faced her. He put his hands on her shoulders, fingers digging in a little to keep her still when she moved to pull away. "I'm sorry. I didn't know, I promise you. This guy, he's a blip, he's a nothing. Yeah, those soccer moms with their sexual predator websites might've known about it, but trust me, on the greater scale, Stan Andrews is a nobody."

"Not to me," Effie said.

Bill pulled her against him, and she let him, though she didn't soften into his embrace. This time he caressed her hair instead of yanking it. Effie preferred the pain to his feeble attempt at comfort.

"It's all going to be okay," Bill said.

Effie closed her eyes and breathed in the scent of his skin. She turned her face a little, let her mouth press his bare chest, but she didn't kiss him. After a minute, his hand moved from the back of her head to the small of her back, and she took that moment to step away.

Clear-eyed, she gave him a neutral smile. "Thanks."

Bill looked as if he was going to say something, but instead he gave a low, long sigh and nodded. "You know I wouldn't let anything happen to you."

As if he could prevent the world from turning. Could she be angry with him for breaking a promise she knew was impossible to keep? Irrationally, yes, but she wouldn't show it. She gave him another faint smile and, at the front door, stopped to blow him a kiss.

"Shit," Bill said miserably. "Effie."

She answered him with the closing of the door behind her.

There it was. Effie had spilled all of it. The entire story of her abduction, the years in the basement, the reason for the clocks in her paintings. The paintings themselves. Her love for Heath, and the reasons for that, too.

Mitchell had listened, frowning at first, then sitting back with a look of stunned disgust he made no attempt at hiding. When she finished and took a long, deep breath, Mitchell didn't say anything. Effie gulped ice water, glad she'd asked him to meet her here in a public place where she could hope to count on his good manners not to make a scene.

She hadn't thought he would. Stupidly, Effie had thought good-guy Mitchell would tell her how understanding he was of her problems because he had a sister who was fucked up, because his brother had died, because... Just because. Now, looking at his curled lip, Effie could clearly see how wrong she'd been.

In a way, it was a relief.

Mitchell was who he was, as Effie was who *she* was, and here they were. He'd fucked her once, he'd slept in her house and eaten off her plates and used her toothpaste, and all she could think of was that even though she'd spent almost an hour spilling her guts to him, how much there was still to learn about her that Mitchell did not know.

How weary she was of trying to hide it.

How little she wanted to explain any of it.

"If you want to know more details, you can look them up on the internet," she said finally. "They're not hard to find."

"I think I've heard enough," Mitchell said. "Shit. And you say he's out now?"

Effie nodded. "Yes."

"Living in the same house? The one where he kept you guys?"

"Yes," she repeated.

"Shit," Mitchell repeated under his breath. "That is really, really messed up."

"He made parole. His children had kept the house. I looked it up online." Maybe she should reach for his hand, Effie thought, but she didn't move. "I went past the house. I saw a light. He's living there."

"You went past the house?" Mitchell frowned. "That's a little creepy. Damn, Effie, it's kind of creepy that you live so close to it to begin with."

"I've lived close to it my entire life," she said in a low voice. "I bought my house because it was close to my mom."

She could tell her explanation hadn't made it sound less weird to him.

"I didn't knock on his door," Effie said. "I just walked past it."

He studied her. "Maybe you should."

"That's... No." Effie shook her head. "Wow. No."

"You obviously have a lot of unresolved issues about all of this stuff." Mitchell rubbed at the back of his neck and gave Effie a narrow-eyed glance she couldn't read. "You should've told me this before."

Effie snorted softly. "Sure, riiiiight. That's how to start off a date. Tell me, Mitchell, what would you have done if I'd laid it all out for you the first time we went out? If I'd introduced myself, shook your hand, ordered dinner and then regaled you with the reasons why I can't bring myself to eat like a normal person, what would you have done?"

"I wouldn't have asked you out again," Mitchell told her flatly and crossed his arms.

Effie sat back in the diner booth. "I see. Because I have some fucked-up stuff in my past? It makes me too damaged."

"No. Because I was up front with you, Effie. I was looking for something long-term. You told me that you were, too. And I thought you were maybe playing a bit of a game with me, but I figured, give it time. See what happens. There are a lot of people on that site, and it's still really hard to find someone you connect with. I thought maybe we did. Or could."

She furrowed her brow. "I *was* looking for something serious. I am. I know it took me a while to open up to you, Mitchell, but it's because I want to make something of this. I…like you."

Mitchell shook his head. "Like."

"Yes. I like you," Effie said firmly. "Isn't that a good place to start?"

"It would've been, before."

"And not now?" Her fingers curled into fists below the edge of the table, and she put them in her lap.

"I don't know, Effie. It's a lot to deal with. And Heath. You're in love with him. You didn't have to tell me," Mitchell cut her off when she tried to reply. "I could see it all over both of you that day I came to the house. Maybe you should've told me all of this that night."

Effie nodded. "Yes. Maybe I should have. But I didn't lie to you. I told you it was over between me and Heath, in that way. And it is."

Mitchell's laugh barked out of him. Snide. He shook his head again. "I'm not that stupid. You told me that night he was in your life and always would be."

"For Polly's sake," Effie began but stopped at the look on his face. "Mitchell…"

He put up both his hands and pushed the air as though he wanted to push her away. "No. It's fine. I get it. You love who you love. There's no way to get around it. I just…well, I'm not the guy who's going to take second place for the rest of your life, that's all. And it's pretty clear that second place is all I'd ever be. Unless you can tell me you'll never see him again."

It was actually a promise that seemed more likely to be possible than it ever had, but the fact that Mitchell had asked her to make it only set Effie's jaw. "I won't promise that. He's important to my kid, and to me."

"So, if I asked you to choose between me and him, you'd choose him?"

"It's not a choice I should have to make," Effie said stiffly. "You and I, we're barely starting out."

"No, Effie. You and I, we're over." Mitchell sighed. "I'm sorry. But I really want to find someone I can trust."

That stung, and she recoiled. "Okay."

Mitchell stood, picking up the check. "I'll get this."

"You don't have to."

"Yes, I do. And listen, Effie…" Mitchell paused. Effie looked at him. He sighed, and his expression softened. "You're a great girl. Just not the right girl."

"Wow. Thanks."

He sighed again. "I'm not the right guy for you, either. I'm sorry."

Effie pulled her coffee mug closer. She hadn't taken even a sip. It was cold now. She stared steadily up at Mitchell, then smiled. "No. Don't be. You're right. You were up front from the start about what you were looking for, and I really thought I could make it work. I wanted to. I hope you believe me."

"I do." Mitchell looked thoughtful. "You know what, I do. And I hope you find a way to make it work with him, Effie."

She didn't stand. It would be too awful to fend off a hug or, God forbid, a farewell kiss. He was trying to be nice, but he had no idea what he was saying. A way for her and Heath to make it work? It was called a miracle. "Thanks."

"Good luck."

"Thanks," she said again and half turned, dismissing him.

"More coffee, hon?" the waitress asked, looking expectant but also a little anxious, as though she wanted Effie up and out of there so she could fill the spot with other paying customers.

Effie shook her head and slid out of the booth. "No. Thanks."

"You didn't eat very much. You want a box?"

Effie didn't even bother to look at the uneaten meal. "No. You can throw it away."

She'd grown very good at that, Effie thought as she left the diner. Throwing things away. It seemed it was all she was able to do.

chapter thirty-eight

Effie had dressed as carefully for this moment as she ever had for any date. A dozen outfits pulled from her closet and tossed aside. Nothing seemed right. Too dressy. Too casual. She'd settled on a pair of skinny jeans tucked into knee-high boots. A tank top and a cardigan over it. A scarf. Her leather jacket.

A hundred times she'd driven past this house and never stopped, but she stopped today. She didn't park in the driveway, but along the street. She sat there for twenty minutes, waiting for someone to rap on the window and demand to know what she was doing there, but nobody even passed by on the sidewalk. She stared straight ahead, hands on the wheel, until she couldn't stand it any longer. Then she got out. She went to the front door.

She knocked, hard. Three times. Then again when nobody answered.

She didn't have a story ready, in case it wasn't him. She hadn't thought she'd need one until right this second when she could hear someone on the other side, shuffling. A faint voice, muttering, "Hold on. I'm coming."

The door opened, and there he was. He did not look the same. He'd shrunk throughout the years. Shoulders hunched.

His dark hair had gone gray and thin, brushed over a bald spot.
His skin sagged, circles like bruises beneath his eyes. He'd become an old, old man, and clearly one in ill health, but it was
him without a doubt.

Daddy, she thought but didn't say.

"Help ya?" His voice had grown as old as the rest of him.
Raspy and clogged. He looked at her without expression or
recognition.

Effie opened her mouth but could find no words. The old
man in the doorway frowned. This was not how she'd imagined it would happen. He would see her, he would blanch,
maybe stumble back. Or he would smile and wave her inside,
though no, no, of course she would not go. She would scream
at him, or she would turn away without a word. She'd even
imagined punching him in the face. Kicking him. Knocking
him down while she knelt over him, battering until he bled.
Instead, she stood there and gaped like a fish while he stared.

"I don't need Jesus or a vacuum cleaner, and I don't read
magazines," the old man said. "So if you're selling something,
you can go right on along out of here."

Effie found her voice. "No, no… I'm sorry. I thought this
was… I knocked on the wrong door. I'm so sorry."

His smile had not changed, though the teeth inside it were
dingy and yellowed. She backed up from the sight of it, her
heel catching on the step. She almost fell backward off the
concrete stoop but caught herself.

"Careful. You don't want to hurt yourself now." He gave
her a curious, up-and-down look that shifted into sly wariness in a second. He straightened. "What do you want? Who
are you?"

Who are you?

Who are you?

Effie answered something meaningless, a scatter of words

as careless as a handful of gravel thrown at a window. She turned. Back straight, not shaking. Down the two steps and onto the sidewalk. Furtive, embarrassed glances from side to side, making sure nobody could see her leaving.

He shouted something after her that sounded like a question, but Effie had no answer. She could not speak. She could see nothing but her car in front of her. Her fingers fumbled with the key, setting off the car alarm for a horrifying second before she could hit the button to stop it. She was behind the wheel moments after that, key in the ignition, foot on the gas. She didn't look for traffic, but fortunately she didn't hit anything as she sped away.

Effie always made sure not to drive and text, but today she pulled her phone from her pocket as she steered with one hand. Dialing Heath. She needed him, but he wasn't there, and she'd done that. She'd fucked that up. She'd forced him away from her, she'd been so stupid and prideful and awful, and now when she needed him, he would not answer her calls.

"I saw him," Effie said to the voice mail. "I saw him, and he didn't…know me. Heath, he didn't even recognize me. Call me. Please. I need you. Please, Heath, I'm sorry, I'm so sorry. Please call me, baby. I miss you so much and I need you."

Then, although she'd been lucky up until that moment, the light turned red before she was ready for it. Effie slammed on the brakes. She dropped her phone. Her car skidded on the damp road and came to a stop so hard she hit the steering wheel with her chest because she'd forgotten to put on her seat belt.

The car behind her hit the rear bumper hard enough to knock her forward again. Her teeth clicked down, catching the tip of her tongue. Stars. She saw stars.

In the next moment, her car rocked forward again as the second car in the line hit the one behind her. Glass shattered this time. A horn blared. Through it all, Effie sat stunned, not sure what had just happened, and she sat there without moving until someone finally knocked on her window to ask her if she was okay.

When she faced him, the man outside the window recoiled, face twisting. It wasn't until she looked into the rearview mirror that she understood why he looked so startled. Her grin had gone wild, fierce. Her teeth, outlined with blood from her cut tongue.

"No," Effie said around the taste of blood. "Nothing is okay. Nothing is okay at all."

chapter thirty-nine

Everything hurt, but ice and some ibuprofen would take that away. Nobody had been injured badly in the three-car fender bender. Effie had not admitted to talking on her phone and being distracted, and nobody, so far, had said otherwise. Wet roads, a red light, cars following too close to each other. Her car needed to be repaired, but it was still drivable until she could get it to the shop. It all could've been so much worse. It was an accident, and they happen.

Mom had come to take care of her, of course. Clucking her tongue and muttering, but she'd done it. She'd made sure Effie was tucked into bed with the ice packs and the television remote, and she'd warned Polly about what had happened as soon as the kid got home from school, and she'd managed to do it without scaring her, which Effie appreciated. Polly had sat with her for a while but had grown bored of Effie's choice in TV. Now Mom and Polly were in the kitchen playing cards. Effie could hear the slap of them and their laughter, but she couldn't bring herself to get up and go out there to join them.

Heath had not returned her call, and Effie would be damned

if she called him again. He'd let her down in the past, and to be fair, she'd done the same to him. But never like this.

"Mom?"

"Yeah, Wog. What?" Effie opened her eyes to see Polly in the doorway.

"Nana wants to know if you want something to eat."

Effie held out her hand, and Polly came over to take it, sitting gingerly on the edge of the bed. "No, thanks. I'm not hungry."

"You sound funny."

"It's because I bit my tongue." Effie stuck it out to show her, laughing when Polly made a face. She squeezed the girl's fingers lightly.

"Does it hurt?"

"Yeah. It hurts." Effie smiled, though. "But I'll be okay. What's Nana doing?"

Polly shrugged. "Cleaning the kitchen. She said if you don't want any soup, she's going to go home. Unless you need her to stay."

"No." Effie shifted under the blankets. "That's okay."

Polly hesitated. "Mom…"

Effie waited. Polly didn't say anything. Effie sighed.

"I want to go over to Julia's house for a sleepover tonight. She asked me." Polly looked slightly defiant, which didn't make much sense.

Effie shifted again to prop herself higher on the pillows. "Can Nana drive you over? I'm not up to any driving."

"I'll ask her. But, Mom…"

"What, Polly?" Effie's tongue hurt too much for her to bite it, so she rubbed it against the back of her teeth to stop herself from getting irritated.

"I don't want to leave you alone." Polly frowned, for a moment looking as though she might cry.

Alarmed, Effie pulled her daughter close, careful not to groan at the aches and pains. "I'm fine. A little banged up, but I'm okay. You can go to Julia's house. I'll be okay to pick you up by tomorrow."

"Are you sure?"

Effie stroked Polly's hair. "Yeah. I'm sure."

From the doorway, Effie's mother knocked lightly. "I can take her to Julia's house, if you're sure. I can pick her up to-morrow, too, so you don't have to run out."

"Thanks, Mom. That would be great."

"You sure you don't want any soup?" Her mom frowned.

Effie laughed lightly. "You two, both of you, I'm fine. I promise you. Everything's okay. I'm going to lie here and watch bad TV and take a hot shower later. Really, I'm okay."

It took some convincing, but at last Mom and Polly both left. Effie settled into the blankets, dozing until her phone rang. She picked it up at once.

It wasn't Heath.

"What the fuck, Effie, what happened?" Bill's voice cut through the distance, sharp as shattered glass. "The guys at the station said you wrecked your car."

"I got rear-ended. I came up too hard at a red light. I'm fine. Damage to the bumper, but that's it." Effie clicked off the television, cradling the phone against her shoulder.

"Shit. Why didn't you call me?"

"For what?" she said. "Would you have come over and made me tea?"

"Maybe."

Effie laughed without humor. "Sure you would've. You're a regular fucking Mary Poppins."

Silence. Bill sighed. Effie pressed her lips together, closing her eyes, thinking of the way that door had opened.

Who are you?

"You could come over, if you want to." She kept her voice light. "My mom took the kid. She won't be home until tomorrow. We could watch a movie. Order pizza."

He wouldn't agree to it, of course. This was Bill on the line. All at once, though, Effie could think of nothing but having him there next to her. Having someone. Anyone.

"Never mind," she whispered, already steeling herself for the refusal.

"I'll be over in half an hour."

He was there in forty minutes, two frozen pizzas in one hand and a paper sack with a bottle of Bushmills in the other. "This won't fuck with your meds or anything, will it?"

"I'm only on ibuprofen. And I could use a drink." Effie still wore a pair of yoga pants and a slim-fitted T-shirt with a hoodie sweatshirt. She'd brushed her teeth, but not her hair. Looking at Bill now, she thought maybe she should've put on some mascara, some eyeliner, something. She'd been less than glamorous in front of Bill many times before, but somehow she was now made shy by the way he stood in her front room.

In her kitchen, she sat at the table while Bill preheated the oven and slid the pizzas onto two stoneware pans. He cracked open the bottle and poured them both a glass.

"Oh, the ice maker doesn't work," Effie said when he tried to get some through the fridge door. "You have to get it from inside."

Heath would've known that already, she thought and shoved it immediately away. Heath was not here. But Bill was.

He handed her a glass rattling with cubes and brimming with whiskey. "Here. Sip it. Don't gulp. Pizza will be ready soon. You need to eat something, and I don't want any bullshit about it."

Effie managed a small nod. "Thanks."

Bill took the chair across from hers. He held his glass in

two hands, spinning it before taking a drink. The whiskey made him grimace, but he drank again almost at once before setting the glass on the table. He looked around the kitchen.

"Nice place."

"Thanks," Effie repeated. There didn't seem much else to say.

Fortunately, she didn't have to think of anything. Bill took over the conversation, regaling her with stories about his job and the wacky things he'd had to deal with in the past couple of weeks. He kept them light. Funny. She appreciated the effort he was making.

After the pizza, Effie took Bill into the den to pick out a movie on streaming. When he put his arm around her shoulders, Effie stiffened for a second or two before relaxing into his embrace. Bill looked at her.

"What?"

"Nothing. I just…" Her shrug sent a soft wave of aching through her, despite the medicine and the booze.

Bill took his arm away from her and put an inch or so of distance between them. "I get it. Your boyfriend might not approve."

"I've told you a million times. Heath isn't—"

"Not Heath. That other guy. The one with the glasses." Bill frowned. "That guy."

"Oh." Effie chewed the inside of her cheek for a moment. "I'm not seeing him anymore."

Bill put another inch between them. "Oh. I get it."

"Get what?" Effie frowned and wished she'd poured herself another glass of whiskey.

Bill's brow furrowed. "He dumped you, so good old Bill's here instead."

"That's a stupid thing to say, and you know it."

"Why's that stupid? I know you've been dating him. That

guy. Like he mattered, like he made a difference. Next thing I know, you're inviting me over here. I should've figured it was because he dumped you."

"He didn't dump me," Effie snapped, defensive, because part of what Bill was saying was true. "We agreed not to see each other again. It wasn't working out."

"No surprise there," Bill muttered.

Effie got off the couch to stand in front of him. "He wasn't the kind of guy I could be with long-term, okay? I thought he was. I wanted him to be. But he wasn't."

Bill sat forward to put his elbows on his knees. "So you come running back to me."

"My God," Effie said, stunned. "You're acting like you care."

Bill stood, forcing her to take a few steps back. "What makes you think I don't?"

They were quiet then. Effie crossed her arms over her chest. Bill went into the kitchen and brought back two more glasses of whiskey, but Effie didn't want any now.

The problem was, she had no idea what she wanted.

"Do you?" she asked finally.

"Of course I do." Bill sat on the couch again. "Sit down."

She did, one knee tucked beneath her so she could turn and look at him. "I never know, with you."

He reached to push her hair off her face, then over her shoulder. He let his touch linger a moment or so on her cheek before dropping his hand. Bill shrugged.

Effie closed her eyes for a second, thinking hard. Then she leaned to kiss him. Soft. Sweet. A brush of lips, the tentative hint of tongue. Bill pulled her onto his lap.

Effie groaned, though not with pleasure. "Ouch."

Bill kissed her again, too hard. Effie turned her face just enough that his mouth skidded to the corner of hers. He pulled away.

"You want me to leave?"

"Did you just come over here to fuck me?" Effie asked.

Bill's eyebrows went up. "Why else would I come over?"

"To take care of me. To make me tea. To make sure I was all right?" She tried to push off his lap, but she was too stiff and sore, and Bill grabbed her wrists to hold her still.

"I brought you pizza and booze." Bill smiled, charming. Sly. "Isn't that better than tea? And making you come would be better than pizza. C'mon, Effie. Let me get my mouth on that sweet pussy. You'll forget about everything else."

For an hour, she thought. *Or less than that.* She'd used him for that purpose in the past, but now the thought of him touching her turned her stomach. She pulled at her wrists to free herself from him and got off his lap.

"I'm an asshole," Effie said. "I thought maybe… Shit. I thought that just maybe…"

"Ah, here we go again. You thought what? I'd be your hero?"

Effie looked at him. "You've rescued me before."

Bill said nothing. He rubbed his mouth for a moment. Then he shook his head. No light in his eyes. No love in his voice. He got up and paced for a moment in front of her, then turned.

"That first time I saw you in that bed, I was sure you were dead. You know that? You were so still, lying there in your own mess. Like some kind of fucked-up Sleeping Beauty. And I thought, there's no way that girl's alive. Or the kid, either, the one on the floor. I was sure I'd walked in on two corpses. And then you opened your eyes."

"We would've died, if not for you." Effie swallowed bitterness. "A week without food, we could've gone longer, but four days without water? The drugs in our systems? We were both almost dead when you showed up."

"Sheila Monroe was the reason you didn't die," Bill said

flatly. "If she hadn't come to the house looking to score drugs from that creep Andrews and found you both, I'd never even have stopped there. She came running out screaming, alerted the neighbors, left all the lights on upstairs. Door to the basement with all those fucking locks... Christ. The locks..."

Effie and Heath had never told anyone the part Sheila had played in what went on in the basement. It was true that if she hadn't come looking for the drugs Daddy had so often given her, Effie and Heath would've died. It was also true that implicating her in the abuse Daddy had heaped on them would've ruined her already pretty shitty life. Heath had been the one to plead for Sheila's clemency, and Effie had gone along with it because it had been important to him. She'd never really understood it—but then she'd never been the one forced to do the things Heath had done. If he could forgive Sheila, so could Effie.

"You were the one who answered the call. She left us there. You're the one who came in and found us. We're alive because of you. And then, later, when we started fucking. You saved me then, too, more times than I can tell you. When I look at you, that's what I see."

"When I look at you," Bill said, "I see that door with all those locks. And I think, there's no way anyone can ever get past all of that and be all right. But you managed, didn't you? Got yourself a house, a career. A kid."

Effie stood up straighter despite the aches and pains. "There's something I never told you, Bill."

"I'm sure there's a lot of things you never fucking told me," Bill said.

"Polly is yours."

Bill shrugged. "I know."

Effie flinched. Then again. She wanted to sit but forced herself to remain standing. "What do you mean, you know?"

"You think I couldn't look at that kid and not see it? She looked just like I did when I was a toddler. She's got my hair. My eyes. Fuck, Effie, do you really think I didn't know?"

Effie shook her head, the world rocking. "You never... How have you..."

"I'm a fucking cop. You think I never did one of those school programs at her school? You think I never saw the two of you together? You think I can't do the math, Effie? I knew that kid was mine the second you turned up pregnant." Bill laughed, harsh and rough.

Effie blinked back tears. "But you never said anything."

"I told you, I don't want to be a father. I don't want to be a husband. I don't have it in me to be that. And besides, you were cozy enough with Heath, weren't you?" Bill sounded bitter, though he was still keeping his expression flat and neutral and bland. "He stepped in. He's the one you went to anyway, wasn't it? Not me."

"I thought you would ask me to get an abortion. Or give it up."

"I would have," Bill said. "Not that you'd have listened to me. You'd just do whatever it was you wanted anyway. And I guess I thought maybe you'd lose it the way you lost the other one. By the time I figured out you were too far along, there wasn't much pointing in letting you know I knew the truth."

"All these years, you had a daughter, and you never said a word. You let me struggle." Effie had to cough against the sudden uprush of bile.

"You didn't struggle. You always had him. You ran to him. You always did, and you always will. You can't get away from him." Bill tossed up his hands. "Shit. If we aren't going to fuck, I'm out of here. This was stupid."

"You came here! You said... All those times, you acted like..." Effie couldn't breathe. Choking, she whirled on him. "You fucking molested me! You used your power and authority or something, I don't know, I was a kid and you took advantage of me!"

Bill was across the room with her in his grip before she could even take a step back. His fingers gripped hard enough to hurt, even if she hadn't already been in pain. "You seduced me. You remember that, Effie? Begging me to fuck you? Sliding all over me, your shirt all wet and see-through? You put your tongue in my mouth and your hands down my pants."

"You should've said no," Effie gasped.

Bill let her go so suddenly she stumbled. "Yeah. I should've fucking said no to you. That first time and every time after."

"But you didn't," Effie said.

They stared at each other. Had she ever loved Bill? Had she ever thought, for a second even, that he could've loved her?

"Why?" Effie asked. "Why?"

Bill sneered and ran a hand over his hair, looking away from her before fixing her with a solid, steady gaze. "I don't know."

"There could've been other women."

"There have been. Plenty."

Effie nodded and wiped at her tears, hating that he was seeing her this way. "But they always expected you to try harder with them, huh? They weren't satisfied with your whole deal with not wanting to settle down."

"Yeah. I guess not."

"So…you figured I would never make you do something you didn't want to do? Is that it?"

"Shit, Effie," Bill said quietly. "Can't we just stop? Can't we just go back to fucking and pretending that's enough?"

"It's not enough. Not for me," she said. "What if I said, let's try? We have a child together. She's amazing. You could get to know her. We could see what happens. We could make an effort."

"We can't try anything together, you and me. It will never work. You can pretty it up however you want to, or say whatever you want, but that's the truth," Bill said. "Me and you? Never going to happen, not like that. And you know it as well as I do, and you know why. All the wishing in the world can't change it."

She went at him with both fists, and he let her smack his face first, then pummel his chest, before he held her off with one hand. Sobbing, Effie collapsed against him. Bill held her for a moment before pushing her, hard, a few steps away. Without another word, he left her in the den and headed for the kitchen. He came back a minute later with his coat in one hand. Effie hadn't moved.

At the front door, her shout stopped him long enough to face her.

"How do you know?" Effie asked.

Bill looked...sad. For a moment, something glinted in his eyes before he steeled his expression. Gave her nothing but cold.

"Locks, remember? All over that fucking door. That's what you are, Effie. A locked fucking door. And it's all you'll ever be. At least for anyone else but him."

After that, she had nothing else to say to him.

chapter forty

"How do you get the ideas?" Heath asks, watching her. He's been quiet until now.

Effie's not sure how to answer him. She uses her fingertip to smudge the lines. "My imagination. How does anyone get any ideas?"

"I have loads of ideas, but none of them could become a drawing. At least, I couldn't draw it."

She looks at him with a smile. "You could, if you tried."

"Nah. You have talent. That's not something you can learn. You have to have it already." He gets off the bed and looks over her shoulder. He points to something she'd tried on a whim. "What's that?"

"It's us." She looks at him, then touches the tiny marks she'd made inside the bark of a tree.

"A clock?"

"Yes." Effie waits to see if he will understand.

Heath is quiet for half a minute or so. Then he says, "It's… time. It's all the time we've been down here."

"Yes." Effie looks up to the orangey, blurry lamps and blinks hard, but it doesn't do any good.

Her head still hurts from concentrating so hard on the

drawing in such horrible light. Yesterday the soup had tasted faintly metallic. She's still fuzzy from the pills that must've been crushed up inside it. They'd saved it the longest because it was the least likely to spoil. It's been three days since the bright lights came on and that song, the one that makes her stomach sick. It's not the longest time they've gone without Daddy coming into the basement, but they have started to portion out the food in case it goes on a lot longer.

Heath looks at her. "It's a secret."

"Yeah. Like we are." Effie puts down the broken nub of her pencil. She's used up all the paints in the set. "It's all the hours we've been down here."

"All the lost hours," Heath says.

The phrase stabs Effie in her heart. "Yeah."

All the lost hours. She works awhile longer, smudging and shading. The clock in the tree doesn't have regular numbers, one through twelve. She uses thirteen, fifteen. Their ages when they were taken. She uses one hundred and four, the number of weeks she's been able to count so far. She adds some other hidden figures, just for fun.

"I wish I had something better to use. I could probably make really great paintings if I did." She faces him before he can say a word. "I'm sorry. That's ungrateful. I don't mean it, Heath. I'm sorry."

He shakes his head. "It's okay."

Effie sits next to him to take his hand. Her fingers are dirty with the remnants of her picture. "No. I know what it takes for Daddy to give me new supplies. I won't have it."

"It doesn't matter, Effie," Heath says in a low voice. He won't look at her, but his fingers squeeze hers, tight. "I'll have to do it anyway."

Effie curls up next to him, her head on his shoulder. "Not for something as stupid as paints."

"You hungry?" Heath asks. "We should eat before the lights go off."

She's always hungry, but all they have left is tiny portions of disgusting food. Yeah, sure, they picked through it all to try to get rid of anything truly foul, but sometimes she thinks eating in the dark would be better. At least then they wouldn't have to see what Daddy's laced the food with.

"I guess so. A little."

"I'm thirsty." Heath gets up to open the creaking cupboard. He pulls out a bottle of lemonade. He shakes it, holds it up to the dim lighting. "It was opened, but it looks okay."

They share the drink and a package of stale pretzels that taste slightly bitter but don't make her feel sick. Effie makes Heath take more than she does. He's bigger and needs it. Besides, though she can't say so without making him feel bad, he deserves more. He's the one who works for it.

It's too warm. She's very thirsty now, but there's no more lemonade. Effie blinks and blinks at the orange lights, which have begun to grow bigger and smaller, like some kind of *Alice in Wonderland* trick.

"There *was* something in the lemonade," Heath says. "I'm sorry."

Effie's laugh is the burble of a brook rushing over stones. The bones in her hands have gone translucent. She's growing wings. Something is happening.

"There's always something in everything," she says.

She doesn't mean to kiss him. They haven't talked about what happens when the lights go off and he gets into bed with her. How he touches her, or the things he likes her to do. She shouldn't kiss his cheek, his ear, his neck, his mouth. She shouldn't open his lips with her tongue and push herself onto his lap.

It is the first time they've done this with the lights still on.

She has seen him naked, of course. They don't have much room for modesty down here. It's different now, though, with her hands on his body and the sound of Heath's moaning in her ears.

Something has overtaken them, a force neither of them can fight against. Because this feels good, and down here in the basement, almost nothing else does. They should stop for so many reasons, but all Effie can think about is getting that feeling back, the one that erases everything else.

Being with Heath blocks out the world.

They are stupid with it. Sating themselves and going at it again, then falling asleep curled in each other's arms without bothering to put their clothes back on or to pull up the blankets.

There is music, that song, the song, and the lights, and Effie struggles up and out of sleep as if she's swimming through marshmallow fluff. Sticky, suffocating, she can't breathe. She's covered in sweat.

"I knew it," Daddy says from the doorway. "I always knew it. Get up! Get up, you disgusting brats!"

He has Heath by one arm, yanking him. Heath falls out of the bed. Effie finds her way to consciousness. She launches herself from the bed. Bare feet hit the filthy concrete. Her ankle twists.

When Effie comes at him with windmill arms, all it takes is one strong crack of his fist against her cheek to send her down. She hits her head. There is no pain. Everything is soft-edged, blurry, floating. She is on her feet again, though. Screaming.

Screaming.

If they can get him down, they can run. Find the key. In his pocket. Open the door. Up the stairs. Break the door, they can break the door, they'll break.

Something breaks. Glass. No key, no door, no running, her head spins, and Effie falls back when Daddy hits her again.

Leaning over her, spit flies from his mouth. His face is red.

He stinks, sour breath. Dandruff in the part of his thinning hair. His eyes are red, with slits like a cat or a lizard. Oh, shit, oh, shit, what's wrong with his eyes?

Her wrist breaks with a crack louder than the shatter of glass. Now there's pain, instant and ferocious and all-consuming. She can't even scream with it. All she can do is fall back.

"I knew you were a little whore all along, I knew it. I knew it! You've been fucking him this whole time, haven't you?" Daddy hits her again. The same arm. More pain. Effie's scream is thin and breathless, a tin-whistle teakettle shriek.

"Leave her alone!" Heath hits Daddy over the back and shoulders with the rickety chair. It splinters, pieces flying. Some hit Effie in the face, scratching.

Daddy turns. He's so much bigger than Heath, his fists are hammers. Punching. Heath lifts the chair leg, the end jagged.

Daddy goes to his knees. The chair leg sticking out of his stomach wobbles. There is blood, not as much as you'd expect, until he pulls it out, and then there's a flood of it. Daddy gets to his feet. Again, he punches Heath in the face, sending him to the floor with a thud as loud as thunder. He kicks. Again. Again. Hand over the hole in his belly, blood gouting.

Effie can't move. Her arm is in agony. Her head swims. This is a nightmare, she thinks, crawling to Heath, who won't wake up. She can't wake up, either. She wants to wake up.

"Both of you, just like the other ones. Sick little fucks. Lying little cunts. Like your mother, full of filth and lies, oh, oh, you stupid little bitches."

Daddy spits. Frothy blood curdles in the corners of his mouth. There's more shouting, but Effie can't hear it. Her ears are ringing, ringing, there's a conflagration, a tintinnabulation, and then...

There is darkness.

And it stays dark for a long, long time.

chapter forty-one

The house was not on Effie's way to anywhere she ever really had to go, but she drove past it anyway, at least two or three times a week. Snow fell, nobody plowed the driveway. She drove past on garbage day and never saw a can at the curb. The mailbox never had the red flag up.

But the lights were always on inside.

She never stopped again. If the weather had been warm, she might've jogged past to get a closer look beyond the living room curtains, but winter had sunk in its teeth at last and wasn't letting go. She satisfied herself with slowing as she passed. Once or twice, a silhouetted figure twitched the curtains, or at least she let herself imagine so.

She never meant to drive past with Polly in the car, but like an addict who promises only one drink, only one pill, never when it will get in the way of life, just a little hit to keep things going…that was Effie with that house. Of course that was the day the ambulance sat in the driveway. That was the day the traffic was blocked by a cop car, not Bill's, thank God, so that Effie had to slow and stop to wait for the cars coming in the opposite direction to pass before she could drive on.

"What's going on, Mom?" Polly looked up from her phone,

where she'd been busily trying to beat the next level of her favorite game.

Effie rolled down her window to say to the woman standing on the sidewalk, her dog on a leash, "What's happening?"

"Guy died," the woman said, all too eager to share the information. No shame at all. Sort of gleeful, actually. "Guess his daughter came in to check on him when she hadn't heard from him in a few days, found him dead."

"Gross," Polly said.

Effie looked at her daughter, who'd been made immune to the random deaths of strangers by too much violence on television. Or something. "How did he die?"

"Stroke, I think someone said." The woman shrugged. "He was pretty old, and it was a shame, to tell you the truth, that his children left him alone so much. The house was in total neglect."

"How long have you lived in this neighborhood?" Effie asked.

The woman looked surprised and a little affronted. "Five years. Why?"

Effie rolled up her window and drove on without replying. Polly's phone bleated and beeped. She finished the level and turned to her mother.

"Mom."

"Yeah, Wog. What?"

"Mom, was that the house?"

Startled, Effie twisted to look at Polly. Her fingers gripped the wheel hard enough to hurt. "Why do you ask me that?"

"I know it was close to Nana's house. And this isn't the way to the mall." Polly looked solemn. "And…I saw a picture of it on the internet, when I was looking at that stuff I wasn't supposed to see. I'm sorry, Mom, I didn't look again after you said not to."

Effie swallowed and concentrated on the road ahead, mindful of what had happened the last time she hadn't been paying attention. She'd barely gotten over the bruises. "Yes. That was the house. I shouldn't have taken you past it."

Polly looked behind them. "He's dead now. Doesn't that make you feel better?"

With a small gasp, Effie pulled to the side of the road and slammed the car into Park. She turned to take Polly by the front of her puffy winter coat. "Don't you ever say such a thing! Wishing someone dead is wrong, Polly."

Polly didn't flinch, though when Effie let go, she did shift a little toward the window. "Sorry."

"No, I'm sorry. I just..." Effie drew in a deep breath to keep her voice from shaking. "It's complicated, Pollywog. It's hard and it hurts and... I'm sorry. I'm so sorry."

Polly reached to hug her. "Don't cry, Mama. It's okay. I mean, maybe you can be okay now, right?"

Effie clung for a moment to her daughter before pulling herself together by sheer force of will. Traffic passed them, going too fast. A car horn blared a complaint. She'd be lucky if they didn't get clipped.

She put on a smile for her kid. "Yes, honey. Now I can be okay."

Of course she was not okay.

How many times had she dreamed, literally, of Daddy's death? She'd fought nightmares for years about throttling him, watching his face go blue and then his tongue, black, lolling out of his mouth. She'd dreamed about the fire, the three of them burning to death while Daddy laughed. She'd dreamed of watching him carve Sheila into tiny pieces and forcing her and Heath to eat them. Years of horrible dreams, and yet now that he truly was dead, all she could think of was that she'd never had the chance to confront him.

Worse, the local news hadn't mentioned even a word of it.

No coverage of the ambulance or police car's flashing lights, no quotes from smug, self-righteous neighbors. Nothing on the television, nothing even on the websites.

Nothing on the forum.

Effie had ignored this forum for years. Even her curiosity about what they were saying about her latest works had not been enough to prompt her to dive into what she thought was a cesspool of almost-salacious voyeurism. She had a log-in, though. Ancient, tied to an old email address she hadn't used in forever. She knew the password, had no trouble recalling that. It was, of course, *thelosthours*.

That fucking forum where the freaks hung out dissecting every tiny thing that had happened to her and Heath in that basement, and not a single thread had appeared about Daddy's death. There were posts about his time in prison and his release, information about the house itself and who'd owned it all that time. Nothing about him dying in it.

Days, a week, another week passed. Still nothing.

Nothing anywhere. She scoured the local newspaper's site for an obituary, a notice about a funeral service, a memorial. Something, anything to note that the man who'd changed her entire life had passed on, and someone, anyone other than she herself to notice. But nobody seemed to.

She called Heath. "He's dead. And nobody cares. Nobody notices. It's like he didn't exist."

She filled the rest of the message with silence, praying that somehow he'd pick up the phone, but of course that wasn't how voice mail worked. He didn't call her back. He was the only person who could possibly understand why this upset her so much, and she'd lost him.

If Daddy didn't exist, Effie thought, if what happened to them together didn't exist, then…did she?

Without Heath, did it matter?

chapter forty-two

It had taken her the entire morning to convince herself to finally get in the car and drive here, but now that she was here, all Effie felt was calm. Blank. Daddy was gone. Nothing would bring him back.

She needed this, though. To walk through the front door of that house and walk back out again, free to do so as many times as she wanted. A dozen times. A hundred. Proof that there was nothing there to hold her any longer.

A couple cars had parked in the driveway and some more had taken up the spots in front, so Effie found one across the street. She watched a couple with a young child come out the front door and get in an SUV. She waited, but the front door remained closed after them. This was it. Now or never.

She tugged the hem of her blazer over her hips when she got out of the car. Smoothed her skirt. She'd raided her closet for an outfit that resembled upscale professional, someone who looked as though they could afford the ridiculously reasonable asking price for this house. Effie had never gone to an open house before, but she had an idea that the Realtor would be able to spot her right off as a looky-loo, and she didn't want to have to answer any awkward questions.

Did she knock? Or go right in? Her hesitation was rewarded by not having to choose when the front door opened to reveal an older couple on their way out. She stepped aside to let them pass, then went into the foyer.

Everything was so…small.

It was also bright, airy, clean. Freshly painted. The smell of vanilla wafted toward her from the kitchen. Effie forced herself to walk down the hall. No pictures on the walls. A sunken living room to her right contained a few pieces of carefully staged furniture and a cheerful fire burning in a small woodstove.

"Hi, there!" A woman who had to be the Realtor greeted Effie with a chipper grin. "Thanks for stopping in. There's some literature on the table there, and help yourself to cookies and punch. If you have any questions, please let me know."

The floor creaked as the woman took a few steps toward her, and Effie flinched. She knew that sound, though she'd always heard it from overhead. It was so much quieter from this spot. She pasted a smile on her face and managed a nod. "Thanks."

The Realtor turned her attention to a young couple, the woman pregnant, who'd come in from the dining room. Effie took the chance to take one of the brochures, skimming the house's specs to look as if she was interested. Cookies and punch? As if she could eat a bite of anything in this house, ever.

She'd been in this kitchen, but there'd been no cute dinette set. No flowers. The floor had been dirty, scuffed, faded linoleum, but now gleamed with brand-new laminate. The appliances looked new.

"Everything's been updated and upgraded," the Realtor was telling the other couple. "The owner is really motivated to sell."

Effie looked at the brochure. "Who's selling it?"

"The original owner's daughter took over the property after he passed away." The Realtor gave her a glance and another of those too-bright grins and turned her attention to the other couple, who wanted to know about the plumbing.

Effie crumpled the paper a little in her fist. Four bedrooms, two baths, kitchen, living room, dining room. Garage.

Full, finished basement.

The basement door had not been replaced, though it had been painted and the knob looked shiny and new. Effie touched the fresh white frame and the small marks and dents where once there'd been an entire set of locks and now there was nothing. She touched the knob. Turned it.

The stairs beyond were well lit with brand-new bulbs, clean of even a cobweb. The wood was splintery, the stairs creaking, and her stomach lodged in her throat when she descended. She used the handrail, convinced she would fall headfirst and split herself open on the concrete floor.

The lights come on overhead. Bright. White. Glaring.

The song. The song is playing. That song about the boats, sailing, it's awful and cruel, they are down here in this room, and they will never sail away. Not ever.

Effie's arm hurts. A dull, solid ache that flares into agony if she moves it too much. So she doesn't move it. She doesn't move at all. It's wrong of her to wish the drugs hadn't worn off, but she does. The bed beneath her has gone clammy with sweat, and though it disgusts her, she can't make herself get up to strip off the sheets. They have nothing to replace them with, anyway.

Heath has been quiet for a while, though the soft huff of his breathing reassures her that he's still alive. It took him so long to wake up after Daddy hit him to the ground that Effie was sure he was dead. For a while she thought maybe she was dead, too. Now she wonders how long it will be until she is.

It had always been hard to keep track of the passing days because there was never any consistency to when the lights would come on and off, or when Daddy would visit. All Effie knows is that he hasn't come back into the basement for so long they've now definitely run out of food and water. They've even used the small amount from the toilet tank, barely enough to wet their throats.

"Effie?"

She doesn't open her eyes. There's nothing to see. "Yeah."

"I'm going to try again."

"It's locked," Effie says wearily. "The door's still locked, it will always be locked, you can try it as many times as you want, but you can't break it down and you can't get it unlocked."

"I'm going to try."

She manages to sit. She can feel him through the darkness, though they're not touching. "I can help."

"Not with your wrist, you can't."

"If the two of us try…" Effie says but stops herself. She doesn't believe it will work, and it will hurt her arm. She lies back on the bed.

Time passes. At least, she thinks it does. The ache in her belly grows as fierce as the throbbing in her arm, at least for a while until both fade. There's only darkness. Only silence.

Effie is very, very cold.

"Effie. I want you to know, I love you. I hate Daddy for all of this, but if he hadn't taken you, we'd never have met. You know that?"

"I know it," Effie answers, or at least she thinks she does. She feels as though her lips are moving, but it could be her imagination.

"I love you, Effie. I will always love you." Heath's hand in hers.

His fingers are like ice, or maybe that's hers. Either way, there's no warmth between them except what she remembers from when he kissed her. Heat is a memory.

And there is light, faint, from the other room.

A woman's voice, querulous, curious. Calling out a name. Then a strangled cry. The thud of an overturned table. Shadows stretch and tease. Effie sees a silhouette. Long hair. The sickly-sweet stink of a familiar perfume.

"Oh, my God! Oh, my God! Oh God, oh God!"

God stopped caring about them, Effie thinks, while beside her, Heath struggles to get up from the bed. The light stays on. Heath is on the floor. Someone's in the doorway, and then they're gone.

More time.

Another voice. More light. Bright, this time. It hurts Effie's eyes through her eyelids, and she tries to cover her face with her hand, but she can barely wiggle her fingers.

"Hello? Holy shit." The voice is garbled. Staticky.

A figure looms over her. He wears blue. He has a gun, but he puts it away and puts a hand on her, gentle, but the pain flares and Effie screams. Or tries to scream. She has no breath for it.

"You're okay," the police officer says. "I'm Officer Schmidt. I'm here to help you both. You're going to be okay."

Blinking, Effie gasped for breath. She was going to pass out. Her fingers gripped the wooden railing hard enough to make the wood creak. A splinter gouged her with a small sting, but no real pain. She misjudged the last step and went down too fast, onto...

Carpet.

Soft, thick carpet in a plush royal blue. The basement was well lit with hanging pendant lamps in multiple colors. One big space broken up by several wooden pillars, but nothing else. No other rooms. No walls.

Everything she'd been expecting was gone. She moved forward on numb feet into the center of the room. Here it was, their living space. Here, that fetid bathroom. Here, the tiny decrepit bedroom where they'd spent so much time. All gone, replaced by fresh white walls and the lingering scent of floral air fresheners. From one corner, a small dehumidifier hummed. Two small windows hung with pretty, gauzy curtains let in a bit of filtered light. Like the frame of the door upstairs, the wood around these had been painted, but if you looked closely enough, you could see the places where nails had once punctured the wood to hold in place the boards that had covered the glass.

It was gone, everything was gone, there was no remnant here of what had happened, and this was worse, somehow, even than Daddy not recognizing her. Effie went to her knees there in the middle of the room. Then her hands, too. Bent over, pressed her forehead to the carpet, waiting to see if she was going to scream or wail or faint or die.

With her eyes closed, it was dark, but she could still sense the light. Above her head came the familiar creaking step, step, step. That had not changed, and oh, what fuckery, that she should take comfort from that. Effie pushed herself up onto her hands.

Get up, she told herself. *Get up, Effie. You didn't come here to be a prisoner again. Get the fuck up and go upstairs and walk out that fucking front door.*

There are no more locks.

Shaking, she managed to get one foot beneath her. It wasn't enough. She couldn't make herself stand. Her fingers dug into the carpet, all the way to the scratchy base. A staple poked her. She dug her fingers deeper, seeking that pain.

"…Miss? Are you all right?"

Get up, Effie. You're making a fool of yourself. You need to get up right now.

She turned her head, trying to smile. "Yes, yes, I…"

"I know you," the woman said. "Oh. God. I know who you are."

"My mother left my father when I was twelve and my brother fifteen. She wouldn't tell us why. There was no joint custody. We never saw my dad after that, except maybe once or twice a year for holidays, and then he always came to our house and sat in the living room while we opened our presents or whatever. My mom wouldn't talk to him, but she never left us alone with him, either."

The woman's name was Karen. She was older than Effie by about ten or twelve years, but you wouldn't have guessed it if you put them side by side. They were about the same height. They had the same color hair. Karen's eyes were deep brown, but aside from that, they might've been sisters.

"He'd been in the hospital for two weeks before they found you. The infection from that untreated stab wound. It almost killed him." Karen paused to pour them both mugs of tea. She'd chased out the Realtor and everyone from the open house so she and Effie could sit in the kitchen and talk alone.

Effie was lucky Karen hadn't called an ambulance. Or the police. As it was, Effie could barely string more than a few words together. She took the tea and warmed her hands on the mug, though of course she didn't sip.

"It might've been better if he'd died then." Karen's voice shook a little, and she drank a gulp of tea. "Someone would've come in. Found you sooner."

"Someone found us anyway, thank God." Effie blew on the tea and let the steam bathe her face.

"I asked my mom, when he went to prison, if there was something he'd done that had made her divorce him. I was almost thirty by then. Married, two kids. I'd allowed my dad to see the kids. Never alone, like I somehow knew without knowing, but still..." Karen shuddered and shook her head. It took her a long minute to speak again, but Effie let the silence hang between them without trying to fill it. Karen got up to wipe her eyes with a paper towel she tore from the rack beneath the cabinet. She stayed where she was, leaning, before she cleared her throat. "He took you and that boy to replace me and my brother. And I finally got out of my mother why she left him. She'd found diaries, drawings. Sick things of what he'd intended for us. He wanted to keep me safe, so I didn't become a whore. And my brother was somehow a replacement for him, to do things he wasn't able to do. He was impotent or something. I just... I didn't want to ask her more than that."

Effie pressed her hand to her mouth. She wanted to hate Karen. She wondered if Karen hated her.

"He never touched me," Effie said. "I know that we testified something different in court. I know it's what everyone thought. But he never actually touched...me."

Karen looked sick to her stomach. She breathed in and out a few times, then shook her head. "I'm so, so sorry. He was a sick man. I'm so... If there was something I could do, I would do it."

Effie looked toward the basement door, shut but not locked. She gave Karen a faint smile. "You've done a lot."

Another silence spun out, longer this time. Karen came back to the table, but not to sit. She took her mug and dumped it in the sink, rinsed it and put it on a dish towel on the counter. It was a signal, Effie thought. Time for her to go.

"What ever happened to the boy? The one who was with you? Is he okay?"

There was a question without a straightforward answer. Effie hesitated, then decided there was no point in launching into a life history. "Yeah, he's fine. We keep in touch."

"Well, you look like you've done all right, anyway," Karen said. "You look...good."

"Sure, other than totally losing my shit in your basement, I'm great." She'd meant to joke, but Karen flinched. Effie stood. "Sorry. I was trying to make light."

Karen wouldn't meet her gaze. She wiped her eyes again with the paper towel, then crumpled it into a ball she shoved into her pocket. "I wanted to make sure there was nothing left of what happened down there. He's dead. There's no reason for anyone, ever, to remember anything he did."

Except there was every reason. There was Effie. And there was Heath. They lived it, survived it, and they'd done it together. They were the only two who knew what it was like.

Effie didn't say that, though. It wouldn't do any good to castigate Karen for what her father had done. If smiling blandly and leaving meant Karen got to go on with her life without carrying more of a burden than she already did, well...there were times when giving someone else what they needed meant doing just that.

So that's what Effie did.

chapter forty-three

"I never wanted this for you. You know that." Effie's mother stroked her hair off her forehead with gentle fingers. "As a mother, can't you imagine how it was for me? How horrible and terrifying, and how I did what I could to keep you safe, because I'd failed you so miserably?"

"It's not your fault that Stan Andrews took me, Mom. I never blamed you." It's a tiny lie—the blisters from the shoes, that Effie had blamed on her mother. But not the abduction itself. Not for real.

Effie leaned against her mother's shoulder with her eyes closed, thinking of all the times she'd done this when she was young. Of how often Polly had leaned on Effie's shoulder this same way, how she sometimes still did, but how mostly she'd started leaning away more often than moving close. Polly was growing up.

"But you have to understand something," Effie said and looked up at her mother's face. "What we went through... it can't be erased. We can push it to the past and get over it and move forward, but it happened. And, Mom...if I tried to pretend it didn't, that would negate what was probably the most influential experience of my life. What happened in that basement made me who I am."

Her mother hitched a broken sob and shook her head. "But I don't want that to be what made you who you are. I want me and your father to have made you who you are. I want your other life experiences, the good things, to outweigh all that bad."

Effie put her head back on her mom's shoulder and said nothing for a moment or so. Her mother stroked her hair the way she had when Effie was young. If she kept her eyes closed, maybe she could pretend she was ten years old again. Eight. Six. Maybe she could be a toddler in pigtails, a birthday balloon in each hand and cake smeared on her face.

Effie sighed. There was no going back. Not to good times. Not to bad.

"I want you to be able to move on," her mother said quietly. "I'm so proud of you with your art, but every time you sell one of those paintings, Effie, all I can think about is how you have to put yourself back in that place. With him."

Heath.

Effie sat up then. "All the best art comes from the broken places, Mom. And I love him. So does Polly. So I wish, for our sakes, or at the very least for hers, that you would try to accept him. Because I can't live without him. And I don't want to."

"Oh, Effie." Her mother shook her head.

Effie got up and stood in front of her. Not weeping or shaking. Calm. Smiling. Confident.

"You don't understand. Heath is my world. If everything else in the universe disappeared and Heath was left, I would still find a way to live. Without Heath, everything else is a shadow and a strangeness that I can't ever be a part of. I need him, Mom. I need him, I love him, and I'm not sorry about it anymore."

Her mother got up, too. She took Effie's hands and squeezed them. Tears in her eyes, finally, she nodded.

"All right," her mother said. "Because I love you, too. Because you're my daughter and I want you to be happy. All right. I will try to accept this, and him."

Effie hugged her mother hard. "All I can ask you to do is try."

chapter forty-four

Seeing Heath with Lisa would be hard. Perhaps far from the most difficult thing Effie had ever lived through, but it wasn't going to be like riding a unicorn along a rainbow into a swimming pool full of kittens, either. All she could do was straighten her shoulders, put her chin up and make the best of it, since most of it was her own damned fault.

"I want to go to your art show." Polly frowned and kicked at the table legs until Effie gave her a frown.

"Wog, it's not for kids. I told you that."

"Me and Nana could go for a little while and then stay in the hotel. I never get to stay in hotels."

Effie laughed, though the thought of exposing Polly to the possibility of any of those wackos from the forum wasn't funny at all. "I promise, I'll take you to stay in a hotel with me another time. And besides, you've seen all my paintings already."

"Not in a fancy show. Mom, are you going to be famous?"

"I don't think so. Hardly anyone gets famous for their paintings." At least not while they were alive. "You and Nana are going shopping anyway, so that will be more fun. Do I look all right?"

"You look pretty with your hair curled. You're wearing heels," Polly said. "You're probably going to have sore feet."

Effie looked over her shoulder. "Yeah, I know, but this is a fancy kind of party. I have to try to look like a grown-up."

"You need lipstick." Polly got up to stand in front of her mother with a critical look.

"I have lipstick on."

Polly rolled her eyes. "Lip *balm* isn't the same, Mom."

"Okay. Okay. I'll put on some lipstick. If Nana gets here while I'm in my room, tell her I'll be right out. I need to get on the road. Long drive. Shit. I'm going to hit traffic—"

"It's all going to be okay, Mom." Polly took Effie's hand and waited for her mother to look at her. "You're going to have a fantastic show and sell a ton of paintings, and then you can buy me an iPad."

Effie took a deep breath and focused on her child, the delight of her life. She hugged Polly close, expecting resistance, but the girl squeezed her hard. She stroked Polly's blond hair and breathed in the soap and water scent of her.

"I love you, Pollywog. So much. You know that?"

"Yeah," Polly said with a sigh. "I know."

Two hours later, Effie had avoided most of the traffic and arrived more or less on time at the gallery. Cursing the light misting rain that threatened to weigh the curls Polly had insisted she try, Effie let her car idle in the parking lot without getting out. This was it. Her big night. Her time to shine.

"Dammit," she said aloud. "You're going to get through this night, and it's going to be great, and you're going to enjoy it."

Still, it took her another ten minutes or so before she convinced herself to get out of the car and stagger like a newborn colt across the parking lot in her too-high heels. Inside the front doors, she let an attendant take her coat. She found the restroom. She fixed her hair and her lipstick. Her eyeliner, courtesy of Becky, looked fucking amazing. She straightened her shoulders. She was going to do this, ready or not.

"Effie, hi!" Elisabeth waved at her from a short distance down the hallway. "You made it."

"I made it," Effie agreed, self-conscious in her fancy clothes.

Elisabeth gestured her closer. "You look so beautiful. I love that dress. The vintage style is so flattering. And your shoes. Wow."

"If I don't break an ankle, I'll call it a good night." Effie looked down at her feet, then at Elisabeth. "So…am I the only one here?"

"No. Absolutely not. I told you we would advertise and promote the hell out of this event. We have a room full already." Elisabeth grinned and looped her arm through Effie's. "You've already sold two paintings."

"What? No. Really? What?" Effie had been allowing Elisabeth to lead her toward the gallery, but now she stopped short. "You're kidding."

"I would never joke about something like that. You just bought me a week on the beach." Elisabeth looked solemn. "This show, Effie. It's going to change your career."

Effie let Elisabeth lead her another step or two before she faltered again. "Are any of…them…here?"

"The forum people? Maybe. If so, they're behaving themselves. And if anyone bothers you, let me know. I have security here tonight," Elisabeth said with a confidence she obviously meant to ease Effie's fears, though it didn't help much. "I mean it. Anyone who gives you a hard time or in any way makes you feel nervous, they're out."

Effie laughed. "Wow. Okay. That's full service, right there."

"C'mon. It's going to be great," Elisabeth said.

Effie had seen the photos of the room layout Elisabeth

had sent in advance, but nothing had prepared her for how it would all look in real life. Fairy lights, gauzy fabric, candles, soft music. And, oh, her artwork everywhere. Her fingers and wrists still remembered how fiercely she'd worked, but seeing the number of pieces hung in frames or set on easels was still somewhat shocking.

"Let me get you a glass of wine," Elisabeth said. "White or red?"

"White. In case I spill it all over myself." Effie looked at her black dress. "Though I guess it wouldn't matter."

"There's a cheese and fruit table back there. Desserts in the other room. Catered hors d'oeuvres. Mingle," Elisabeth encouraged. "I'll be right back."

Before Effie had time even to worry that nobody was going to talk to her and she'd stand alone in the corner all night looking like an asshole, Naveen brought someone to meet her. To her surprise and relief, Effie had no problems after that. People came and went. Some asked about her inspirations on certain pieces. Nobody mentioned the forum or the basement. Most of them, Effie realized, didn't seem to have any idea that any of that had ever happened.

With a second glass of wine in her, Effie had relaxed enough to have something to eat. With a plate of cheese and crackers in one hand, she waved at Elisabeth from across the room with the other. Elisabeth, though, was deep in conversation with someone and didn't notice her. Effie watched them a moment or so. The way they stood, angling toward each other but with enough distance between them that to touch would require an effort. The guy never took his eyes off Elisabeth's face, and she looked at the floor. Never at him.

"That's Will Roberts. He's a photographer," Naveen said from behind Effie's shoulder.

She turned. "Ah. One of your artists?"

"Sometimes," Naveen said. "Should I rescue her?"

"Do you think she wants to be rescued?"

Naveen laughed a little. "Don't all women want to be rescued?"

"No," Effie said. "Sometimes we don't need saving."

She hadn't meant it to sound bitchy, but Naveen gave her a slow, assessing look before he nodded. "Yeah. I guess you're right. If she needs me, she knows I'm here."

The conversation shifted after that. Naveen introduced her to some more people, including Will, who complimented Effie's paintings so sincerely that she blushed. She kept herself from returning the favor with nice words about the photo in Elisabeth's office—though she was kind of desperate to watch his face when she did. Elisabeth had disappeared, and Effie hoped she was all right.

Heath had not shown up yet. Effie couldn't decide if she were upset or relieved. Still, every time someone walked through the door, she found her attention dragged there.

Maybe he wasn't coming. Effie had included Lisa on the invitation to be nice, but what if the other woman had refused and forbidden Heath from coming, too? If he didn't come, Effie thought, could she blame him? She'd pushed him into Lisa's arms, after all. She'd told him to make it work. If that meant not being here for Effie, well…it was what she deserved.

Trying to put the thoughts of him from her mind, Effie ate cheese and sipped at a third glass of wine. With only an hour or so left in the evening, she was looking forward to getting out of here. The boutique hotel Elisabeth had booked for her was a short walk that was going to seem much, much longer while wearing these shoes. But the wine would help with her aching feet and a lot of other aches, too.

"How's it going?" she asked as Elisabeth approached. She looked tired, but her smile was genuine. She held up her own glass of wine and shifted from one foot to the other with a wince.

"Ready to get these shoes off, I'll tell you that."

"Me, too. Listen, Elisabeth, I can't thank you enough. For all of this." Effie gestured around the room. "This has been more than I ever dreamed it could be."

Elisabeth clinked her glass to Effie's and drained the rest of it. "I'm so glad."

Over her shoulder, Effie caught sight of that photographer. Will. She tipped her chin a little in his direction. "So...?"

Elisabeth didn't even look. She smiled, shiny as a diamond and as hard. "I didn't know he was invited."

"You could've called security," Effie said, and they laughed.

Her laughter stopped at the sight of a familiar lean, tall figure. Heath wore a suit—had she ever seen him in a suit? A crisp white shirt, a tie, his sleeves not too short and showing off his wrists. Polished black shoes. His hair, smoothed back from his face in an actual style.

"Oh," Effie said. "He's here. Alone."

Elisabeth turned to look. "A friend?"

She would not cry. She would not. Effie blinked back tears and nodded. He was here. He came. He hadn't forgotten. He had not abandoned her.

Heath was here.

chapter forty-five

As always, no matter how long they'd been apart, when they were together again it was as though nothing had changed. Heath followed Effie from piece to piece to look at everything she'd done. They drank some wine.

"You're eating…? Is it good?" he asked when she offered him some cheese.

"Yeah. It's good." She ate a piece to prove it.

Nobody else in that room would've understood what a personal accomplishment that was, but Heath did. Right there, in that room with all the people who'd come out to praise her, the only one who mattered was him. It took her breath away, literally; it left her gasping with her heart thudding so hard in her ears that for a moment all she could hear was the thrum of her own pulse. Heath took her hand, his fingers warm and strong, and everything came back into focus.

"Hey," she said. "Do you want to get out of here?"

She took him down the street two short blocks to her hotel. When she stepped too carefully because of her aching feet, Heath, laughing, bent so she could get on his back. They were still laughing when they got upstairs to her room and fell through the doorway in a burst of hilarity that felt so fucking good…that laughter…that Effie almost started to cry.

"I thought you weren't going to make it tonight." She tossed her shoes into the corner and stretched her toes with a grateful sigh.

Heath hung his coat carefully on a hanger. "I wouldn't have missed it. You should know that."

Effie paused, thinking she should keep her voice light and hoping that at least it wouldn't shake, embarrassing her. "I didn't know… I thought maybe Lisa wouldn't want you to."

"Ah. Lisa," Heath said, then nothing else.

Effie looked at him. Heath shrugged. Effie's eyebrows rose. "She broke up with me."

"Oh." Effie went to the bag she'd packed with bottled water. She took one, offered him another. Drank.

Heath drank, too, then set the bottle on the dresser. "She said there was no point in trying to make something work with somebody who, she said, could only make it work when someone was hurting him."

"Ouch." She tried to feel sympathetic, or upset for him. She really did. But all Effie could do was smile.

Heath nodded. "Yeah. She was right, too. It wasn't good with me and Lisa, not the way she wanted it to be."

"You tried," Effie said. "At least you did that."

He was silent for a second or two before shaking his head. "No. I didn't. Not really."

With someone else, there would've been more words, but Effie and Heath didn't need any. She was in his arms in the time it took her heart to beat three or four times. Kissing him within a breath after that. He picked her up and took her to the bed, where the pillows scattered and neither of them cared.

So many times they'd come together with a clash and crash, their lovemaking a battle. This time, he undressed her slowly, piece by piece, leaving her in her pretty lacy panties and bra long enough to sit up to admire her. Effie preened, arching her back on the bed, then laughing at the look on his face.

Heath didn't laugh. "You're so fucking beautiful."

Effie quieted. "I feel beautiful, with you."

She reached for him, and he covered her with his body so he could kiss her mouth. She rolled them, but gently, so she could get at the buttons of his shirt. Effie took her time in undoing them, one by one, letting her lips and tongue follow the path her fingers made. He shivered when she kissed his bare flesh.

He always did.

They'd been naked together many times, but something about this time felt like the first. Effie kissed the ink on the inside of his elbow. Then the pulse throbbing in his wrist. The scar. She kissed the palm of his hand and curled his fingers around it, then brought his hand to her face. When he cupped her cheek, then slid his grip to the base of her neck to grip her hair, Effie sighed and opened her eyes.

Heath kissed her mouth. Her chin. Her jaw. His mouth slid along the curves of her face and the soft vulnerability of her throat, where he pressed his teeth until she moaned and arched and offered herself to him. Then lower, nibbling and nipping over her collarbones and the slopes of her breasts. He took a nipple between his lips through the lace of her bra. Effie shuddered at the pressure and the wet heat.

"Lower," she whispered with a smile and ran her hand over the dark brush of Heath's silky, thick hair.

He obeyed at once. His lips traced circles on her ribs and belly until Effie gasped and tangled her fingers in his hair to keep him from tickling. She felt his smile on her skin.

"Lower."

Heath nibbled her hip. Her thigh. He brushed his mouth

across her lace panties and paused to blow heat against her. His fingers hooked in the waistband and tugged them away. He hooked her knee over his shoulder and slid his hand beneath her ass to lift her to his kiss. His tongue found the seam of her cunt and parted her to his caress. Steady, steady, gentle and steady, unwavering, Heath used the flat of his tongue to stroke her clit. In minutes, Effie was on the edge, and that was where he kept her no matter how she writhed and moaned.

"Please," Effie said.

Heath lifted his head with a grin. The sight of his wet mouth sent another surge of pleasure through her. She let her fingers drift through his hair, no longer so neatly combed. She took his chin in her hand, tight. Their gazes met and held. Slowly, deliberately, Heath tugged himself from her grip to give her another long, deliberate lick.

"You taste," he said in a low voice, "so goddamned good."

The adoration in his voice made her want to laugh or weep, and Effie did a little of both. She opened herself to him, with more than only her body. She gave Heath all of herself, and he feasted on her until she cried out, over and over. Her body tightened, tense, and released, only to be swept up again in another wave of pleasure that overtook her and left her gasping.

When she stopped shaking, Effie let her hands fall to either side of her head. "Oh. My. God."

Heath laughed and kissed the insides of her thighs before moving up and over her. His cock pressed her belly as he kept himself from weighting her, his hands denting the bed on each side of her body near her ribs. He kissed her lightly before pushing up on his hands again.

"I want you inside me," Effie said.

Heath's breath hissed. "Yes. I want that, too."

She pulled him back to her, urging him to cover her even though he resisted. "Kiss me."

"I don't want to crush you."

"You could never," she told him, still urging, until he gave in and lowered himself full on top of her.

Heath kissed her. He fit himself inside her slowly until Effie tipped her hips to draw him in—he filled her, and they both groaned. Heath pressed his forehead to hers for a moment, his eyes closed. He throbbed inside her, and she wanted to giggle, but it felt so good that she chuffed out a small sigh instead.

At the taste of salt, Effie used her thumbs to press away the tears—his or hers, did it matter, when they'd so long ago become one person? She drew him against her. "Hold me close."

He moved inside her, and though she'd already had a dual orgasm, the pleasure built inside her again as he took his time and played her body the way only he had ever been able to do. They rocked together for a long time. She didn't expect to come again, but the longer he drew out his climax, the closer she got. Every thrust pressed him against her clit, until Effie gasped and moved and raked her nails down his back to urge him to fuck into her harder, faster, deeper. When she hooked her heels over the backs of his calves, Heath laughed, low against her neck. The noise muffled. He nipped her throat, sending a shock wave of delight all through her.

"I want you to come with me, Effie."

"I am. Oh…shit. Yes, I am."

So many times and with so many men, Effie had lost herself inside her own head at this moment of orgasm. Taking her own pleasure without sharing it with her partner had been more than a habit; it had been a practice. But not with Heath. No, here and now and always with Heath, Effie gave and opened and shared. They were in this together. For all of it.

Breathless, she let the waves overtake her. She held him close as he shuddered. She kissed him, sipping at his breath and giving it back to him with her next exhale.

Finally, Heath collapsed. For a moment, his weight did press her a little too hard, though she'd never have said he'd even come close to crushing her. A few seconds only, before he rolled to her side, and without the time it took for a heartbeat, he'd pulled her snugly against him with his hand on her belly. He kissed her temple.

They stayed that way awhile, dozing. Effie's stomach rumbled. She twisted in his embrace to press herself against him.

"We're sticky."

"We could take a shower."

Effie yawned. "Bleah. Okay. In a few minutes. I'm lazy."

Heath cuddled her again. She drifted, waking with a start to the beginning of a nightmare about lying tucked up in his arms with that man standing over them. Her mouth was too dry, and her pulse pounded, but unlike the many other times Effie had woken from a similar dream, this time, in Heath's arms, she simply settled back against him and let the dream fade.

Her stomach rumbled. She laughed. He pressed his mouth to her hair, and she allowed herself to melt once more into his embrace. When he kissed her, though, Effie put her hand between them so her fingers could cover his mouth.

"Hungry," she said. "C'mon, let's raid the mini fridge. No. No, let's order pizza! There's a take-out menu over on the desk."

Heath pushed up on an elbow to look down at her, his brow furrowed. "You're going to order pizza delivery. From a place you don't know."

Effie sat. Naked, she crossed her legs and leaned forward to run her fingertip down his sticky chest and along his thigh. "Yes. I told you, I'm hungry."

"What happened to you? Where's Effie?" Heath looked so concerned she couldn't tell if he were joking or not, so she swatted him. He ducked from the swing and captured her hand, then pushed her back on the bed to pounce. He held both her hands with one of his so he could pat her all over, tickling.

She fought him, but not fiercely, then offered her mouth for a kiss. When he took it, Effie rolled, breaking his grasp, and ended up on top of him. She straddled his hips and put her hands flat on his chest. She bent to kiss him but kept her mouth just out of reach.

"I'll give you something to eat," Heath said.

"I didn't say I wanted sausage on the pizza."

He laughed and kissed her, rolling her gently off him so he could sit up and swing his legs over the edge of the bed. He looked at her over his shoulder. "You want pizza? For real? I'll order it."

"I do." She put a hand on her belly and watched him find his phone in the pocket of his discarded pants pocket.

He'd called her beautiful, but to her eyes, he was so lovely it hurt her heart to watch him move. She knew every inch of that body and had never grown tired of it. She was never going to.

"Heath—"

But he was talking to someone on the other end, ordering a large pie with mushrooms and pepperoni, and whatever Effie had meant to say got lost. She went into the bathroom with a lift of her brow and a quirk of her finger to get him to join her, and grinning, he did. They splashed and teased, until Heath went to his knees in front of her to press his cheek to her slick, wet belly. There in the shower he put his mouth on her again, teasing and tempting, until Effie had to gasp out a plea for him to stop.

"I can't," she said. "I can't again. Three is enough."

That made him only all the more determined. Carefully, so she didn't slip and fall, Heath pushed her against the tiled wall and held her there while he licked her with that same steady pace that never failed to get her off. She wasn't going to manage, she couldn't possibly…and then oh, yes. There it was. That moment when nothing would keep her from it. Effie slipped into pleasure shaking and crying out his name in soft, breathless gasps.

The sound of knocking at the hotel door got him to his feet. With a grin, Heath kissed her on the mouth and slipped out of the shower to wrap himself in a towel and pay for the pizza. By the time Effie came out of the bathroom, towel drying her hair but not bothering with anything else, he'd set up a small picnic at the desk in the corner.

"You want a soda? I can run down the hall." He looked at her expectantly.

"Like that?" She pointed at the towel that was all he still wore. "Uh-huh. No, water's fine."

Heath shifted his hips from side to side. "You never know. I could end up on the evening news."

"Been there, done that," Effie said.

"And we didn't even get a freaking T-shirt," Heath replied.

They stared at each other, both smiling.

"I love you," Effie said. "You are everything to me. I don't want to be with anyone else, ever again. I want to be with you for the rest of my life."

Heath took her hand and kissed it. Then her mouth. "It's a deal."

Nothing fell away all at once. Their world didn't change. She didn't even feel that different than she had in the moment before she said the words aloud. And all of that made sense, Effie thought as Heath kissed her and kissed her and kissed her again. Because the world *hadn't* changed.

Only she had.

★ ★ ★ ★ ★

author song list

I could write without music, but I'm so glad I don't have to. Here's a partial playlist of what I listened to while writing *Hold Me Close*. Please support the artists by purchasing their music.

"Waiting Game" – Banks
"Call and Answer" – Barenaked Ladies
"Skinny Love" – Birdy
"Beautiful with You" – Halestorm
"Break In" – Halestorm
"Hurt Makes it Beautiful" – Hugo
"Without You" – Jason Manns
"All of Me" – John Legend
"What You've Done to Me" – Needtobreathe
"You Won't Let Me" – Rachael Yamagata
"Everything Changes" – Staind
"Last Love Song" – ZZ Ward
"Before I Ever Met You" – Banks